$\mathcal{V}$OICES OF THE $\mathcal{S}$OUTH

THE DAUGHTERS OF NECESSITY

Also by Peter Feibleman

NOVELS
A Place Without Twilight
The Columbus Tree
Charlie Boy

NOVELLAS
The Only Danaid
Fever
Along the Coast
Eyes

PLAYS
Tiger Tiger Burning Bright
Cakewalk

MEMOIR
Lilly: Reminiscences of Lillian Hellman

WITH LILLIAN HELLMAN
Eating Together: Recollections and Recipies

OTHER NONFICTION
The Bayou Country
The Cooking of Spain and Portugal
Creole and Acadian Cooking

PETER FEIBLEMAN

The Daughters of Necessity

LOUISIANA STATE UNIVERSITY PRESS

BATON ROUGE

For Susan

Copyright © 1959, 1987 by Peter S. Feibleman
Originally published by The World Publishing Company
LSU Press edition published 1999 by arrangement with the author
All rights reserved
Manufactured in the United States of America

08 07 06 05 04 03 02 01 00 99
5 4 3 2 1

Library of Congress Cataloging-in-Publication Data
Feibleman, Peter S., 1930–
    The daughters of necessity / Peter Feibleman.
        p.   cm. — (Voices of the South)
    ISBN 0-8071-2388-9 (pbk. : alk. paper)
    I. Title. II. Series
  PS3556.E4D38 1999
  813'.54—dc21   98-51109
                                     CIP

. . . these are the Fates, daughters of Necessity . . .

PLATO: The Republic

Here's much to do with hate, but more with love.
Why, then, O brawling love! O loving hate!
O any thing! Of nothing first create.
O heavy lightness! Serious vanity!
Mis-shapen chaos of well-seeming forms!
Feather of lead, bright smoke, cold fire, sick health!
Still-waking sleep, that is not what it is!
This love feel I, that feel no love in this.

SHAKESPEARE: Romeo and Juliet

Contents

Around Town

IT DID NOT HAPPEN most recently, but one past pendant summer this decade. In a medium small Southern city a man was taught the meaning of death by his own child. The man was maimed, he was even killed, the city still exists. It is a paved dampish swampland place, set by a nameless bog along the ragged lower part of the eastern United States.

The city is caught in a swirl of the river.

From high, the riverline looks aimless as a trickle of melted ice in a dry dust path. It loops and folds, cringing from its own way for nothing: having no way. It is a line that shows no purpose nor reason but proper being. And you see its glare and its darkness.

Then you will have to go down to the water's edge when the day ends; sense it slide by in the dusk. Squint at the fading whorls and feel the dim river tuck around the land—sparkled with fireflies, locust-loud—holding things there for the night. There is an understanding in the feel of it.

Living in the crook of the flow, some say the summer sun is nearer to earth over this city than anywhere else. But such claims are often made; they are not proven facts.

And you might hear too that the white sun in August can make even the plants swell bigger. For the sun then is a watery round hole, whiter than the sky. It does make people and people's deeds soar up—sharp and twisted, colored too high for the eyes: like anything through heat waves. If the sky is that bright, people look at the ground and at the river and at each other. They get sweat in their eyes wherever they look. Those who do not work stay in their houses to talk, drinking—fanning hot air against oily powdered necks, and telling stories. And the summer stories can last all year round. By the second year they are so distorted, no one pays real attention to them. Minds acute for memory aren't much use so far South.

They aren't any use at all on Melpomene Drive.

It is wide, and it is the greenest street in town. It runs from the cemetery in a long smooth curve down to the river, and the winding canal cuts over it a little more than halfway up to produce a kind of wilted cross. There is a neutral ground in the center of the Drive, with baby magnolia trees—four to each block—and a streetcar track set between. So it is divided in two; the west-side traffic sweeps downtown to the business section, and the east side heads up to the cemetery. You can go in either of those two directions, and still be on Melpomene Drive.

There would hardly be many residential streets over the world to match it; not in grace or odor. The spread is flat, and the curve so gently perfect it looks more infinite than straight. If you stand on the Drive, you can see it has no end. You don't believe the cemetery stops it unless you go up all the way.

On either side, under oak trees and the dappling shadows of maple leaves strung gray with moss, there are certain houses. Any one of them would be the right address to give—known far on the river, and in other places too. These houses have an elegant deep green gloom, spaced well apart by spaded mounds of lawns and bushes and garden paths, offset with bird fountains and pink marble pedestals, and all such things as men admire to live with. They are sighs of houses, clutched in ivy; and they are real.

The first few up from Bank Street show their worth. But those nearest the canal crossing are most grand. That is where importance set in: powered money is there from the past. The houses could be on plantations, and some gardens are orchards. The sated breaths of sere gardenias rot righteously, slow, in the air. Ambition isn't merely social there; it is natural. You almost have to shrug, or be rude, when you say you live on Melpomene near the canal. And the people who live there are rarely rude. They try to shrug each day away.

Houses are burgundy brick, and summers are dusty. Clamshells sift white powder that blows and cakes you in your sweat for August. The heated wet from swampland slicks the skin. Then you get a drop hidden amongst the eyelashes; and if you blink before you wipe, through the salt of pain you will have spots that stay like mildew in your eyes. For the sun makes the dust: the land is wet. Summer cool is man-made, bricked, wine-colored, stroked with ivy, like the houses. And unlike the houses, it is only a wishful green.

That is August; but for October there is comfort before the ice. Not much color, though—besides the general white of flowers, autumn is dull brown. Hard leaves scrape on roofs, and they come to a shriek on the sidewalks. At night they whisper over each other in their fall. Hackberries pop and smear underfoot. The undecided wind tilts the moss; and the gray mourning moss flutters, indecent and coy, on the naked trees.

Then the silt-slow river is cold where it pits the land.

There you have most of the weather. Life seems to turn in it, and usual events take place along the Drive. They are placid, sudden, light, they are sometimes brutish. They are themselves immobile as unconsidered facts.

Yet live gossip can never resile. This must be chewy and shapeless to fit each mouth; and the same as any living thing, if it isn't growing it is dying. So when the events are talked about, you wouldn't want to swear by what is said. Then you know, whatever it may be, it won't be said for long. There are always new happenings.

. . .

There are two empty houses that stand on Melpomene Drive. Both have been vacant for some time, though one has been recently sold.

This one, the Choate mansion, borders the canal. It is the biggest house in the city. It runs from Melpomene to Melrose, through its own orchard, and it takes up the entire block, except for the caretaker's cottage which was sold many years ago on a half-acre of land for eight thousand dollars. The set of the house is towards the Drive, and its long north wing is partly reflected in the black canal water. There in the water on a windy day, a graying façade of thick-choked ivy will creep green. Soiled old brick, dull and crusty, ripples to blood. And up, swaying chimneys with heavy tops menace the sky in reflection—fisting the house against heaven. But if you look at it straight-on, the Choate house has splintery boards on every window; and it is fagged as the moss beards that hang from branches over the roof. And you can sense the old air sealed inside.

Then across the bridge, three blocks up on the other side of the Drive is what was once known as the Legrange place. That is quite different. It has been renovated since it was built; the house is a third smaller, and the grounds are perhaps half as big. The whole property is worth less, and sold first. It has sold now for the second time. And now its two particular attentions of other days—a formal gardenia garden and a possible ghost—are gone; they have both disappeared. The last owner was a woman who didn't like gardenias, and the ghost didn't like the last woman owner: so people say.

It was before, decades ago, that these were houses fresh-toned to smooth living. The Legranges were worth half a million— enough to exist most carefully then. For two generations, the Choates had been careless-rich. Their houses made known their means.

And in the passing of the years, counting everything that happened, the two properties had one story, whispered as it unwound in the city. Told, and changed, and filigreed—never the same. The properties are unoccupied now because of one man. He and the story are both dead.

And the ghost is not remembered. She put in a final off-season appearance and ceased to exist permanently on one July the twelfth. But that fact would not be recalled even if it were known. The day was memorable and horrible for other reasons.

This ghost was a young female, and she was nameless. Edmund Choate buried two wives in his lifetime and nobody around town was ever exactly sure which one might have enjoyed to haunt over at the Legrange place. There was little agreement, for she was not often seen. Only two persons actually perceived enough of her to recognize; and neither of them could claim to have known her in life. Mostly she was a fierce chalk face that might stare from back of the garden when the light was pale certain evenings. Or she would walk through the gardenia bushes, white like the flowers, staring back at the house. It was the sort of face some people can see in a cloud if they know it's surely there—while others can't, no matter how carefully it is explained to them. The house was empty then too, and some said she meant to keep it that way. But she never did anything besides walk. It was her eyes that frightened. The second of the witnesses especially noticed her eyes.

The first was a neighbor boy, seven years old at the time. He sneaked over the splintering fence to pick a giant gardenia on his way home from school. The Legrange gardenias were the largest in the city, unkempt and dying; and as he broke one off its stem she walked around from behind a bush and eased right past him. She hurried around the house and faded into a lucent quick breeze. The boy was not scared because he didn't know about ghosts; but his insides humped at the touch of her dress. And when he focused on the flower again, it appeared to have turned dark brown. That was how the talk started, and the boy was made to repeat his story many times. Three years afterwards, a passing tourist got in there with a camera. He was a lean-boned blond man with a very small but pertinent nose, and he was traveling through the South taking pictures. He wanted photographs of whatever he could find in moneyed decay. And even then almost all the city was kept new, excepting the poorest districts; there were many views that could have made handsome pictures. But this particular man was after decay. He was the sort of man who is so out of place in the world he feels he must give it his constant approval by peeking unseen through an all-seeing camera to stop it on sterile film. He was adjusting a light meter to the pale shadows towards the end of a milky afternoon; then he looked into the lens, and there she was. She stood stiff, glaring at the house as if she wanted to spit on it. A light wind nuzzled the blooms and the branches around her body. But she was all still; and the hard-sheathed hatred from the piths of her eyes to that empty house cut solid through the air. Her eyes, he said later, were two black holes into hell. Of course the man had no reason to imagine she was not a live person living in an old-style Southern mansion, boarded up, which would be a pleasure to a tourist. He lowered his camera to be sure. And then, in the passing of a second, she shifted only just her eyes and looked at him. And she went right on looking: she did not disappear that time. He did. His little nose turned cold. He broke a hole in the fence to leave town the same dull day.

In the days when she walked, the ghost was seen every several months—once, or at most twice a year. And always in the autumn. When the crisp leaves buckled and moved like rivercrabs over the dead lawn, anyone from town passing the Legrange house would glance behind to the edge of the garden, then beyond. She was expected in the autumn, for this was when the gardenias had singed out of bloom. Still, it wasn't precisely if you looked to see her that she was there. Edmund Choate wearied of hearing talk about the place; he went once and wandered through the entire house alone, and out in back, with a small crowd waiting in the street for him—and she never showed. It was said he did that to prove there was nothing but rumor, so everybody would stop talking and forget. But nobody forgot. Not before she really left. She had a way of staying in the mind.

No strangers and no known friends found out who she was, because no one ever asked why she was there. They asked who; people discussed which of Edmund Choate's wives might have secret cause to burst her grave with hate. They wanted to know many things. But not why. Right up until July the twelfth, that day of the year the accident took place, no one ever asked why.

But most people are like that. People are wary of why; while science tells them how. And they are made like that by necessity.

Even with the river, a man can be fooled. Standing off from a map, he sees where the twisting water goes, sees how. Sees it wind to the Gulf and empty there: he finds that it has direction. Then he will think such wheres and hows make reasons, he will be rightly fooled.

Yet *why* is not a question for a curious man—not even for a scientist. It is not a question at all. Why is a poet's word; it is the missed beat of the heart. And it cannot hold a light.

It is a wonder for children, and idiots, and atheists, and story-tellers, and some certain lovers of the river.

PART ONE

The Day

I

One Young Morning

1

STILL HE KNEW it was a dream, but that did not help; he had known from the beginning. He had announced it to himself. And knowing was no help.

Edmund Choate jerked from inside his body, and woke up.

It was the soft part of the morning. Not quite dark nor day, but a gentle grayish blue, blushed white, smothered the dawn.

Cool and unrosed the high eastern sky cupped around Edmund's aching eyes and made them film. The color in the sky was deep, unbroken: fresh full of emptiness. Without a star or a sun or a piece of moon, this was a sky to reach out and feel, like the other half of swollen shiny sea water asleep in the Gulf untouched by a breeze. It was something to touch and then be inside.

Far up from the Gulf, the city paled in the thin beginnings of early light.

Edmund rubbed at the wet crusts around each eye with the underpart of one thumb; he blinked at the flat-blistered window panes between the wide curtains. He had left the curtains open all night. Then he leaned on both hands to swing out of bed. The wrinkled sheet was cold and damp underneath. He sat up. He sat heavily there for three limp minutes.

Now the high full gleam—the blooming white of a blatant,

colorless dawn was a burn in the sky. It wrapped white back of the man's eyeballs, a fervid cloud, and pushed them forward. Then when he swallowed, the same burn turned sour and sank into his stomach to fester there. And a quick cold thrilled vaguely through the rest of his body—fluttering at the joints—pointless.

Edmund squinched his eyelids tight, and felt the sharp sting and then in a while the answering flush that trickled out warm on his face. He snuffled twice, and swallowed again. He made a noise to clear his throat. There was a soft dizziness in aftertaste of sleep that circled through the dark of his head to weigh him down, forgetful. Weak with ease, his elbows broke out; he sank heavily back.

And he thought about the day before and his short visit in the hollow house. The Legrange house, unlit, stark black; a flashlight spot ahead of him. Stale dust and moodless rooms. Marching up to memories that had no more meaning. A house he had never truly known, and a high tangle of garden in back, damp around his feet. No ghost; and surprised faces waiting for him on the street. Looking bored for them: no fright; no ghostly lady. A half-hour spent walking in a boarded house he could not sell—with the ghost of a rumor of a ghost.

Edmund lay and thought about that as he smiled himself back to sleep.

Then he remembered the nightmare. It was arranged there, in detail, still bilious and still with him. It still made sense.

He snapped ahead and stood up, rocking on his feet. He said, "Damn." Burning under the gut and breathing fast he stood to face the clock. Edmund said, "God damn." And he let his weight carry him forward into the bathroom.

Stiff-armed, leaning over the slick washbasin, he put his head two inches from the mirror and stared blankly, breathing small puffs of clouds over the lower half of his own reflection. Then he curved his big neck; he rested his forehead against the cool. His palms and his brow felt sticky on the dry shined surfaces.

Edmund's hair shone an unclean gray, highlit in the room. But he had stood long ago in the same bathroom when it took him minutes to make a dry forest of dark brown grow in one direction. He had kept more hair than most men can show at fifty-four; now cut short. It covered three-quarters of his head, an area shaped like a half-moon, running into the thick russet flesh on his neck. His shoulders spread wide under the damp white pajamas, and Edmund had a hard body. He was tightened; he was not draped with age. His legs were muscular; the blood escaped from two long contours of muscle in heavy purple veins that ran back between the bones on his feet.

Edmund turned the cold-water faucet full to the left, and watched the wild splash rush below him. Then he ducked a hand in the icy October water. The spray tickled up his sleeve. He cupped the water in both palms, and rolled his face in it.

And he looked up at his rosy eyes—at the dark skin, threaded red in each cheek, bloated with sleep and dripping. He said, "Now look, man." And he exhaled a sort of voiceless chuckle. He said, "Man, you do get older all the time."

When he turned off that faucet and opened the other one, the new water was too hot too quickly. The shock came under his wrist; then there was a second and a half of numbness while he waited; and the pain finally came and lasted for two seconds more. He held up his wrist and looked at it.

With the wet hand he began to unbutton the top of his white pajamas.

Dressed, as undressed, Edmund's eyebrows were noticeable. A man should have one feature to check a slippery upward gaze, and Edmund did. He had violent eyebrows. Lighter gray than his eyes or the hair on his head, they swam up long and high and snarled to float on the close-waved tide of his forehead. And whenever you glanced at them, they were able to stop that rippling movement. They fought, and played, and then they posed. They were there to watch; and most people watched them.

By the time he had finished in the bathroom the day was come. It was soggy and fresh through the windows, stretching solid, a palpable clear light of bright blue. Strings of birds screamed into it and swung down to make busy on the naked earth of the patched, growing lawn.

Edmund studied them while he dressed. He put on the dark blue pants from an old double-breasted suit, and fastened them over a neat white sportshirt. His shoes were black and polished; his socks were blue.

And everything matched except one finger. Part of this finger was brown. It was the index on his left hand. The finger he had mashed in a Roman taxicab when he was woolly-drunk, singing, and twenty-four. One knuckle had been stained for thirty years.

Up over the birds, the color of the morning went feminine. It had softened while Edmund washed; it was densest bright. It was the inside blue, edged with pink and gold, of one great bland eye over the earth. Trees in the orchard and the outlined roof on the other wing cut into the sky. That coolness of blue gave way and held around them.

Edmund saw the color of it there. And his body carried him back; he backed away from it. Meticulous, unknowing of any particular fear, he walked backwards across the room to watch the morning. Then he bumped into the bed and stood still. He felt the mattress spongy against his legs; and he could remember the live smell of used bedclothes in different times. The smells of personal cold-dried sweat and warm spent perfume that had mingled and come to be one in the night. Wild nights, and sleepy early mornings, and a round completion of manhood to begin the day.

He turned to see the bed, and he looked over the room. Dark oak darkens with time; some walls are always the same. He saw the easy chair covered as before in cracked, deep brown leather, then the small chandelier that was for sprinkling slivers and prisms and broken pieces of white light around the rich textures of his private bedroom after the sun had set in blackness. And he remembered when the bedroom had not been so private.

And now there were only dreams, and the last one now was

burst. Just fragments of his night's dream lay loose in his mind, with that chalky skin from a missing face, familiar; but unrecognizable and senseless with disorder. Then fear, the mother and child of hopeless dreams, outlived it whole.

Cold outside and singed within, he shivered slightly once. There was a slick around his mouth. He sucked air through his teeth till they were iced dry, and he closed his lips over them. The skin caught, stuck on the frozen enamel; Edmund pushed his tongue in between to lick wet the fluted enamel of his teeth.

Then he pivoted. Sour and somber like a mourner, he walked out the doorway into the hall.

Edmund could carry himself direct down the center of any passage. Exactly down the middle, never wavering, and without looking to follow the pattern in the carpet or to measure the space from right to left. He kept his eyes pointed ahead at the other end, and he followed his own gaze. Edmund Choate naturally walked the shortest distance from where he was to where he was going.

As he went by Adrianne's door, he slowed. He sensed his daughter's out-breaths and her warmth, in sleep, even through the closed door: a delicate heat of love that folded around him and turned his long night's horror to escaping, invisible steam. A love that made a hot band of air in the hall. And when he had passed it, he could smile—the heaviness had quit his body; the fear went out and left him buoyant and ageless in his walk.

The end of the hall was his study, and that was open. He went in to stretch there, surrounded by the sudden cold gaiety of early sunlight. The pale burst of light settled over him, and Edmund twisted his arms in it, flexing his big shoulders—swiveling on his hips. Standing planted with his legs widespread, he writhed awake into the day.

But the sour that was left of the burn held like a round film of poison. It sent waves to slide up the inside of his stomach, and his tongue felt too large. When he tensed the muscles below his chest and tried to belch, he was not able. He tried several times.

Then he sat down in the low oak chair—the old swivel chair,

ribbed up and down behind—and put his hand under the edge of his desk and rang for his coffee.

Some of the furniture in the study was fairly new, but most had been put there with all the things belonging to the other rooms just after the house was built. It was all dark wood, waxed, and it gleamed. The pieces were big; they were fine antiques. But there was enough space around to set each piece off, regal. The carpets underneath looked right to be worn.

And there was that special odor of luxury in the house. Not dusty, nor only from wax; not unkempt wealth and not too cared for. It was just rich—the quality in those materials, the walls, the house itself smelled rich. Like the velvet odor of roses, without the sweet. It was a cool smell, even in the dead of summer. Smooth from the slick tiles and the black marble and the white marble staircase, cool with the cold taken off for winter by the tan tapestries threaded in color to match the upholstery and the patterns of streaks in the winter carpets. The Choate house was built for fine living; it smelled that way.

In his north-wing study facing Melpomene Drive, Edmund turned to the left and looked at the painting set high over one enormous bulbous-backed wicker chair. Adrianne's portrait was the biggest painting he owned, half again as high as any of the portraits in the main hall; it was the only one he kept with him in his study.

It had been done on her eighteenth birthday—eighteen years after her mother's death; and it was even bigger than Adrianne. The painter had worked for seven months. And Edmund spoke of it as being the closest any artist could come to representing his daughter with some truth. But more often and privately he thought otherwise: he thought such an effort was by nature doomed. He liked sometimes to recall how that artist had bowed away from Adrianne's sky-black eyes, and how the man had looked then at his lifeless new tubes of paint.

Edmund said quietly, "That is not you. That is not your smile."

He looked at the rigid neck and shoulders, the hard back; the empty face. And for a second he understood how the painter had come to make her look stiff. An artist without the right tools was worse even than everybody else: a man who had been awed by the depths of her humility, a man unable to represent an angel in oil had produced a blackboard queen.

But it was done four years ago, and unimportant. No such things had any matter. And wearily, Edmund drooped; he said to her there, "Princess." He had had many chiding names for his daughter. And he said, "My lady, you never knew such a dream."

Adrianne's face in the portrait was the wrong tone of white; it held no translucence in the skin. It watched out above Edmund through the window to the far side of the jonquil garden bordering the sidewalk.

He said, "Now don't ask me to remember, but somebody did it. Some half stranger," he said. "Someone. I had a pasty nightmare, Princess; imagine me in a big white dream. And a stranger came walking. You wouldn't ask me to remember." Edmund chuckled, and he worked his eyebrows together.

He felt again that difference in the passage by her door—the change in the air that had wiped out the deformed, murderous face from his midnight mind. Then he said, "You hear, Princess? Hear?" he said; "strange as she was, I knew her. No-eyed. Some vacant lady."

And in the pale damp air of early morning—twice a widower at fifty-four Edmund could chuckle and he could frown for love watching the sad attempt at a likeness: the stiff, pastel-souled figure meant to be his daughter on the wall.

2

Tufted clouds were skeetering. They rushed from the edges of nowhere up into the clean high blue. It was not going to be that kind of day after all.

And the maid was late with the coffee. She was hardly ever late, Opal; which made it that much more annoying when she was. Edmund emptied his lungs through round pointed lips and allowed himself to get angry. He brought his hand down spread open under the desk, and aimed part of it at the bell with minute care, as if he were about to kill a fly.

Three mashed grunts in the oak door behind him sounded way faraway.

Edmund's anger choked, and joined the dark sourness. "All right," he said. "Fine."

The door groaned to open. Opal looked down; she stepped up over the carpet fringe. She came to a stop, and looked back at it. Then she started moving again. She rocked the tray at a queer angle to keep any coffee from sloshing out of the cup; but a little slop did jump into the saucer. "My," she said.

Edmund watched her.

"Morning," said Opal. And: "My," she said. Each word was a thoughtful product like each step. She came and laid the tray over the desk. Opal was moving in a thick private world. She straightened the tray until it was exactly parallel to the blotter, which was crooked.

"Good morning," Edmund said.

She said, "Mr. Choate, I see the coffee is half in, half out."

"It is."

"I will get you a fresh cup. A clean cup. I have been thinking how I came to pour it; that is the use of the pot."

"Let it go. Never mind," he said.

Opal was aware of Edmund's eyes; she studied the black tray. Next to the cup there was a tall silver coffeepot, and next to that a silver sugar bowl full of lump sugar with the tongs hanging on the side. There was a plate, and two dry pieces of toast, uncut. No knife, no butter; no milk or cream. That was Edmund's breakfast every day.

Opal was made of a peaked face flat on top of a long, thin body. She was light Negro, fifteen years younger than Edmund; but she could claim she was still thirty-four.

Lifting the cup, she said, "Let me." The spilled coffee made a big filmy suction bubble, and she scraped the bottom of the cup on the saucer and spilled the liquid back inside. Then she slapped the cup into place, and put them both down.

Edmund said, "I wish I knew what to say to you."

"I was thinking how I came to pour it."

"You been pouring all night?"

"All night, no," Opal said.

She stood with her shoulders to the sky, and waited. And she blocked a lot of light.

Just for her job, Edmund had said Opal's greatest feature was her refusal to make excuses. She did not acknowledge excuses. She also possessed some natural faults, and one in particular was blossoming. But it was not easy to outbalance that first feature.

Opal was a widow; they shared an unspoken quality of sorrow. Yet this was buried to forget, and they did not need to speak of it.

"Who is in the kitchen?" Edmund said.

"No, sir. She is in my bed."

". . . She?"

"Mrs. Fitch, my mother."

"So I gathered. Anybody else up?"

"Some are up and working," Opal said.

"Got here early, I suppose. She must have got here at three in the morning."

"She didn't," Opal said. "Mrs. Fitch won't go out in the morning. Got here last night. She come to visit with me and stayed the night."

Edmund stirred two lumps of sugar into his coffee, and took one swallow. He could feel the heatball wash all the way down.

He said, "I do not know what to say. I don't ever want to fire you, you are aware of that."

"No, sir." Opal's eyes and her lower lip were directed at the desk. The inside of the lip was dry pink.

"Break anything?"

"No."

"I'm surprised. Well, you will want to get her out now. I mean now. This morning."

"Yes, when I serve everybody their breakfast."

"That will be time enough, you think?"

". . . Yes, sir." Opal frowned on one side only.

"Has she come to yet?"

"Come to in the middle of the night," Opal said.

"And she passed out again?"

"She always does," Opal said.

". . . She didn't get into my liquor cabinet?"

"She wouldn't."

"It isn't locked."

"She wouldn't do that."

Edmund lifted his shoulders, and let them settle back, of their natural weight. "She would do anything," he said. "She does. She has been ordered by me personally not to come here, and she still never misses a month. A woman who wishes to drink her own daughter out of a job into this state."

Opal licked her mouth. "I slept it off last night, Mr. Choate. She wouldn't steal from you." The lower lip was puffed. "She won't touch it if it's over a year old."

"I see what you mean," Edmund said.

"Mrs. Fitch has a few homeless principles."

"Evidently."

"That's right," Opal said.

Then they stopped talking again. But she stayed where she was; the white apron of her uniform was stiff and clean.

The sky behind her head was thickening fast.

Edmund finished his first cup of coffee. He poured another, and sat back. "It's the third time since I told you she wasn't to be allowed to come here."

This was true, and they both knew it. This was not what you would call a necessary announcement. Only now it appeared there was really nothing more he could say.

Edmund said, "Are you waiting for something?"

". . . No, sir."

He broke a piece of toast in two. The bottom piece. "What can I say?"

"Not much," Opal said.

"What, for example?"

"Not very much," she said.

Edmund chewed, and swallowed dry. "We'll have to wait and see what has to be done," he said. "I can't say at the moment. I'll talk to my daughter about it. I don't want to fire you, I like you, Opal. But I can't say yet what has to be done."

"Course you can't. I like you too," Opal said.

"Is my daughter up?"

"No, sir. Nor Miss Aunt Clothilde." Opal didn't start to move. "You don't look so good, sir, neither," she said.

"I know I don't." Edmund looked at the sky. "You have something to tell me?"

". . . Not worth telling."

"Then why are you waiting?"

"I have been thinking about it. Mrs. Fitch arrived with an aid."

"Not a very practical one, I imagine."

". . . I didn't think so. She wanted me to give it to you."

"Then don't."

"I have been thinking not to."

"Good for you," Edmund said.

Opal said, "I am going back to work, Mr. Choate. You want some Bisodol or something?"

"No. Why should I?"

"You don't look very good."

"I had an unpleasant night," Edmund said. "Why Bisodol?"

"I don't know how you could sleep after going into that house yesterday."

"I slept."

"The talk about that house, and those two ladies. Why can't they leave the dead buried? They should leave the dead alone."

"They should," Edmund said.

"They should talk about their own dead. Instead of which of those two ladies. They have very little respect in this city."

"Right, they don't. Now get back to work."

"Picking at a person's sadness; you didn't have to go in that house."

"No, I didn't."

"Enough to give anybody a bad night."

"It was," Edmund said.

"Course it was. Enough for anybody. You wouldn't take some Bisodol?"

Edmund lifted the second piece of toast, and dropped it back on the tray. He said, "Do you consider having any work in the kitchen?"

Opal was given to waddling. She was flat-bone thin and never had to, but she cared to. It gave her a sense of filling more space. "Yes," she said.

"And get your mother out."

"Yes, I will."

"And shut the door."

Outside, the weather was gathering. It was interfused and unattractive, and the sky looked like somebody had been throwing clobber.

At the closing of the door, he made two fists. He put them together on the desk beside the tray. Then he opened one and hooked a finger in a cup.

After that he couldn't stop a grin.

Edmund said, "Where would you fire her?"

But the amusement was cheap, too soft: it died on his face. His eyeballs were warmer than the lids. They burned, then he felt heavy.

He said, "Which of those two ladies."

The coffee was full of chicory and faintly bitter. It was deep brown and opaque; and it was cold.

The Romance of
Melpomene Drive

1

EDMUND CHOATE was once young.

The city of those years was a sudden place to stop on the river. All equally hard, coreless, brash with color; waved with the steam of hot chicoried coffee rising out from the swamps. High-dressed ladies wilted, crushed around town with the summer's weight; fall was when a few last burnt greens faded, together with the heavy heat. And towards the middle of autumn each year, un-snowed, the city froze.

There was never any spring, even then. On this part of the river it's cold, or it's not cold, or it's too hot. But it won't be new—never fresh like spring; it can't be, not under air so thick with wet. The outside of a plant nor animal, a person's skin won't breathe in such air. Where the river twists towards an end, spring is a reference. Freshness is a simple idea, trapped in certain people's minds.

While he was young, Edmund Choate was one of those people.

The Choates, his parents, were known for a banking concern, and they owned stock up in New York. But if they were not yet quite the richest, they were considered the best-bred family in town. And they had no other child but Edmund.

They were board members of the two important clubs; Mr. Choate had founded one of them. Mrs. Choate nursed the city's social life and made it grow into a particular, secure system. She was frail and full of hollows, fine-looking, with a long straight nose —and finger tips like new grass, shaped like that, always pointed at you. Not many people ever cared much for her, she was not a lady who admitted that kind of caring. But nobody acknowledged active dislike for her even to their own mirrors, except a friend or two such as Mrs. Legrange, who had a habit of personal poisonous reveries. Lily Legrange wanted her daughter Anne to marry Edmund; she kept her hate private.

But Edmund was worse than disordered. The way he behaved, at first it appeared his purpose to shock everybody and then be righteous about it. Not until he was nearly twenty-four would people begin to say he had no negative purpose: he just went out and did what he liked. At that age he was hard and smooth-skinned and handsome, and there was a kind of gloomy, overt sexuality about him that would have made his mother uneasy whether or not he used it as he did.

Edmund could make some women blush just by looking at them. He didn't often try, but it happened all the same. When he sat in on one of his mother's gatherings, she sucked at her cheeks and covered her mouth with a knotted lace handkerchief every time he raised his head. If a silence formed for him while he spoke, she tried to fill it from the other end of the room. As long as she lived, Amelie Choate was never alkaline in her mind about Edmund or what he might say next. Most usually he stayed pleasant and charming, at least quiet; and then perhaps once an evening he opened his mouth and licked out a word or an idea that made her breath change its natural direction. He would actually get up while someone else was talking and ease his body to the nearest open doorway—both hands balled deep in his pockets, head down, shoulders bunched; and leave like that in a stark, yawning carelessness, as if he wanted to be rude. Edmund alone had the means to upset his mother's perfect balance—that interested and withdrawn presence of a lady in society. Without him, she was like some feathery slight reed floating dry down a riverload of other people's lives. But Edmund splashed. He embarrassed her so, she sometimes felt her heart beat. He almost made her live.

But he didn't often try. There was at least one other source he could use to make sure of his own breath.

Edmund was seen from time to time around the red-light district downtown, in more than a modicum of daylight. He would not then limit his visits to once a month at the proper secret night-hours, like a few other young men of his standing. He went when-ever he wanted to. And once he took a woman from down there out to a good restaurant, and they both got drunk, and Edmund stood up and held that woman's head while she vomited publicly on the floor. His father heard about it; he lectured Edmund from two o'clock till seven—one whole Sunday afternoon. In and out of fury, he tried to explain the exact difference between what was acceptable taste and what was not. Edmund listened carefully, weighted within and quiet, more polite than usual. Under shining dark eyebrows that heaved heavily down, his shapeless gray eyes began to glow with a dry brightness: a silvery glint that kept the old man standing to circle the room, in nervous, quick bursts of choked energy. Then when the lecture was finished, Edmund thanked his father with a serious empty voice, and low—before he got up and went out of the house. And that night was the first of the whole nights Edmund spent away from home.

Still once a week, every Friday evening, he went to visit Anne Legrange. They sat on the porch of her parents' house, three streets above the canal on Melpomene. The porch was back of the house looking out over the formal garden. They sat there into October each year, till the damp, excited odor of gardenias was too cold to smell. Then they stayed inside the living room, their backs to the fire, watching to see the winter grass tip in the wind under those white flowers; and the green of the grass was brighter and deeper than the slick, powdery leaves in the fading winter days.

Anne talked; Edmund did not. He listened and at times he watched her. She was of slight-boned delicacy, with tawny eyes and beautiful dull hair the color of late summer dust on the ground,

and features so right and regular for her face they were uninterest-
ing. Anne was said and thought to be beautiful; but she could not
make herself felt in that or any other way. Her voice was small,
and it was clear as a water bubble, and it contained nothing; she
kept her manicured hands gathered neatly on her knees as she
sat, ankles touching. She talked without looking at Edmund, in
an icy whining shyness that no one knew for what it was. She
talked evenly, and she hardly paused; she held her voice within a
studied range to speak of whatever mattered only to her mind:
ideas. Anne had hundreds of ideas about the world because she had
not yet learned to be a part of it. And she kept them neat and
well-placed, trim, and unused, like her hands. It seemed to Edmund that she matched the filigree tan-thread doilies crocheted
by her mother Lily and pressed with delicate attention always
under thick glass. But she loved him, though she did not show it.
She could never show her feelings, least of all to him. She just
talked and she talked on.

Edmund heard her words and attended her ideas. He sat beside
her once a week, indoors or out, sometimes eyeing the ivory profile, listening to what she had to say: not knowing what she felt.
The lone person ever to tell Edmund that Anne loved him was
her aunt—a youngish spinster called Aunt Clothilde by everyone,
who lived in the Legrange house because she had no other place.
Aunt Clothilde was unable to breathe well through her nose and
she had limped badly all her life from some accident right after
her birth. She liked speaking to a man of another woman's love.
Her first private session with Edmund was the first time she had
talked of love at all, and she thought she did it nicely. After that,
she would often stop him in the hall when he came to visit, and
whisper a few words or smile and squeeze her eyes at him. Aunt
Clothilde did as much as a lady could without telling Anne.

And Anne talked a tuneless song and never told him anything.
Still she knew she would not ever care for another person, and
she was more than afraid. She guarded her love in her personal
turn of day to night and back to day; it was her balance on a whirl-

ing earth; she kept it from the world and from starvation. Her waiting life was strung on Fridays: the time between. It was as if she were sealed inside herself with her love. And there was no breaking in or out. Some nights, asleep, she could feel the shell shiver her breast, and she rolled over on both arms and laughed and screamed into the pillow. But when she stifled herself awake she was crying, and she only remembered the fear. Time was like that. On Friday, each hour before he came was like one of the six days before. When the doorbell rang, it might have been wired to her veins.

Yet when Edmund's eyes filled the doorway, her fingers curled back out of the wide heat from his palm; and she dared not look full at him once again in the afternoon. And she could not stop talking.

Anne knew of, tried not to think about Edmund's nights in the wrong part of town. She had heard people whispering, and the maids told stories. But with her he was always gentle and respectful. Then too, her mother said there was a wrong part of town for every young man—Edmund simply was not tactful. Her mother said a young man has a wrong rawness of nature to clean out from his system before marriage, and there were places to do that. And Anne still used most of her mind for storing such ideas, things that she could not feel to believe. She loved and lived as she was able.

So Edmund had those Friday visits. And he had the other nights, lost in the freedom of his body, unmindful; spending hoarded heat from his muscles and his mind. He teased himself that way with his time. Until one afternoon when he and Anne were together.

It was late November, and they sat in their places by the window, waiting to see the day demur and die above the garden. The chandelier was not lit. Wafts of white flowery air sucked through the dark Legrange house, too strong for sweetness. There were three heavy glass bowls of cut gardenias covering doilies in the living room. Anne studied a bush through the windowpane as she talked.

Then from an easy slump, Edmund rocked forward to his feet. He stood for a minute, bulging—growing bigger and hardening his body, as though his feet were pulling up juice from the wood of the floor. And he walked behind Anne's chair, and was gone from her view.

Only her mouth moved; it made words. Hushed, as she watched, the day was deepening fast into night. In the garden even the near flowers dimmed softly. The different greens joined in darkness.

And she paused once then. Wide around the room she heard the thick-edged clucking of the clock; and over that, his breath seemed to act like starch on the air. She felt him tall behind her there; and she was aware of the heat from his thighs on her back, she stiffened not to shiver. And Anne began smoothly to talk again, with the same tone as before. The chain of words formed in her mouth to say themselves—apart from her will. The worded ideas she had never felt came out alone without feeling.

Edmund set his big hands, one around each of her shoulders; he pressed her backwards. Then he moved against the wooden slats of her chair.

There was a purple cloud above the garden, bigger than the house. Black at the center, moving down as the sun set, it turned suddenly silver. Colorless light splashed in the garden for a quarter-second; unreal and metallic, it shone brilliant on each dusty leaf, and slipped in to separate grass from bladed grass. Then the dark took its place. Other parts of seconds went by, timeless there. The cloud growled.

Anne Legrange drew in one fist and held it over the pounding between her breasts; she covered it with the other hand, and pressed hard to relieve the pressure from inside.

But the thuds burst through to her voice. They hit it out of its usual range, and she spoke too high. They filled her throat until, for whole heartbeats, she had no voice at all.

Edmund said, "Stop talking now."

And another cloud made a long, sighing growl.

He said, "Do you want me? Lean," he said. "Whatever you want. Stop talking now."

Anne pushed her folded sharp knuckles into her ribs until the ache spread. She thought about that particular ache.

Waves of darkness were rising from the garden back up to the cloud. She saw them float. She saw the darkness rise.

Edmund said, "Now. Do you know I'm here?" And after it was stopped, his voice echoed a rumble in her ears, like the voice of the cloud. "Do you know now?" he said.

The echo was one held: Now?

He said, "Now lean back. Lean back. Lean."

But the darkness was in her eyes, and she was sleepy or dizzy, she didn't know which. She could not move. The black air thickened around, and her eyelids sank, spidery, through the dark air. They caught midway, so that her eyes were neither closed nor open. Then her neck was not going to support her head.

Standing behind her, Edmund said, "No. Lean," he said. "Lean against me."

But she could not willfully move, and she felt her body sinking; in the rise of the darkness she was sinking. Yet she knew she would not faint. And all she could think of was one thing after another like that day in high school when Ada Roan Simpson had stolen her new eraser and then lied and laughed about it. Because she had seen Ada Roan steal the eraser.

Edmund said, "Will you lean back? Lean back and feel me here." He said, "I'm here. I want you to kiss me now."

And she could see Ada Roan's face in her lap just as plain. Big and plain and laughing there in her lap, that Ada Roan Simpson. A flirt, and a liar; a flirt. A thief, and laughing about it. Ada Roan Simpson. And then there was the time Aunt Clothilde was limping through the garden and tripped and fell in a gardenia bush. Anne had watched her from an upstairs window. Aunt Clothilde wasn't hurt any. She just lay there in the gardenia bush. She didn't holler or do anything. She just lay there in the bush looking up at the sky. And Ada Roan Simpson hadn't been there then, but she was laughing about it now. Ada Roan had died one year at school, and everybody said it was a shame that girl died. Ada Roan Simpson was an awful flirt, and she was a liar and a cheat and a thief, but everybody said it was a shame she died when she did. And she was laughing now.

And Anne knew, she actually knew these were stupid awful things to think about at this moment.

But they were the only things.

Edmund said, "Stand up."

Now perhaps there was worse thunder outside. Thunder might have been what it was.

He said, "Stand up here with me."

He was in front of her, bent over, with his hands like warm wood underneath her armpits. Holding her; tipping her back. So she was made to watch right at him, full at his face in the air above hers. He was breathing rough, he was breathing weird: the world was all weird. With his mouth open and his face in the air. Only it was not his face. It wasn't. It was Ada Roan Simpson up there. It was that dead girl's face up there in the air. Still laughing.

Edmund said, "Stand up to kiss me."

And he pulled her straight up to the thunder.

East of the house, on the river, where the water curls above the city and then swoops into a wavering line for maybe four-fifths of a mile—up there somewhere a shrimpboat wailed. Such a sound at night is not a peculiarity.

Yet you hear them at night, sounds you would never notice during the daytime. Boats are leaving all the time for New Orleans and other places, different boats are coming in. When these pass or when there is a blind curve in the river—or if it is just a blinding fog, whistles are always blown. There is a different kind on each kind of boat: you will know what you are hearing. Then on the land the day is full of sounds, and you don't separate one from another. You wait till night. The dark does that for you.

It gives the bugs and the frogs, car horns, and the boats, and all such sounds a definite position in every person's world; and a certain meaning. You won't think one is peculiar because you happen to notice it at night.

It is the same with many things. That is what the night is for— to hold sound from sound, and smell from smell, and heart from inner heart. Some nights are needed to keep feeling out of thought, or thought away from feeling. A man is constructed to have his sky blacked out those few hours in every turn of the earth. True light lies to every soul; there must be whistling blindness for another kind of truth. A man needs the night for that.

Then let him hope to remember, and he will close his eyes. Let him try to stop remembering, and he will close them to sleep. A few wise persons shut both eyes to feel; and this is not peculiar.

If you please, a man is born in doubt, and he should be. Fear is always with him: though it may not be a proper thing, a man must use it properly.

Only a child can be afraid of the dark. Allow that then. And a man must fear the light.

So on the particular evening when Edmund Choate kissed Anne Legrange in the living room of her parents' house with the lightning bursting outside, and the shrimpboat's wail in the distance, the most unfortunate event that took place was that he kept his eyes open.

Then to him—and just to him—did it all appear outrageously peculiar.

In the sound of the weather, she went limp. Her arms and head swung back. She felt him around her waist, and under her neck, and on her mouth; and full in front she felt his whole body standing hard for them both. There was no strength in her. Tides of blood ebbed—shrank back in a long full swell to her heart, and she was lifeless cold. But there was his heat to live by, and although she could not breathe, there was his breath. There was Edmund to hold her.

And she knew then she would never see that laughing flirting lying schoolgirl's face, that Ada Roan Simpson, ever again. Because that girl was dead; and Anne Legrange was alive. She could not see the dead face because she was going to be alive.

First from the storm her chest filled; all the blood; then no more air would fit inside. Then, an instant before it happened, she knew it was going to. She wanted to scream. She wanted to. And she was not able. She did want, she tried to scream. But she could do nothing. The storm was Edmund and she was mute and going in that storm. And it would happen. There had to be lightning. And the lifelong shell sealed in her breast shivered and exploded—the blood rushed free.

Her heart gorged her body. The weirdness of the world was soft away. She and her love were whole, and Anne was one for love.

It wasn't till Edmund took his face up that she began to laugh. She laughed and she sobbed, and went right on like that and knowing it was herself who was laughing. She was not limp now, not any more. She stood firm in his arms. Caught and strong in joy, she let loose her fresh-freed care. Sobbing, she laughed this one time in her life to unleash her love.

And she laughed her love away.

Edmund let go, and stood back. He strained to see. He watched her there.

Another shrimpbarge came to pass a ferry on the river. Both boats wailed.

The noise of the clock ran rampant around the room. Ran fast, unfettered, ran clucking wild; a chicken, escaped out of the clock.

And in that time Anne quieted. It was slow. The heaving of her breast went easier, longer. Then it was uneven. Her lungs spasmed as though she had choked. And she was panting, newborn —newly gathering air in the gloomed silent room. She and Edmund waited. These two people faced each other across the near darkness.

Outside there was a gentle sprinkling splatter and then a loud flush in the leaves, as the rain began. There was that sound; and almost immediately the smell of rain was in the house, shifting cool and floating to the floor. It fell like the water, half as fast; it wiped clean the tight black, used black air. It was a good, green, right, smell.

Edmund said, "I beg your pardon." He said, "I forgot."

And the lightning was pale silver through the air.

"I didn't . . ." He said: "I did not mean . . . please, I . . ."

Anne was looking for a way to connect her lungs to her fresh voice, she looked and found no connection. Talking, talking all those years. And now the need; now there was no sound in her.

"Wait," Edmund said. He made a movement that started like a shrug, and got stuck. "Wait," he said. "I forgot. Please. I forgot it was you."

Came the thunder. Abrupt. Then high around the house the thunder came to warn him.

Anne rocked backwards and stepped behind her to where the storm was. She moved into the long gray curtains, leaning through them against the French doors that overlooked the garden. The wall of windows trembled around her in the fading voice of the thunder.

Edmund said, "I'm sorry."

He followed her. The table top dug into one thigh; he muttered. Then he walked around it, testing the way with his hands.

He said, "I'm sorry."

When the air shone again, it lit the curtains around Anne's body. She was holding one arm out, stiff, in front of her face; with the fingers closed and the palm sharp-angled up to hold his words. She was cased in blooming gray, shelled white in the mother-of-pearl curtains.

"I did," Edmund said. "Don't look like that; please. Wait, I wouldn't . . . I won't. I forgot."

But she had become herself too soon or too late, she had no speech yet. Anne pulled her hand in quickly and gripped it with her teeth. Then she made four little noises, something like a day-old baby.

"Don't." Edmund said loud: "Please don't. I said I was sorry. How many times do you want me to say it? I'm sorry."

He swiveled then. So hard he lost his balance and almost fell. There was a faint yellow sheen in the front hall from upstairs. He aimed his eyes at it, and began to walk.

Anne stood in the dark and watched him go. The gray velvet fluttered softly around her.

With the open front door in his grip, Edmund said one thing more. He said it as he left, he said it back to her. He said, "I forgot." And his voice filled the sky and crashed down over the whole house.

Then he was gone.

She was a sore face in the soft fluttering gray. Her eyes groped out; they pushed out, paling, like the eyes of a deaf mute, hungry and hard. And he was gone.

Washed yellow light hung suddenly from the ceiling. The chandelier seemed to crackle. The old living room was not quite the same as before.

Aunt Clothilde took her finger off the light switch, and limped across the carpet. "Now, fool," she said. "Go after him. You know what you just did?"

Anne dropped her stiff arm to her side.

"Fool. You awful fool." When Aunt Clothilde spoke, she snuffled. Always: she always was like she had a cold. "Go on," she said, "right after him."

Anne said, "No."

". . . Why?"

"No," Anne said, "I won't."

Aunt Clothilde nodded. "Now that's a new voice," she said. "Listen at you here, that's a brand new grown-up voice. Stop smiling. Go after him, I told you."

"No," said Anne. She started with her left foot, and went directly to the center of the room. Then she stood there and looked at the clock. She said, "It's raining."

"Of course it is. What do you care about the rain? Go on."

"I won't, no."

"Why? He wants you. Can't you see?"

"No."

"What?" said Aunt Clothilde. "Of course he does. That man wants you."

"Oh no," Anne said. "What a silly mistake. No. You are mistaken."

"I don't make mistakes; not likely, not about that. He does want you."

Anne said, "Me?" She said: "*Me?*"

"Yes, you."

Then she said, "He just forgot."

"He did not," said Aunt Clothilde, "don't be a fool. Hurry."

"No," said Anne. "It isn't any use hurrying."

". . . But he wants you."

"No," she said. "Not me."

Aunt Clothilde was quivering. "Damn fool. You don't know what you're doing. Fool, you don't know what you just did." She rested all her weight on her bad leg and swayed towards Anne. "You want me to do it? I'll tell him. You want me to go and get him for you?"

Anne took her eyes off the clock, and turned slowly to face her aunt. She lifted the same arm, but in a different way. Delicately, she held it out. Then, with careful precision, she slapped Aunt Clothilde, hard across the left side of her jaw.

The yellow light shivered.

"Now," said Anne, "get back upstairs."

". . . I . . . I wasn't upstairs," said Aunt Clothilde. "I was there all the time. In the hall. The whole time."

Anne said, "Then go up now."

Aunt Clothilde moved from under the chandelier and headed for the doorway. Her short leg bowed out; it made her rock when she walked, worse than a common limp.

From the hall, she said, "You awful fool. It's you he wants."

"Does he?"

"Yes. He does."

Spine arched, face to the light Anne whispered, "Then let him come back and get me."

"Oh no," Aunt Clothilde called. "No, he won't come back. You godawful fool. He won't ever come back. Not this way. Not like he was just now."

Anne smiled. It was not a pleasant twisting of her mouth. "That's right," she said. "He won't."

Alone in the living room, she went and sat on the sofa, facing the mantelpiece. Anne sat straight and strong, like a person should. And she watched the clock.

Behind it, spaced between the ticks, she could hear the laughter just as plain. Though she couldn't see that face. But she knew who it was.

Clear, loud, deep from her chest and even, Anne said: "Laugh."

Edmund was nearly downtown. He was marching fast—iced and dripping, in the languid winter rain.

2

Italy froze that year. Practically the whole country, so the Paris papers said. It froze late; right down to Naples, where snow at any time was a wet unearthly wonder in the wandering eyes of children.

Edmund first saw it on the train from Genoa, fourteen hours to Rome. He saw snow for fourteen hours. It made whirlpool bursts in the air when the train stopped. And it raked a diagonal skein over the crawling land from town to town so that the trees leaned forward. When the engine bucked, he thought the trees would fall.

He sat alone on one side of the first-class compartment, by the window. At the other end of the opposite seat sat an old backboned lady in seaweed-green with a damp brown fur muff and two small girls. The lady kept her hands in the muff and one girl tight to each hip. Every few minutes she gargled something silky in French to one of the girls. Otherwise she stared at the laden dust in the empty seat across from her. There were steam coils hidden under both seats; heat blasted out through the splits between the backrests and the dusty bottoms. But the window was not well sealed, and a draft of iced air hit the ceiling over Edmund and swept around the compartment as the train went jiggling on. The place was both uncomfortably hot in certain areas and too cold in others. The two never fused; except, to the same purpose, in the old lady's face.

Edmund rested his head on the yellowy lace napkin laid out for it. He slipped four fingers in the split back of the seat where the heat came from; then jerked them out, burned. The train hit a bump, and the draft sank for a second to play on his forehead. Then it was up again. Thick snow hit the window in fierce silence. Snow beat on the leaning trees.

He watched the bare branches claw at the soft snow that came to crack them. He thought the trees would win and live. Edmund thought they must win; and he was thinking how to explain that to the French lady when she was his mother.

He pulled himself from sleep, and shook his head. Then he grinned at the little girl who had been watching him. She was apple-pink and slickly combed, and she looked up at the French lady for permission to grin back. But the lady only took an ancient hand out from her muff, and shook its bones in the air before she replaced it. The girl drooped; tried not to look at Edmund. She frowned deeply at the window, and pretended not to mean a glance, and was not going to smile. Then, shyly, she smiled.

The French lady coughed, and watched the place where it had happened as if she had made a pearl or a smoke ring.

Edmund could still see his mother.

He saw her face on top of the old lady's neck, and he saw it in the snow. The slight, loose relief around the shrunken mouth when he had said he was leaving for Italy. And the relief showed there before she had been told whether he was taking Anne Legrange with him. She never asked; she left him alone when his father put the question. Because it was known that Edmund had not visited Anne for over a month. And because his mother knew those visits were ended and the engagement broken. His mother could sense many things: more than she could receive in the fragile tentacles of her caring. A lady touches, she does not take: a woman is not a lady.

And Edmund had noticed the same difference even among unladylike women. There were good ones—and there were interesting ones. You couldn't really respect an interesting woman, and you couldn't really be interested by a good one. You needed them both. Then you needed ladies too.

You needed them all.

The French hag was a lady. Edmund was always aware of each difference. And the two girls would soon be proper ladies.

There had been that lovely dark young female on the boat, pale and black and feline almost; still, quite fully a lady. With her husband and an infant so small it was a lump in a bundle. Edmund saw her just once, but he played pinochle with the husband every night. Walking down the passage from his cabin in evening dress, and when he turned the corner he side-stepped to avoid smashing into her, and nearly toppled his pinochle partner. Not quite, but nearly. And she lifted the baby and kissed it while he apologized; and she said never mind, no harm done; and the boat rocked from a big sea. Then that night over cards he congratulated the man for having such a lovely wife. A sweet lady, British. Definitely a lady.

Better to wait.

In Rome his friend Jergen Wilson would be on the platform waiting. Jergen was from Melpomene Drive at Wilkins, and he spent six months of every year in Rome. He lived there with a woman. Then he went back to his lady wife and his business in the States.

Always better to wait.

Anxious, pulsating snow seethed against the frosted glass. The circle he had made with his fingers for seeing outside was clouding over. There was one round clouded circle of swirling white closing on both iced eyes.

When the sliding door banged, he stood on his feet. He woke up that way—standing and watching the door.

Then she laughed.

Edmund sat down again. He collapsed into the seat. It was still snowing.

He flattened his hair with his left hand, and stretched his shoulder muscles.

The French lady and the two girls were gone.

He cleared his throat. Thick-voiced, he said, "How long was I asleep?"

The train rattled.

"I don't know," she said through the rattling, "I have no way of knowing."

"You don't?"

"Actually not, no."

"Oh."

"You were asleep when I got on, I got on in Florence. Two hours ago. With six pieces of luggage and two porters. That didn't wake you. At least that long."

Edmund said, "Oh." He looked at her hard, but she didn't disappear. Maybe she wouldn't disappear; it was just possible that she didn't want to.

He said, "I am awake now."

"Yes," she said, "I expect you are." She seemed about to giggle again. Not giggle: laugh.

(But how could she be in a dream and out of the dream? Unless it was like always.) Edmund said, "They say dreams are opposite. But I never in my life had a dream that didn't come true."

". . . I see," she said. "You mean you live a dream."

"No," said Edmund, "I don't."

"No? Then how do you explain it?"

"I wouldn't try to explain it," he said. "But that's the way it is."

"So," she said.

The snow hadn't changed. It was violent as before, silent. It still did want to get in at the window.

The oiled black hair was pulled tight back in a bun. Eyes nearly as dark as the hair, larger than any other eyes, sloped upwards. Deep hollows on either side of her mouth, from high-arched cheekbones with an oval pink flush on each. Full hard breasts from nursing. Pallid. And a shiny melted mouth. Thinnish. The same black dress. Or the same kind.

The train seemed dustier; Edmund sneezed.

"God bless you," she said. She had a brown mole under her left nostril, and a silk fringe mustache.

"Thank you." He took the show hankerchief from his coat pocket, and blew his nose. It honked. It didn't usually honk.

He looked at her, ashamed.

"You must be very careful," she said, "of the weather in Italy." Without turning her head she gripped the edge of the quilted gray box on the seat next to her. And that was where the baby was, asleep.

Edmund said, "Where is your husband, Mrs. Hutchinson?"

Now she was leaning over the box. She said, "My name is Silvana. People like to say Silva. Mr. Hutchinson is in England."

"That's right," said Edmund, "he said he was going to England."

"Did he?"

"That's right," said Edmund.

"I see," she said. Then: "I say. It is most unnecessary of you to be so polite. You are American."

Edmund frowned. It made one thick black line across his forehead.

She said, "You have remarkable eyebrows. But you mustn't try to be so polite."

". . . Aren't the English polite?"

"Some of them. Indeed. Yes, the English are polite."

"Mr. Hutchinson . . . is polite."

"Yes, he is," she said, "Mr. Hutchinson is indeed polite." Flat and edged.

Edmund said, "Plays a good game of pinochle." He had to keep talking.

"Yes, I expect he does. He is English and he is polite and he plays a rousing good game of pinochle. Admirable," she said, "he is quite admirable. In every way. I have nothing bad to say about him. You will have to try something else."

Edmund sat up, and swallowed. He said, "The thing is, I was dreaming about you."

Then she did laugh. She did it from the stomach. It was very strange because it was not like a lady at all: it was a woman's laugh. She said, "Yes, that is rather better, I think."

"How, better?"

Silvana said, "You are remarkably polite for an American. No. Shy. No . . . awkward. Yes, you are awkward. Of course yes. That is proper; all Americans with manners are awkward. They are awkward when they make friends, and they are awkward when they make love. Americans should never attempt adult manners, they are far more acceptable as children."

". . . Is that true?"

"Quite true," she said.

Edmund thought about it. Then he thought about the snow. His mother's face had gone. Gone out on the French lady.

Now things were strange, and they were too strange.

Silvana said, "This is your first time in Europe?"

"Yes. I mean except when I was a boy I came with my parents. It's my first time alone." Edmund thought he had never sounded so infantile.

"Yes," she said, "I imagined so. Too young for the war. You are twenty . . . six?"

"Twenty-four," Edmund said.

"How old do you think I am?"

". . . I don't know."

"Obviously not. I said think, not know."

Edmund coughed. He told her, "Maybe . . . twenty-nine. But you don't look it."

"I am thirty-five," said Silvana. "You have come to Europe because you had an unhappy love affair?"

"No. Not . . . well, no."

"Yes," she said.

"It wasn't a love affair. I mean not the way you mean. But what . . . how did you know?"

Silvana said, "It is one of the four reasons. You don't sleep like a student, and you don't act like a businessman. And you don't carry a camera. Tell me, how could you dream about me if you only saw me for one second on the boat?"

"I don't know," said Edmund. He could not get that nursling sound out of his voice.

She crossed her knees. There was a slipping of silk, and Edmund looked at them. When he looked back up, she was watching him.

She said, "You are not a liar. Are you?"

"No."

"Remarkable," she said.

The train was slowing; it was swaying.

"Why?"

"Why remarkable? I think I have known only one man who did not lie. He died."

"Then what makes you believe me?"

"I am not certain," Silvana said. "But I believe you. You . . . I believe you. Simply that."

Edmund smoothed his hair again. Then he took his hand down, and scratched it.

"You are sweet," she said.

Edmund said, "I am not."

Silvana chuckled. And the chuckle stayed inside. She never smiled. She said, "What exactly did Mr. Hutchinson say?"

"About what?"

"Me."

"He didn't. He didn't talk about you."

"No?"

"No," Edmund said, "he didn't talk about you."

"He did not explain why I remained in the cabin?"

"No."

"Did you know Mr. Hutchinson before the crossing?"

"No," said Edmund, "I met him on the boat."

"Are you acquainted with Mr. Hutchinson's family in America?"

"No."

Silvana said, "And he did not boast of me. Remarkable," she

said. "He must have seen the same quality in you. That is remarkable, he is stupid. No, you are not that kind of man. He must have seen that. Even he."

Edmund coughed.

Silvana said, "Do you think he did? Would you like to know about me?"

"Yes."

"How much?"

"I would like to," Edmund said.

"Yes, but how much? Very well, I shall tell you. Not all; I shall tell you as much as you want to know. But no more. I shall explain exactly as much as you want. It is an hour to Rome," she said. "You can have your dream for an hour."

The train started up faster. The swaying was rough now.

Silvana bent over the baby, and pulled at its blanket.

Then she said, "I am Italian. That is why I speak English so perfectly. I speak it too perfectly, I am aware of that. You would be aware of it too, if you weren't an American. I loathe the English, and I loathe their language. Therefore I am most careful to speak it perfectly."

"You're not . . .?"

"I am not what?"

Edmund said, "You're not . . . British?"

"My father was British, I think," Silvana said. "He was a British count. I never knew my father. My mother is in Rome. I lived in London for eleven years, from the time I was nine. Not with my father. I learned English there."

Edmund said, "You were just in America."

"For three weeks, with Mr. Hutchinson. He took me to America for three weeks; he has a married sister there. Then I stopped in Florence to see a friend. The boat docked five days ago. Where did you spend the last five days?"

"In Paris," Edmund said.

"That is fortunate. Paris is an oblique city. Young Americans who stay longer than five days in Paris acquire beards and affected accents, and poetry. And very often venereal disease. When they have not already fallen in love with other men. The beards smell worse than the French and are greasier than any Italian; then they stop bathing entirely. They pass two hours every day writing beatific and dirty adolescent verse; fourteen hours drinking absinthe and insulting Frenchmen, and whatever time remains they spend tolerating any Negro they can find who will put up with it. While you were in Paris I was in Florence with a friend. Now I go to Rome. I live in Rome."

"With your family?"

"My mother lives with me. I have told you I never knew my father."

"And Mr. Hutchinson . . . ?"

"Does not live in Rome. Not permanently. He travels a great deal."

"Oh," Edmund said. He cracked the knuckles on his left hand.

"Are you trying to find out whether I am married to Mr. Hutchinson?"

"Yes."

"This would not spoil the dream?"

"No."

"*Either* way?"

". . . No."

Silvana said, "I am not married to him."

The dust on the seat beside her looked deep and slippery. Like dust in velvet.

"I am not married at all," she said. "I will never marry. Particularly not if I were asked."

Edmund looked at the box.

"Mr. Hutchinson's," Silvana said. "It is his daughter. He would not like to believe that she is, but she is."

Edmund said, "I don't understand."

". . . What, exactly?"

There were two slivers of red in the blacks of her eyes. Edmund was staring, first at one, then at the other. But he could not focus on them both together—not see them at once. And this upset him. He could feel a cold knot harden inside, and the knot was around his bowels. Because he had never noticed before in his whole life that it is impossible to focus on both a person's eyes.

He said, "You're a lady."

Silvana sucked a lump of air in to laugh with; and then she didn't use it that way. She let the air escape evenly. "No," she said, "how young. How young, how young, how very young. Young American. You are more than sweet," she said.

Edmund said, "I am not."

"But you are. You are sweet and you are young. How must it be to be so young?" Then she said, "I was never quite so young as you."

"I'm not . . . sweet."

Silvana said, "Now look at the snow. Watch the snow. Is it the white makes you dream?" She said: "Sometimes in the winter I go north to the mountains. Not to ski, not to do anything. To see the mountains. When I think I am hating too much, then. I like to watch the mountains, just below the snowline; the rock is gray there, all the rock is naked and gray, cold. Clean. I like to watch the gray rock clean under the snow."

"I'm not; I'm not sweet. Not the way you mean."

"What way do I mean? There is only one way." Silvana put out a long, pale fingernail and scraped at the frost on the window. "What is a way? What is clean? What is sweet?" she said. "How is your dream?"

"Stop it," Edmund said. He said: "Stop it." His hands were shaking.

Silvana sat back and guffawed. Harder and deeper than a man—a wrong noise for her. She said, "I think I like to travel because it is not the same as living. Is that it? Is this why I like to travel?"

"I don't know," Edmund said.

"Why don't you know?"

Edmund lifted his shoulders. He said, "I don't . . ."

"Can't you like your dream? Can't you like it? On this trip I am a lady and you are sweet. A most agreeable dream."

"I told you. I'm not that kind of sweet."

"I am not that kind of lady."

Edmund put all ten fingers around his skull, and pressed them there. "All right," he said.

Silvana squinted at him.

She said, "Would you like to kiss me?"

". . . Yes."

"I say. And you haven't even made an effort. You must ask me, or you must pull me up. Young American. How long have you been conscious of the fact that you would like to kiss me?"

"I don't know," Edmund said.

He had to cross his legs. Then he had to fold his hands over his lap.

"Well." Silvana lengthened her neck. "Now you have my permission, you see? More than permission; I ask you to do it. I beg of you to kiss me."

The train was bumping to a stop.

"Wait," Edmund said.

"Please kiss me."

"Not right now," he said.

"Why not?"

"I uh can't . . . yet."

"Why?"

". . . Wait."

"Why? Young American. Why? My American, why?"

Edmund shut his eyes and tried hard to concentrate on nothing. "You're sitting down," he said.

"Did you never kiss a lady sitting down?"

"I . . ."

"Or you mean you are embarrassed to stand up at the moment?"

Edmund opened his eyes. Silvana kept her arm on the baby's box. And they stared at each other. Then she bent forward.

She said, "You would never know I hate so much. Would you?"

Voices in the station sounded thick. Shadows picked their ways quickly over the ice. Their voices sounded muffled in the snow.

Edmund whispered, "I hope nobody comes in here."

"Someone doubtless will," she said.

And nobody did. Passengers walked past the compartment from

both directions. Some paused, and looked in. Edmund held his breath till the sound of the blood filled his ears.

And nobody opened the door.

The train hooted, and jerked. It jerked twice more.

Fresh out of the station, a black sooty cloud mixed with the white in the air. Edmund sat still, and caught up with his breath; he could see the wafting black from the corner of his eye. It grew darker, soft and shining—much like the sheen on her dress.

He wondered why he had not seen that cloud before.

They were married in Rome one week and six days after their arrival. Jergen did everything he could to stop it.

Jergen Wilson was five years older than Edmund. He was not attractive to look at, had never been, and knew it. But he had willfully tried to improve on God's will: kept himself dressed in the most subtle combinations of wrong strong colors, unbathed, and nose-thumbing fat. Jergen had chosen a whole character for himself, and he spoke in a colloquial manner as he thought he must. Because although he was educated and intelligent, he was a very wrathful young man. Yet he meant intensely everything he said. And without this obese character to express it for him, he would certainly have had to lie about his truth.

Jergen said, "Man, you don't plain steal another man's mistress like that. Not without his permission. His wife all right, but not his mistress for chrissake, it isn't proper. Not in Rome."

And then Jergen said, "Well, take her if you want her, for crying out loud. If you want her so bad, go ahead and take her. We'll fix it up some way with Hutchinson. Sure, take her. But don't marry her. Crying out loud, you can have any woman you want on this earth with your looks, you don't even need money with your looks, do you know what she is? Take her if you got to have her. Just don't marry her. Take her on a permanent basis, put her in a palace on the Grand Canal in Venice, or buy her a house in Paris. Your papa'll give you the money, what do you care? He'd give you more than that if he knew what you are planning on. Anyway it isn't as if she wanted to get married, it's you, not her. Edmund, you don't know what you are, you can have any woman you want with your looks, you could have them paying you. Or use your money if you'd rather have it that way, either one. Look how ugly I am and look at my little Bruna. Happiest Bruna is in her life is when I just let her sit on the sofa and arrange dollar bills. She just sits there and counts American dollar bills, and you'd think I'd up and gave her the Pope's teeth or something. Tickles her to death. And grateful? My Lord. But if I went and asked her to marry me, she'd flip. She would, she'd faint away right in my face, I can see her now. And she doesn't even know I have a wife. And she hasn't been in the business half as long as yours, not half as long. That's another thing, look at your woman's age: that woman's upwards of thirty. A good ten years older than you. All right for now, but what are you going to do in another ten years? And what about the baby? What you planning to do with Hutchinson's baby? Hutchinson doesn't want it. You couldn't even make him admit it was his, much less want it. You can't marry her. No, you cannot, don't you shake your head at me. Edmund, what do you think, you imagine you are being honest with yourself? Well if you do you're wrong there too. Consider. Nothing honest about marrying that kind of woman. It's the worst type of crusading, and nobody's going to respect you for it, not even her. It's dishonest to everything you were ever brought up for, and it would unhinge your mother's feelings. What you got to do is go back and make an honest respectful wife out of the Legrange girl, whatever happened between you. She deserves to be a loving wife to you. It's what you got to do, it's the only honest upright thoughtful thing. Then if you still care to, you can come back over here and get this woman and do anything you want with her. And you won't be hurting anybody at home. You can set her up right now if you really have to, she'll wait for you. With dollars you can set her up like the Queen of the May. And I'll take care of Hutchinson. I will. Me, personally, I will see to it. But you can't marry her. Edmund, believe me, that's the most horrifying thought you ever had, is marrying that woman. My

Lord. Aside from what it means to you and your family. For crying out loud, no, man, no indeed. Not on any count. No, sir. Now consider. You absolutely may not marry that woman."

They were married in a church on the outskirts of Rome. A pitted gray church, poor and made rough by the wind. Silvana dressed in dark gray, and she wore a gray lace veil. But she carried her baby in a glistening new white blanket. She never put it down, not even to give to her mother, and she stroked it during the entire ceremony. Under the blanket she held a bouquet of long-stemmed, dark red roses; she had spent an hour alone removing every thorn with her fingers before she left for the church. And she had not permitted Edmund to give her anything for the wedding but those roses and a plain gold band. By Silvana's request Jergen was best man, and there was another man, fleshless and gawky, from the American Embassy. Silvana's mother stood behind. Jergen had trouble keeping on his feet through the whole thing. He was so drunk he dribbled when he kissed the bride. But Silvana let him kiss her nevertheless; serious, almost grave, as she became the second they entered the church. Before that she had laughed hard —long and hard, all the way from her apartment in a taxi; with that queer unsmiling laughter.

Precisely this much was known about Silvana Bufardi:

She was the daughter of a professional prostitute and a British count—or so her mother admitted, and claimed. She was among the most beautiful women of Rome. Her mother raised Silvana to the age of nine; at that time she was seen by a wealthy older Englishman who was spending the weekend. He noticed with outspoken awe her quick mind and charming curiosity for all things. The Englishman stayed on longer than he had intended. Being himself childless, he came to love Silvana; he made a financial arrangement with her mother, and took her away with him to London. Silvana lived there as his daughter for eleven years, and much care was given her education. When the war was over she came back to Rome to live with her mother, though she could have stayed in England. Her adopted parent had died, and left her well-read, rich, and in eleven years groomed almost beyond his own expectations. In Rome alone, Silvana received four propitious offers of marriage and six to go into business, and these offers came within a month of her return, and all were legitimate. She rejected every one. She refused to better her social standing. Further, from then on she began to live in a wild, outlandish way. Silvana visited the capitals of Europe and the Orient, spending months in each, seeing each with a different man. Always in the winter she came back to Rome; and always then there were huge parties given at her three-storied apartment on the Via Claudio Monteverdi. Silvana paid for each party, accepting no assistance. She stood at the bottom of the staircase with her mother—the old lady covered in gold cloth, dripping gold and bright-stoned jewelry; being present against her will, as she hated and feared the spending of money— and Silvana in plain black with a few scattered diamonds. She made her aging mother stand beside her without the comfort of a chair, and she made her welcome every guest. Her money went like that, and it went in other secret ways. She took costly presents from men, but she would take no cash—not until she had spent her entire bank account, and sold the presents too. Then she selected another lover. Her notoriety increased; and Silvana was known by name and by sight among the most and least respected kinds of people throughout much of Europe. Her lovers were generally offensive to look at, and mostly old. Men said that Silvana, given to choose between a rich handsome man and a rich ugly one, would take the ugly one. The most recent was Claude Hutchinson, and he attained the distinction of making her pregnant. Women said that Silvana was inevitably unfaithful to the man who kept her; but she had not been seen pregnant before. Claude Hutchinson offered to pay for an abortion, and he offered to pay for much besides. Silvana had the baby.

Such were the facts in view. No one knew any more about her.

No one including the groom knew why Silvana Bufardi married Edmund Choate.

. . .

On the sidewalk outside the church; after the ceremony. Vague, damp sun, insipid and dead yellow, through the gray mist over Rome.

Edmund bent his arm and took the child from her.

Jergen was humming, privately. He was leaning on Silvana's mother. Spasms of tears wandered like milk in the old lady's thick white powder.

The skeleton man from the American Embassy shook everybody's hand, and walked away.

Several little boys, ragged, and one girl, climbed over a wall to swarm around. Yelling. Dirty. Stretching up.

"They want money," Silvana said. She faced Edmund, and all her fingers were moving over the baby. She was afraid he would drop it. Her face looked anxious—the way Silvana looked whenever she watched her child. She said, "Give her back to me. You must throw them all the change from your pocket."

And Edmund said, "No."

He switched the baby gently to his left arm. After that he turned his right pants pocket inside out. The coins sprinkled and rolled across the sidewalk.

Every child except the girl screamed; they chased the spreading coins. The dirty small girl stood by herself. Like Silvana, she was watching Edmund hold the baby.

Then the taxi exploded twice and backed up, grunting and bouncing.

"She's mine now," Edmund said. "What's her name?"

". . . Don't you know?"

"No. I had to write it on that form three times, but I don't remember. All you ever call her is darling. Or *carina*. Same thing."

"Her name. Loris Licia," said Silvana, "that's her name. Loris Licia Bufardi."

"Too long," Edmund said.

"Not so long. Like all Italians. Be careful there with the blanket, for God's sake."

Edmund said, "Loris Licia Bufardi Choate."

Between grunts the taxi exploded again.

Silvana stared at Edmund. Then she looked at her mother. She said, "Yes, I think we might dispense with the Bufardi now. *Non è così, Mamma?* Loris Licia Choate." She bowed; turned, expressionless, and stepped into the taxi. Seated inside, she opened her pocketbook and took out a ten-lira note. She handed it to the girl who was standing on the sidewalk.

Edmund bent to follow her.

Silvana stopped him with her eyes. "Just a moment," she said. Using her right hand, she held out the bouquet of roses. They dropped darkly, crushed from her elbow in the misty light. She pointed her hand, and scrupulously, exactly, aimed the flowers.

"*Signora,*" said the taxi-driver, "*felicitazioni. Felicitazioni a tutti e due.*" He smiled to congratulate them.

"*Grazie,*" said Silvana.

And she flicked her wrist and tossed the bouquet. It did a short rainbow arc high over Edmund's head, to fall into two outstretched, trembling arms. Silvana's aim was perfect.

She slid over, and made a space for Edmund.

When they were seated together, Jergen knocked on the window. Edmund rolled it down for him.

Jergen put his head in, and belched. "My Lord," he said.

Then the taxi bumped off like a camel and left him there.

Edmund put his free hand over one of Silvana's. He said, "You haven't smiled yet."

"No," said Silvana. "Actually I hadn't planned on it. As a rule I never smile. Would you like me to?"

Then she opened her mouth and kissed him.

Edmund tightened his hand.

She said, "That girl was watching you."

"What girl?"

"On the sidewalk, she had eyes like my baby. She wouldn't get out of the way. She wouldn't even go after the coins; I gave her ten lire. I had to throw the flowers over all three of you."

The gray city was endless past.

"I didn't notice any girl," Edmund said.

"She was there. She was watching you."

Edmund turned and stared out the back window. Three blocks behind he could see the church. All the children were gone.

Silvana said, "That was an awful little girl."

But there were no children left. Jergen was next to the old lady again, with his back turned; he was being sick on the church steps. A second taxi waited for both of them.

Silvana's mother must have seen Edmund staring from the window. She lifted her arm and solemnly waved the flowers. She made long strokes up and down with the red-tipped bouquet.

It looked as if she was trying to paint the air.

3

Several weeks before he came back to the city with his new wife and adopted daughter, Edmund's father died of a heart attack.

His mother Amelie went on living for four years and ten months after that. And there was a sense to Amelie Choate while she lived. She was a sorrowful lady.

She was in a certain sense like Anne Legrange; and in another sense she was not. Amelie was a lady because the definition fitted her—never because she conformed to it. She had the desperate strength of an untouchable soul, and she even enjoyed her unhappiness.

You might feel the inside of a well—which isn't square like a room nor four-walled. You might feel one round surrounding endless barrier wherever you reach out. Floating there, you have enough space to move; you can arrange your hair and your ways. Feel no fear, for there is no danger: it is a well nobody uses. Don't mind the dank darkness and ignore the slippery mold. Just be in the center. Only just be.

Amelie had an arrangement like that around her soul, and she had it when she met Edmund's father. They were married. And he was not a man to crack a lady's apparatus.

He was not a man at all, and she punished him for that. In the thirty-one years of their union, Amelie effected polite discussions with her husband once a day. She asked his net opinion on every subject and every object within her vision; and then she showed him he was wrong every time. She was asking him to be a man, but it was her own manner of asking, and he did not understand.

And finally at the end of that cold winter, after one late discussion, he gasped, with his right hand over his mouth, and died with a contradiction thawing in his heart.

Edmund was born long before. It took seven years from the date of their marriage. Then here was a child more frightening than any being Amelie had ever known. From the time Edmund first cried, she developed a habit of staring at him—and at anybody—for a full five seconds before she could speak. It was a kind of optical stutter. Because Edmund was a threat; he needed what had never been exposed. He demanded what was inside the well. Amelie could either believe in him, or she could go on having that protection. And if she lost that, what might the day do—and what would she offer her child?

So she offered him everything else, and saved herself.

There is much talk in the city of children who are *spoiled*, and there is little understanding of the word. People do not know what they mean by it. They use it when they find a child who has been laden with luxury and who is always wanting more and who is never satisfied by what he has been given. Then people say the child is spoiled; and they say he will not ever be sated because he has already been accustomed to too much. They do not say that no man's gift on earth, not even life, matters of itself—but merely for what it means.

Amelie Choate gave Edmund life, and she gave him the world. She gave him toys; expensive clothes; the best training; a square golden watch with round diamonds for numerals; the most money. She shook her husband fastidiously until he jangled empty, and what fell from his pockets she gave to Edmund. And she gave it all in atonement. Each gift was a gilded substitute for real giving; every new package sparkled bright as the cold helpless glitter of her eyes.

And Edmund was never content. He wanted more, and when he got it, more. The first few years, he was ill-behaved on purpose; after that he simply did what he felt like doing at the time. He was his mother's dread.

So the city people said she had spoiled him. They said Amelie had given him too much, and they said Edmund's temper was the awful ungrateful result of being overindulged in his upbringing. They were sure of what they said, and they seemed sad at being sure because the Choates were such a fine, well-bred family. Talkers are only morbidly sure when they are right for the wrong reason.

The last discussion Amelie shared with her husband was about a letter from Edmund announcing that he had taken a wife.

After his death, she got into bed. Many friends and acquaintances came to be miserable with her; Amelie was still lady of the city. That way she had of staring at a person before she spoke was considered to be genteel, and it was discreetly imitated by women all down Melpomene Drive. They sat around her canopied bed in adumbral dress and outstared her in dismal understanding. Now she hardly spoke herself. Some dear friends, and the servants, noticed a strange new behavior. Amelie would suddenly get up from her bed in the afternoon and go off into the internals of the house trailing black chiffon and vague violet water; then she would come back with a book, or maybe a vase, or a small painting. She climbed under the satin covers and placed the object next to her about a yard off. And she watched it fiercely there for fifteen minutes, without speaking. If she were asked, she either didn't answer, or muttered something about its being an object she and her husband had once talked over together. But she said that in a wooden dull voice, and clearly didn't care to be asked.

Then when she finished watching it—she looked up and dismissed the thing as if it were not on the bed at all. And someone would have to take it gently away and put it back where it belonged. This was her way of missing him. It was thought to be more delicate and elegant than anything Amelie had yet done; ladies held a remembrance of it for future reference.

Edmund and Silvana moved into the second floor south wing of the Choate house, with her child. That upstairs wing was cut off spiritually by Amelie, and they occupied it alone. They lived there for close to five years.

Amelie never accepted Silvana as a true daughter-in-law; not even before the facts were known. She had not trusted Edmund since the day of his birth (which was the actual reason he had spent so much of his time proving her right). Now, though, Amelie was weary and grieved, and she felt old; she stayed in bed most of the day. She took no action against Silvana, and if she passed her in the house she nodded. Still she made her feelings known by all. She allowed that the marriage be taken as valid, because she could do little else. But valid, in Amelie's mouth, did not mean acceptable—not by a colorful distance. And any woman who was even half received with favor in the city against Amelie Choate's decided judgment had done a practically impossible thing.

Silvana did it. One by one she charmed every person she met. Her manners and her educated speech, her admitted age; her wearing of black, her humble pride, her taste in all things were noticed by Amelie's hidden enemies and whispered about to closest friends. Yet Silvana made no obvious effort to be accepted; and that also was noticed. When she offered no excuses regarding her child's father, word spread she was a widow in mourning. And the fact that she preferred to dress in black even after her marriage to Edmund was seen as another quality in her favor. It took almost a year: by then, Edmund's tailored wife was a recognized figure in society—though both she and Edmund spent their evenings closed in their rooms, and disliked invitations, and hardly ever went out to a restaurant.

After Jergen Wilson got back from Rome, it was discovered that he had been best man at the wedding. Jergen was a shop owner, and therefore not of the highest social layer. He was permitted to appear in certain circles because he lived on Melpomene Drive; the right people looked down on him with amusement, and he knew it and played to it. He was the globular clown, but because he did not presume to be anything else, his somewhat ostentatious taste in his own dress was overlooked; and these same amused people bought at his shop. He had nothing to say of Silvana; he and his wife were not as friendly as they might have been. They never came to call.

One day not long after settling down, Silvana and Edmund went for a first formal walk on Melpomene Drive.

They wheeled the baby's carriage down the sidewalk, each with a hand, and their hands touching, on the round metal bar. Summer was wide then; dust shone by the sides of the street under a molten white sky. The sore tops of trees were pleading green in the open heat, and their heat waves were like smoke. The sparkling asphalt on Melpomene Drive sizzled at the feet of shambling dogs as it had always done towards August. Edmund and Silvana moved slowly through the dusty shade; he was watching the soft wide warm part of the baby's head. When he looked up from that he stopped so suddenly Silvana nearly fell over the carriage.

Edmund took his hand off the bar.

She was coming down the same sidewalk. A new quality of person: differently toned. She was different even in her movement.

Edmund stood still to meet her. Then he forgot to open his mouth.

But when she came closer, she crossed to the inside; she ignored him and went straight to Silvana.

She said, "I am glad to meet you, Mrs. Choate. My name is Anne Legrange." And the directness of her look and her smile were new in that face.

Then she said, "You are even more lovely than people say."

"Thank you," said Silvana, "how do you do?"

Slow as a lighthouse beam, Anne turned the smile to Edmund. The round beam flashed, and passed. She said, "Good afternoon, Edmund."

She bent her right forefinger, and touched the baby's cheek.

"Hello," Edmund said.

Anne smiled at her wet finger. She slipped by, and went off down the sidewalk.

A block later, Edmund was still silent.

Silvana said, "She is regal."

"What?"

". . . Miss Legrange."

"Yes," Edmund said. "Her. I guess so, yes. Now. I guess she is."

But Silvana was not paying attention. She told him, "Wait a minute," and walked to the front of the carriage. "Have you got a handkerchief?" she said.

Edmund gave her one.

He did not ask why she had used his rather than her own to wipe the baby's face.

She taught him to be tender when she taught him what a bed was for. Then Edmund was no longer embarrassed or ashamed with her. Sometimes in the heat, after he came home from learning to run his father's business, they would walk the halls naked and sit around like that for the rest of the evening. They locked the doors to the south wing, and she told him stories of what her life had been long before. She talked of the Englishman who had tried to be nice to her, then explained what she had done in her hate. Other later men she listed too; she gave them numbers, laughing, so Edmund could refer to them easily when he wanted. And after he was at last able to forget them, she told him she had not loved and would not love any man but him. When she said that, Silvana stopped laughing in her flat, frozen way—and Edmund believed her.

Once some handsome friend of Jergen Wilson flirted with her in the street. Silvana acknowledged the gesture, and she thanked him. Then she expounded gaily and with great charm her specific reasons for suggesting that he choose a male sexual partner rather than a female. She wheeled her baby all the way down to Edmund's office to inquire the name of the man she had insulted.

Even after the scandal of her past life came to town—when men eyed her wherever she walked—Edmund had no reason not to be sure of his wife. In the time they were married he had one rival: Loris Licia Choate. Silvana never let him hire a nurse for the baby. She prepared the food and formulas, and washed the diapers. The child had her own bedroom two doors up the hall from their own.

And no other person mattered to Silvana but him. By the start of the second winter, Edmund knew he could trust her with his love. He even thought he might begin to believe in himself.

The scandal arrived quietly. Lily Legrange was the one who found out and spread the news. She had a friend in Europe who was acquainted with many people.

She came one day to see Amelie with a letter. When she left, the skin over her cheekbones looked white, and she walked fast.

In a single day the wind of many mouths blew it all over town.

It made little difference. Edmund and Silvana were close to no one in the city. They did not go to parties. A few old women now crossed the street to avoid them; and some men Edmund knew winked at him or passed an occasional remark. The society column of the morning paper tried to be sly and humorous about "The News on Melpomene Drive" for a while, and then dropped it. That was all; they had both been expecting it, and neither cared. Silvana only said they would have to go somewhere else to live when Loris Licia was old enough to go to school. And Edmund's love was stronger than the wind.

The last person who came to call was Anne Legrange. She stood just inside the doorway. Then with the same tranquil moon-gaze she explained that she never had anything to do with the letter. She said it was her mother's doing, and she herself had not known about it and didn't care when she did know. This was a mottled morning, a weekday, and Edmund was at work; Silvana was alone.

Then Anne said, "I would prefer to be sure you believe me."

Silvana nodded. Both were at the door of the south wing. "Be quite sure," she said; "now please come in."

"I was to have married him, you know. He has told you that."

"Yes, he has," Silvana said.

"They like to think I would shame myself to disgrace you."

"Do they? How presumptuous on an earth to have beings who *like* to think about it."

". . . About?" Anne was watching some sunlight fade on the floor.

Silvana flicked a particle of dust from a square black button of her sleeve. "The earth," she said evenly. "Won't you come in?"

"No. Thank you."

Anne stared down the long hall to the open bedroom, and she apologized again for her mother. She smiled; stepped back, and shut the door in her own face. She never came back to the south wing of the Choate house.

And they lived alone for three years more. Edmund was blissful; Silvana was more beautiful, and she seemed younger. Loris Licia had not taken more than one winter's cold when the diphtheria scare began five years after they were married.

Lily Legrange died among the first, overnight. She died of a burst appendix; but nobody accepted that explanation. House by house, the doors of Melpomene Drive had already slammed and were chattering. The city was panicked; schools and public houses closed. Downtown, the shops and restaurants and most offices stayed empty. And at first there was no true epidemic.

What there was then came from the river, on an oysterboat. The boat docked one morning, and a gray-skinned bearded man with red swollen eyeballs was carried off and taken to the hospital. By night they had not yet been able to stop the contractions in his throat. Four hours later he screamed so loud you could hear him in a bar a half-block south. It was the kind of sound that stays in your ears, and people still thought he was screaming when the man was dead.

Doctors could not check the hysteria. Whatever it was, of that particular disease six people died in the whole city. But gossip listed eighteen by the second week's end. The remainder of these were actual deaths from ordinary flu or flu followed by pneumonia. By that time in their tumble to leave the city, people did not heed a slight fever. Influenza was the real danger, and had been since early December. Influenza was accountable for the queues outside the cemetery; Silvana was buried through a gray mid-morning rain. And Amelie Choate contracted it from her just in time to follow Edmund's wife out of his world. This was the only thing they ever did together.

And it was undeniably Silvana's fault. The day she heard some-one mention diphtheria in the upstairs foyer, she changed; she behaved from then on in a way Edmund was not able to com-prehend.

She forbade Loris Licia to go out of the house. Then she ordered Edmund to make plans for an immediate departure from the city. She packed their things in one day, though they could get no train reservations for a week. When Amelie declined to go, Silvana went up to her room and silently filled three suitcases with whatever she thought the lady might need. Edmund could not cope with her. Amelie, who was in bed fighting a series of head-aches, stopped being polite and said many things. Silvana paid no attention. She intimated a knowledge of what diphtheria could do, from having lived in Italy, and then kept silent. The servants except for the cook were not coming to work because of the scare, and Silvana minded the house and cared for Amelie during those last days. By then she herself was coughing so that there was a low squashy echo in her chest.

And the weekend before the trip, Edmund found their bed-room door locked. He hit it and shook the handle. From inside,

Silvana's voice was barely familiar. She said he was not to come in again: Edmund was to take the train with everyone else, and she would follow when she could. He hit the door once more; then she yelled at him. She said she had taken the mortal disease.

He got a doctor, and Silvana would not allow the doctor in until Loris Licia had left the house. Edmund walked to see the Jergen Wilsons, who were going to New York with their three children. He told them that he and Silvana did not care to leave because of Amelie, but were both very worried for the child. Jergen began by politely refusing to take Loris Licia and was told to be quiet. Then Edmund asked Mrs. Wilson to depart from her own living room; and when he had finished with Jergen, and Mrs. Wilson came back, her husband had changed his mind about accepting the new responsibility.

Back at home the child was shut in her bedroom as Silvana had left her. The cook had brought breakfast and lunch, both, and put them on the bedside table, where they still lay. Loris Licia never ate without her mother. When Edmund came in she would not speak. She was dressed and sitting on the edge of a chair close to the corner, with Silvana's china figurine of the Virgin across her lap, and the white china was smudged and stained from fingering. Loris Licia's heavy winding hair was matted around her face. She stared at Edmund through a fringe of black with gray eyes that were lighter than his own; but she would not let out a sound. He felt clumsy and too big trying to explain because she went on staring like that, without a movement. She neither moved nor spoke until he touched her. Then she hit him in the neck. Edmund's neck and one cheek and both wrists were scratched to bleeding by the time he got her to the Wilson house. He had to carry her all the way, and she beat him over the head till she broke the china Virgin into two parts. But she did not make a sound.

Silvana lived a week after that, and still believed she had diphtheria. The doctor told her otherwise but she laughed at everybody. The hospitals were full; Silvana refused to allow an oxygen tent brought into her room, and she wouldn't let Edmund touch her for fear of infection.

In the last days Silvana spoke mostly Italian. She was not then the woman Edmund knew and trusted. He sat on a straight wooden chair in her room and passed the hours watching a white-faced girl who tossed and tangled wild in her own loose hair; and this was a girl he had not ever seen before. Distempered, enraged with fever, Silvana died thinking she was in Rome. She laughed constantly and spit on the floor, though there was a clean basin always by her side. She was something like his bride only twice. One of these times she sat straight up in bed and in perfect English accused Edmund of wishing her dead. She looked at him and told him to bring Loris Licia to see her right away; she requested that he bring a priest as well. And then she said very seriously that if he brought either, or did anything else she requested, she would kill herself. She swung back on the pillows, and before Edmund could think of an answer she was talking in Italian again.

But on the last night she was singing; hardly able to breathe. The song was French. It stopped, and started again; and Silvana laughed. After that she was quiet. Towards midnight she called Edmund's name six times, in a strange thin voice that was young and high, and frightened, and she did it with a noticeable accent. Edmund squatted by her open eyes, but she did not see him, and she went on calling his name. Later while she slept Edmund sat in his chair wondering. He could wonder things like whether he might smoke a cigarette after she was dead, for he had not seen a cigarette in eight days, and did not want one now. He looked at his gold watch and noticed the minute hand move between the diamonds. And he thought it was impossible that he could see the hand move. Then he scratched his chest, and there was something wrong—and when he took it out it was a pencil with the point broken off long ago. And the air felt like rain, and it was not raining. There was a dull spot in the wax on the floor; he studied that spot for a half-hour. He compared it to things.

When it didn't change, he got up and went out into the hall. He walked down the hall to his study and to the window on the far wall. Only there it was not raining either. But he knew what was inside the closet door, having attached it there himself personally, and he went and opened that door, and slid the pencil in, and used it. And it seemed to him that this was the first time he had used it, because he was certain he could not remember standing this way and turning the handle that way; and he would certainly have remembered had he ever done this before. On the way back to her room he looked at his watch again, and he thought how ridiculous to have thought the hand had moved that fast. Then he went in and sat on the chair. She had not stirred, and he was sure she was probably dead, but he was too tired to get up and look, and there was no use doing it anyway. There was no purpose in a lot of things. But Edmund was positive there must be some use to something; only he could not think what it might be, because all he could think of was that there was no purpose at all in looking to see if somebody was dead. So he sat and watched the sawdust on the sharpened pencil, and when he blew it off the point was shiny black in the thick orange light, like jet earrings, or like her eyes. And when he woke up the rain was sliding down the window behind him, and he could feel it there against his neck without looking. And Silvana was dead.

The days around her death were wet and wintry. Upstairs Amelie Choate was dying too. Before his wife died, Edmund had spent a few minutes of each day up with Amelie; but when he sat by her bed he was usually thinking about Silvana. And sometimes when he sat with Silvana he was feeling sneaky about his mother. He remembered this sense of badness from when he was very little. It was the same as when he was a boy and had done something to upset her, and then wished she would hit him or punish him, or at least show anger. But she would not. And now sitting watching her cough and gasp, ladylike, he wished somehow she would slap him. He wished she would reach out and scratch and punish him for everything bad he had ever done, and tear at him with her fingernails and shake him and call him names before she died. Because he could not even weep. He wanted his mother to punish him for his life and their two deaths and to make him have tears before it was too late. Because he could not place what he had done that was so bad but he knew she knew, it was her secret. His mother had always known why he was bad, this she knew now, and now she was going to die with the secret. And Amelie lay there using one handkerchief after another, ordering him to turn his head away every occasion she had to spit up, and asking what time it was. Then the trained nurse got the flu and left, and after that the doctor took away the oxygen tent because anyway Amelie didn't really have trouble breathing, they needed oxygen in other places; then Edmund saw for sure she would die. He saw it for sure, and it made him sick at his stomach. Then he remembered and it made him want to vomit what he had not yet eaten to remember how frail and delicate his mother had always been like she was right now when he had done those worse, disgusting and slimy things. And now right now there was nobody to care for his mother in a nickel-plated, slobbery domestic open bedpan death where she couldn't even defecate sincerely—after her waterproof dustproof antimagnetic and shockproof and eighteen-carat Swiss-timed life with imported diamonds for the tickaway days: nobody, Jesus, but him and the cook; and Silvana downstairs dying Silvana, Silvana, Silvana, who was not Silvana, Silvana who had made his mother ill.

But the morning two days after his wife was buried, Edmund went up to Amelie, and when he walked into her room that day he thought possibly now he might weep. She was lying there with the covers up to her neck, frowning and whispering. There was a new crocheted afghan over her bed; it was thick wool and colored all the many different shades of brown that got left out of the rainbow. The sheets were clean, and the frilly canopy over the bed had been taken off. The room looked fresh and dusted: shiny tops reflected light from the newly wiped windows. And sitting next to his mother holding her hand, dressed simply and in mourning, without her make-up, was Anne Legrange.

She glanced around when he came into the room, then looked

back at Amelie. She said nothing. Across on the other side of the room Edmund saw Anne's Aunt Clothilde. She limped to a brown velvet chair and sat down. Aunt Clothilde's hair was bleached and fuzzed loose blond around her head, and she had pink plump skin. Snuffling, she pretended to wipe her nose. She carried a piece of radiant white material to do that with. She was shiny in the steam heat. With her emaciated left leg and her hair and the pink sheen, she looked like a broken dissolving kewpie doll.

Edmund chewed at the inside of his underlip. He leaned on his hands against the wall.

Amelie had been discussing something private. She pushed herself up a few inches on the lacy, satin-covered pillows. Her head strained forward; all the puckered skin pulled back from her eyes, and she blinked three times. Then she could not speak normally, so she preferred to whisper, "I am reminded of the summer we went to Europe. I cannot say why I bring to mind that summer. It was so long ago. You may sit down, Edmund. Do you remember?"

"No," he said.

"You were quite little. Your father and I took you to Europe. And we went to Lourdes. In France; don't you remember?"

"Not very well," Edmund said.

"You should. What an experience. A terrible place. We went there to see the pilgrims. To Lourdes, you know. It was your father's idea. It was his father's idea. Won't you sit down, Edmund? You can hardly be very comfortable standing up."

"Thank you," Edmund said, "I'm comfortable."

"You see, we went to see the pilgrims. I don't know what I expected, but I did not expect anything like it turned out to be. An experience. And I said to Edmund's father before we left Paris, I said, 'Really,' I said, 'I don't know what to expect,' I said, 'but I'm sure you are wrong.' And my dears. An experience."

Anne said, "Really?"

"Well I mean you really can have no idea. What a place. I had no idea. After the pamphlets Edmund's father obtained from the

Syndicat d'Initiative, you know. Crystal pools and what have you. Crystal pools indeed."

Aunt Clothilde said, "Where is all this?"

"Lourdes, dear; we're talking about Lourdes. And he was entirely fooled, you know. But I can't say I was. Still I did not expect anything quite like that. I mean one does expect at least a certain cleanliness from a pilgrim, don't you know, one doesn't think a pilgrim would look like that. I mean merely the word, *pilgrim.*"

"Like what?" Aunt Clothilde said. Then she sneezed into the white handkerchief. It sounded like the last rites for a small locust.

Amelie said, "I'm not going to go into the details now; you can take my word. I had to send the maid out for two bottles of Argyrol. Two large bottles. And I never thought I'd be so happy to see Argyrol in France. Don't you remember any of it, Edmund?"

Edmund shifted his weight to the other foot. "I remember the Argyrol," he said. He bit into the rubbery inside flesh of his lip until he could taste live salt. Then he looked down at his sock, and he had a hole in the top of it. The hole was like a bloodless flesh wound: it was obscene.

"I should think you would, indeed. I washed you with it every place you'd been exposed. I washed us all. And used it for nose drops too. We washed and we took it as nose drops. And I wiped the door handles with it, and we left for Paris on the morning train. I should rather think you would remember."

Aunt Clothilde swallowed aloud. She said, "I never believed in Argyrol nose drops. Never did me any good at all. No nose drops I ever heard of did me any good at all. So I just simply don't believe in them."

"That's because you haven't been to Lourdes to see the pilgrims, dear," Amelie said, and she exposed two yellow teeth. "Anybody who's seen the pilgrims *has* to believe in Argyrol."

Then she began to cough.

Edmund slapped his hands over his ears, and he got out into the hall. He stood in the hall holding his head. But he did not yell; or cry either.

Amelie's fever came back that night. She gave up breathing sixty-five hours later.

Anne stayed till it was done. She sent her aunt to the Legrange place for clothing, and they slept in a guest room on the same floor as Amelie. Anne did not speak to Edmund; Aunt Clothilde went to ask if they needed something for his mother.

Edmund was out of the room when it happened. He came back to find Anne standing alone by the bed. Aunt Clothilde was not there. Anne had pulled the sheet over the dead woman's face, but she had not covered the arms. She stood facing away from Edmund.

Amelie's left hand was a centipede, clutching out at the air: there were extra fingers on it. The right hand was a knot.

Edmund felt he might be on stilts walking around to the opposite side of the bed. He stopped there and looked across at Anne; but she went on watching the cornflowers in a faded oil painting on the wall. Then he bent down and undid the finger-knot, and he took out the crumpled paper ball. It was only paper, but it crackled when he unfolded it, and he thought they might hear that noise in many places. He tore one part smoothing it out. He did not need to study or even read the letter, because he well remembered writing it to his mother the day before he was married.

Anne was watching him now. He could feel the difference. He raised his head, swaying forward, and her brown eyes were close—very close and bright, the shiny brown inside was pitted and ringed and harder than the slick pustuled face of the moon. Anne made a slow pivot and walked out the doorway. Her footsteps were soundless on the carpet.

He folded the letter in half, and then in half again, neatly.

Three weeks afterwards the scare was off. Shops opened to gray hands; those who were alive came back to work.

Winter pulled off from the streets and left them damp. Plants put out teasers that turned into buds. The sky held green; if you stood on Melpomene Drive and looked upwards you could not feel your shoes. Most things washed clean, and the new green was yellow, and old life made fit to repeat.

Jergen Wilson wrote from New York. They were going to stay there through the heat of the coming summer. He asked when he might send the child back.

People did not come to commiserate, there were too many deaths.

Edmund was alone in the house. He was there with the servants and the empty rooms, he was alone. He was not washed; he had not shaved in many many days; his crusted jowls were greasy with hair. They crackled and felt dirty if he moved them.

He could not find a reason to shave, and another month went by; Jergen wrote again.

And there were two quiet rooms in the house worse than the rest. More hollow than empty. Edmund spent the round hours wandering into one and then along to the other as he had done when there had been someone in each. And when he could not stand it, there was no place else; he was not angry. He was worse than angry. He was lonely and dirty and acheful, and he had nothing left inside him echoing but a wide bottomless cavity of fury.

And he had to pay penance, yet to whom and for what he did not know. And he did not understand.

Then they called him from the office, and if they had known what he looked like, they would not have called him from the office.

It was with this smelly rotting infinite spiteful emptiness that he did it.

Because otherwise it reached just one notch more than tragic: it became offensive. If God wants a wreckage, then He creates a mess—and this is His right; but to root around like a pig in it, to nose around for something to salvage, let Him ask you to do that too. Then hand Him His penance in kind.

First Edmund took a clean fountain pen, suave in his oily hand, and his shirt cuff was dirty. He took a clean sheet of paper and wrote his name six times—six different ways. He practiced, and he did not like any of his signatures, including the one he was used to using, and he had not done that since he was sixteen and first got a checkbook. There was a bottle of ink eradicator in the second drawer. He took it out and made puddles. Then he signed his name again in one of the drying puddles and that was a proper mess. There was lots of clean writing paper, which explicitly said

EDMUND CHOATE

on the top in the middle, with black embossed letters because he had no middle name. He lifted off a clean sheet, and it said explicitly

EDMUND CHOATE

in the same place just like all the rest, this piece of paper did. They were the finest kind of very expensive paper. Then he pressed the point of the pen into that piece, and went on pressing until it curled back double and made a hole through the blotter and the ink splattered on the paper and on the desk. He raised the broken pen and dropped it carefully in the wastebasket, and he had two other fountain pens just as good to do that with if he wanted to do that again. He opened the drawer and spread out some of the paper which had no box, so that it said

EDMUND CHOATE
EDMUND CHOATE
EDMUND CHOATE
EDMUND CHOATE
EDMUND CHOATE

six hundred million times or so, then he picked up the open bottle of ink eradicator and let it fall in the wastebasket, and then fished it out and washed his hands with it. There was the telephone: so he picked up the phone, dripping, and called back his office. He heard a voice answer and he started arrangements for a trust fund to be set up in the name of Loris Licia Choate to be given in full at her coming of age.

With a new fresh piece of paper and another fine fountain pen he wrote a neat nice explicit letter to Jergen and had the child shipped to her rightful grandmother in Rome, where she had been born.

And if it did not any of it make sense, then let somebody else make sense of it; at least this was his right and just as good as anything else; so at least it hurt and was evil.

Then, bearded and greasy, with his teeth unbrushed he went out trembling calmly onto Melpomene Drive. A light wind was blowing north, towards the cemetery. He followed the wind across the canal, and followed it three blocks further. His heels scuffled, but so did his love, and they carried him on. As he approached, he could feel the tears slide down in streams to tickle around his beard. Then he stood on the sidewalk crying, and watching the dark wreath on her door; and he wondered why he should be this way now with no reason, after he had wanted to cry for so much and been unable.

There were lights like soiled yellow stars from the windows of the Legrange house. It was a dim afternoon.

4

Anne Legrange changed Edmund Choate quicker and further through than anyone in the city thought was possible. People were awed; she showed the man what he was made of. She taught him how to exist properly—how always to live in the middle of the road. She took the last wildness out of him, or she pushed it far enough in for it never to show again. And she made him learn all the values of money she knew about, and some of these were values that money was not ordinarily known to have. In a short marriage Anne taught Edmund more than a person might expect to learn in a whole long natural life.

The wedding took place six months after the deaths of Edmund's mother and his first wife. It was done at the Legrange house— all gardenia-white, like the bride; and the bride and her aunt were the only dry-eyed persons there. She sent very few invitations, and every one was accepted. Edmund and Anne were childhood sweethearts joined anew in sorrow. It was most honored, and generally pleasing.

Afterwards they moved into the disarrayed Choate house with

Aunt Clothilde. Anne put things in order and made them function as things should by the end of the third day. She was careful not to disturb Amelie's last systematic arrangements unless she could better them; and she could.

Anne and Edmund had separate bedrooms, one on either side of the hall. Aunt Clothilde was given the downstairs south wing to herself alone. The three ate their meals together in the main dining room at the same hours every day.

Evenings were spent in the drawing room of the north wing. Aunt Clothilde liked to knit, while Anne read out loud. Anne had decided that Edmund's education was not yet perfect for a father, and she set him in the path of literature; she did what she was able in the time allowed her. Through two years and three months she read him the complete works of Dickens and Austen and Wordsworth, and she was halfway through Trollope when the labor pains started.

Anne shocked him daily by the mere texture of her being. He found nothing left of that tight, shrinking girl—the girl who talked endlessly, and never looked and did not seem to know he was there. Now she was the opposite in each definitive way. Anne was a lady who did not talk except when she had something worth while saying; who looked straight at him with a round unblinking beam that occasionally made him blink; and who not only knew he was there, but showed him why, and how, and what he could do to improve his position. Edmund thought it was almost as if somebody had turned her core the other way around.

And she did not change again during the years of their marriage by so much as the amount of cream in her morning coffee.

Edmund's metamorphosis came simply. In his new life with Anne, he ran his father's bank and business so well people said he must have been born with a green dollar thumb. At Silvana's death business had been quiet; and after that it had declined. A single year with Anne doubled his holdings, and what Edmund had up in New York nobody could tell. He made few enemies, and never boasted. The birth of his child occurred during the same season

Edmund was elected chairman of the most powerful club in the city.

He was a permanent man, and now he knew it. And Edmund lived happy with his second wife. This was a happiness distinct from any he had wanted or known before, less intensely felt—but it felt more solid too. It was an ease. It was a sort of pure contentment.

Silvana's name was never used, and the second floor of the south wing stayed closed. Anne helped him to forget the lost child. She promised that he would have a new baby of his own, and Anne's word was like Anne.

Edmund was in love again. He loved her voice when she read to him, and the way she ordered his salad without oil. He shaved twice a day for her, and would have done it three times if she had asked him to.

He loved her steadfast sameness—a thing nobody, not even he could alter. Evenings when Edmund knocked and went into her room, he found her always standing off the carpet, beside the bed. She would be dressed in her high-buttoned housecoat, and under it a pale blue nightdress. That nightdress: the color of an early morning sky. And she looked at him full with her clear round stare, and she would not speak because this was not a time for speaking. Then he could walk straight into the beam of her eyes, the brightness all around him, and she did not move an inch while he slipped his hands inside to feel the blue silk soft as petals there over her. And the close blinding sheen of her eyes. There was no shyness—Anne left all the lights on when he took her to bed. She let him do what he wanted; ivory-cool, she lay and lifted her long loins high for him and she stroked the dip of his back with silvery fingers and she did not shut her eyes until he had emptied himself of his pleasure. Even her breathing did not quicken; she was the same when Edmund stood to kiss her cheek as when he heaved, verged to eruption and panting, against her pointed hips. Then after that, after he had used her, she lay quietly looking at him just the same, watching like that till he was gone from her sight. Anne appeared to live in a deep coolness for his passion; and in them both, the one increased the other. On a certain occasion he ripped the pillowcover over her head reaching for control. When he left that night she was smiling.

Aunt Clothilde did say there would be trouble. She said, "You won't live through it."

The day was bright, and they were in the dining room.

Anne made no answer. She was three months pregnant, and the swelling large. But her walk was no different; and she stood without counterbalancing, as if the added weight meant nothing. She left the table to go upstairs.

Edmund yawned. He rarely attended anything Aunt Clothilde said; she very often said things that made no sense at all. It had long been public knowledge that her physical deformity was the same in her mind. He asked, "You knitting panties for an elephant?"

"I am not," said Aunt Clothilde, "and I can make do without the sarcasm too. I am knitting a skirt."

"At breakfast?"

"You are watching me," she said, "you ought to know."

Edmund set his wakening gaze on a gleaming white coffee cup, and got foggy in his thoughts.

". . . looking so happy about?"

A boy would be named William for Edmund's father and it would be his own child and

"I would appreciate to be told . . ."

if it was a girl

"Just exactly what you think you have to look so happy about. Forget it, I already know."

Edmund said, "Sorry?"

Aunt Clothilde made a roll of her knitting, and pulled one

needle out. It was the wrong needle. Then she jumped up and spread the roll flat, and in doing that she unraveled some of it. "Now witness there," she said, "just look exactly what you made me do." She sounded as though she might be going to cry.

"Easy now," Edmund said.

"Easy what? I haven't got any ease. That's three inches work. You damn fool, I never saw such a godawful fool."

Edmund set his face to keep from grinning; but he felt too good.

"What do you think you have to feel so good about?" Aunt Clothilde said. "That's right. Laugh at me."

"I'm not laughing," he said.

"Yes, you are."

"No."

"Of course you are. Think I'm blind?"

"No," Edmund said, "I don't think you're blind."

Aunt Clothilde leaned on her palms over the table. She said, "You recall eight years ago when you used to come calling at the other house, and I took to sneaking around downstairs to tell you how much she loved you and all? Bring that to mind?"

"Yes."

Aunt Clothilde freed one hand, and wiped her nose. "Why didn't you laugh then?" she said.

". . . I love her."

"I know you do."

"I love her . . . like . . ."

"Doesn't matter like what," Aunt Clothilde said, "words are words. You just love her, that's all. You just do. Now."

"I wonder if she knows. Sometimes I can't believe she sees how much. Do you think she knows?" he said.

"I know she knows."

"How?"

"Doesn't matter how; I can tell, that's all. I can tell about those things."

He grinned again, and let it subside. He said, "I don't think she'll ever know how much I love her now."

"Don't you? What do you think makes her spit up from time to time?"

Edmund's eyebrows slid together. ". . . She's pregnant, Clothilde," he said.

"That's right; she is. Think that's what makes her have to spit?"

Edmund tapped a spoon on the tablecloth several times. He said, "I hope you didn't ruin your knitting. Better watch it."

"I am watching it. And I am also watching you sit there and tell me how much you care about her and all just so I'll go up and repeat it to her. Which I am not going to do, so you can stop. I wouldn't make her any worse than she is."

"Worse? There's nothing wrong with her."

"Isn't there?"

Edmund said, "There's nothing wrong with her. She'll have the baby. And she won't die."

"Yes, she will probably die," said Aunt Clothilde. "She's not prepared for babies, and she's not doing it the right way. She will probably die. Which would be the kindest thing she could bring herself to do for you. But that wasn't what I was talking about."

"What are you talking about?" Edmund let his head fall back on the wood slat of the chair.

"Forget it," Aunt Clothilde said. "For all the good it would do you to remember." She took her shaggy knitting up, and limped away. As she left, she said to the wall, "Did you see what he made me do to my knitting? I don't know why I spend my breath on such a godawful fool."

Straight above Edmund's face, there were angled splats of sunlight on the ceiling.

5

Fall of that year came like a cold brown veil over the city. People bought new warm clothes, and many evening clothes. This was the first functional year of the Civic Opera League. Five productions had been planned; the season might have exploded with a dizzy glow of wealth and social gaiety uncorked in vintage and unequaled. The city's pride could have burst with its champagne. But Anne's funeral hushed Melpomene Drive.

After all that had already come to pass, Edmund Choate was looked upon as noble when his second wife expired in childbirth. The man had seen too much sorrow. It was true Edmund had misbehaved long ago more than he should have; but that was in his youth, and no man is perfect, and he had repented and suffered enough already. This new grief was not just. The man was not a criminal for God to strip him of two wives, and leave him thirty-two years old with a motherless infant daughter. It was too much. People did not know what to say even among themselves.

And the Drive was black with mourners the day they carried that coffin up to the cemetery. It was a solid black procession—the finest in anybody's memory. Four blocks long, it moved silent and slow, bleak as the shadow of some great cloud. Edmund walked ahead, behind the hearse, and Aunt Clothilde held to his arm. He was rigid and gray-faced. He did not weep and he did not have to: the city wept for him.

Aunt Clothilde's wail was the loudest of all. It had a bad sound, almost angry. Everybody was of course aware that there existed a peculiar defection to her mentality. But even so, a number of friends were upset when the procession passed the Legrange house; because she suddenly stopped wailing and began to giggle out loud. This was the worst kind of hysterics to have in such a silence. Then she made a disturbance at the grave. People formed a line to give their sorrows, and Edna Wilson got to Edmund before Jergen and murmured something about Anne's having loved him so much at the end—and Aunt Clothilde started giggling all over again. Nobody could shut her up no matter what they did; she went on like that as though she truly might have been amused.

On his way back, Edmund's eyebrows shone like fur in the autumn light. All the lines of his face sloped down; it was a glowering sadness. But he was clean-shaven, and remarkably handsome—a man with a purpose. His thin gray eyes flattered his black suit better than the buttons. Many said he had never looked so handsome.

. . .

The lost love of a man can be many things, and still it is his personal nowhere. It is the same as a first breath; it is what he gains, and loses, and does not comprehend.

Now in his second loss, Edmund Choate despised the damp sweetness. He loathed kindly looks and wordful comfort from people who had never felt what he had felt, or wanted as he had cared. Each solacing gesture of every good citizen in town made the fuzz crawl up and down inside his intestines. For none of them had ever known the real love that tides a man wild. And not one of them was a person who owned a heart big enough to break.

So Edmund kept to his home and his business; he did not see friends. He was solemn and polite with everyone, because no one mattered. In particular, Jergen Wilson's sumptuous sympathy addled him more than any other; but that was not of true importance, and he tried not to let it show. He became dark and dignified, ancient in his ways. It came to be that Edmund's daily walk to and from his office, and Wednesdays to his club, was unobstructable as the thick living gray water of the evening river flow.

And what he had left for power and love changed, and it grew. This core was in quality a soft thing—a richness; it was a new final reason to live. There was peace in it, and tenderness. And there was wonder. Edmund set out to care for his daughter, Adrianne Legrange Choate.

He was not seen with women, ever. By two years after Anne's death, people expected him to mix in female society—perhaps take to a dinner companion. And they thought he would someday take a third wife. He was still young and very rich, he was eligible wherever he chose to seek. But Edmund surprised the gossips again. He elected only to be with Adrianne; and he existed only to keep her from pain. In living for his daughter, he undid himself. He strove straight to his goal, and raised her as her mother would have wished: always in the middle of the road.

When Anne was five years dead, people had not stopped talking. They went right on with Edmund Choate, his fashion, his deeds, his money. He was always the one man who had not conformed in any way to the regular flux of high life in the city. First he had gone on as if there was a slew of Mexican jumping beans playing politics inside him; and now you could set your watch by his morning shadow. So stories varied with new facts, but people's interest did not. And disgusted at his unebbing vogue, Edmund took his daughter and her great-aunt Clothilde and himself out of the city. They went up North to New York, and they all lived together there for fifteen years. He never wrote his friends a post card. He was finally gone.

Another war came and the winter ice settled over Edmund Choate's house, the Legrange house, and their remembrance. Now in the city he was the man you once knew, caught between two hateful wars—a man too young to fight the first, too late for the second—and caught the same some say between two loves; and he lived now someplace else. Time dragged, or didn't; but it was full of what breathed in the world—full of happenings. Children grew up and had children. Grass grew in the cemetery, and some of it had to be mowed. The earth around the city and the city's sky had new business.

Yet the taste of a birthplace sits under a man's tongue. Like a recollected smell of childhood, it is not a thing that allows itself to pass away.

And he did return. Through the heat and the blowing, shifting dry dust of one late summer, the three came back to live in this city. Aunt Clothilde was old, and the girl was a woman, and Edmund looked older than he was. They stayed at the Hotel Washington till that great house of the Choate's could be fixed and furnished, have its age painted over.

Several reasons were rumored for their return. Some friends wondered if the girl might not have made an uncomfortable choice in men—possibly as uncomfortable as Edmund's early choice had been. Those that could recall said there might be a wildness to her like her father showed when he was her age. But that kind of rumor didn't last very long. The girl was too gentle. She was too gracious and seemly—too much of a lady; she was another lady in line to occupy the Choate house. And Adrianne had a soft, quiet tenderness—a profound humility that her mother and grandmother perhaps would not have recognized. Adrianne Legrange Choate was as intensely attentive to the garbageman as she was to the leaders of Melpomene Drive; and with the same dignity of caring. She could be approached and loved where her own father could only be respected. For no one had any real nearness to Edmund, or mattered to him, except his daughter Adrianne; it was said they shone together like the sun and the moon. It was said that one lone word was never uttered between those two: the word "no." And within a month people snickered to think that rumor might concoct foolish tales about the young lady Choate. They sighed, and they wove other stories through the warp of loose threads picked up from old Aunt Clothilde, who talked overmuch: stories better suited to quality like this young lady, the finest born of the city, come back in gentle glory to her own people. The stories, every one, had lost all venom by the start of that first winter. The city's tongues turned as sweet and as regal as the smooth crystal smile that always gleamed, sharper than silver—for anyone to see—in the soft black of those black eyes.

Then at last there was no one in town looked up to like Edmund Choate. And there was no one awed and reverenced like his only daughter Adrianne.

III

Letters and People and a Little Air

1

IT WOULD NOT RAIN. It would not be that decisive.

The study was choked with sluggish silver light pressed downwards from a bloated gray sky. The sky had filled in just fifty minutes.

Edmund said again, "Which of those two ladies," and he was immediately sorry for having said it, because he had not wanted to the first time. It was one of the things you say when your mind is focused down to such a small point you can't use it any more.

He pushed his chair back in a swell of annoyance, and bumped his knee, and got mad. You do not seek unsuccessfully through your obfuscated memory with a brilliant beam the size of a hair tip for fifty minutes and then bump your knee.

Edmund said, "God damn bad mornings."

And there was the old feeling of reversal that comes to a man on these occasions. A sense that all the important things in the world were now become shruggable details; and the everyday things like respiration and batting the eyelashes were hulking efforts. If he did not specifically remember to breathe now, Edmund thought he would die. It was one of those mornings.

But with the unpleasantness and in that useless sour air, it was somehow agreeable to ache. It served him right, he thought; although there was no particular reason why. Yet some cause did always lurk just beyond the orbit of consciousness. This he knew because he could see it there at times—faint-faded and yellow—like a cluster of dull stars, to be believed but not to be looked at directly. An ancient twinkling scattered wish for penance. Or even say a child will take pleasure at punishment if this punishment lifts off the weight of immortal sin by allowing him to feel sorry for himself. Then young men change their habits; but they hardly lose them. And at fifty-four by Jesus if the conditions are right it only takes a bad night to make a bad boy again.

Edmund got up and went to the near window. And how do you bury a love when you do? Then what does that mean? Melpomene Drive was dipped dusty upwards into the inverted sea of gray; winter rippled across the street, and back, and it was spring. Where do you love from that you can love twice? three, four different times?—what is the quality of your caring?

You go from your mother through to your daughter, still you do it; and divided in between you bury other people, and parts of what has died came out of you. And still you love. Then they call you Mr. Edmund Choate.

And another bright, bloated spring is the gray time of sharing.

Opal coughed; she didn't knock.

Edmund swung around.

"It's Mr. Wilson," she said.

"What is?"

"The phone."

"I didn't hear it ring."

"You turned it off in here yesterday. But it's Mr. Wilson."

Edmund moved heavily to his desk and reached for the receiver.

"No, sir," Opal said. Pushing in, she took a calculated step over the carpet, and then two more. She leaned way over the desk; each flat eye had a little telephone in it. "He hung up," she said.

". . . Why?"

"He got through talking. He is coming over."

"No."

Opal said, "He is coming over to visit with you."

"No, he isn't, damn it."

"Oh but he is," Opal said.

"Lord." Edmund turned to the side and sat in the wicker chair under Adrianne's portrait. It was his favorite chair in the house. "I told you to say I was at work."

"Mr. Wilson knows you don't work on a Saturday. Everybody in town knows. Besides, he would have come over anyway, says he got something to discuss with you."

". . . He does?"

"That is what he says."

Edmund said, "Jergen Wilson. There's the man. Rounds out a perfect morning."

"Yes, it does," Opal said.

The tray was centered under her long level breasts, and the silver coffeepot peered up between them, and its lips drooped. Opal couldn't seem to see enough of the telephone.

"How do you feel?" Edmund said.

"Foolish."

"You are drunk," he said.

"On four glasses of ordinary faucet water?"

"I'm sick of this."

"Uh-huh. Foolish as disgusting. I feel like a mammy in the movies."

"You are beginning to act like one. I'm sick of it," Edmund said. "Opal, really sick. It's the last time, Opal; it is the honest to God last time. Now get the hell outside and get a little air."

Opal unattached a blurred gaze from the telephone, and got it to wandering over as far as Edmund's left ear; it stuck there, on the lobe. "The color of blind," she said, "and dead alive, and the color of blind."

". . . You escape me."

"Unborn blind. And born; Mr. Choate, I am thirty-nine years of age. I am forty next year."

"You're drunk right now."

"Not even that. She is," she said.

Edmund said, "All right. Jesus. Never mind about breakfast. Go on, get her out." He scratched his ear.

Opal let her neck sag.

And Edmund could feel his hair catch and pull in the holes of the slick varnished wicker. When he moved his head, it made a sound like tearing or grating. He measured time to get up, and turned to face the chair. "Go on," he said.

"Yes, sir."

"Well, go."

"Yes, I plan to," she said.

The spoon rattled on the saucer.

Then Opal was plodding like the first slow beat of a distant locomotive along the empty passage.

This now was his desk:

The top center drawer under him had no lock; in there he kept a photograph album and several loose pictures—all of Adrianne. Below, locked specially in the bottom left drawer, there were two folders of old letters. The letters had been read by no one in the house but Edmund, and had not been read by him for possibly two years. Between these two drawers he stored copies of some impersonal business correspondence he was privately pleased to have made.

There were pencils that fit his hand, and objects the right color.

Now a man who is disturbed within himself will like a hold around his world.

And a man can want to grip the things he has, good or bad; to look up from there. This may even be when he has already sensed a nebulous, forming threat approaching somewhere beyond to match what he feels within.

So when he heard her footsteps, Edmund was sitting at his desk, and he was holding it. His hands were placed like vises over either end of the stained mahogany top; both arms up past the shoulder were hard as the wood.

But the footsteps unloosed him. He had not seen her, and he

relaxed. Because there was no necessity for a hold on anything with those footsteps in the hall.

He let go, and sat back, and felt it happen. The last of the night's threat pulled off, fatuous; receded in direct proportion as Adrianne came closer. The rancid sourness dissolved.

She walked at a special pace, she never varied, she did not move faster or slower; Adrianne walked in her own way. It was a sound Edmund could count on better than his own time—inflexible; a rhythm that remolded every other sound and rhythm and feeling for him, wherever he might hear it.

And she was coming down the hall. It was like listening to his pride and his future at once. He thought: all dreams should end like this; and now she is coming down the hall.

When he swiveled in his chair Adrianne was standing in the doorway. A white angel is real, he thought. There was a new morning.

Aunt Clothilde came in to find them sitting on the window seat, and Adrianne was dressed in white. She was finishing her coffee.

It was a plain pure white dress, she did not wear fancy clothes. She could have, but she didn't. It appeared to be tinted. It looked that way; nothing had ever looked white next to Adrianne.

Edmund said, "Morning," the same time they did. But he kept his eyes on his daughter.

Aunt Clothilde studied the sky while she put on her gloves. "How is it you got up so early?" she said.

Adrianne's neck was as disproportionately long as the calves of her legs, and smooth—where that much extra length should be.

"You got up early?"

He was watching where the harsh light from above turned soft in her hair. Adrianne's hair was cut short—the sheen of the sun through summer dust; it was almost intangibly curved, and it was true.

Aunt Clothilde said, "Question number three, why did you get up so early?"

Adrianne put a light pressure on his wrist.

"Sorry," he said. "I wasn't listening."

". . . You got up. Early."

"I woke up."

Aunt Clothilde took a white silk cloth out of her purse and held it up to her nose. "Well," she said. "That explains it."

"It . . . isn't very early."

"It was. When you came out of your room."

"How do you know?"

"I heard you," she said.

"Oh. Sorry."

"No, you are not," Aunt Clothilde said. "You don't have to be sorry." She moved to join them by the window.

Edmund looked at her. The light that was clean on Adrianne got into Aunt Clothilde's fuzzed hair and made it a dirty bright halo. Her hair matched the clouds. The wrinkled tan skin around her neck could have been part of her dress, only leather and older. She was ten years older than Edmund.

She said, "Get your coat, if you're coming."

Adrianne rose and set her empty coffee cup on the sill. She went off into the hall.

And the fresh morning began to dim.

". . . Noise wake you up?"

"I just woke up."

"You said that. Particular noise?"

"No," he said.

Aunt Clothilde sat sideways on the window seat, and shut her eyes. She kept them shut for fifteen seconds. Then she said, "Gray turns blue." And: "It was stupid of you."

". . . Waking up?"

"Going into that house yesterday."

"Let's skip it," Edmund said. He rubbed under his eyebrows with two contrary circular motions.

"It was. It was stupid. I didn't say anything yesterday because I don't like to waste my breath. But it was a godawful unattractive dumb thing to do."

"Fine. Now let's skip it."

Aunt Clothilde said, "The only thing more unbecoming than a man who enjoys to make other people suffer is a man who enjoys to suffer himself."

"Fine," Edmund said. "I had my reason. Forget about it."

"I already have, and I know you did. And it isn't fine. And you haven't forgotten, and you won't. It was a stupid thing to do."

Edmund swung his head from far left over to the right.

"You want a cigar?" Aunt Clothilde said.

". . . You know I never smoke till noon."

"Then what are you looking for? Stiff neck?"

"I'm not looking, Clothilde. I know where everything is. I'm tired."

"You ought to be."

"Drop it."

Aunt Clothilde snuffled hard. "I already have," she said.

Edmund got up and walked to the tapestry wall; he kept four fingers of each hand in each back pocket.

If it became much darker, he would have to turn on the electric light. This would throw yellow at the sky.

Then things might look as dreary as they felt.

He said, "Going shopping?"

"Yes, I am going shopping. Don't imagine you are expected to keep me amused here," Aunt Clothilde said.

". . . Need any money?"

"Not while they still have charge accounts; thank you just the same. I am going to buy two slips and a pair of stockings."

"Buy anything you want," he said. "I didn't ask."

"You wouldn't. You are so delicate, it isn't even polite."

Edmund cleared his throat. He coughed first. "I gather you might be in what's known as a touchy mood."

"I generally am," Aunt Clothilde said. "You haven't noticed recently?"

"Yes. I've noticed."

"That's accurate," she said.

Edmund settled against the wall.

". . . Coming back for lunch?"

"Yes, I am coming back for lunch. This is a catchy conversation here. I am coming back to have lunch. Adrianne is not coming back for lunch."

"She told me."

"Know where she's going?"

"I don't want to know," Edmund said. "That's her business. Not yours and not mine. She has her own life."

Aunt Clothilde stroked her nose with the silk cloth. Then she folded the cloth. "That isn't even delicate," she said.

Then they both kept silent and waited.

Before leaving, Adrianne came back to kiss him. She stretched up and touched his cheek with hers—and again the day bloomed. When she had left, Edmund stayed where he was. He watched to see her cross in front of the house on her way out to the car.

Aunt Clothilde was standing next to the window seat. She walked to the desk and stood there.

Edmund said, "Hurry up, you'll be late."

"For what?"

"She's just ordering dinner. Then she'll be expecting you in the car."

"Let her expect," Aunt Clothilde said; "she's young. Not like us. She hasn't done a lot of expecting."

Edmund blinked. "What are you staring at?"

"You. You look awful."

"I had a bad night," he said.

"I can imagine."

"No, you can't. I had a simple nightmare."

"I don't know what you think I meant," Aunt Clothilde said. "But you're confused. A nightmare is what I meant. Two nightmares."

"I'm afraid not. Just one."

". . . One?" she said.

Then she said, "Yes. Yes, of course."

Adrianne moved smoothly across the lawn under the sagging sky. Sterling the chauffeur held the door for her, and she didn't seem to pause when she bent to get in. But Sterling backed up a step; Edmund could tell she had smiled at him.

"Better hurry," he said.

Aunt Clothilde shivered, and buttoned her left glove.

Edmund said, "You cold?"

"No."

He faced the new lawn. "Well, she's waiting."

"Yes. She is."

The two of them watched while Sterling shut the door. The light had gone dismal. The sky might have been blackening in the east.

Aunt Clothilde said, "Nightmares."

". . . Didn't you ever have one, for heaven's sake?"

"Yes. Certainly. Of course."

"Well?"

"When I'm awake," Aunt Clothilde said. "That's a funny thing; it's funny you should ask at this exact minute. I only have them when I'm awake, you see."

She made a puffing noise with her nose and the cloth. "You could know that by now. But you wouldn't remember."

Edmund frowned, and he held his breath to stop the rise of a sigh. He tried to think of something to answer.

But long before he turned, there was no one else in the room.

2

Jergen came at a quarter past eleven. By then if it wasn't raining it was because it didn't want to.

Edmund had been seated at his desk with the two folders open in front of him. The brass desk-lamp was a glare on old paper, and made a layer of greenish glow between him and the weather. He was not meaning to read the letters, only to look at them. He had not taken them out since he couldn't remember when. That was the way it usually started. And he always finished reading every one.

Now, though, it was done; he would not sense the need to see them again for another year or so. They were copies of letters and they had been sent to him by a lawyer from Pittsburgh. They were not fileable because there are some things in life a file will not hold. Someday somewhere they might have a use—though that did seem doubtful; until then or if not the letters got kept in the bottom drawer.

Edmund closed the folders; he slid them into place, timing himself to avoid Jergen's pudgy curiosity. He locked the drawer, and looked out.

And it definitely should have been raining.

Jergen squeezed down in the wicker chair, and settled into his fat. "Glad see you," he said.

Edmund nodded. The sky was one dirty cloud, beginningless. It was all there. No single word would hold with such a sky.

Infinity has three too many syllables.

Jergen said, "You did it again."

"Did I?"

"You sure did. Smoke?"

"No," Edmund said. "What did I do?"

"The same thing," Jergen hardly took a cigarette out of his teeth once he put it in. He licked the paper first, all around, so his lips wouldn't catch on it when he talked. Then he let it hang there and burn, and the ash fell on his vest. His wife had often told him he would catch fire one of these days, but his wife was mistaken in many things. "I swear to God," he said, "I never saw such a man."

Jergen was bald except for a gray shaggy horseshoe, and his fingernails were long and manicured with thick colorless polish, and dirty. He had on a bright blue suit over a hand-painted orange tie.

Edmund said, "The same thing as what?"

"Just like . . . now you know what I mean."

"If I knew what you meant, I wouldn't ask. There is an ash tray by your right hand."

"There always is," Jergen said. And without looking, sadly he said again, "There always is."

Edmund rubbed his neck and got ready for an unpleasant hour.

Jergen was in town about half of every year, and came to pay a visit maybe three times during that period. It had never been pleasant or less than dull yet.

At fifty-nine, Jergen still insisted on being the vulgar clown; he still had much to say about anything and meant it all. You got the feeling he thought of himself alternately as too honest, too clever, and too awful for this world. He presumed an intimacy that was distasteful to Edmund, and Edmund was the only man in the city who suspected Jergen of rehearsing at night in the bathroom.

Edmund said, "How is your family, Jergen?"

"They're fine, I didn't come to talk about them. They're just fine. They always are. Thank you."

"How's the oldest boy, what's his name again? How's he like medical school?"

"He likes medical school," Jergen said, "he likes medical school just fine. I didn't come to talk about him. Name is Jergen Junior."

Edmund coughed. "Right. I keep getting him mixed up with . . . William?"

"I don't have a William," Jergen said. "I have a Warburn, and I have a Justine. But I don't have a William. I don't occupy my mind with any of them, and they're all three fine. Not much to notice; nothing to talk about, considering your Adrianne. I didn't come to talk about them."

Edmund slid open the top left drawer. The new cigar box was sealed in red and gold; the seal had the same design as the band on each cigar inside, only larger. He shut the drawer. Then he said, "I know what you came to talk about."

"I hope so but I don't believe it," Jergen said. "My Lord," he said . . .

"Does it hurt?"

"Naturally," Edmund said. "Damn right it hurts." He held his wrist with the other hand, shaking. He was chuckling.

The finger was bleeding steadily. First there had been a spurt, but now it streamed out. He was covered with blood, and they were walking up the stairs.

Jergen tripped; he caught himself on the banister. "Frigging

Italian wine," he said. "Hits you like four whiskies. I should known better."

"We had the four whiskies," Edmund said.

"We did?"

"Before the wine."

"Before lunch?" Jergen stopped and thought. "That's right," he said, "we did. I should known better. Course, I never figured you to have your finger in the door. Slammed it before I figured. Frigging Italian taxis. Does that hurt? That's right, it does."

"Here we are," Edmund said.

"We are? We are not. One flight more."

"No," Edmund said; "here we are."

Jergen stopped again, and came back, and looked at the door. He stood wavering in a kind of fractured ellipse. Then he reached close for Edmund's shoulder. "You right again," he said. "Got to give it to you. Man, you sure always do know how to get where you want."

After pressing, Edmund snatched his good hand away from the bell button. He wrinkled his nose and began to laugh in a new way. It was extremely funny that a little winter spark should make him jump, and the pain of a mashed finger mean nothing.

"What you laughing at now?" Jergen said. "You're not going to marry her. You can't marry this woman."

"I can," Edmund said. But he couldn't stop the chuckle. It was all so funny.

Then there were several clicks. And a rattle. And instead of the door she herself was there.

Edmund said fast, "It's my finger, now. It's my finger; only one finger. Don't be frightened."

Silvana kept still.

"I won't be," she said. "Come in."

She stepped aside to let him pass.

And he heard Jergen ask her, "That invitation good for two?"

"No," said Edmund.

"No? Hey. Hey, I thought you weren't mad at me."

"I'm not. Now trot along."

"I didn't mean to do it," Jergen said, "I told you I didn't mean . . ."

"Run along, I'll see you tomorrow. I know you didn't."

"Hey," Jergen said.

Edmund put his foot back, and kicked the door shut.

Then he held Silvana against him, just inside the apartment. He kept his bad hand close to his side and his right arm around her waist. There was a lemon smell in her hair. It was a full minute before he thought of the rug or her clean gray dressing gown.

After that, she led him into the bathroom. She said, "I see no need to apologize."

"But I got you full of . . . and, and the carpet . . ."

"Yes," she said, "do keep your apologies. It is tiring of you. Blood washes out with cold water."

And she made him stick his finger under the faucet. She took a full bottle of iodine from the cabinet; and she poured the entire bottle slowly over the raw flesh.

It didn't burn. It didn't burn at all.

"It won't burn," she said.

". . . Why?"

"The cut is too deep. Far too deep," she said. "It only burns when you have a shallow surface cut."

Edmund said, "I love you."

"Hold still."

"I love you."

"I cannot do this correctly if you are going to be childish."

". . . I love you."

"You've had too much wine. Americans should never drink wine."

"I won't ask you to marry me."

"Please hold still," she said.

"I'm not going to ask you: I love you."

"Now stand there while I get the gauze."

Edmund said, "Tuesday is a good day. I'll go for a license on Monday. Don't know where; have to ask at the Embassy. I'm not going to ask you to marry me," he said. "We'll do it on Tuesday.

With the baby. I love the baby. Know what?" he said, "I love the baby too."

"We must get you to a doctor immediately. It won't stop bleeding."

"It's too deep," Edmund said, "I love you."

Silvana unrolled a long white filmy strip, and tore it apart with her teeth. Then she put one end on the side of his finger and began to wrap. "If you don't keep still you are going to get blood all over the floor."

"You're shaking."

"No. You are."

"You're dripping on the floor."

"That doesn't matter," Edmund said.

"What?" Silvana looked up. "Why not?"

Edmund grinned. He said, "Blood washes out with cold water."

"I'm just crazy mad about talking to people when I know for sure they aren't hearing a blessed word I say."

". . . I hear you," Edmund said.

Jergen slid down and tried to cross his legs. He made a show of managing to get the left ankle over the right knee, then got a cramp on one side. He let the foot fall back on the rug, and set both legs sticking out in a parenthesis. "O.K.," he said. "What was I talking about?"

"You are about to burn your lip."

"No, I'm not." Jergen picked up the ash tray and spit out the tiny glowing butt. A string of brown saliva came out after it. "Well?"

"About my going into that house yesterday."

"You were," Jergen said. "I could of swore you weren't listening."

"Could?"

"Yes. I could."

Edmund worked his eyebrows. He yawned, and pushed the air out in a rush. He said, "You are waiting to ask me why I did it?"

"Course not. I'm not that stupid." Jergen had caught the yawn, and was chewing at it.

Edmund thought about saying suddenly: You are a little less

clever than you think; what you are not is what you pretend to be.

Jergen said, "About time you got the Legrange place going. House has been up for sale ever since you came back. Two years now. Nobody that counts really believes in haunted houses, naturally, but nobody's going to pay good money for a place either with a creepy reputation like that one has. I bet you haven't had a decent offer since you put it up for sale. You did it to get the place going."

"What time is it?" Edmund said.

". . . Eleven thirty. Why?"

"My watch is broken, I don't smoke till noon."

"Well, so? Isn't that the reason? That's why you went and paraded through that old house like a frigging general."

"Yes," Edmund said.

"I knew it was, same way you do everything. You were always the same. I never knew such a man. You conceive a mind of what you want, then you just go and get it the quickest way. All your life," Jergen said, "even before you changed so much. No compromises. Mr. Edmund Choate. I swan. I swear to God I never knew such a man."

He wouldn't stop talking. But she listened. She always listened to everybody. Aunt Clothilde attended too, and knitted, and looked bored.

The Wilsons had come over for coffee. Anne was eight months and three weeks pregnant, but she always listened.

Jergen's wife Edna balanced her coffee cup perfectly with two fingers. She was a nervous breather. While Jergen spoke, Edna found Edmund looking at her, and she grimaced. This gave her the stunned appearance of a cow just before it moos. She was very pretty and she meant it as gracious.

Edmund got up from the sofa; he excused himself, and walked out. He tried to seem as if he were heading for the bathroom. But he went straight out to look at the night. The darkness was blowing.

He stood in the garden for five minutes watching the sprinkled glint of the stars; thinking how he loved her.

When he came back he stopped in the hall to comb the wind out of his hair. And he heard Jergen say: "He's changed."

"Is he?" From Anne.

"Sure is. I mean he has. Hasn't he, Edna?"

"What?" said Mrs. Wilson. "Oh. Yes."

Jergen said, "Two years with you, he's a different man. I swear to God. Everybody says so; can't help to notice it. And on top of that now he's a businessman. I never saw such a one for investing money. In just these two years he's married to you. He wasn't anything like that before."

"Wasn't he?" Anne said.

"Now you know he wasn't. He wasn't a financier. For crying out loud, he practically owns the city now. Runs it anyway. In just two years. Nobody in town would make an investment without seeing Edmund Choate first. And he'll make even more before he's through. Course, I don't know how; he's done so well up to now."

"Yes, he has, hasn't he?" Anne said.

"He's done fabulous up to now." Then Jergen told her, low, "But he's worried tonight. I can see he's worried. He is worried."

". . . Truly?" Anne said.

"I'll say he is. Course, everybody worries for their first child. Only he's specially worried, I think. More than I was. I didn't worry that much. Did I, Edna?"

"No," Mrs. Wilson said.

"You just better make sure nothing happens to you," Jergen said to Anne, and Edmund could hear a smile in the voice. "He wouldn't know how to live without you."

"Wouldn't he, Mr. Wilson?" Anne said.

"I certainly wish you'd remember to call me Jergen. No; he would not. After these two years? He surely would not. Not without you. You know that." The smile could be heard more plainly now. Jergen said, "That man would not know how to live without you."

". . . He wouldn't?" And then Anne's quiet voice sent a quick strange chill out into the hall. It wasn't her words. Just the emptiness—the lack of quality in the tone. It was a voice Edmund had not heard since long before their marriage.

She said, "He has done awfully well up to now."

But when he stepped into the room, the smile was on Anne's face, not Jergen's. Jergen was nodding.

And Aunt Clothilde was about to have one of her spells.

"Got you," Jergen said.

"Who?"

"Who yourself. I got you. This time I got you."

"No," Edmund said.

"You have not been listening and I don't care what you say."

Edmund said, "You were talking about the way people like to decide . . . which . . . of those two ladies . . ."

"I'm a sonofabitch," Jergen said.

Edmund interlaced his fingers behind his head and looked at the window.

"I wish I knew how you manage to think your own personals by yourself there and keep an ear open at the same time."

"Practice," Edmund said.

"My fat Aunt Tilly. It's a born talent. You never practiced a thing in your life. Throw me the matches. Far as that goes, I wish I knew how you lived."

Edmund picked up the oblong brown leather matchbox. He rattled it to make sure, and then tossed it over; Jergen was a big target. But he missed.

Edmund said, "Sorry. How do I live?"

Jergen made a noise in his throat. He was leaning over part of his belly to get at the matchbox. Just as he lifted back, he broke wind on a very high note. Then he said, "Cue me."

"You're excused," Edmund said, "you always were. And for Lord's sake stop trying to be picturesque; how do I live?"

"Don't know. Wish I did."

Edmund lifted his shoulders. "Middle of the road," he said. "That's about all, Jergen."

"No, not all." Jergen licked the cigarette, and lit it. "I mean even before you got married the second time."

"Yes. Well, skip it." Edmund pulled forward.

"Don't care to skip it. Interesting subject. I was thinking about that all night. It can't be done, it can't be. Know that? Course you don't. You are the impossible."

". . . Let's just skip it," Edmund said. He was watching the cigar drawer.

Jergen struggled three seconds audibly to get up, and then relaxed from the effort. He said, "You been reading about this new antimatter?"

"No."

"Well that's what you are."

". . . I see."

"No, you don't see. That's what you are, you can't see. You are the new antimatter."

"I see."

"You do not. I bet you don't even know what it is. And quit talking about what you see. You couldn't see it if you did know. Because you are it. Antimatter is the opposite of matter. It's what can't exist. Because when it comes into contact with matter, wham. See? Energy. Nothing. They destroy each other, stop yawning at me. It has been stated by scientists that antimatter can't exist with matter. And you do it. You are it."

"Am I?" Edmund said.

"Yes, you are. Listen at me."

"I'm listening."

"No, you are not. Now just listen. Edmund, you go the opposite; you go straight, you are anti the matter all over hell and gone, you go your own way. That's what you are, you are all made up of antimatter."

Edmund let his eyes slip over the bulging swollen mold of Jergen's body in the chair. "One of us is," he said.

"That's right, and it's not me and you can quit looking at me that way. It's not me, it's you. You break all the rules, not me. It's you. I stick to the pattern. In my own way but I keep to it. It's you."

Edmund nodded.

"I wish you would quit agreeing with me," Jergen said, "when you don't even know what I'm talking about. Now wait. Now put it this way. By the straight line."

Edmund said, ". . . What time is it now?"

"Oh, for crying out loud, go on have a cigar. Eleven fifty."

Edmund said, "No. Ten minutes more."

Jergen bent ahead in the chair, and waved his feet. He heaved his pendulous weight out onto the floor. Then he achieved his balance, and walked stiff-legged to the window.

He stood in profile against the blinding gray, pointing north to the cemetery. "What kind of a line is that?" he said.

"What?"

"You heard me. What kind of line is that?"

Edmund set an elbow on the desk, then rested his head in his hand. "Straight?" he said.

"Wrong."

"Am?"

"You are. You are wrong. That's what I mean, you're wrong. It's curved."

"Is?" Edmund said.

"Yes, it is."

Standing outlined as he was, Jergen's bulbous stomach and his belly made two loops: the top one small, the other large. The great swelling started from no chest at all and set him leaning back to compensate as if he were with child. His lumpy weighted buttocks seemed to hold him on his feet. The outline was a sort of tuberous S.

Edmund grinned. He said, "You are."

"I am what?"

"Curved."

"I am and I'm not," Jergen said, "and I know what I am. But I'm referring to the Drive."

". . . Which is straight."

Jergen said, "Which is not. That's where you're wrong. Looks like it, but it's not. You want to know my theory?"

Still with his head on his hand, Edmund scratched his nose with the little finger. "I have a sibling sense I'm about to."

"Just don't talk so colorful," Jergen said. "Everybody has got a right to state his own theory. Like you and your middle of the road. Now I am informed on this subject. My theory is that the world has to be curved."

Edmund shut one eye.

"Get what I mean?"

"More or less," he said. "Dangerous."

"Why dangerous?"

"They tortured Galileo."

". . . So what? They tortured anybody that told the truth. They burned Joan of Arc."

"That was different," Edmund said, "she was a communist."

Jergen made a face. "I certainly wish you would not always laugh at me." He leaned over a round silver ash tray and spit out the second cigarette.

"No, you don't. You wouldn't have it any other way."

Jergen said, "People just always do."

"Do they?" Edmund said. Then he twitched his eyebrows, and raised his head to stare at Jergen's watch.

". . . Five minutes of twelve."

Edmund leaned back and folded his arms.

Jergen said, "I'm trying to tell you the truth here and pay you a compliment, and all you do is watch for the time and laugh."

"No. You don't amuse me, Jergen."

"Talk about communists. All you do is laugh, you know something? Know the only thing the big communists and the big capitalists got in common?"

"You tell me."

"Both think the world is flat."

"Say."

"Yes; say. And you know what Einstein proved?"

". . . You tell me."

Jergen said, "Proved that space is curved. Plain ordinary space.

Like inside of a glass, for instance. Take any glass, the glass might be straight; you know? But that's because a man made it that way. Otherwise it wouldn't be. The space is still curved, because everything God made is a curve. For instance, a tree might be straight. A tree might be almost straight." Jergen squatted, and set himself on the window seat. It wasn't really wide enough and he looked uncomfortable. Then he looked pleased. "But the earth is covered with trees, isn't it? Well, answer me. Isn't it?"

"Yes."

"And you know what you would see if you could stand back from the earth?"

". . . I'm trying to think."

Jergen nodded from the neck. "A circle of trees," he said.

Edmund said, "For heaven's sake."

"Course you would. That's what I'm telling you. It's made up of curves, understand? The world. All curves. And a normal body has got to move on a curve. Can't go along by the straight line because it isn't possible. Lot of people talk about it, but they don't do it. Because they can't. Because it isn't possible."

Edmund nodded. He said, "Possible."

"Except you're the opposite. You don't talk about it, but you do it. The whole way you live. Whole bunch of improper lines. Every time you decide where you want to go, you just go, that's all. Like yesterday. Like when you got married the first time. You just up and go straight there. No compromises with anybody or the world, not even with yourself. You just do it."

Edmund swallowed a yawn. It came back up, and he had to swallow it again. "*Grazie*," he said. His eyes watered; they were starting to scald again.

"Thank you yourself. Look at me. You just got past breaking the rules, that's all. It's one minute of twelve and shut up. Look at me."

"I'm looking."

"I bet you never even told a lie. In your whole existence. I bet you never once up and told a lie. Did you?"

". . . I can't remember," Edmund said, and he sighed. "I don't think I ever had to. And I wish to heaven at nearly sixty years of age you would not sticky your Harvard diphthongs trying to sound colloquial."

"Yah, you see? No dark side. You go and you come back, you got no ordinary dark side."

Edmund rubbed his chest. He said, "No, Jergen, not in a goldfish bowl."

"What's a goldfish bowl?"

"This house," Edmund said, "on this street."

"It is? And who watches the king goldfish?"

"You, for one."

"I do not. Look at me. I just go where I have to, that's what I do. And I go the right way. I go curved. Or crooked. But I get there the right way."

Edmund said, "Crooked is right too?"

"Feasible," Jergen said. "Crooked is feasible. Curved is right and crooked is feasible. Understand? But straight is wrong. Least it's antieverything. That is my theory; see? Now that's my rule. And you know what the exception to my rule is?"

". . . You tell me." Edmund groped to his left, and opened the drawer.

Jergen had time to say: "You." He sat forward.

Then the narrow cushion on the window seat gave way and slid him down quietly onto the floor. Feet out wide and head thrown savagely back, he looked like a limp marionette.

Edmund put a hand over his brow.

"My Lord," Jergen said, "go on; I can see you. Next time I'll come and bust my frigging skull. Just to keep you amused."

Edmund said, "You wouldn't have to go that far."

He lifted his cigar box out, and took a silver letter opener from on top of the desk.

Jergen got both elbows behind him. He grunted.

"My Lord," he said.

Gathering careless—made weak by unvoiced, mirthless disgust, Edmund slit the red and gold seal.

3

There she was, and alone on Melpomene Drive.

She was alone, standing still and approaching forty. Mrs. Fitch had gone home.

And there was no sense to the day, and no core in her life; and she could not remember or believe she had yelled being born.

Once Opal had three sisters, all named for precious things because Mrs. Fitch's Christian name was Lipithy and she did not want her children to suffer as she had for a name. So they grew up to keep in mind what they were called. The oldest was Star; she married a well-off Chicago undertaker and lived there. Ruby sang in night clubs in the North, without a surname, known just as: Ruby. And Pearl was engaged to a traveling man who took her all over California, up and down California, for eight years, and still would not marry her. None of the three ever came back since they first left home.

Opal drank with Mrs. Fitch from a floating sense of duty she could not explain. Her second stepfather never drank. He beat Mrs. Fitch sometimes, but not too hard and no longer very seriously. Opal lived where she worked; she went home only on Sundays. Sundays were heavy going because Mrs. Fitch would not touch alcohol on the day of the Lord's collapse. And when Mrs. Fitch did not touch alcohol, it was heavy going.

Around the first Monday of every month Mrs. Fitch came to visit Opal at her job, and quite often stayed overnight. Then Opal drank; she felt bad about this, but it was a question of feeling worse if she refused. Mrs. Fitch was a woman who made you feel you could never do enough for her—made you hurt worse because you were not able to take over the pain of her troubled, lost life. Which was why her husband beat her, and Opal drank with her, and it was for the same reason the other girls would not come back to town.

Mrs. Fitch never had too much religion, but she was superstitious in different ways. She was the most superstitious woman Opal had known. She believed in voodoo, and owned fourteen gris-gris charms of various kinds; and she claimed to have more information about ghosts than she did about people. Last night she had come with a gift—she brought a special charm to keep Opal's employer free of haunts and danger during his intended walk through the Legrange house. But she miscalculated and came a day late, having been a little unsteady the day Opal told her about it.

And now she was gone, and Opal had the charm.

Opal Fitch Reed was a sensible woman; she would not try to unconvince her mother about such things. She was sensible in thought and in action. And yet she was not capable of life by her own definition; and there was no answer to that.

She had been married for six years. At present she was a widow. Her husband Mr. Reed was a man passing through town who stayed, a man everybody had joyously approved of but her. She had been patted into marrying him, mainly by Mrs. Fitch, who liked his manners. He had the nicest manners from the North, every place but where they might count; he was extraordinarily handsome, a man from the North, not very dark, and most educated. He was the kind of husband every other woman thinks is the best kind of husband except his wife. He was a very Boston pansy, and he died.

And nobody understood why Opal didn't rant or rave, but this did not matter. What mattered was that her suffering had not taken the form she herself expected and wanted when he let go his last breath. There was no intense pain, there was no tossing. Fact there was nothing that coffee wouldn't stop; she felt sorry for him, had to, kept her mouth shut, took too many baths awhile and that was that. No piercing pain, there was nothing; for she was not in love. She had never desperately loved a man, though there had been opportunities, and no man but her father ever loved her to her knowledge. But recently she had begun to look twice at herself: Opal. And Opal did not think she had very much to see.

Adding it up, she thought Opal was Opal. She thought she had one quality, this being that she liked to take care of people.

She sometimes played with dolls, wanting somebody to care for, and then the one real chance she got, had not really wanted to do it with her husband. Now she had nobody else but Mrs. Fitch, and there was no other way of taking care of Mrs. Fitch but drinking with her. Otherwise apart from that she was not alive, not in her own sense of the word. Inside she was like her name, the color of blind—and no core and nothing to live out from.

On the Drive, the texture of the air was thick and soft. Cool, the air was flushed around her; she had a sense of taking up space. She could feel the steady wet; dew around the swamp stales in rising, for it truly has no place to go. And neither did she.

Knowing and wanting was not having, and the sky, the loaded sky—muddy gray, bent in the wrong direction and spilling down from the middle; the worst kind of gray. The worst kind of sky, its stomach burst down, blinding, going on forty and no more a lady can do but know; and want; and work. And hope for luck.

The air was fresh anyway. Opal opened her hand, and let the dirty woolen voodoo doll fall into the gutter. It bounced out, then stuck on the lip of a crayfish hole. She put her foot on it and took a breath of the air.

She saw Jergen Wilson come out of the house; and she started back to work. He was a horrifying man to look at, Opal was aware of it, but she was not horrified. She was not anything, she thought. And she could not really believe she was even unhappy. Like the sky inside and the color of blind, she thought. She was Opal.

Jergen had trouble squeezing into his car. He usually did, and it made him short of breath. The interior was specially constructed, but still he had a time getting in behind the wheel.

But he could not yet hire a chauffeur. One chauffeur meant two —his wife would need one for herself and the children. He was not in a position to afford two chauffeurs. Not now; possibly next year. But he was not in a position yet.

He let off the emergency brake and turned the ignition key and pulled the door to. He waved at Edmund, who was standing in the first window of the north wing.

If you looked at the Choate establishment from the outside, you had to pause and think which room was where—even though you might have been in it often enough to be familiar. A castle of a house; Jergen became more admiring on each visit. Except for seeing Edmund in that window, he would not have said that was the study. From the street you wouldn't say the place was comfortable, it was so formidable. Yet it was both. A house of a castle. A refined and distinguished home.

Jergen said, "How would you like it?"

Rolling backwards out onto the Drive, he said, "I might not after all. Have to redecorate. It and me. Maybe I wouldn't."

"That's my boy," he said. "You tell stories." He braked, slipped into first gear, and smoothed off. He drove extremely well. It was most easy handling an automobile after managing his own swollen body.

"I actually might not," he said.

"You actually might not be full of shit," he said, "is what you *might* not be."

"That is a possibility," he said.

"Now," he said, "don't get mad again. And stop talking."

He had always wanted to own and live in a house like Edmund's: specifically Edmund's. But that was the least of it, and there was not much grace in vexing with particulars.

The grand issue was a different matter, and he had to keep silent about that too. For he had always been jealous of Edmund Choate's looks; but too achefully jealous to make a game of saying it out loud to himself. He did not mind Edmund's business sense or his money, or even his way of living—these things were concomitant niceties. It was the handsomeness of the man. And in secret Jergen believed that any man who looked like that could break all the rules and still make out. The rules did not hold for the truly beautiful people, because such people themselves were exceptions. The story was this—most people were plain; some unattractive; some were distinctly ugly and a few most ugly. It was like that. And which you were—the careless touch of the fates. There has to be a scale to any quality, and there must be instances on either extreme of any scale. And that was the story. That was all there was to it. He, Jergen, was born on the ugly side, quite far over. He was naturally ugly. Not the most, absolutely not the most; but enough. He did not deserve to be that way, nobody did, but it was not a question of deserving, it was luck. His father and mother had not been ugly, they were attractive. His father lived to be a rather handsome one. Not like him. Yet there were millions who looked like Jergen in the world, men who did not even consider, much less mind it—and this really made him mad. Sad and crawly and furious all at once. It was when he couldn't stop eating and got so hideously fat, in seven months, in one of those long malignant moods. So fat he nauseated himself to look at. And he stayed fat; and chose the most subtly harsh contrasting possible shades in clothes, with hand-painted nauseous ties. And if he ever took sick and grew thin from being sick, he would get fat again. He could never be handsome. But he could show the fates to be careless.

His wife Edna was lovely to see. She idolized him, and that was the last insult. His skin began to ripple when he thought about it. All the men to pick from, and she wanted him; it showed worse than no taste. Right after the wedding he suspected Edna must be idiotic or deficient in some way. She looked right at him, and she melted in his arms. She adored him in and out of bed. And after the first ten years he no longer touched her—the idea made him want to puke.

He saved up his love activities until he left on his business trip to Rome before each spring. There in the very early years he had kept one boy after another, all painfully handsome, and all needing money. Then after his fatness he matured and preferred girls. He never found one quite as lovely as Edna; but the Roman girls had taste—they never would have come near him were it not for the dollars. He could tell they felt about his ugliness almost as he did, they had at least decent vision. Only the money brought them in. He kept several, for varying periods of time, Bruna the longest; and she had got too old along with the rest, and now his mistress was named Marcella. But his manner of love-making never altered. That was the same with them all, very well explained beforehand. He and Marcella would stand naked, and he would have her chase after him, swatting where she could with a silver-topped thin ebony cane—an exquisite thing, a family heirloom. They ran around the bedroom like that and sometimes through the apartment, Jergen galloping ahead over the bed and between the chairs, like a shaved bear, swaying dangerously, and little Marcella swinging the cane, and her kinky black hair tossed long behind; she missed him most of the time. Then Jergen would turn around and grab her and try to knock the cane out of her hand. And he rarely had time to do much more than that.

In the fall he came back to Edna and their three children; he hibernated in his fat through the winter. He owned the best men's furnishings shop in town. The shop was not his whole living (he had stocks in various concerns, and held them secret), but it kept his lone conscious self busy during that part of the year. Jergen personally chose all the clothes that were sold there, and they were all beautiful things, for his only love was beauty; he had mellifluent taste. But because of the way he looked and dressed, no one who came into his shop ever asked him whether this tie went with that suit or shirt. The customers asked the salesmen or bought what they liked, selecting from among the carefully displayed splash of colors and materials and weaves. And Jergen stood by observing with pleasure the mistakes in judgment—the hideous combinations people thought were true. For a wrong shade of difference showed like an angry wound to him. And such wounds were his pleasures through the long dull winter hours, they really rather broke up the day.

His children were not ugly—were cast more like their mother; but plain-looking. He could not love them because they were his children. Perhaps, if she had been unfaithful, she might have borne a child for his care. But she had not the sense to be unfaithful. She did not have any sense at all: it appeared clear to him that Edna could never have wanted a real man. This was a disappointment in its time. He'd waited three years to find some sign indicating that she might have married him for other reasons. But no such sign ever came. And Jergen was forced at last to realize that he had taken to wife a tasteless woman who was just as revoltingly deformed in her heart as he was now in his body: she loved him.

Of all his friends, Jergen knew Edmund was hardly able to bear the sight of him; and that was another reason why he admired Edmund the most. But Edmund Choate was a man of taste in many areas—taste and refinement, you just had to see how he fit into that house. Except for Edmund's heavy-featured masculinity, Jergen in his adolescence might have worshiped such a man. And now he still regarded Edmund with the greatest wonder and esteem.

It made him start to smile.

Gliding with an integrated hum down Melpomene Drive in his bright green bulbous Cadillac, Jergen softly wet his upper lip.

Aunt Clothilde saw him pass. She was alone in the rear of the limousine. She said to the back of Sterling's cap, "Did that man stick his tongue out at me?"

"No, ma'am, he didn't," Sterling said.

"I thought so. I thought I saw him stick his tongue out at me. Not the first time, either."

"No, ma'am," Sterling said.

Aunt Clothilde said, "Where did he obtain that green color?"

"Had it painted."

"Of course. Where?"

"Don't rightly know, ma'am. He don't have a chauffeur, I don't know much about him. Around town somewhere."

"Green on the outside and orange on the inside?"

"Orange upholstery like. Probably Mrs. Wilson."

"Don't be so stupid," Aunt Clothilde said. "It was his own idea. His wife couldn't have had anything to do with that."

"She couldn't?"

"Of course not. Don't be stupid."

"Yes, ma'am," Sterling said.

Aunt Clothilde said, "The poor revolting man. He has a right to stick his tongue out; that poor man."

Sterling made a docile curve on the wide asphalt, and drove up the cement entrance to the Choate residence.

The sky had got so thick it was losing its dark gray brilliance. It hung, dull and wet, over the city.

"That poor man. Somebody ought to help him, he's pitiful." Before she got out of the car, Aunt Clothilde held her white silk handkerchief next to the skirt of her tan dress. She had knitted the skirt herself. She craned her head back, and sniffed. "Now *that* does match," she said.

"Yes, ma'am," Sterling was holding the door open for her.

"I wasn't asking. I can tell for myself."

"Yes, ma'am. You right, too."

"Of course I'm right."

"Yes," Sterling said, and meant it: the colors matched.

Aunt Clothilde limped past the jonquil garden across the flat white stones of the path, towards the house.

Then she was in the front hall.

The hall was a bad place to limp in. When you did it there, the walls rocked.

And you could see the end, where you were going, and it was an intentional, bouncing tease.

But even if she had not limped, Aunt Clothilde was sure she would have considered moving to be a waste of time. She'd considered the problem for years; when you wanted to get someplace, the thing was to be there without having to go. You spent three-quarters of your life traveling from here to there, and with nothing to gain, no inherent value in motion. Exercise yes, but your mind. Not your body. What is a body? Tell it to a plant. You go through the same hallways a thousand times in your life. Only to get there again, not to go. *To go*, two words, a verb you would be better off doing in French. Move. Move is funny. Moving is a funny thing for a person, and nobody laughs at that. Nobody does anything about it, either. They invent airplanes and things to get you there quicker, but those things move too. You want to *be* there. Be there, not be here, whenever you want. But no matter how quickly you move, you are still moving. And it's the concept that's stupid, not the speed of it. Let a plant tell you. Just let the earth do your moving. It is stupid. It takes a man's mind to make a telescope, takes a mind to use it, it takes a mind to think about what you saw; and then men stop using their minds right there, and they go right ahead and move. As if they couldn't invent something. Of course they could, they do, all the time, the wrong way. They come up with television, which swaps shadows around and leaves people exactly where they were. They go to all that trouble to take a shadow apart and put it back together again, and they leave people sit. Whereas if they had any imagination they'd make the shadows watch the people. They'd take a person apart where she didn't want to be, and put her back together where she did. Whether she limped or not; that doesn't matter. That has nothing to do with it.

Whether she limped or not.

Edmund began to chuckle.

"What's the joke?" Aunt Clothilde said. She stopped in the hall, and looked up, and looked around.

Then she heard Adrianne join in. This was happening around the bend up ahead, in his study. It would take her a good two minutes to get there and by that time the funny joke would probably be over.

"Wait for me," she said, "wait." And she said: "How did you get home without my seeing you? You said you'd be out for lunch. Adrianne? Where were you? You-all wait for me."

She started for the study. But the chuckling was going to leak off and disappear before she could get there; and she never got to share a joke with them.

She said, "Wait for me. I have to hear. Wait."

But they weren't either of them going to.

And she could only move just so fast.

IV

Post - Mortem

IT WAS LATE. All in all it had seemed to him an unnecessary day, and that is what he told her. An offensive, meaningless day; no positive quality, no essence; a day you were pleased to see spill off into night.

Edmund and Adrianne often sat together to share the hours past. The library with only the fire lit became a special place. Firelight by itself was the color of being; it made negative whatever was not touched by its own fluttering glow. It singled life, and held the mold of the mind separate and still, unaging. Or else it melted those few minutes with the whole of time—so wound and fused there could be no outward movement. Whichever, the effect was the same. Even the marking of the clock was an inert beat, involuted; an arrangement of hours within minutes. A spiral made from the outside, and everything traveling in. Winding smaller to an infiite point of darkness, an end in a center—a beginning: a thick cottony crystal-black center like the black pith deeps in her eyes. And these were the conditions a man could use to shake his brain after eight hours of living.

Aunt Clothilde knew that Edmund liked to be alone with his daughter when dinner was over, so if she made an entrance this was not accidental. Sometimes she seemed to enjoy just ruining the atmosphere.

Aunt Clothilde said, "I am only here to say I don't think that story was funny. I didn't and I don't. I've thought about it. It isn't funny at all."

". . . No," Edmund said.

Adrianne was watching the fire.

"The way you two were going on I thought it really must have been amusing. As stories go. But it wasn't funny at all. Jergen Wilson is sad, he isn't funny. The poor man."

"No," Edmund said. "He isn't."

"Then why were you carrying on like you were?"

"We weren't."

"You were."

"Fine," Edmund said, "we were."

". . . Adrianne wasn't. She was just trying to make you feel better."

"That's fine," Edmund said.

He shut his eyes.

Aunt Clothilde said, "I understand. Just don't give me notice. I'm going now."

". . . You don't have to," he said.

"Of course I have to."

Aunt Clothilde changed her weight from the cane to the bad hip.

Then she said, "And another thing. I don't think I'd let her go near that house. You shouldn't have gone there yourself."

"Please," Edmund said. "Clothilde, please, I ask you; I'm tired."

"I'm not going to lecture. I am going upstairs and take a pill and go to bed."

". . . Maybe you take too many of those pills."

"I take enough of them to be sure."

"Well; so they work."

"So say your doctors," Aunt Clothilde said. "Doctors. Just so they do."

Edmund lay his head back and listened to the night. He said, "You haven't had a spell in a long time."

"No," Aunt Clothilde said. "Not so you'd notice."

The fire was high, and was making a tishing noise.

She said to the door, "No, I would not let her go near there. It can't be. You should never have gone in there yourself; melodramatic and you were stupid. Now don't be a worse fool. Keep her away from that house."

"Stop it, Clothilde."

"I've stopped. I'm just saying what I have to say."

Edmund said, "You're being pettishly rude and on purpose."

"I'm always pettishly rude on purpose. I don't do it just for fun."

"You do," Edmund said, "and don't tell me you've started to believe in ghosts."

Aunt Clothilde leaned on her cane. She said, "Not started. Hardly; not started. I believe in everything there's a word for. I just like to collect my own definitions."

"I see." Edmund was working his shoes off. "And what is your definition of a ghost?" he said.

It was later than he had thought. Soon he would be sleepy.

". . . I won't, I won't have one. I will not have one." A last loose thread of Aunt Clothilde's knitting disappeared around the edge of the open door. "Forget it," she said. "Just keep her away from that house; use your rational heart, not your rationalized morals."

The door stayed open.

Then they were alone again.

But of course it wasn't the same yet; the air wasn't.

The touch of the fire was timid, in soft shadow against the walls of books, and uncertain. It had lost all its personality.

Edmund said, "Your turn tonight. Yesterday she was after me."

Aunt Clothilde's saying what he should or should not allow Adrianne to do was improper and pointless, and she had done it quite thoughtfully. Aunt Clothilde had always liked to tinge the air.

And now they were forced to wait for the air to clear.

"She likes to think she's obscure but profound," Edmund said. "It'd be pathetic if it weren't cloying. A wasted life is pathetic."

They had a secret together belonging to Edmund, and this was a moment to think about that.

It had been the kind of dreary day better gone anyhow. Nothing to value, nothing truly worth their tenderness. Every evening when they could, they compared time in the old way; and each was mindful of the other's care. It had started long ago—the day Adrianne was six, when she first went off to school and they had to be separated for one entire passing of the sun. Then he understood her shyness at the end of the day. Without need of speech he understood the hard hollow ball back of her throat: the emptiness she had tried to swallow all through the turning hours, because his throat had been no different. And they sat together on the sofa then, he sent the nurse out tapping her wrist watch, and they shared as much as each wished of the day that had gone. After that Edmund and his daughter almost never lost this end to each evening. It was not exactly a habit, but something both wanted and expected when the sun set. They might sit side by side, or she might lie down. In the winter they lit the fire; and for them the color of flame was the rekindled light of a twice-born day. And time to each was truer in the telling. This was Edmund's freedom— no questions ever asked and none allowed—no need to question. They were careful to expose only what might bring pleasure there. They were mindful of a dreary dead day.

And they had a baby secret.

The secret was Edmund's; but they both knew and had even talked about it; still it remained his. It made his own simple, secret lack of worry.

It had to be secret a) because it was so nonsensical to hear, and b) because it might sound arrogant rather than proud, and c) because they knew it was true. A fact like a private soft warm rock, a thing for him to hold—a belonging thing.

It was the plain solemn absolute fact that Adrianne's well-being was inflexible. And she was like that: inflexible. And she was.

Not a subject to discuss or argue. There did exist accidents, disease, earthquakes, maniacs; a million other unforeseeable threats; these were there for other people. The generic threat of the world, it was there for Edmund himself—always in the universe of possibilities—irresponsible, always ready to take form. Anybody could be walking faultless down the street, and have something bump him in the gut and maybe even kill him; something he didn't cause, or select, or deserve. An ever-present potential in nature, *the threat*—there for every person of every age. Edmund had lost a mother and two wives by reason of it. No one could deny its existence, and he least of all; Edmund had more cause to be aware of it than most. The threat was there for everybody.

It just didn't happen to be there for Adrianne. Except for the passing of time, nothing could and nothing would ever be able to harm her.

And Edmund would not have said why he was sure of this, even if he had known how. If you can give determinants for a faith of fact in the heart, then you have no faith and there is no fact. Both were sure, there was no more worth knowing.

He had kept it to himself a long time now; had not worried about Adrianne since years before her full growth. While other parents fussed and fingered their children, Edmund and his daughter went their way. For such a faith like an egg to a bird is warmly private, and it is shelled; you can get off it to look at, but then you sit back down. It is a thing to be protected and it is not a thing to show.

Now he was examining that, listening to the crickets and a locust out in the night. The bugs sounded angry for the sun; there had not been much burst of brightness to stretch in since early morning—only an instant. And the winter bugs wailed, they did not chirp. Not until the river and the swamp began to heat again with April. Cold rot makes a wailing discord in live sounds.

So rot must be warm—or must not be at all. You say which.

Still watching the fire. A profile; she had one. Not many people have a profile. A thin, straighter nose than was ever invented, the truest nose in the world. Plus one soft sweeping and deep ebony eye.

And in that stillness she said, " I forget, you know." She said: "I forget."

And she said it to the fire, with a heated softness which held the color of the flame.

Adrianne said, "Sometimes I am content and I know it isn't right."

Edmund sucked a medium-deep breath. He gathered in his stomach. But below that, his abdomen was beginning to glow, and he was sensible of it. Her voice had crept down there inside with a torch.

She said, "I walk, and I ask why I should be she. It isn't right for me to be content, not this way; not . . . this way. With everything else running on in the world. It isn't right, it's as if there were two of us."

Adrianne said, "So many people. I don't think I've ever met anybody who wasn't trying to be happy. And people can't because they try, and they try so hard. But who am I?"

Edmund lay his hand palm-up on the empty sofa-cushion to his left. It had only been there a few seconds when he felt Adrianne's cool fingers settle gently inside.

And each individual finger was a separate reason to live.

In a sudden blazing heat the useless day began to curl.

She said, "I forget. I do it purposely, I know. I go walking and I think, and soon I will forget. It seems only right like that. Not often; at times. When the weather turns cold and I don't feel it, then . . . and the people without houses. Sometimes I'm watching that big tree where the river turns. Or I'm by the canal, sometimes it's downtown walking, just passing between the people. And I will forget where it is I've just been or who with, or why. I won't know where I've been. Because it doesn't seem right to remember. It doesn't seem right I should be the one. Everybody tries. Why should I be she, who am I? How much can I deserve? I haven't done anything. You know I haven't."

But Edmund was thinking she had; and he was thinking how

often. Not a single time of distress in the city or an unhappiness for somebody, without his daughter there, immediately: people always said so. She could not know of an unhappiness without doing something.

He lay his head back and watched the fire turn to smoke. There was no use answering Adrianne when you wanted to tell her all that she meant in the world. Many persons had wanted to; and it was no use.

Edmund held the quiet to her in his palm.

And none of the day was left with them now. Before the darkness had come, that thick gray above had parted in the west like curtains, and the late afternoon sun had shone. It was big up there, and a sluice of orange light spilled out from it over the Drive to frighten the first raw cool of evening.

But nothing now was left.

He said, "Listen to the crickets." He could hear them around close.

And: "I hear them," she said.

"And a locust."

"It too."

Edmund told her, "The river is quiet now."

"Yes."

"I wonder where the boats are. Listen. They needed the heat," he said, "they were angry for the sun, those bugs."

"Did they?"

"Sure. Still do; they want it. They're still angry, listen. The bugs still are."

Adrianne stretched a little, and kneaded his palm lightly with the tips of her fingers. She was smiling.

She said, "How can they be when it's so peaceful? It's better to forget," she said. "Sometimes it's better to forget."

PART TWO

The Reflection

I

Talk and Skillful Scandals

1

A YEAR AND A HALF LATER. Then gossip was limp and dull, heavier than the approaching summer. And with the early heat, she came to town.

Now a visitor in any city who is classified as a tourist will be treated directly with the best there is to offer; or will not be treated. Only a true invader is ever allowed to see pure clannishness close enough to call it dirty intrigue.

And to that sort of stranger, a large residential avenue may seem smaller than the smallest private drawing room. Then it is no different than a room swarming with people who know each other well, but not as well as they think; and none of whom the stranger knows at all.

Such a street is Melpomene Drive, and such a city is this. Here people die, some persons change; but talkers talk on. If there is no topic for discussion, they can accuse each other of making something out of nothing. It is when a thing actually arrives, and from the distant outside—some sudden trespassing, unannounced and with no explanation; it is then that tongues threaten to choke their owners, and go dry.

So on these occasions you can often find out a great deal about the invader simply by listening to the invasion.

And though the degree of truth may be slight; and exaggeration great; and you might never be sure just how much is true, still you can often learn more by listening than by doing anything else.

Now it was public knowledge that the Legrange place had been bought for some unnamed person who was not of the city. Bought not long after Edmund Choate confronted all the past rumors and marched through that vacant house from top to bottom; and bought for a sum said to be enormous. An amount of money that was quite ridiculous considering the true value of the place and its evil reputation.

But Edmund Choate was admittedly the best businessman in town. And besides, the city was growing fast; people winked and said he had done right again. If a collection of strangers was going to take over the local industry and incorporate the commerce, they should be made to pay. They should pay like that—before arrival.

And many strangers did come to live and do business; they kept arriving. But they never came to live at the Legrange house.

She was there almost before it was known she was in town. She just came on a morning train, and took two taxis, and went with all her suitcases to see her lawyer, Mr. Samuel Vine, who had bought the house at her orders in her name. She hadn't ever met him, but she took two taxis to see him. And Mr. Vine was an honest lawyer; he explained again what he had been telling her in letters all along—that the price she'd paid for the house was far too high. Then she stood there tall and listened, and did not answer—dressed as she was in a suit of fine undecorated cloth, giving no hint of color, with her baggage piled around. And afterwards when the secret of her identity was out Mr. Vine's wife liked to tell how much they had been given to keep it; and she liked to speak of the moment when she had first looked on the woman's face, and had seen for herself that the most blaring simplicity and the hardest pride were perhaps not so opposite as some ladies thought. And Mrs. Vine was the first to know there would be a kind of queen on Melpomene Drive.

. . .

They gave her the grandest suite at the Hotel Washington for four weeks. It took that long to put the Legrange place in order. During those weeks, before she moved into her new home, she used a name that no longer belonged to her—one that went unattended around most of the city.

So the whispers started about other things. They began with her money.

She spent so much, people became uneasy. She paid every bill as soon as it arrived, and she paid in cash. The reconditioning of the house had been ordered by Mr. Vine; but she waited to choose the furniture on her own, from Craig's Department Store and from a custom carpenter and dealer in antiques on Magdalene Street. She got five hired help who worked until the house was cleaned and decorated, refurnished throughout. All the old stuff was carted away and given to the impoverished colored people in the Gerville shanties down the river. And the only objects she allowed to remain were some bathroom fixtures and the chandeliers. Every day there were trucks lined up to her door, and men carrying tables and beds and easy chairs, and in every truck there were at least three mirrors. People on the Drive do not like to appear outwardly curious to strangers. But some of them couldn't keep from standing by when those mirrors started coming in. After it was all done, she let a lot of the help go, and a maid who left told about there being one of those mirrors on each single wall; that maid said there wasn't one wall in the whole house without a mirror on it. Only the strange woman wouldn't make friends, though she was most polite to everybody, and no person was invited in to see.

Then at the end of the fourth week, Mr. Vine came to talk to her. He came to tell her he couldn't go on like that. He said he would have to take a vacation out of town if he had to go on like that, and he didn't want a vacation unless there absolutely wasn't any help for it. But he said the way things were going, if he as much as left his own house to get into his own car, he'd be stopped twice and asked the question; and that was after he'd had the phone disconnected; and so many people came to visit with his wife—people she hardly knew to say hello to—and she had a cold, and they brought her little presents like rum cakes and half-bottles of old brandy and the like to see if they could get the secret out of her that way, he absolutely couldn't go on. He explained it all. He said with the effort it took his wife not to tell, she was all one nervous disturbance, she had ceased speaking to him: she spoke to everybody but him. And he said it wouldn't make much difference if she were speaking to him, because by the time he came home at night she was usually reclined on the sofa or somewhere with an empty bottle next to her, and she wasn't in any proper condition to speak at all.

The woman listened to what Mr. Vine had to say. She let the maid serve him coffee; sat, and listened, with the light from the chandelier glittering in two long mirrors—crinkling over her in a wrinkled sheath of electric-yellow—touching cut gleams into the thickness of her black hair, pulled and rolled in a low chignon. When he had finished, she got up and went to the rosewood secretary. From the top section she took a square copper plaque with three initials etched, large, in the center. She took the plaque in one hand, and walked to the front door; and she felt over the doorknob with just the underskin of her large fingers for an instant before she twisted it and pulled. A thin whisper of hot air passed around her, circling into the room. Then the woman turned to Mr. Vine and asked him politely, not very loud, if he would be so kind as to have the carpenter sent that day to screw that plaque to that door.

The word exploded right away, because the woman was already a fashionable curiosity. For four weeks stories had spread wider than the truth. She had been the sort of visitor any slow, settled avenue might enjoy to stare at—a gray-eyed young stranger, friendless; and a beauty. A woman who could dress all in black for the rancid, choking, soul-bending heat of August. It was Eddie Reese the druggist who said she didn't sweat. He said she walked down the sunny side of Russrose Street, coming from Melpomene to his drugstore in the middle of the day, and the dust lay up behind her;

and the sun got in the dust to make an orange cloud that glowed off from her blackness like a liquid spilling sun streak—like she was melting the air as she came. And when she walked in, she was smooth and dry, cool as a late fall night. She got up a bill for more than twenty dollars in soap, Kleenex, toothpaste, mouthwash, that type of thing, and she paid cash and had it all sent to the Legrange house. She wasn't living there yet. Only when Eddie asked her whose name should go on the package she just spelled out Legrange for him, carefully and perfectly, with that transparent cast of an accent, and then left. And Eddie said there was something about her look that he had seen before, and something else about it he had never seen in his life. He didn't even notice the perfume she was wearing till she had gone; then he noticed it so much he closed up the drugstore and went home and shut himself in alone with his wife for the entire afternoon. And the next day he did talk.

The woman smelled of jasmine. Real jasmine, not at all the same as a bottled perfume.

She always smelled of jasmine. This was most apparent.

The Hotel Washington generally always looked damp. The hotel was at the foot of Melpomene Drive. It was large, full of filmy white marble statues and two fountains and a small Viennese-type band, and one great hip-deep goldfish pond slung in its ivied patio slicked over with patches of green scum. Around the patio, the hotel sat old and splendorous, the color of thinly spread curds. Between the patches, the pond was seen to be occupied by gasps and bubbles and the biggest goldfish in town.

While she stayed at the hotel, the visitor was known as Miss Bufardi. She dropped this name the day she moved into the Legrange house. She never used it again.

Everyone at the hotel was awed by her; she was treated there like visiting royalty. She tipped too much, but that was not the reason. She did not seem to know the value of money.

What she knew, among many more surprising things, was how to take care of the hotel personnel—or anybody else—by the mere tone of her presence. She could show how to dress so that both men and women were forced to admire; and how to sit at a table in admiring public and eat unawares. How to solder a man to his chair and make him cross his legs by looking at him, and how to say maybe yes with her profile and definitely no full face, and how to redirect every male swallow in a crowded restaurant along with a few female ones just by getting up to leave after lunch. She could; but you would not say these were calculated or even conscious effects. She just could.

Miss Bufardi was given the greatest consideration by the hotel manager. He came at her daily with a wet-lipped deference, bowing as if he had the cramps. He had a certain sense she would recognize the one person in town capable of dealing with a European personage as such a personage was used to being treated in Europe. And Miss Bufardi did not disturb the order of his belief. He wished to be regarded as the finest carpet under her feet; she was respectful of his wish, and looked on him precisely that way. This happened the first week, and for days afterwards even the headwaiter was embarrassed at the phlegm in his voice when he had to speak to the foreign lady. But then something else was noticed enough to be considered and discussed. The lady was most formidable: at particular times and to particular people. She could also be the opposite. One morning a bellboy walked into her suite without knocking. He brought her Monday roses from the management; and this time he thought she was out. He was busy in his mind with a personal problem, so he just used his key and walked in. Then the lady was standing five feet away from him in a black lace blowy dressing gown, filing her nails. Her oiled hair was loose down her back. And the hair was not combed. Now the bellboy was young; he was so mortified by his error he could not apologize. All he did was stand with his legs apart, bunching the muscles in his body up to his ears, as he might have done to look his best before a firing squad. He waited like that for her outburst, and he crushed the long white flower box till it buckled under his arm.

And the lady stared at him a long time—interested; serious. The gray of her eyes unfroze and swam out, and there were green specks like moss-sprouts floating in the gray. After that, she put the nail file down, and came and took the box from across his chest. Again she stood in front of him, holding the broken flower box tenderly like a dead body in her arms, and she said, unsmiling: "Thank you very much." She said it as though the roses could have been a private gift from him to her. Then she turned and went into the bedroom, and she shut the door. And three minutes ticked off before that young man could think to leave the same way he had come.

It was not a trick; it was a quality. It was not anything you can learn, or teach, by instruction. But the lady had it. Some said it was a special sense for people's secret insides. And some claimed she had a feeling for the hidden parts of others because she was so very queer, like inside out, herself. In Miss Bufardi it was as if the usual social sparkles were buried deep within her; and the dark blind unadmitted hopes that most persons keep and protect from the world, and sometimes from themselves—those she wore like her clothes.

However she came by it, the ability was there. Her stark ability was her quality. She was able to tell which one of his private personalities a man would most prefer to believe in; and then help him to believe. She seemed to admit without shyness or unwilling-ness or cotton-touch style that every man is the proof of his own imagination: that each single man is a single group of all the men he would and would not like to be. So she showed you to choose. She was impatient with ordinary defenses, and she ignored the other kind. And this simple spectacular lack of tact was more tactful than any usage. It was not this, but her silence, that scared the night clerk.

Then to a woman she spoke without refraction; and no sense of rivalry could last for very long, because there was never a sense of any mutual goal.

Before she came, people in the city used to talk of *piercing* eyes.

Old Mrs. Rhale who lived on Melpomene just off Ramiene was said to have a piercing, intelligent gaze. But Miss Bufardi brought a new concept to town. For her eyes did not pierce. They unhardened. When she really looked at you, they spread into a gray open mist: like they were out of focus. And in their openness they swam right through sealed wonderings past the lining of your soul, and made you itch where there was no place to scratch.

Her suite at the Hotel Washington was four rooms long. Decorated in gold satin and brown, it had carved yellow carpets and thick curtains that folded on the floor over windows looking up the Drive. In the main room there was a heavy wall-mirror set in gold-lacquered wood with two golden angels kissing on top. Each angel had the painful, constipated expression of a man with a heart attack or one who is trying to blow up a balloon. Everything sopped dust, and the satin was slick. The chairs did not wobble. The gold curtains caught on fingernails that were not very well manicured.

The sixth-floor maids said Miss Bufardi was the cleanest, neatest guest in the hotel. In four weeks, she never left a door open: she did not push a single ash tray out of place. Her clothes—excluding the ones she had on and those in four unpacked trunks—were left hanging in perfect order. She rarely wrinkled a dress even if she wore it all day. There was no occasion to pick up a towel after she went downstairs, and there were no spots to clean off anything.

And when Miss Bufardi left there were only two differences to show she had ever lived in the sixth-floor suite of the Hotel Washington. Both were discovered when she had gone, and she paid for one. She added two hundred dollars to her own bill. It was the last morning, the day she moved into her new home and dropped the name Bufardi. As soon as the manager had said goodbye to her, he came up to examine her rooms. He found them in excellent condition—brighter-seeming than before. But one heavy bronze statuette was lying off its pedestal next to the main entrance. It weighed so much, he used both hands to pick it up. It was lying below what had been the mirror, and behind it like the tail of a comet spread widening over the carpet and glistening was a big burst streak of shattered glass. Just three pieces of the original mirror remained, jagged, in the wood frame—and those looked like they had pressed cobwebs inside.

The other difference was the odor. Luckily it was pleasant, and something more than pleasant; but according to the maids, no cleaning agent was ever able to get the smell of jasmine completely out of those rooms.

The manager went to watch her from a window of the suite. She had sent her luggage on by car, and then had refused to be driven herself. She was walking alone up Melpomene Drive. And her way of doing that was as individually striking as the woman herself.

2

When Loris Licia Choate walked, she moved from her flanks, and you could feel that movement with your eyes, beneath her black skirt. She went smoothly on, in a full rumbling roll that never bounced and did not waver—plain forward.

Mr. Spewack who runs the grocery store on Rennet was meaning to be funnier than he sounded when he explained it. He said after his little boy once saw her walking along the street, his little boy never asked what made the thunder any more.

An epidemic of talking can last longer than many other diseases because people never seem to develop an immunity to any form of it.

And on Melpomene Drive as always, if not the subject, the object of discussion was Edmund Choate. This time it was by means of his foreign invading daughter. And also now it was to help him protect Adrianne Legrange Choate—his and the city's heart; so all-loving in her gentleness she would not recognize evil if she saw it.

But Edmund made no public sign, and said nothing. Under the magnification of a hundred stares, everybody at the Choate house behaved as they had before—just sharper and more so. Only Aunt Clothilde took a summer cold and did not go out or receive callers. And no person in town would dare to anger Edmund, much less hurt Adrianne, with a personal question.

Except Jergen Wilson, and now he himself was involved. He was also gone.

Jergen had stayed in town much later than usual because of the tourist parade that year. Business was five times better. And while the woman was still living at the Hotel Washington, she passed a shirt that pleased her in the window of Wilson's Everything For Men—and went in to ask whether they sold women's wear as well. She was standing in there talking to a salesman, when the owner witnessed the sleek full shape of her figure from behind, and started up to get a better look. Jergen was two aisles away by the time the woman turned and saw him; and he never moved any closer than that. His feet came to a stop before he did, as if he had stepped in wet cement. Then his bulbous body swayed forward so that he looked like one of those balloon-men with weighted legs. He reached to the Italian-silk ascot counter for his balance. And he and the woman stood watching each other over the silk until not just that one salesman but every person in the store hushed to silence. Out on the street some workmen were using a power drill, tearing up the asphalt for repairs. Then the sound of the drill seemed alive in the store: a solid pounding from wall to wall, floor to ceiling. And the woman removed her gaze.

She thanked the salesman for his trouble; and she headed down the aisle towards Jergen Wilson. She went directly to him. When she got there, she put the shirt up against the top of her dress, and said: "Please. Will you tell me what you think?" She was including him again with her eyes.

Jergen opened his mouth, and nothing happened. Then he said, "Mr. Jameson."

"No," the woman said, "I have already spoken with the salesman; thank you. No, I am asking your opinion. I know it is a man's shirt. But the size is mine. Do you think it suits me?"

Jergen was wearing a brown suit that had huge checks in it, and a speckled blue tie. He looked down at himself and grinned like a painted clown. He said, "I don't seem . . . to be the uh, the one here to ask about . . . a thing like that."

The woman was quiet awhile, watching, and it appeared she was thinking.

She said, "You are the only one."

"Me?"

"Please."

"Well, I . . . uh, black looks good on anybody, right? And any . . . and most anything would look good on you. Right?"

The woman said, "That is not what I asked, please."

Jergen licked his mouth. She did not take away her eyes.

"No," he said.

"Ah," said the woman. "Now. Because of the material? Or the cut?"

And then, at the same instant, the power drill outside was turned off; and Jergen Wilson's body relaxed and slumped. As if he had been attached to that current.

Much too loud he said, "Both. The pattern isn't right and the tone is wrong. The shirt is wrong. It would look awful on you."

"I thank you," said the woman quietly. "That is very interesting." She folded the shirt twice, and gave it to him. "Very interesting," she said, "that is most interesting to me. Thank you."

She turned in at the counter, and followed it along—examining each silk pattern with her gray spreading eyes. She followed the ascot counter to the Fawdon Street exit.

The same afternoon, Jergen went to visit Edmund Choate; he stayed three hours.

It became known later that he had urged his friend to join him and his family on a long vacation cruise, with the two other occupants of the Choate house. And four days afterwards Jergen left town for a prolonged trip to Rome.

A few old ladies could then remember how Jergen Wilson had been the last person of the city to see Loris Licia Choate as a child. But they would not speak of it more than to bring it to mind. In leaving now, Jergen had acted sensibly. Edmund remained the center of things, and for a time Edmund did nothing.

After that the woman began to behave in a way that alerted and excited the most unexcitable people on the Drive. Only one other Melpomene resident had ever presumed to conduct himself with equal freedom; and that was a long time ago and nearly forgotten now.

Then the enigma was complete. For not only did she act more like the young Edmund Choate than his real daughter—she looked more like him. The slant in use and the depth of those gray eyes were unmistakable. Anyone who was not acquainted with the situation, just from seeing both women, might think Edmund had denied his own child and adopted somebody else's.

And like Edmund in his youth—though in a different way, and perhaps for different reasons—Loris Licia Choate lived without recognizing the social laws of the city. Just according to each daily dawning spasm of her will. She began those scandals.

3

Now it must be understood that opinions around town were often outspoken, and were not often correct. Always there had been happenings that caused people to consider.

There had been for instance the death of Hercules Jackson.

He was a railroad engineer, a white man, and Irwin Humphrey Jackson had so many cords and slabs of muscle in his body, he was known to acquaintances by the name of Hercules. They said he was so strong he could twist a straight flat metal bar to make it look like a Maypole—and not twist himself doing this, or even get into a sweat. He had tattoos all over his body, and each tattoo was from a different port in the world; he had been a sailor. There was one on his upper left arm of a man and a woman standing close together. When he rolled up his sleeve and flexed his arm the man and woman took on suddenly in a comic, obscene manner.

Hercules Jackson was about forty-five when he became an alcoholic and got fired from his railroad job. Then he sat around in bars all day and most of the night, though he had a wife and three children to support. Finally, he was always drunk. You could see him any time you wanted to, in one bar or another. Only most people had the sense not to want to, because now Hercules had developed a couple of unpleasant habits. First was the way he would hit with his fist on top of the bar. He did this often, maybe every half-hour, in a sort of trance. He started blandly and steadily, and maintained the same rhythm while he increased the pressure until every glass and bottle down the entire bar jumped to a rattle. And no barman could stop him, or make him hear; he stared in wonder like a baby at his own fist. Then, in between each series of poundings, he insulted people. He called anybody names. He might be in a friendly conversation with a person several minutes; withdraw from the conversation in the middle of a sentence, and frown, and then call that person an insulting name. He got a new reputation quickly from his new, ugly behavior. But no time would anyone get into a fight with Hercules Jackson, regardless of what he said or did.

Except one day and one small man who didn't came up higher than the muscles under Hercules' solid collarbone. A man from out-of-town, traveling by. Hercules called the man a fairy, and then got to laughing like he used to after he had made an insult. And the little man clambered down off the barstool, and told him to take it back. Hercules just laughed louder. Then the man flicked open a knife nobody knew he had in his hand, and said he would kill Hercules unless Hercules took back the bad name. But the laughter went on, and it developed a fresh sound of excitement in the last stillness. And the little man reached back, and aimed his knife at Hercules' chest. When he swung, Hercules could have stopped him by lifting one elbow to block the blow. He could have lifted one elbow. But Hercules Jackson didn't budge. The little man killed him.

He lay on the floor dying for twenty minutes, and he still had his strength and wouldn't let a policeman or a doctor come near him. People only guessed he was dead when he stopped laughing. The man from out-of-town was taken away to jail. Then Hercules Jackson's wife came in. She stood with one hand and all her slight carriage on one hip, looking down at the body. After a while she went out and got their three children, and brought them back into the bar to see. The two older ones screamed and cried till they left; but Mrs. Jackson and the baby didn't. They never dropped one tear between them. And before walking off, she stripped Hercules of all his clothing, to sell. The police let her do it because she really needed the money.

Then he was naked there on the floor, and the red in his tattoos was brighter than the dried blood. And people looked and didn't have a comment. The newspapers did not know what to say. All who saw or heard about it were honestly amazed. Not by his refusal to fight, or his dying that way. It was another occurrence; one that was most amazing of all, on account of its having no proper place in the order, or the accepted disorder of things. This was the fact that under all the swelling powerful muscles in Hercules Jackson's wondrous body were ten clean white toes—and each one had a toenail on it recently painted perfectly with a crimson nail polish shinier and even more brilliant than the red tattoos.

Now Hercules Jackson died in a bar in the cheapest white part of town. But these toenails caused so much discussion, for weeks he was the main topic on Melpomene Drive. And the same happened backwards with Loris Licia Choate, around the city: she lived in elegance on the Drive, and she was talked about down to the saloons on Tilette Street.

But there was a more important difference. For Hercules died with a secret—a private preference for a version of himself that he kept under his soiled socks, and that nobody ever imagined he had dreamed of no matter how drunk he got. He kept that version there.

And Loris Licia Choate allowed all hers out in the open. She did what most appealed to her at any time and in any way;

without the aid of liquor, her actions seemed wild and contra-
dictory. It was as though, having brought all her hidden selves
into the air, she was still unwilling to decide on any one.

Yet about Hercules, people had agreed at last that the toenails
constituted a big joke. He was probably senseless with drink one
night, and playingly painted his toenails for a gag. They did
not take a thing like that seriously; it was a morbid joke to be
discussed as such; they said there was no secret at all.

And talking of Loris Licia, they claimed the fabric of her
behavior was highly suspicious. A woman would not be so wild-
willed or so ignoring of normal public criticism unless she wanted
to hide something else; people said she was out to guard a shock-
ing dark personal mystery.

In this city it is almost impossible for two individuals of some
general wealth not to see each other occasionally. You cannot
help it. There are not that many places to go. And still Edmund
had not been to see her. This was known because, inversely, it
would have been known if he had; Edmund Choate was never a
man to disguise or hold off his actions from anybody's view. So
friends lived in expectation of a public encounter between Edmund and his ex-adopted daughter.

But now the woman did not frequent the restaurants or the
cafés. Her favorite servant took care of all the shopping. The
woman was consistent in limiting her excursions to an hour's daily
walk along Melpomene Drive.

Once each afternoon, at the same time, she left her house by
the front door and went to the sidewalk. There she turned to the
left and headed north for the cemetery. And she started her walk.
She did it without hurrying; and a man who saw her said she did
not slow even for a passing car, though of course this could not
have been true. The first day it was imagined she was going to
visit her mother's grave. A few neighbors peered out of their
houses to nod and make faces with understanding. She went by
each house, trailing a long shadow behind her, and the fierce

intent she focused on the path of her direction was noticed by all. In time this might have changed some ladies' natural antipathy to a sort of sympathetic testy attitude. And some stood out on their lawns to watch her after she had passed. But on reaching the wide white entrance at the head of the Drive, Loris Licia Choate made the one move nobody expected. Without going in, and without seeming to stop, she reversed her body so that her feet pointed south—and she came back the way she had gone. There was no change of speed, and no evident weakening of intent. She walked to the same spot and turned as she had before. She went into her house, and did not appear again until the next day.

It was the same every day after that. You got used to seeing her on the sidewalk in the afternoons. She was thirty minutes going in each direction. After awhile, one or two courageous persons who happened to be on foot there even acknowledged her passing with an attempt at a smile. And on those occasions, Loris Licia nodded faintly in return. But she did not stop, and she spoke to no one.

And the purposeful mien of her walk never altered. She seemed to be going someplace. It was not considered the manner of a lady only out for some exercise.

Then several residents noticed a movement on her lips. This, people said, was next to imperceptible, and she made no sound; so it was not of general remark for awhile. But a Mrs. Heppleton saw it, and started the rumor that the woman was praying. Mrs. Heppleton's interpretation was popular right up until old Mrs. Rhale of the piercing eyes unleashed one all her own. Mrs. Rhale said much more likely the woman was just counting the number of steps to the cemetery.

4

Within a month after Loris Licia Choate had moved into her new home, the place looked different from all four sides. For one thing, it stayed scrubbed; the bricks around the ivy had a rich deep reddish glow. But more evident was the change in the garden. The biggest Legrange gardenia bushes, famous long ago for their size, had been cut down. Only the smaller bushes remained, in a big rectangle stretching back from the house. Loris Licia's maid announced that the lady did not care for the odor of gardenias.

And with the flowers went the ghost. It made no show of disappearing; yet those who had once believed said it would not have stayed on after the bushes were cut down. Actually no one could conceive of any haunt occupying the same house with this kind of lady.

Many stories were spread; a few held some truth. But gossip was furtive. People were waiting for Edmund Choate to make a sign as to what sort of action he might take. And while they waited, a doubtful fear drifted like a light rivermist up the Drive. It settled on your skin, a tingling wet touch in the tight air. Everybody felt it, and it alone remained unspoken. Friends were all wondering what could be done to keep Adrianne Legrange Choate safe from whatever harm or insult might come to her through her lawful sister's presence in the city.

Then one day, they passed each other on the Drive, the two sisters. Towards the middle of September; the last hot breath of a dusty dying summer still sulked under the sky. It was around five of an afternoon, and the Drive had open eyes to see them. Adrianne with a pale violet dress and skin that was near transparent, her short brown hair curling like a live crown; Adrianne walked and you thought her feet would chip on the pavement. You wanted always to be close and take care of her, even though you knew she surely didn't need you. But Adrianne's strength grew out of her delicacy (that was most difficult to comprehend and accept); with her sister it was just the other way around. And as Adrianne passed her sister, she stopped, and lowered her head, she stood right on the sidewalk with her head bowed down. Black Loris Licia kept her hands close to her body; she locked her eyes ahead and went on up the street. She left the dusty sky to shine over the violet, bowed figure behind her.

Word of that must have got back to Edmund very fast. It set

the whole Drive talking. Starting with old Mrs. Rhale, and from her on down, an impossible woolly situation became suddenly clear—then solidified itself into a concrete public dilemma. How (she said) could any man live with his pride and his shame (Mrs. Heppleton changed it to his future and his past) on the same street? Then everybody knew things couldn't go on as they were.

Days later, Edmund sent for Mr. Vine to come to his club, and they spent the morning alone together. And Mr. Vine left with his coat over one arm, wiping inside his shirt collar with a balled handkerchief; he was soaked through.

And then without warning, Edmund took overt and decisive and blunt action, as he had done ever since anyone could recall. This was in the approach of October. And there were Edmund and Adrianne and Aunt Clothilde going up Melpomene Drive in the early daytime.

They went on foot, nodding to friends, but not stopping; and Edmund, a vibrant shine from his face, had the look of a man who can know how to do the right thing in the right way. They went to call on Loris Licia Choate like that, out in the open— the two ladies, one on each of Edmund's arms, following his strong lead. They marched down Melpomene to Number 16, and swerved in at the walk, and Edmund Choate himself rang the bell.

And at that moment it came to pass. The maid called Luthella left them standing outside and went upstairs.

Loris Licia Choate sent the maid back down to say that she was not at home.

And that was that; the surprise inflated gossip too large for people's mouths. There was nothing to be said if you had already heard it. It would not have been taken seriously as a rumor. And it had happened.

The thing was witnessed. On the way back down the Drive, Edmund's legs floated him forward. They took him past trees and timid people as though he were wearing a miner's lamp to see by. His morning's righteousness eviscerated, he looked empty as a shopwindow Santa Claus left after Christmas. Aunt Clothilde showed every sign of being in a savage mood, and was. But Adrianne, holding hard to her father's arm, smiled softly and warmer than the clear-edged morning sun.

Mrs. Rhale's married daughter, Leonore R. Le Vey, was head of the Civic Opera League. She made them stop, and talked to them on her way out to her car. Afterwards she told her mother that Edmund had carried the conversation well: he was polite— and politely, distantly sick. Edmund's manners were not frangible. But while speaking with him, Leonore Le Vey was watching Aunt Clothilde's round milky eyes, puffed up with tension in their sockets. And Aunt Clothilde turned then to the side and in a perfect chiseled whisper, said to Adrianne: "Now stop smiling."

Before everybody had time to savor all that had taken place, the situation got conglomerated. Downtown, Loris Licia went out and located one of the poorer brothels in the growing red-light district of the city. There she made friends with two anemic white prostitutes—one young, the other oldish for the profession.

She took them both back to live with her in what was no longer the Legrange house.

And Loris Licia Choate, though she looked, dressed, and was in appearance the same as on the day of her arrival, lived a little differently.

Parties were given not less than twice a month at Number 16 Melpomene Drive. Small intimate parties, gleaming wide through wide windows; pale, then lustrous in the evening air that filled slowly with night as winter began. The parties were attended by a few men, fewer women, but were undeniably attended. They were given Thursday or Saturday nights. If it was Saturday, there was a three-piece band that played in one of the back rooms, and people danced. They moved by the windows; the men were seen, and sometimes recognized. The lights on the second floor stayed lit as well, and it was said those rooms were used for card games. And it was also said those rooms were used for worse than card games.

The two newest members of the household now dressed expensively, but without much color. For some reason they and the maid too often copied Loris Licia Choate's preference for unadulterated black. The women were quiet; were usually with Loris Licia wherever she was, at home or not. The house itself was surprisingly quiet, even when it held visitors and during the parties. Of all that was watched, and more that was suspected, not a great deal was truly heard.

Leonore Le Vey resided with her husband and her mother five houses from Number 16 on Melpomene. In bed she often listened to the breakfast stories her maid had got from other servants in the neighborhood. Loris Licia double-locked her front door now according to one Sarah Wirth's butler and had a chain put on it, and Leonore heard tell. When three young men came in the afternoon and didn't leave the house till long after the dinner hour, Leonore knew. She knew when one of Adrianne's elegant beaux, Lydell Wainscott, came to call and was regurgitated from that house within ten minutes of the time he entered. It was Leonore who caught up and spread the rumor that Loris Licia had found an old photograph of Adrianne's mother, Anne Legrange, in the attic—and had placed the photograph in a silver frame on the mantel for anybody to see.

And it was Leonore Le Vey who said out loud that Loris Licia Choate differed from her own mother only in class—not in classification; that of the two, Loris Licia showed desire, and blatant lack of taste, where her mother had demonstrated necessity and great savoir-faire; and that this daughter of a famous foreign demimondaine was, by nature, a plain local whore.

Now the fact of her coming was a public scandal, openly discussed. Melpomene Drive decided that Loris Licia Choate meant to cause violence and harm: she must have evil things in her mind. Further, people at last concluded that the ghost of the old Legrange house had been an unfounded rumor in very poor taste. For this present inhabitant, this creature, this woman was the true haunt. She was a vengeful black wraith who took her being from Edmund's past; and she was come only to haunt him and to do him wrong. She could have no other reason for buying property in the city, when she wished not to make contact with

Edmund, nor with his real daughter—nor even with the other socially acceptable elements around town.

Five young families of the Drive, not including the Choates, had a friendly coffee meeting. Edmund would not be called upon to take any part in a service directed against his adopted daughter, although that daughter was doing him and his family—and everybody else—so tawdry an ill. The most to be expected was Edmund's silent, unsolicited co-operation in his own defense.

Step one of the service had to do with the two women house guests. A dependable man was hired to come across the type of information which might be of interest to the police. He made friends with the two women on the street; discussed his curiosity with them; by and by made clear that he could pay for a few documented and detailed facts; and was obstreperously giggled at. The two women, Miss Mady and Miss Viola, left him in Relasoire's Restaurant during the second course. They wove in a single colorless path through the steamy room around four tuxedoed waiters to the door and outside, and the older one was still giggling. The detective specified afterwards that Miss Viola, the older, had not struck him on the forehead with the champagne bottle only because Miss Mady expressed a burdening fear of waste and took it home with her.

Then Loris Licia's Negro maid Luthella was approached, not in quite an equal manner, but with quite equal, if rather more aggressive, results.

The committee decided that Loris Licia Choate had a means of inspiring fierce loyalty in unexpected hearts. They then decided to hire a few more men who would attend one of her parties and find, or if absolutely necessary lay out, the facts for themselves.

Not long after this, Loris Licia had a new kind of evening. The party was attended by half a dozen important members of the city's law force, and two from the Board of Health. Some unrecognized women also attended. It lasted later than usual, and this was the only party she had yet given which might have been accurately termed noisy.

Her next visitor was Mayor Salten. He arrived for Wednesday luncheon, and towards evening was led out to a taxi and driven home; he called for his own car the following day. And Mayor Salten was heard to say in various places that the manner in which Loris Licia Choate had taken those two unfortunate women to her bosom and shown them a fresh life was not remarkable only when you considered the other remarkable qualities inherent and apparent in the benefactress, Loris Licia Choate, a great woman and a great lady.

The committee did not meet again. They agreed by telephone that no further action could be taken until the specter disclosed some tangible intentions. Loris Licia continued with her gatherings, no larger than before, and then one day she was no longer amused by them and stopped. Awhile after that, some sore things that were said of her even began to sound as if they might be edged with jealousy. The ladies on Melpomene Drive spent much expensive time collecting for charities and doing purposeful good in each others' eyes. They now found themselves having to speak of one who lived by her own standards. New terms ranged from "cheap tart" to "venemous and unloving," depending on who used them. And they all talked, these ladies. Yet they could not lose a lonely sort of milked respect for the woman. And Loris Licia Choate allowed them their loose-tongued lives. While persons have surely been known sometime in history to spit at the moon, it is doubtful they looked down—or ever looked anywhere but up—for that purpose; and when city people look up to spit, it is not always the moon that gets moist.

There was some more natural stir when Loris Licia's Negro maid took to dressing as elegantly, coming and going as freely as Miss Mady and Miss Viola and by the front door. It had been said for weeks, not believed, that all the women in that house lived together as friends on an equal basis. But by then she was considered just too lewd, odd, and outlandish to be taken seriously. Her general erratic behavior was obvious, and that was enough. Some who had and many who had not met her swore that Edmund's former adopted daughter was insane.

Yet she lived on there; the faint wild smell of jasmine was more lasting than the gardenias around that house. If she still caused talk, this meant she had a place in the city. Consider that she came to shock, or to do worse things. And there was a whiff of doom in her coming. Then let her be a lunatic, a black usurping phantom, or a whore: let her be. Now Loris Licia Choate was at home.

The House Without Time

ON A DAY IN NOVEMBER, five months after her arrival, Edmund started down the main north hallway with the two neat manila folders set like schoolbooks under his arm. Not quite past evening, and the hall was dark, and dimly cool, and lazy. This day had been the same; he left the light off with reason. Edmund pressed his elbow against the folders. Then inside the jacket and shirt, along the left side of his chest, all the muscles recognized that touch.

There were blocks of wintry evening gray lying in at each window. They fell in even-cornered patches on the carpet: quickly fading faded films, overexposed, of a lost sky. They did not make nearly enough light to see by. But Edmund followed his vision to the end of the hall.

The letters had reached him through a lawyer; a man from Pittsburgh, efficient and honest, a worthy trustee. He had chosen the lawyer as a result of business connections, and Edmund's perception was never untrue when he examined a man for integrity. The lawyer was dutiful and just.

Excepting the war years, there was a letter for every four months of Loris Licia's growth from the time she entered the convent until the full amount of money went to her free on her twenty-first year. There was nothing after that.

Silvana's mother died when the child was seven. Loris Licia Choate was sent from Rome to a distant relative in France. But this cousin was not a responsible person; a Paris associate of the lawyer made a report. The cousin wasted the money given to him each month for Loris Licia's upbringing, and the child was neglected. The Paris associate suggested that she be consigned to a convent—one where she would be well treated and educated. A particular convent was chosen in the Midi, not far from Dordogne.

Most of the letters were written by Mother Superior Leulie, who ran the convent; sometimes a Sister Rose or a Sister Leone wrote in her place, and two letters had been signed by a Sister Angélica, who was Spanish. The tone was usually the same, though Sister Angélica did demonstrate a distinctive feeling for people. She was killed early in the war. The letters were all written in French, and translated by a Pittsburgh school of languages. The lawyer sent one copy of each translation to Edmund upon receipt.

The trust expired and Loris Licia was given her capital the day she was twenty-one. Good investments and accrued interest had more than doubled the sum; she received over a half-million dollars. She left the convent, and there was no official word of her from that time. It was believed she had gone to Spain. Six years later, the lawyer clipped and mailed to Edmund a British newspaper item he had received describing the scandalous breaking of a formal engagement between Lord Wilfred Duncan and Miss Loris Bufardi. The Miss Bufardi referenced in the article could have been Loris Licia Choate. The clipping was attached to a note from the lawyer saying it might just as easily be a coincidence.

Edmund had saved each letter, and shown them to no one. There were twenty-four in all. Adrianne knew of their existence; he did not keep secrets from her. Both knew it was not right that she be made to read them.

Three months now had passed since they went to attempt a

visit at the other house. Before having that door shut in his face, Edmund had written Loris Licia five notes; all were unanswered. She would not answer the telephone.

And now there was something to be done, and it was not a pleasant thing.

But Edmund did not come to action for pleasure, or for the lack of it. Certain ends were called upon to meet; he came to his calling. And if his thoughts were turbid, his will was not. He could follow an aim of necessity to any end. He was that kind of man.

Through a door into another short hall bearing south, and three dark rooms. Then a swinging door with a round glass porthole that beamed deep yellow. The light was on in the pantry.

He stopped inside, and squinted, and blinked. The pantry blared cream from its shiny walls. Enamel paint; and when his eyes balanced, Edmund saw that the painter had put it on so thick the gleaming contorted brushstrokes were still there.

Opal was in the kitchen. He saw the back of her head, and heard her slap a plate onto the counter, and he wondered if she were alone. Then he thought it should have been the cook, not Opal. Unless it was because dinner had been served. Some of the other servants might be with her.

And it made no difference.

Between tiny green starched curtains with white lace fringes set chastely around one small window over the sink—night was a hole. Now the gray was dead-black and endless deep. It held no object, not a tree, not a moon.

Edmund felt it slip past his shoulder as he moved. He went between the icebox and the wood sideboard into the kitchen.

Opal was alone, facing the stove, with her profile to him and her head turned away. And she was humming. The door on the other side of the kitchen was closed; there were voices beyond.

The kitchen was a large room, almost square. At the right

as you entered was a short passageway leading to a door and three steps out. The kitchen faced the back garden.

He looked then at the steel box with its black handle, set in the passageway wall. But there was no way of knowing whether the fire was on below. It should be; it generally was at this hour. You couldn't tell though, by looking, and there was no smell of smoke. You had to pull the handle or ask.

Opal's hum mangled itself. She stopped whatever she was doing and peered at the floor under her right armpit. But she didn't turn.

Edmund said, "It's only me."

". . . Yes, sir."

"Fire lit?"

"Yes," she said.

A greased swatch of gray-stringed hair stuck out of her cap. It pointed out, high; more grease than hair. She still hadn't turned.

Edmund stood as big as he could and pulled out the balled muscles of his calves. "How are you doing?" he said.

"I'm fine, sir."

The fire was always lit once a day.

". . . You are?"

Opal put the plate down and looked around to face him. "I don't rest well, sir," she said; "but I'm fine."

"Sure?"

"Fine, sir."

Since she had given up liquor and got engaged, Opal was the most formal and proper, and the saddest of all the servants.

The fire would not go out, being lit; for fires very seldom do that.

"Do you want something, sir?"

He didn't want anything.

". . . No, sir?"

"No," Edmund said, "I don't want anything."

Next to her head, another window; and the night was dead there too. So say it was the fire that killed the night.

Edmund said, "Maybe you ought to take vitamins." He tightened his arm on the lumped folders.

"Sir," Opal said, "I don't need them."

"Vitamins will prevent a cold."

"Yes, sir."

Edmund said, "How is your man?" And he thought he could feel it from below. Through his shoes. This was not possible; but he *thought* he could feel the heat from below.

"He's fine," Opal said.

"I'm waiting for you to get married."

"So is he," she said.

"Then do it."

"Sir. I keep thinking."

"Can't decide how you feel?"

"Oh, yes."

"Then do it."

"I don't know, sir," Opal said. "There's Mrs. Fitch. And Mr. Reins is thirty-two. He's deaf."

"Deaf? Do you mind?"

"No."

"Then do it. You think too much," Edmund said, "you think too much. Do it. If you know how you feel. Go ahead and do it," he said, "just do it."

And he would have said again: just do it. But his voice was getting out of control—Opal was frowning.

Edmund stretched his hand out for the black handle as he moved. He went fast; it was warm. The heat made it feel alive. He pulled it to him.

The inside of the incinerator was caked with black. Now he could hear the growl of the fire, and he could smell the burn. There was an orange glow—wastefully warm as sunlight in a new-dug grave. But he did not see the actual flame.

A burst of thin black ashes rose on a draft; wafted; fell back singly, and fluttered in the light. The edge of each ash glowed with angry live sparks that grew to flash in clusters and streaks, most bright just as they died. Sparks make a show.

And one wide ash held, floating, to be last.

Edmund watched it sink. He lifted the folders and tilted them forward, and the letters slid out while Opal said: "I could have done that, Mr. Choate," and he shook the folders loosely. The letters dove out and down—swooping, rattling. The letters lost their order before they burned. And when every one was gone, in the sudden consuming glare, there at last he could see the flame.

"I could have done that, sir."

"No," he said; "you couldn't."

He let go the handle, and the door of the incinerator slammed. It bounced open, and closed again.

He had intended to drop the folders too. But he was still holding them. He still had them in his hand.

"I . . ."

"I know," Edmund said. But the phrase *do it* would not stop rolling around and catching in his mind, like a sticky piece of a song. He turned and moved through the pantry towards the darkness.

From this side the same porthole in the swinging door was black instead of yellow.

Then he had to stand in the dark dining room till his eyes got accustomed. It was a bit better than turning on the light. So he waited there.

One whole window must have been open; though he felt no draft. Yet in the vacuum of an unoccupied room at night he heard a wondrous noise. The noise came rich and violent, and it came in thick long spurts, throbbing to Edmund's own time. These were all the separate night-sounds gathered hard together to match his rhythm. And his mind was uselessly empty as those folders.

He was thinking about vitamins.

A while later he moved; he went to the sun porch. He went to sit and be alone. He did not know Aunt Clothilde was out there until he sat down next to her. Then it was too late.

Edmund breathed deep. He lay the flat folders across his lap, and placed one hand on them. There was a moon.

But Aunt Clothilde was silent. She even seemed as though she might stay that way.

There was most of a moon in the night after all. And the sky was still fading to pure blue. It had only looked black from inside because of the yellow light. Out on the glassed sun porch things were different. No truer perhaps; but different. Things here showed in relation to themselves. You could for instance be an observer.

And here you found no senseless man-made quality like: *at the same time*. Your time was your own. Here it always was. It could hardly be shared, even when you wanted to. And when you do not want to love you can watch the moon alone.

Edmund studied the stroke of spilled light caught on the cold shrunken surface. This was a clear night, and the moon looked like it had been left too long in water. He asked himself what sunbeams would have done if that moon had not been there; how far sunlight travels in spaceless space before it shines again.

When a thing is burned, it may live in the mind. But when the mind is gone, there seems an end.

And there was a night. He tried to remember:

The girl is more intelligent.

And left of the moon and down, one side of the pond rippled silver through the trees. Pine needles and bare branches were shivering in the late breath of winter. But the sun porch shut out all the weather. Thick sloping panes stopped the feel of the night, and held a sheet of glossy silence over the world. It made you want to whisper for the wind.

She is very well behaved and quiet; the girl is more intelligent.

Down from each branch the moss was moving. In a few places it swayed, and other parts merely trembled. The moss was full in the trees, dripping with dense gray weight. Like pieces of clouds hung around in the dark to dry. Where does moss come from?

As you know, Loris finished her ninth year of age the day before yesterday. There is some change. She is inclined to ask questions.

The deep blue had come and gone, and the sky was a black empty husk of the day. And now no stars. Now things were darkening in.

Such a way of looking at you. Such a way she has.

Frankly, we were disturbed, she is always quiet. Were it not for Sister Angélica . . .

There are so many sides to her character, she is really quite amazing. She conducts herself like an adult, and she is only fifteen.

And things were buzzing in.

Grass at night can be gray, or it can be dim silver. Depending on the sheen of the blades, and the texture. But green at night is not wasted. Because you cannot see it, because it is not, these facts do not make waste. Nothing is wasted for having been. A lack is a true quality; and *nothing* is a word which takes its meaning from time. Do you see?

Grass at night can be gray.

And the ground is a flat patty substance sprinkled with brittle leaves. Up under the hump-backed leaves in sudden licking circles and fountains, this is the way the wind plays.

But when will the wind want a color? Grass at night should be green.

The Sister and she often had long talks. One expected to see them together whenever Sister Angélica was free. She enjoyed being . . . almost to a fault . . . we were happy to note her calm acceptance when Sister Angélica passed away. The girl has a profound faith in God. At present she prefers to be alone.

Aunt Clothilde had not spoken. But she wasn't dead. She was unnatural. Such quiet around her was peculiar.

She knows that we are in contact with you, her trustee. I did not believe that she knew, but now I am convinced . . . The subject of money is strangely distasteful to her. Yesterday the Mr. Laurignac from Geneva came to meet her to discuss the impending financial aspects of her future. However as soon as he had begun to speak, she left the room. Loris has not ever behaved badly before . . . You know how surprised we were when she refused to answer your kind letter to her. She refuses to deal with any of the trustees, but only says "they will know their duty." But in less than a year she will be a wealthy woman. Sister Rose also is unable to approach her with this idea. She remains quiet, she is a reserved girl, obedient in every other way, and she is an honor to her instructors. But one would think the very subject of money has a special effect on her.

Outside the wind was increasing. Branches bent, and the moss bounced. Layers of leaves leaped over the ground now, all in one direction. But the glass held out the sounds; Aunt Clothilde held hers in.

She might have been going to market as she used to do with Sister Angélica before her death. She kissed my hand and left. I spoke for quite an hour, and told her much I thought to be pertinent. But frankly I do not know whether she listened. One never knows how much she listens. She remains respectful as ever, but frankly one has no way of knowing what she feels. She had nothing to say, and answered all our questions by saying she did not have any plans. I do not know, sir, whether that is true. It is what she said . . . Without doubt she is capable of dealing with the world. We have always been happy with her response to all training, spiritually and mentally, and we can say that we have done our best . . . It may be said that she is a little unusual, she is an unusual girl. But her profound faith in God and adherence to her religious training cannot be doubted . . . However as you know she has been with us fourteen years from the age of seven. Sister Rose and I have been here since then and we have seen her every day through these years. She demonstrated no emotion of any kind at leaving us. When I had finished speaking to her, Loris kissed my hand. One would think there was nothing extraordinary about that morning. She kissed my hand, and left.

The folder under his wrist was sleek. Edmund moved his arm over it, feeling the top. It gave under his palm, personal and slow, like the touch of a used pillow in the morning. After that he felt paralyzed—all but one hand.

Then he knew he was close to being asleep.

Aunt Clothilde's voice sounded dusty. She said, "I have been thinking."

". . . Have you?" Edmund needed only his lips to talk.

"Sometimes I get lazy when I think too hard; you know? My whole mind gets occupied. I disbelieve in the moon."

Edmund practiced a smile. "Surely," he said. "I was watching too. Don't let it upset you."

"No."

". . . A day over full."

"No."

"Yes, it is."

"That's not what I meant," she said.

He arched his back, strong. This had no effect.

"Not the kind of thing upsets me," she said.

"Good."

Aunt Clothilde said, "To me the moon always looks like an X-ray picture of something else."

". . . . Of what?"

"I don't exactly know," she said. "That's what I was thinking about. I never thought about that before."

"Well. Don't worry."

"I told you, it isn't the kind of thing upsets me." Aunt Clothilde did not turn her head. "I've known you Edmund Choate longer than anybody else, and you still don't know the kind of thing upsets me."

"Afraid not. Just . . ."

Aunt Clothilde said, "Doctors."

And their two voices met in the glass-cased porch, and passed. Then there was no sound.

He thought that she might be silent again; Edmund listened for her snuffle as he would for the unsure drip of a faucet.

"I can't help it," she said. "The moon just always looks to me like an X-ray picture of something else."

The porch was bloated with warmth. Against the cold of the night, an invisible cloud had begun to condense over the glass.

It spread an opaline sheet on the view, like dead skin. And where the wet came from you didn't care; to be there with that heat watching through it gave you the mental representation of sitting inside a fever blister.

The story was simple, and this was it: the letters had had to be burned.

There were many more ways of explaining it than were necessary. Because every notion, every thought, every feeling-lane, and many of them unimportant, had led to the same place. You could name it; define it; call it what you liked.

Just say the letters had had to be burned.

In past years sometimes he felt the other child's face, her echoing silence. And other catches of things came along, more brilliant in hue than before. One neat document to Jergen—a single unctuous sheet of directions, inked in bile. The bleary day; a breeze on Melpomene Drive. Then the walk—tossing to a lost sea tide, lit from the shore by dirty yellow stars in exquisite panes of expensive, well-washed windows; truly the best glass. All these seemed to go as one. They were inseparable parts of the same sequence. And at the end of that sequence—and because of it—came Adrianne.

The gossips were right, Loris Licia Choate was his shame. He had not ever been able to undo her from his mind. Yet they would also have been right in saying he had no shame at all; for if he did, it formed the base—the solid substratum of his pride. And inside there could be no division.

He had sinned, he was aware he had sinned; he had been aware of it at the time. Yet out of the rot had come the angel. True too, you cannot explain right if you don't know wrong. Light is born of darkness; then you don't produce an angel without protecting her from evil, and you have to be on the most familiar terms with evil if you want to separate it out for someone else. He himself had sinned, that was wrong, he never wished to excuse it. But now above everything there was Adrianne. She was not an excuse; she was a reason to live. And she would not be a whole Adrianne if he were not one whole Edmund.

This he knew, and Adrianne knew it—had always known what she was for him. And Adrianne had not let him be ashamed.

It was Adrianne who answered Jergen Wilson for her father; standing next to Edmund, speaking clear—standing straight, not stiff. She would not leave the city; not let him come to shame. Then neither would she listen to anything unpleasant that might be said of her sister, no matter who said it. She took the sympathy that cloyed in people's faces, and she put it back where it came from. Adrianne did such things in her own way; no one ever went away insulted. But with the passing of two short weeks, people came to realize she did not care to hear gossip or criticism about the goings on at the other house. She never allowed a single censure; though the sisters had not met. And Adrianne took her behavior from an essence of dignity that was not known before in the city. Thereby old Mrs. Rhale announced needlessly around town that Adrianne Legrange Choate was made of love.

And there had been nothing left for him to do but what had to be done. The burning of the letters loomed in on Edmund's awakening for three joined months. Each day he expected the idea to disperse itself. And every morning it got worse. It was a gesture, and Edmund did not like gestures.

Yet this one became a need. Then of course he had numbed himself for the doing of it; and the actual doing proved much less painful than the mere thought.

His annoyance now was a package emotion. It came from a different area, all wrapped up and damp, with no apparent destination, and no return address. It was not of importance; and that made it worse. The kind of impotent, pathetic, wet anger that leaks out and confronts you when you have willfully choked the tender spring of rage.

Aunt Clothilde said, "A penny?"

Edmund raised his eyes to the top of the fogged glass.

". . . No," he said.

"Not worth it?"

"No."

"I doubt that," Aunt Clothilde said.

Now she had been watching him from the side. She still was. The right side of Edmund's face was getting itchy and disarranged. A lonely moonlit trysting-place for two ectoplasmic horseflies.

Edmund said, "I was thinking how much I dislike do-gooders and smug curiosity, both. The little people who can't mind their own business."

"I doubt it," Aunt Clothilde said. "You didn't start with that. But I catch your swathed meaning. You are so tactful when you want. And I appreciate it. I have no business," she said.

"That is because you never wanted any."

Aunt Clothilde swallowed and looked closely at her knitting. "No, she said. "That's not because of that."

Edmund held his lips together with his teeth. Then he swung to the left, and faced the window nearest the open door that led to the winter dining room.

He said, "Sorry, Clothilde."

"Another bad day?"

"No. Not really."

"Nobody would blame you."

". . . That's nice to know," he said.

The film of wet over the night had got thick. It stifled everything outside. Only the moon came through it, spreading, like the white-fuzzed center of a pretend.

Aunt Clothilde said, "I didn't intend to squelch your personal thoughts. I just wondered what you were thinking."

Edmund grinned a little.

"Not what you were feeling. What you were thinking, exactly. Before all that."

"Naturally. You have already conceived of the other."

"Yes."

"Naturally. Clever," he said, "how?"

"I've told you for thirty years."

"You just know."

"That's right."

"You just do."

"That's right."

"Clever," he said.

Aunt Clothilde coughed. "I always appreciate the sarcasm too. I just wondered what you were doing out here with me. You haven't been alone with your daughter yet today."

". . . Wanted to relax."

"Since when don't you relax with Adrianne?" Aunt Clothilde was watching the folders. She had balanced on the left to see them better.

Edmund said, "There are some things I don't want her touched by."

"Such as?"

"If it can be possibly helped. Some things. I don't want *her* eaten at by any of *my* past mistakes."

Aunt Clothilde felt the loose skin on her throat. "I sometimes wonder what happens between what you mean and what you say," she said. She was still watching the folders.

Edmund said, "Better confine your wonderings to the moon."

"I do that too."

"Came out here for a breath," Edmund said. "I might have wanted to think."

"About what?"

"Nothing in particular."

"You are a fool."

"Thanks," he said.

"You don't have time for that. Not for nothing in particular. You should think about what's going to happen. You have no time to pet your pain."

". . . Clothilde, will you for once leave me alone?"

"I generally do."

"You generally do not," he said, "and I'm not in the mood."

Aunt Clothilde picked up her knitting; she fondled it. She said, "You have no time for moods."

"Supposing I take care of my time."

"Supposing you do," she said. "Instead of what you're doing."

"Oh, for God's sake."

". . . More for your own."

Edmund said, "You know, all the pills in the world aren't going to help, if you keep on like this. You've done it for too long, Clothilde. People who think they can see through other people and see into the future are the kind of people that end in asylums. With all the pills in the world. And all the doctors."

"Now don't try to frighten me," Aunt Clothilde said. Then she whispered, "I hate doctors."

"You'll have better reason to if you're not careful."

". . . Don't threaten me."

"I'm not threatening. Simple fact."

"Don't explain. And I can't help it if I see inside people. I can't live; I might as well do something."

"See all you want," Edmund said, "just stop believing you can foretell what will come. If you had any idea how annoying it is, you wouldn't do it. And especially at a time like this."

"Will come?" Aunt Clothilde put her head out and up, in the manner of a walking bird. "Future?" she said, "will come? What a dumb fool thing to say. I don't believe in it. I won't, I will not. Nothing will come, nothing ever was; it's all here now, right now. Don't talk to me about futures and pasts, I don't believe in them. I refuse to. You can't know anything at all about what I believe, you never asked me. It's a shame if you're disturbed, but don't presume to take it out on me. No, it isn't a shame, you should be disturbed. You damn fool. But not about the future. About now. It's now, Edmund, now, it's all here now. There's nothing but now; don't try to cut it up and label it separately, it's just one thing. It's just now. It always is. How do you think I always know? I'm not magic, you damn fool; that's how I know."

"All right," he said.

"It's not all right. And don't tell me to take it easy, Clothilde either, because I haven't got any ease."

". . . I'm sorry, Clothilde."

"I know you are. I am too now. You and those pills."

"Would you like one?"

"I took one before I came out here."

Edmund stood up.

"So don't think about nothing. Think about all that."

"All right," he said.

"And don't be condescending."

". . . I wasn't."

"You were."

"All right," Edmund said. He looked down, and sighed.

The skirt of Aunt Clothilde's dress protruded up, rigid, from her chair. It had a petticoat inside that kept it from going limp. It was smooth shiny white, and frilled. Crimped fluted folds of slick white satin, the same as a party dress, or like the inside of a coffin.

Edmund said, "Coming in?"

"I am not. I came out here to think," she said. "I have that problem with the moon."

Adrianne was waiting in the library. She was asleep.

Whitish light from three strong lamps was there. Covered, and made amber by the shades. And lavings of a smoky hopeless fire made a sheen, gentle and dark, an orange to fade on her skin. A book was open face-down beside the sofa.

Edmund watched; then he went past her, his weight steady in motion. He moved with the trunk of his body on a flat plane, crouching, as a cat creeps, to keep the wood floor from sounding under the brown carpet. The leather easy chair left of the fireplace had a permanent oval dent in its cushion; it was old and stiff, and if it were alive it would have yawned. It did make a sound like dying when you first sat in it—unless you knew how not to let that happen. Edmund put a hand on each wide arm and lowered himself in.

She was robed in powdery blue, lying as though the air sustained her; you wanted to look a minute to be sure that she breathed.

Edmund felt his eyebrows bunch, and it was mostly old habit.

Sometimes the bottom of his stomach did still begin to melt when he met her unexpectedly around the house; but from a different acid than in those early years, and in a positive way. Now it was a fresh suffusion, it soothed and destroyed. And Edmund could count on it. An effect he craved on occasion, if business or something had upset him during the day. Then when he looked at her the upsets shrank down and digested. A slow pulsating, infinitely shy pride occupied the raw places of his system. It swelled up inside. And whatever else had seemed consequential was absorbed in the full flood of love.

So when he frowned from habit, it couldn't mean the same.

Edmund slid forward on the leather cushion and let his head go on the wide back of the chair.

There were shiny areas around the ceiling, and others dull; then marks and faint black fibrous spots, you might say mildew. And then he noticed that the river sounds were again coming in familiar waves. Once, before he was seven years old, playing in the garden, he put his fingers in his ears to shut out all the noise. And he found if he wiggled one of the fingers, the sounds roared and hushed on either side, according to his command. Now the noise of night from the river was doing the same; but not because he had control. The sounds were rolling single in that time because they wanted to. And the splotchy spots tightened and spread, and fuzzed with a cradle rock to his shy-blown pride.

Shutting the eyes at the mildew; rolling them around in semi-darkness. Several mystical various glows—deep yellow to red on the left from lamps, and then way over right you got a pitch-edged taste of orange from the fire. You circle your closed eyes and you reverse the circle; you study each mottled glow.

It was the burning fountain. It was the foundation, and never mind. Where you can't join it, you burn it; so you see you know which is the fire and where. Watch that light through the film of shade and feel the heat of the glow. The witch was right, there is no time; and for an angel, for sending a pure soul to heaven you sleep proudly with some rust on your own.

Inside is in; but when you hold it in your hands, when you can't join it. Then you burn it. When you can't share shame with your pride outside you do not tinge the other with the one. You take it out from under.

And you burn it. The End.

There was a pop and a fuss. Edmund sat forward, and blinked.

The fire was hissing low. The last thin log had broken in the middle, and each center end fallen pointed down. A jet of sparks shot a few inches into the air, and some died. Others settled on the sooty bricks back of the fireplace; they crept there, separating to explore like newborn spiders.

The vacant twin chair opposite faced him with a blank expression, full of some unpleasant hidden meaning, and coquettish. That chair had a definite smirk.

Then when he looked to his left, she was smiling.

But he didn't say, You are my angel. He didn't have to.

He said, "Princess Pea." And cleared his throat. "I wasn't really asleep," he said.

"No."

"You were, though," Edmund twined eight fingers, and buckled them at the joints.

". . . Where's Clothilde?"

"On the sun porch. Sitting."

Adrianne said, "It must be cold."

"No," he said; "not cold at all. Got a little upset. Do her good out there."

"A real one?"

"No, a little perturbed. She must be getting worse, though; used not to make me lose my temper."

"She is worse, I think. Shall I go?"

"No, don't. Do her good out there," Edmund said.

Adrianne stretched her neck. No bones showed. The firelight spread with it; there was smoothness.

There was a long grieving curve from her chin down between the breasts.

Beyond, in the night, probably from the street a sudden series of barks began; held for ten seconds. And they stopped. The sort of intense, self-righteous anger a dog can have for a snake. Only no snake had ever been seen there. Not on the Drive.

Adrianne opened the silver cigar box and rolled the top layer of cigars lightly with her fingers. She chose one, and held it up to the light. After that she looked full at him.

"It's a different size," she said.

But he was busy seeing her. You could not contemplate two things at once if one of them was Adrianne.

They had told him she was born smiling. And they were right.

Edmund took the cigar.

The Nunnery

FROM THE NEW LILT to its barking, that dog had just got wet.

A card table was set up in the living room between the sofa and the fireplace. Three logs were burning, and all the lights were on. Over the windows facing Melpomene Drive heavy ashen curtains shut out the night. On the wall behind the red sofa a tall baroque mirror reflected the crystal-prism chandelier and a second mirror above the mantelpiece and the singing warmth of the room.

Luthella Simms was seated on the sofa with a newspaper by her side, folded backwards. She had been reading; now she watched the fire or the chess game. She was a bony mulatto woman of thirty who exuded a high tension and the faint odor of soap. She washed her face five or six times a day, and more during the summer. Then sometimes she woke herself up at night with this desire to wash. She wore a black wool fitted dress that had been given her a week ago, and an unstarched white cotton apron tied over.

Miss Mady and Miss Viola faced each other across the table, parallel to the sofa and the fireplace. Both were attending the half-empty chessboard.

For twenty-two years, Miss Mady had passed as young and dainty. Pretty was the quality, but she did not have a great deal

171

of it. She did have mournful large eyes, now covered by round-lensed glasses with transparent frames. Her blouse was black nylon, and her hair was natural blond. Though she was thinner than Luthella, her bones were more fragile, and her slimness seemed less strained.

Miss Viola was hitting fifty, hard. She had red-dyed hair with wet-brown penciled eyebrows like misshapen polliwogs laid on carefully over her own. Her eyes appeared naked and tiny, trapped inside the pancake make-up; they looked this way because she had left off her false lashes and did not wear mascara. Miss Viola had a tendency to flesh; she was very recently allowing herself to get much too flabby. Her skirt was black, but tonight she wore an old purple sweater.

Miss Mady said, "It couldn't concern me less what you say, it is not even normal healthy. One hundred and sixty-eight pounds is a crime."

"You and this health," said Miss Viola. "Move."

Luthella uncrossed her legs. She was drinking cold beer from a bottle.

Miss Mady poised her head over a pawn, and looked down at it. "Fatness is a product from thinking. The same as practically everything else. Fatness comes from overeating, which derives from the emotional nerves. Unless it's glands; it could be part glands."

"A lot likely, move."

"I am taking my time."

"Wrong," said Miss Viola, "you are taking everybody's time. Personally I would wish to finish this game this year."

"You see me winning?"

"No consideration."

"Is she winning again?" Luthella said. Luthella had begun to be mildly interested.

Off upstairs a sliding door closed. It opened, and it closed again. A distant dull roll.

Miss Mady blinked. "Back looking in her closet again; how many times tonight?"

"Stop your counting of the times," Luthella said.

". . . I'm simply commenting."

"Stop your commenting." Luthella had a firm, deep voice, with a finished gleam of heat. It was a copper voice. "That's what she has a closet for, is to go into. Much as she likes. The lady don't require comments."

Miss Mady tossed her hair, and caught the back part of it like dead grass in between several fingers of one hand. "My," she said. "You are in a mood."

". . . Am?"

"Shit," Miss Viola said slowly. "Who has got a emery board?"

Eyes steady on the chessboard, Miss Mady said, "It always unnerves you to be the third party in the conversation."

"Wrong," said Miss Viola. "I am not interested. Who said they had a emery board when I asked?"

"Nobody," Miss Mady said.

Luthella yawned. She enjoyed it, and it came out like a gasp. "You ladies please tone down," she said.

"Personally I thought we was playing a game of chess."

"We are," said Miss Mady. "I'm simply working on my move."

"We must of played five hundred games since we came here," Miss Viola said. "You still act like the Queen Mary every time you got to move."

"I win every game too."

Miss Viola made an acutely bored face. "Mercy," she said. "Deliver me. I only ever play to pass my time. All I require right now is a emery board."

"Going to take me a little more while to think this out. You have time to go up and get one."

"Counting back since your last move, I have time to go up and die."

"This you could do right here," Miss Mady said, "and be my guest."

". . . Honey, do not sass after me."

"Then don't criticize."

"I got a lot to learn from you, half my age."

"You could. You never can tell."

Behind her hand, Miss Viola made the hollow-cheek face to Luthella. It was meant to look as though all her blood had just congealed. If she hadn't left off her eyelashes, it might have expressed her opinion better than words.

There was about a minute of free-wheeling silence, except for the rattling of three bracelets on Miss Viola's left wrist while she poured a small pool of Chanel No. 5 into the other palm from a vial.

Then Miss Mady said, "Any more pink gin?"

Luthella sucked, and swallowed deep, "Right by you," she said.

"Oh. How many cocktail drinks I had?"

"One."

"Is that all?"

"It is."

"Must have replenished a little."

"Replenished?"

"You did."

"Feels like more."

"Not much."

"Thought so."

"She did? Replenished?"

"Fancy; I don't really care for any more." Miss Mady scratched at the polished glass pitcher. "Just doesn't taste the same without maraschino cherries. I was sincerely sure we were keeping another bottle of maraschino cherries. The mind can fool you. One never knows."

"That's correct," Luthella said. "You had it for breakfast."

"Them? They were green."

". . . And so?"

"In gin she likes them red," Miss Viola said evenly. ". . . To match her eyes."

Miss Mady sat up straight. "Mind the sassing right now."

"Just returning on score. *One* never gets a chance to open her mouth around here any more."

"I like them red in a cocktail drink," Miss Mady said. "You

can't put a green maraschino cherry in pink gin. Lord. You have got no taste at all. Turns my stomach to consider about it. Simply to consider *about* it."

Miss Viola looked in the mirror over the mantel, and licked some lipstick off her teeth. "What was it you were considering about this morning?" she said, "when you mixed in twelve of them with the Corn Flakes? Green as green."

"Who cares?" Miss Mady waved her hands. "That's a nice one. I have got to tell that to Doctor B. Did you hear her? Sits right there and makes a comparison between pink gin and Corn Flakes. Doctor B. is going to be interested in that one."

". . . Are you going to move?"

"I am making a mental decision to tell that to Doctor B."

Miss Viola chewed at her broken fingernail. "The day you started bothering with your mind," she said.

"Let's ease off, please, ladies," Luthella said. "Both you-all. Don't pay her no concern here," she said. "None at all. They looked real pretty with the Corn Flakes."

"That is not the point. I didn't even take a notice of it. It's the comparison she made I'm talking about between pink gin and cereal."

"Are you going to move?"

"Not now I'm not. With all this criticizing. Now I have got to think about it all over."

There was another far-off roll from the sliding door upstairs. Luthella looked up.

"Shit," Miss Viola said. "Double double shit. We going to be here all night."

"Then we are, that's all. Just keep a hold."

"You didn't have a move anyway. I got a hold on everything I require."

"Yes, I did," Miss Mady said, "I had one. Matter of fact I did."

"Quiet," Luthella said.

"I don't suppose . . ."

"Ladies. Quiet," Luthella said.

"I wouldn't . . ."

Luthella said, "Shut up now, ladies." She got to her feet, and walked around the sofa. She was watching the ceiling.

Miss Viola turned her head. "No," she said, "now we can't even discuss. If you going to call a hush every time the lady makes a excursion to the bathroom."

"She ain't in the bathroom," Luthella said.

"Well, so what? Wherever she is. It's the same every night. Why can't you just let her walk up there if that's what she wants to do? Why don't you go to bed?"

"I will. When she does." Luthella followed a line across the ceiling with her eyes as if she could see the sole of each footstep.

"You been taking on like this for a month."

"I ain't taking on."

"What you worried over?"

Luthella looked at the thick black carpet. "I'm not specially worried. She don't sleep," she said.

"So what? Her business. She don't care to sleep, nobody says she has to. Besides she never did. Nothing new."

"I plain don't like it," Luthella said. "I wish I knew what she was waiting for."

Miss Viola hardened her lips. "Trouble with you, you take this whole thing too particular. Proper job is still a job. All these long talks you have with her are getting on your nerves. You act like you knew her all your life instead of a couple months."

Luthella said, "I wish I had."

"Yes, well some of us don't. Leastways we are not particular one way or the other. Besides she don't pay us good money to make no make-believe about being worried every time she hiccups. She would be the last person to call for a make-believe."

Luthella's upper lashes dipped, and stroked the lower ones. She said, "Make-believe?"

"That's O.K., don't get mad. I'm just telling you what I think. I know my place, and I know what she wants me to do."

"Do you?"

"I make like she tells me, that's what I know. I make like she says. She wishes me here, she pays me, and I don't mention her name outside of this house. And neither does Mady. Do you, Mady? Not even to the doctor. I got my job and I know my place."

"Do you?" said Luthella. "What is your place?"

". . . Are you trying to get my back up?"

"Not likely."

Miss Mady said to a plastic bishop, "Doctor B. is going to be most interested in all this loose disturbance."

"I am wondering," Luthella said, "if you ever considered she could take this town right tonight if she cared to. All she'd have to do is give the word. From Mr. Edmund Choate on down they'd come crawling. They still would. Right from him on down."

Miss Viola put a ringed, pink finger under one eyebrow, and pushed it up. "You know what she said about using that man's name on these premises, don't you?"

"I'm just telling you."

"That ain't the way I look at it all the same."

Luthella lay her mouth open. "How do you look at it?" she said.

"I ain't sure and I ain't saying. But the way she come walking into the house downtown to get me and Mady she didn't look like she was too bothered by crawling friends." Miss Viola took the finger away, and maintained the eyebrow where it was. "Walked in in the middle of the day. Plain daylight."

"Plain daylight is where she lives," Luthella said.

"Maybe."

"Not maybe. There is only one object to keep the neighbors out of this house right now."

"What's that?" Miss Viola said.

Luthella settled herself on an arm of the sofa. She said, "Why don't you figure it out?"

"I don't figure. Neighbors wished to come here, they'd be here. What do you think they strung a detective on her for, friendship?"

"You figure it out," Luthella said.

"Don't keep telling me the same. What is this object in her way, then, if you know so much?"

Miss Mady placed her head on a line with the chessboard, and looked at the bishop from the side. "She means us," she said.

"Us how?"

". . . Just us."

"I swear I don't appreciate either one of you. What you trying to do, make me say something against her? Well, I am not going to. All this mysteriousness. I am her lady friend and that is what I am paid to be, and that is what I am being. And I have got nothing more to say about her."

Luthella said, "And if you wasn't getting paid, lady friend?"

"Then I'd go make my living just like anybody else. I certainly would. Just like anybody. I know my place. I certainly would not be living in a house which it is known was once haunted and which makes my hand clam up to turn off the light. Don't have a thing to do with her; but I would not be occupying any previously haunted house long as I have got another house to go to and work, unless I was getting paid a good amount to do it. And that is all I wish to discuss on the subject. Excepting I would like to know why it is you try to get my back up every night on the same song. That much I would like to know."

Luthella said, "I ain't trying. I was elucidating. I would like to see a little gratitude around here, and I do not care for any referring to a make-believe."

"Why not, I'd like to know. Gratitude for what? I know my place. I don't have to be perfect. And what are you, the Pillar of Epitome? Most things come to a make-believe," Miss Viola said. "Start that way, too. If you wasn't a little flippy on the subject, I'd take you downtown with me one day and show you a whole houseful of make-believe. Little make-believe babies and everything. I guess I ought to know about it, considering. And that is all I wish to discuss on the subject."

"I ain't trying to be personal," Luthella said.

"Mady, I am indebted to you four hundred francs for this evening, and I am waiting to see your next move."

". . . Give me a minute," Miss Mady said.

"A *minute?*"

Miss Mady said, "I don't like the look of that bishop."

Luthella raised her eyes to the northeast corner of the ceiling.

They played chess nightly, and Luthella watched, and she still did not know the game. She was not enough interested to learn, and she had other concerns. But the three women usually sat together after dinner. None of them drank more than two cocktail drinks or two bottles of beer of an evening. They played for French francs, and then settled in dollars. Miss Mady allowed this in order to please Miss Viola, who was made painstakingly honest because she could have cheated with such ease: nobody else wanted to work out the balance between currencies. Miss Viola was once engaged to a sailor from Marseilles who had shown her the right exchange.

Luthella said, "What time is it?"

Miss Viola opened her purse and took out a silver lady's wrist watch with a broken strap. She examined it. Then she shook it and looked again. "Perhaps about one o'clock," she said.

"It was one o'clock an hour ago."

Miss Viola held the watch up closer. "Then it must be about two o'clock," she said.

"She won't go to bed before four or five," Miss Mady said.

Luthella said, "Sitting on the bed now. But she don't sleep."

Miss Mady bent her hand backward at the wrist, and primped a hay-colored natural curl. "She won't try. Not like she had insomnia or something. Like I still some nights get insomnia."

"You got a pain is what." Miss Viola was lighting a cigarette.

"Could be I do. Nothing you would understand."

". . . Course not."

"You wouldn't know about it."

"That damn doctor," Miss Viola said. "Are you going to move?"

Miss Mady looked up. "Keep your preoccupation off Doctor B."

"Wrong," Miss Viola said. "Do not get excited."

"I explained to him all about you on Wednesday."

Miss Viola poured out a cocktail glassful of gin. "Seems to me you and him might have enough to do without talking me into it. At five dollars a day. First time you ever paid a man since you were born. I wonder what he's got. I'm surprised you get any time to talk at all."

"I talk," Miss Mady said. "I talk. He just listens. Then he makes notes. He listens to every single word I say."

Miss Viola picked up her glass. "Who's *his* doctor?" she said.

"He still says I have one of the most fascinating problems he has ever come across."

"Which one is that?" Miss Viola said.

"In all his medical existence. He says I am one of the most interesting people he ever saw. From the first of the insomnia right through these readjustment pains he says he never saw anything so interesting. I am going to be an immense assistance to him on his research."

Miss Viola took a long sip. "You already explained about it," she said. "I am doubtful."

"Couldn't concern me less. He wouldn't still let me pay him except I told him I'd stop going unless he did. He doesn't want my money. I just refused to go unless he takes my money. You would hardly understand the relationship."

"What I would hardly understand is the day he kept you three solid hours over your time and made all those notes just because he discovered about your being fully adjusted to your former life. I could of told him that. Whose is that extra empty glass?"

"I should never have discussed it with you; I should have kept quiet."

"I'm willing."

"He told me I should know better than to discuss it with you."

"Couple more things he ought to discover while he's at it," Miss Viola said. "Concerning how adjusted you forgot you were sometimes."

Miss Mady set her thin shoulders back, and looked up. "For instance?"

Miss Viola took another sip. "Nothing," she said. "Sure. Adjusted. Like that time we had to call the practitioner up to your bed to get the chewing gum out of that Mr. Frazier. He might have a little something to say about it too."

"That's beside the point."

"He didn't think so," Miss Viola said. "I never saw a man so excited when he found out he couldn't walk for the chewing gum."

"Has nothing whatever to do with the subject, and anyway it wasn't my fault."

"If it wasn't," Miss Viola said, "it was a strange place for him to be cultivating chewing gum."

"I explained to you at the time, he told me to put it there. He said he could not stand to see me chew it, and then he himself instructed me to put it there."

"Particular moment you had to ask him, sugar, he would have told you to put anything there. Good thing you wasn't wearing your glasses. That is what you call being adjusted?"

"Not the point at all." Miss Mady waved her hands. "Got nothing to do with it whatever. You don't even know what you're talking about. Just always making these confused comparisons."

"You plan to move the bishop?"

"I do not. I didn't touch it."

"Lordy, move it around a couple places; try it out. I won't mind."

"I will not. A touched piece is a moved piece."

Luthella yawned. "How come?" she said.

"You heard her." Miss Viola smiled, and blew some smoke across the board. "You know what she is adjusted with."

Miss Mady began to bounce slightly up and down in the chair. "Up yours," she said, "up yours, up yours. Dirty mind. I swear I will never discuss with you again."

Luthella rose suddenly, her hands on the table. "Look ladies," she said. " I plain would not like to hear another voice raised tonight."

"Then tell her to lay off her criticizing."

"I wouldn't like to tell either of you ladies anything but I don't expect to see another voice raised tonight."

". . . You right," Miss Viola said. "Anyway, honey. I was only kidding. Don't pay me no mind."

"I don't," Miss Mady said.

". . . I was just fooling."

"It couldn't concern me less what you were doing," Miss Mady said.

Miss Viola poured into both glasses from the last gin in the pitcher. She filled Miss Mady's, and took what was left for herself. "Take a little sup," she said. "I was just fooling." Then she mashed her cigarette in an ash tray, and took out a medium-size jar of cold cream and six folded facial tissues and a round hand mirror from her purse. She put them side by side on the table edge under the shelf of her bosom, and opened the cold cream. When she had smeared a portion of it well into the thick pink make-up between her hairline and chin, she looked as though her face was melting. "I was fooling."

"You are simply another voice to me," Miss Mady said.

"Course I am, sugar. Wouldn't want to go getting mad at my having a little fun with you. You keep on with the doctor if he gives you rest. Know what?"

"I don't care to know."

"I'm just jealous," she said.

". . . Of what?"

"Him. I don't have any doctor interested in me."

"Couldn't concern me less," Miss Mady said.

Miss Viola dropped her head and looked in the mirror. "Nobody likely to be very interested in me that way again."

"He is . . . not interested that way."

"For true?"

"Course for true."

"Queer?"

"He is not. He's interested in helping people. I explained to you, about emotional thinking and things. Like he wants to show people how afraid they are."

"Uh-huh. Might be better off queer," Miss Viola said.

"You would hardly understand."

Luthella said, "O.K. Just don't let it get any louder than that," she said. "It's the same every night; if you going to discuss, tone it down. I'm going on up now and see how she is."

"You go up," Miss Viola said. "We won't make no more noise."

"I plain wouldn't like to see you." Luthella started towards the staircase in the hall.

Miss Viola put her tongue out a fraction and pointed it up while she mopped under her eyes with the tissues. "Then just what does go on every day you pay to see him?"

"Hold on," Miss Mady said. She picked up the bishop and moved it diagonally seven spaces, and set it there. "I count two ways of checkmate," she said. "That's the best. Honey, I keep telling you, I just lay down on a couch and talk."

Luthella snapped her fingers for silence. Then from outside the room she closed the sliding doors to the front hall, silently. It took a quarter of a minute to do.

Miss Viola was perceiving the bishop. The loose flesh of her face had slid down over the bones, and her brows loomed low. Peaceful in relaxation, without her make-up she gave the illusion of being much younger than before because now she appeared her proper age. "You insist to pay him the five dollars," she said quietly.

Miss Mady nodded. She turned the board around the other way, and pulled her chair closer. Then she began to pick up pawns.

The massive carpet covering the wide-curved staircase was filled with shadow. It mounted in a rush of smooth penumbral red, dark as blue blood returning to the heart. Below the chandelier the color glowed. And each single step measured one foot by five.

Luthella Simms went up with a sense of being extra; the carpet and the staircase allowed her, but they designed her out. It did not look right, that staircase, under anyone but Loris Licia Choate. But it looked most wrong under Luthella, or so she always thought. And Luthella was ever conscious of this. When she herself used it she was made to feel even more yellow than usual—and especially at night with that explosive brilliance from the chandelier. Two-thirds of the way up, if her care for Loris Licia had not outplaced the other urge, she would have gone back down to wash her face.

At the top she turned to her right and went along to the oaken door. She set a knuckle into one of the carved channels, and knocked three times. Then she went in.

She saw herself enter; the north wall, opposite the door, was a solid mirror. Her face showed immediately.

But though the carpet in this room was the same as on the staircase, it did not have the same effect. Here the shadow was thinned away; some difference of light at any hour erased the suffusion of blue, and left the red to bask deep—deeply cast, throbbing to the eye, and swimming up over you in waves. Luthella could not figure it out, but her face in that one mirror never looked jaundiced. Every place else she saw it, she might have been living off yolks of eggs. But here in this room anybody's blood was right. If the staircase was a big swooping vein, Loris Licia's bedroom was the heart of the house—a heart that was not partial to any color.

The bedroom was set directly over the downstairs living room; two windows on the east wall with white draperies faced the Drive. The two on the west wall were French doors leading out onto a screened gallery overlooking the garden.

Before and on the left half of the mirror was a long mahogany dressing table littered with brushes and combs, and a jar of hairpins, and smaller combs that were made to stay in the hair. There were two porcelain statuettes on either end: tall white girls holding flowers in opposite arms. Next to the right one stood an empty silver picture frame with a red velvet back. By choice there were no vases in the room and no flowers; no ash trays. There were several lamps; three chairs; an extra-large double bed. The coverlet was white embroidered satin, and it had Loris Licia's three initials round and stark in the center. Her initials were plain on everything that could hold them, including a silver spoon in the bathroom. Over the bed was a square mirror which reflected in the wall of mirrors across the room, and then back into itself; and it went on doing this smaller and smaller until you could not easily imagine the end. On the other side of the bed from Luthella was a doorway into a dressing room one quarter the size of the bedroom, and half of that was closet; beyond it was the bath.

Slung now and cringing over two chairs and much of the bed, like dead shadows, lay eight disordered dresses. They were of various cuts and materials for various occasions, but all were black. Seven hangers were still inside, and one hung loose on a sleeve.

Luthella Simms had shallow dull brown eyes in which no pupil was visible from a distance of over three feet. They were very well placed on either side of her nose like little mud patties. They stared back at her dismally from the mirror; she did not like the look of them at all. And the feeling was reverently mutual.

She shifted to set them on each dress, and then over to the French doors. The white draperies were separated so that she could see one triangular section of the night; a knuckled big hand shaped like a claw held them that way. The wrist disappeared into the floating sleeve of a black taffeta robe with a high upturned collar and pointed shoulders. Loris Licia's hands were wider, more wrapped and ribboned with ligaments than most men's. They had unpainted nails that grew down in sore long curves to tuck under her fingers; her hands were the only ugly parts of her body.

She was standing with her back to Luthella, watching the darkness. Thick loose oiled hair spilled down over the collar to her waist. The night ran into her hair, and the skirt of the robe followed undivided from that down to the floor. Except for the showing of the one hand, and a tone of red inside her hair, from behind she revealed no color.

Luthella's face looked warped when she smiled, it was not a habit with her. Yet she often had to when she saw the lady like that.

Loris Licia did not turn. "What is this noise?" she said.

". . . The garden?"

"Yes."

Luthella said, "Locusts."

"The big insects? Why, I wonder; in this weather. It is the wrong season. What did you want?"

". . . Clean up some." Luthella swiveled.

Loris Licia said, "Locusts. How very curious," she said.

The first dress was a day dress. It lay over the bed, and one side of it was bunched in ripples. It appeared to have a cramp. "You watching something down there in the garden?"

"No," she said.

Luthella brushed down the dress with the back of her hand, and picked up another. "You can't sleep?"

"I am not sleepy."

"You ought to try."

"No."

"You ought to."

"No," Loris Licia said. "I ought not to try."

Luthella shook out each of five dresses, and carried them in to the dressing-room closet. She came back for the other three.

The glass door to the gallery was open now. The set of Loris Licia's body was as before, she kept her back turned. But the robe was waving one bottom corner in the night air.

"Catch pleurisy that way," Luthella said.

"No."

"You're standing in a draft. I bet you don't have a thing on under that robe."

". . . Quite right. And kindly do not begin questioning."

Luthella picked up the third remaining dress. "This one is pretty," she said.

The sliding door to the closet was heavy on rollers, and it made a sound of moony splendor, somewhere between a belch and a yawn. It sounded louder downstairs than up.

"I put them all away again," she said.

". . . You did indeed."

"Need me for anything?" Luthella scratched her left outside ankle through the stocking, with her right shoe.

"Go to bed now."

"I want to get up early. For church."

"Yes."

"You plan to try on any more dresses?"

"Go to bed."

Luthella said, "Guess I'm starting to go to church more. It's a bother. If you have to. I plain guess I have to. Around town," she said, "they still think you're a Catholic."

"Not think," Loris Licia said. She took her hand from the curtain, and slipped it in the pocket of her robe. Then she looked over her shoulder, and back at the white closed curtain. "Please go to bed," she said.

"Can I turn off this one light by the wall?"

"Turn it off."

"Got so much light in here. I couldn't get sleepy myself with all this light."

Loris Licia shifted the position of her head. She said, "You walk upstairs too much."

"Yes."

"Then you drink too much coffee."

"Yes, ma'am."

". . . And the rest of the time you pray for me."

"Yes."

"You see?"

"I know, I can't help it. In church and at night too. Besides what you told me; I just can't help it."

Loris Licia lifted her hair between both palms, and pulled it straight back over the collar, and then dropped it. "I wish you would stop," she said, "it makes me nervous."

Underneath, Miss Mady and Miss Viola were arguing. The voices wafted, tenebrous and angry, and distinguishable from the other sounds of night. They came through the same window. Up here they did not seem to have a purpose.

"They get to fighting over the chess," Luthella said.

"Yes, I hear them."

"Can't get them to tone it down. Always discussing. They get these weird ideas."

"I expected that," Loris Licia said. "The best kind of ideas for them to have here."

"Doesn't bother you?"

"I am accustomed to it."

"And it doesn't even bother you?"

"Praying bothers me," Loris Licia said.

". . . Must be used to a good bit of praying on the side."

"Certain kinds. That is like getting accustomed to apples in salad," she said. "I was against it from the beginning."

Luthella wrinkled her forehead. "Way you talk, Miss Loris, a person would think I do it out loud."

"You do do it."

". . . Yes. "

Loris Licia swirled to face Luthella across a yard of carpet space. Her hands were pushed deep in pockets of the robe, and by her stance she looked both most annoyed and bored. But the gray of her eyes was swarming.

"I wish you would not," she said. ". . . You."

A thing few people were able to explain in Loris Licia's face was the silky soft brandy-colored mole above her right eye, in the hollow next to the nose. It was not by itself wrong; yet it could take away the symmetry of all the whole. It menaced and so it intensified what was her beauty. It moved. In one combination of light and shadow, this mole even made the lady look wild and dimly cross-eyed—the threat was present always. And the mole wanted you to remember many things. It was a hint of destruction, sensual, like the certain possibility of death. It showed wrong for her face and painful. And just because of that it was necessary.

Luthella felt her neck go hot. "I never saw you completely without your lipstick. Miss Mady and Miss Viola do it too," she said; "told me so."

"I was aware they do."

"You never asked them to stop."

Loris Licia said, "I believe the word is coy. Try not to be. I know all about praying," she said.

". . . You watch me with those eyes."

"Theirs is not the same. Your belief is pure. Not habit."

". . . I guess so."

"You do it, you, you say prayers for me because this is important to you."

"Yes, ma'am," Luthella said.

Still with her hands in her pockets, Loris Licia pushed her shoulders up and pressed both elbows against her waist. "So, do not say them for me," she said.

Then she turned to the mirror.

Luthella swallowed a coldness. "Can I shut the gallery door now?"

"No."

"There's a powerful draft."

"No; I wish you would go to bed."

"There *is* a draft."

"I know there is," Loris Licia said, "you make me uncomfortable. You. Not the draft. Why are you afraid of the winter?"

"Anyhow," Luthella said, "you believe in the Lord just the same. Even if you don't have the Catholic religion? You do."

Loris Licia was examining the black slope of her collar in the mirror, against the white skin.

And that dog began to bark again. Way off, and vaguely misty now.

Luthella could just touch her nose with her upper lip. "He's there the same for you to believe. Even without a religion."

"How very curious. I was right. It is badly cut, I think. This."

"You do believe in Him. In the Lord."

"I prefer to let Him believe in me," Loris Licia said. "He has more information. I knew it; I was sure. This is not well cut here. I knew it when I bought it. I explained to the salesman."

Luthella said, "How can you talk that way? You know you do."

"You succeed in making me tired, as always; I have just said I neither do nor do not. I refuse to accept the responsibility. Why must you always come in here like this? Leave your questions at the door. If He exists, He has the power from the information, He has therefore the responsibility. Believing between us is His problem."

". . . Well, it don't matter."

"Doesn't."

"Doesn't matter," Luthella said, "you are going to go to heaven better than anybody of my acquaintance. Better than anybody. You will go to Him. You will meet Him in the other world."

Loris Licia pulled the entire neck of the robe over more to the right from center. "Possibly," she said, "but on equal terms."

"I plain don't comprehend how you can talk like that," Luthella said. "After you yourself went to live in that convent church."

"I told the salesman I can tell immediately. Always. I should give more attention when I know I am right, I told the salesman. What? No, you are incorrect."

"I said . . ."

"I heard what you said. No. I did not go, I was sent."

"Same thing," Luthella said.

"It is not the same thing," said Loris Licia, "at seven you do not go to church, you are sent. When I was seven I had known for two years the difference between power and good. Can you see where this line is wrong?"

"But you did go."

"You make me repeat myself, and you make me tired. No, I was sent. Again: I did not go, I *was sent.* Do we communicate? In London I spent three private hours every day with a university professor on English grammar for nearly two years, and he never thought to tell me which form of the verb was extinct in America."

". . . No."

"Can you see where this line is wrong?"

"No, ma'am."

"You are not looking. I do not like this word, ma'am. It is an unfortunate contraction. Say madam if you must."

"Yes."

"It is impossible to see if you don't look. Go to bed, it isn't important. I can get a new robe. You make me tired, I never liked this robe."

Luthella sucked at her tongue.

"What amuses you?"

"Don't know."

"You are not amused by what you don't know," Loris Licia stared gray at her in the glass.

Luthella rubbed her left cheek once over, using one finger. And they both watched the finger. "I was thinking the way you talk sometimes, it's not much wonder people judge all those crazy things. Not much wonder."

"People like to judge as they like," Loris Licia said.

"Yes, they do."

"People, and other people; and sisters. And, I would suspect, God," she said. Then she looked at the collar again. She lifted it an inch.

"Maybe it's just as well they say you're a Catholic."

"Not in my understanding. They do not say I am a Catholic," Loris Licia said; "they say I am a Catholic prostitute. It is not necessarily the same."

Luthella straightened her backbone, and made a noise like spitting. "You, a prostitute," she said. "And you ain't even French."

"... French too?"

"Oh, sure. Some of them say you are. I wish you'd let me tell them. Some of them drive me crazy. You, who never even let a man dance with you."

Loris Licia laughed. She did it into the glass, and it matched only the feeling you got from her hands. "Yes," she said, "I am. You are quite incorrect. French and Italian, and Spanish too, and I speak English badly, and I am therefore particularly nothing."

"You like Spanish the best. You said so."

"Yes, I do. The best."

"Seems to be you're mostly Spanish," Luthella said. "If you like Spanish the best."

"I do wish you would not so consistently come up here and make me repeat things." Loris Licia leaned stiff-armed over the chair, until her face almost touched the mirror. As slow as falling under water. And she pulled back, and tipped forward again. "Exactly nothing. You make me repeat myself, I said I was nothing. Can you comprehend that? Like the color of white," she said. "Nothing."

"... No?" Luthella snickered to herself. "Couple friends of my acquaintance wouldn't turn down a little touch of that white."

Loris Licia said, "Like that."

"Mentioning no names."

"White is like nothing, my mother loved gray, my grandmother told me. The nicest thing she said about her. Before my grandmother died. I am different pieces inside of white," she said; it was a voiced whisper.

"Could think of a few people."

". . . I am that. The several parts of white."

"Yes, you are," Luthella said. "And you're more besides. It will come together like you want and more besides. Anyway, when the papers come through you'll be a one hundred per cent American."

Loris Licia took her hands off the chair. "That is a condition," she said, "not a quality. Please go to bed."

"Yes, ma'am. But you will. Soon as all those papers come through. You'll be a free white lady American from the South."

"Now you make it so it isn't even a condition."

"What is it?" Luthella said.

Loris Licia was pulling at the black taffeta all the way around her waist. She said, "I believe it goes with gracious and charming. And . . . distinguished. Yes, I have seen distinguished. The journals use it. Gracious, charming, and distinguished. From the South, yes, as you say. But they say old. Of the *old* South, they say. No, it is not a condition."

"No?"

"No," said Loris Licia, "it seems to be a highly flavored lack of taste. There is no way at all to fix this, and I told the man."

"Better not go around saying that."

"I do not go around saying anything at all."

"I know. But I mean, can't nobody comprehend enough without that. Can't nobody else in town comprehend what you are doing here in the first place. Hating like you do."

Loris Licia lowered her hands. They slicked down over the taffeta to her hips, and hung there as if they belonged to somebody else. "Listen to this," she said. "You bore me; I don't. You are wrong. You make me tired and you are more wrong than they are. And no one has to comprehend me, except me. Is that clear? I live to believe myself, this is all anyone has to comprehend. Now if you do not stop talking and go to bed within a minute it is going to be bad."

"Yes, ma'am. Anyway, you'll feel better when those papers come. When you are American. Be just the same as any American is."

Loris Licia said, "Forget this word *same*. The same this and the same that. You like to compare things to themselves, but Americans are not the same. Are you the same as the others? You don't even have the same rights. Even I shall have more rights than you. I shall have as many rights as any American, that yes. The rights. Only I think they told me I can never be President."

Luthella went to the lamp against the wall. "That's a misfortune," she said.

"Yes it is," said Loris Licia. "It is, is it not? I shall just have to choose some other reason to live. In America."

After turning off the lamp, Luthella got a quick tensity through her body. Then her left thigh developed a kind of innocuous twitch in it. But she went on watching the wall.

The shadow was faint and distinct. Loris Licia was standing in the way of one strong open light on the dressing table, and only from there could a shadow be made in the room. A limp breeze, up from the garden and damp, had got around the collar and the high shoulders of her dressing gown. It was making them move, gently.

Luthella put a knuckle on her mouth.

In the mirror behind her, Loris Licia said, "Why do you do that?"

"You would," she said. "Yes, ma'am."

"I would what?"

Luthella said, "Wings. I appreciate it."

". . . What?"

"The wall," Luthella said; "the wings. Both of them."

Loris Licia tried to find it ahead of her in the glass. Then she gave up, and turned to look, and the shadow jumped. Then it changed.

"No," Luthella said. "Not like that, like you were before. Only like you were; you got to face the other way."

Loris Licia laughed. She said, "If you don't go to bed, I shall have to send you home at night."

Luthella was on her way out. "You can't," she said.

"Why not?"

"I moved my home."

". . . Where?"

Luthella went out.

"Come back," Loris Licia said. She walked across the bedroom. "Leave that door open and come back here. You make a ridiculous statement," she called. "You must not, it is a dangerous thing; you cannot say it, you have a home. You already have a home, this is not your home. This is my house. I would not consider it a favor, you make a bad mistake. You come here." She walked fast, lifting the skirt of her robe up off the floor in front—and the robe dragged and crackled behind her.

But she found the hall empty; half-lit and purple, like a sunset over coffee. Luthella had gone to bed.

At four in the morning it was heavy down the Drive. By the swamps there is a weight to a wet winter night that closes most animals in with their own exhalings. The skin does not breathe, it tends to slick and thicken. Bed sheets feel double—and cold, unless they have been slept on, and if they have been they feel like warm oysters. Fifty-watt light bulbs should not be used. These bleed weakly a dark yellow that spreads out and palpitates the eyeball.

And at four o'clock in the morning, people are best asleep.

Melpomene Drive lay back in the dark, indolent and reptilian, and it was wet, to wait for day.

And her bedroom was now the only light. Though she had no idea of this. And it would not have interested her if she had.

Loris Licia could hold still without tensing a muscle for longer than anyone would believe. She had been sitting in front of the dressing table for over two hours. Now she raised her elbows and pulled a black bulky comb through a side of loose hair. She put the comb down, and flipped it over with a fingernail. Then she sat some more.

Behind her chair in broken swells of sound, she could hear a leaf-loud, steady gasp. The late noises diminishing had collected poorly, and shrunk to a low faint note that stopped and started as it wished. Like the rustle of marshwater after evening, when it is crossed by some unimagined body, or by a night wind with someplace to go.

No other sound ranged around from anywhere, and the smell of cold dampness numbed her nose. On a night like that there was no end to your world.

But she was warm there in the room. Loris Licia sat forward after finishing one thought, and looked down at the size of her hands. In the mirror they did not seem so large; this was because of the angle. They were large. They were suited to holding things.

She got up, and pushed the chair off. Placing her hands higher, and low against her sides, she could measure them in proportion to other parts of her body. She turned them profile and backwards too.

Then she reached through the draperies to the cold metal handle of the glass gallery door, and shut out the last of the draft. And something of it whispered in her sleeve.

The material being taffeta, this robe weighed a considerable amount and did not cling. She had only to open it over her shoulders, then hold her arms out behind her. She caught the robe as it fell, and dropped it over the chair.

She had three permanent favorite hollow places. Two were in front, just inside the hips. The other was a small oval dip over the crevice of her buttocks. The three had existed many years; Loris Licia was nearly thirty-two. They were as familar to her as anything. Often, though, in the first inevitable pleasure and shock at seeing herself naked, she touched them to be sure.

Then she returned to the subject of her hands. She had thought several times that she liked them very much, and she did not know why. They were of exactly equal size, this she had noted long ago, unlike other people's; she had no preference for either, and could use them equally well. And her satisfaction in owning them might have come to her differently had they been deformed or badly shaped, but they were not; just very big, wide-knuckled, and masculine. She did not think of them as ugly. They were very private hands. Once Luthella had brought her a bottle of Hind's Honey and Almond Cream, but Loris Licia never tried it. It was on a shelf in the bathroom. She saw the bottle twice a day when she took out her toothbrush. And she might lift it off the shelf, and open it, and smell the cream. She had become especially used to that smell, as she was to seeing familiar cloud shapes around the morning, or the filtering shafts in a noonday on water. Such incidental fondnesses by their nature puzzled her, and they were nice things to have.

Mostly, she liked anybody's hands when in motion, if there was a portion of living in them. But first now she left the mirror and went into the dressing room, because that had been again on her mind.

The suit she was considering was third from the right on the second rack. It had a round scalloped collar with cuffs to match, gabardine and wool. And pointed oval buttons, three, concave and duller black than the material. Loris Licia carried it to the bedroom; she laid it over the white satin cover on her bed.

Standing naked with her toes gripping the carpet, she took two hairpins from a dish on the dressing table, and slipped them between her teeth. Her head back, she twisted the thickness of hair into a heavy tight rope that was shorter at each turn. She wound and pinned that on top.

Then she put the suit on as she was, without anything underneath, buttoning it directly down. The wool made her bare skin squirm; it made her crave to rub herself all around and over. Her eyes would not water, but her hands opened and closed with this desire. She held them tensed away until her body quieted. It was a nice round solid appropriate sort of itching, and it was nicer if left to die.

On tiptoe, not lifting either foot off the carpet, she swung her body from side to side. Then she lowered her heels to stand flat, still oscillating from her thighs in the same way. Under the combined action of gravity and momentum, if she went on like that too long, she knew it would not feel right when she stopped.

In part, her swinging movement did not reflect from outside because without her underclothes the suit was a fraction loose. This suit had been given three fittings by a careful *couturier*, and it was new. He had talked about it while he worked with the pins. A suit only for a woman of known standards and means; undecorated, called Greek and classic by his friend the designer —absolutely Greek and classic, that was what his friend had called it. He and his friend and everyone at the *couturier*'s stood by to admire, they all said what a great pleasure to see the right woman in that suit. And she thanked them and said how agreeable. But now, otherwise naked, she was turning rough against it; she was moving inside the suit. Especially on her nipples and around her stomach she could feel herself moving.

Couturiers all were men who hated women, she had tried to explain that to Luthella one afternoon. She had realized it herself long ago in London—one of them was working on her, and she glanced down and saw his face and his anxious spider's fingers. If they weren't that way, they would be in some other profession. But only jealous homosexual men who hated women could devote long lifetimes to disguising them with clothes. The fashions changed so grossly every year, and got worse. And she, Loris Licia, did not change so with the fashions: she modified them always to her own taste. She would not, because it would seem insulting and pointless to change herself. Next year they will be worse again, while women grow older. Why change?—change what? she said to Luthella. Hairdressers, the same sort of men. Women became older seeking professional advice on how temptingly feminine they looked, and seeking it exclusively from men who hate women. And the fashions altered and worsened. And as long as men who do not know how to touch a woman will continue to design her dresses and her hair, what does one expect? She said to Luthella: me change what?

Absolutely Greek and classic, that was the description his friend had given it, a suit for a woman of standards and means. Such taste madam had to choose this model. A suit for a woman.

Such taste the woman had.

And the girl watching her from the glass could not have been older than thirteen. Young for her age, a girl with hands on her hips, swinging back and forth. Big smoked eyes of a child, and no lipstick, swinging there with her body to the time of any baby song. Without her shoes. And that suit obviously large on her, and the wrong style. A silly suit for a virgin. A girl trying to look as though she had held a man; wishing to appear ten years older and wanton. Ridiculous, with her hair piled like that on top of her head. A thirteen-year-old out in her mother's clothes, and soon she would take them off and run home. If she had a home to run to. But she must have a home or she could not be wearing those clothes.

And the hands. A girl of thirteen; a suit for a woman; a virgin's eyes. And a man's hands. Different pieces of people. All of them waiting for the dawn.

Loris Licia Choate opened her lips and tittered. She breathed out through a slit in her mouth for ten seconds, not ever stopping; and she still swung the same from side to side.

Except for a darkening of the wild gray, the young child's face in the mirror did not change.

IV

Involutions and Facts

It is common knowledge that a blinded bat can fly at length through a complex maze of wires, and remain unharmed. A bat will soar through a treetop after dark to get where it must go; and a person who watches may never sense the shriek that guides it in the night.

Then like a bat's, the darting cry of reason can be lost to human ears. And when its quick-flashed movement is witnessed—the twisting untouched through a world of tangled events—by the time that is recorded in the eye, it has passed.

Yet this fluttering through is the way of the fates, and this now must be considered. For the two years following Loris Licia Choate's arrival were made turbid by a hundred bumpy happenings not worth a thought; there were a few important occasions. And there seemed to be no reason to the end. Then, not because they failed to see it take place—but because the horror would not have made sense if it had been seen, people said the end was accidental.

Now thin the mind or thicken the tongue: ask a man to distinguish between accident and incident. A middle-aged lady is hit by a small meteor, and nine days later dies in a hospital, and friends will say this has no proper cause. They will claim she could as easily have been standing six inches more to the left or right when the thing fell—she just happened during that second to be accidentally placed where she was. And they will make official entry of the event as an accidental death. There that word is used, and there it collapses. It was not used previously pertaining to the lady; and she is dead so it won't be used about her again. Fifty years before her demise, a certain ovum happened to be neither six-millionths of an inch further to the left, nor to the right; the lady got herself conceived, nine months later was born in a hospital—and friends would call this an incident. It, they say, is different, and no one will be likely to deny it did have a traceable cause. No record of an accidental birth has yet been made.

Fear wets the focus in a brave man's eyes. For the fates are only necessary facts; he can but see them after. And no man is haunted by his past, but only by his future.

Now around the start of one uncertain April, it was noticed in the city that Loris Licia Choate no longer took a daily walk along the Drive. She went downtown, or out to a restaurant with the two white women. But she did not take her ritual exercise as she had before. It was noticed too that the postman, who had hardly been to see her, stopped daily with a registered letter demanding her personal signature. Mrs. Rhale claimed the sudden regularity of the postman's visits and the blank discontinuation of Loris Licia's walks had some mysterious relation. Mrs. Rhale could claim what she liked; there was rarely any way of testing a rumor for truth if it concerned either of the Choate establishments on Melpomene Drive.

But before Loris Licia's walks were ended, Edmund had started with his. It was the Sunday morning in that same week; and Edmund and his real daughter and Aunt Clothilde came out from church together, and went up past the cemetery to the country. They were not able to go quickly or far because of Aunt Clothilde's age and her limp; but the old lady could get along when she had to. And Aunt Clothilde did not go with them every day; but unless it rained, or threatened to, Edmund and his daughter did not miss a morning after that. They took different roads out of town, and they would walk beside the asphalt highway that led up by the country hospital and the golf course. They walked out, not back— Sterling went with the car to get them when they had been gone about an hour or so. Sometimes he took them in the car to begin their walk on a road off beyond the city. They liked to go by the river too, past the big cypress; or around the outskirts back of town. They walked all over, changing their route each time, and they only kept away from the swamps for convenience. And while people couldn't honestly say Edmund ever made a point of passing that other house, in either direction—they were forced to see that he did not avoid it.

Then what the city had been waiting for finally happened; and partly on account of its prior appearance as a long-term and lewd expectation, it came into being as a disappointment.

On one of these excursions with Adrianne, Edmund turned a corner and came face to face with Loris Licia Choate walking out of the drugstore.

Two people saw it, and one of them was the sad social rival of old Mrs. Gwendolyn Rhale, Mrs. Ida Heppleton. The other was Eddie Reese the druggist. Their separate stories took off at variance and soon sounded as though they described two separate events. But important people dropped over to hear Eddie Reese's account, among them Mrs. Rhale; and Mrs. Heppleton had to do something. Then when she blossomed, Eddie put his back up, and with people trying to make sense of both their stories the whole thing got to be a fundamental mess.

The descriptions were louder in tone and texture than even that dramatic occasion had merited. They agreed on few details. Adrianne bowed her head; Edmund didn't. Loris Licia did not change her pace or her manner at all and by her face you would not have thought she had seen a thing. And Edmund's look afterwards, whether it represented terrible low sadness (Reese) or cool outrage (Heppleton), appeared to be caused more by Adrianne's bowing—a seeming expression of guilt—than by anything in the other woman's behavior. He did definitely stop and raise his daughter's head up in his two hands before they continued on their way. Otherwise, a lot of these descriptions should be forgotten. The swift cloud over the sun, and Edmund's unbearable weight of perspiration, and the black cat that had been run over and lay alive screaming before them on the sidewalk can probably be dismissed as having been reasonably affected by a greased leakage of imagination.

The stories were famous for a time and died, as famous things, without a gurgle. Neither Edmund nor Adrianne had spoken with Loris Licia since her arrival. Now from month to month, the three passed again in public, and then once again. This was not a common occurrence, but still it ceased to be of great interest. Someone recalled how Edmund used to go walking—with the infant Loris Licia in a baby carriage and her mother, Silvana—and would meet or pass his future second wife, Anne Legrange, in a less tense but similarly awkward situation. He was an unusual man, and unusual events marked his way. He carried power and wide shoulders past them all. He remained Mr. Edmund Choate.

Then, that November, before the first quick sheath of ice, the two men came to town.

It was a sudden cold; and November was the month.

Cold can be a leisurely cry in this part of the South. Inverted smiles come easy. Here the earth should be sogged, or suddenly arid for a baked summer week—and under that crust lies the water. The rich lift their heels and drag their minds. Winter makes a windy flat-eyed awe for those who can play. Camel's-hair overcoats have high collars in cedar closets; no one will need them this year. Expectation grows hair all over its ears.

November was always a month of expecting. There is much to freeze around a city built in the swamps—wet is a constant word that must be qualified; nothing you remember was ever all dry but the hot rising August dust. Yearly towards the middle of October footsteps sound in the leaves, and the harsh white edge of the sky looks too stretched. While the white widens overhead, the low marsh air is beginning to circle. And by the twenty-first you can taste the wind. Then everybody comments it will be a cold season, but not nearly so much as last year which was the exception; all pity the sad souls who live up in the North where they really have winter. This is the talk on Melpomene Drive. Back of town the poor people have to prepare, they do not talk so much. But the wealthy residents have already been overcharged for steam heat and fantasy; and if you can put down a payment on a needless desire, you have time to be disappointed. So it goes on into November—the harshness of white dies dull in the sky. You go on talking, and a silver scum slips ignored down the river; out of politeness you will not look at whomever it is you are talking with, because his breath shows too. Bravely the question freezes in the mind, and hope bursts with the water pipes. Winter is a dirty gleam under your feet when the wet in the streets is stroked thin. For what you paid to forget was just the thing—just the only marshland thing ever truly cold and dry—the new ice. And winter is in.

November was the month ninety years ago before the riverport had got to be a city. You wouldn't have found it on many maps then. Sparsely inhabited, and no one had much money; it was one more port down a big stream. Good food could get scarce, the clothing was handmade warm. This was before Southern women had time to go to the movies and learn they weren't supposed to be wearing anything but slips. In those days every person worked hard to make ready for the winter. You would never have thought this town could find a cause to become a real cosmopolitan city; there was no possible attraction for outsiders or for anyone who was able to live some place else. With the cold, there was trembling and borrowing and praying, and something unknown always came to pass; and on top of it all that November a nice Mrs. Thelma Lafitte's husband was drowned out in the swamps, and then her house began to sink in pure oil.

November was always the month.

So on the sixteenth when those two men came to town for Loris Licia Choate, it was a different kind of surprise.

They came six days before the freeze.

They took a furnished apartment downtown the same morning they arrived, without having contacted anybody. The tall one looked about thirty-five, and the other maybe ten years older. Both were dark, with black brilliantined hair and dark eyes, too studied in their dress and their manners. They had sharp foreign accents that matched their shoes, narrow and pointed. Their shoes always glinted and they had many pairs. The younger man was quite handsome. They went to the best restaurants; at night they went out to the Mallimic Country Club where they gambled discreetly, using small sums, and usually won.

And during the light hours, for the first two weeks and a half, they went to call on Loris Licia Choate each afternoon.

That by itself would have shocked nobody. Loris Licia had established herself in too peculiar a manner; shocks could no longer be admitted. Curiosity had taken a permanent thick grip on her house like the ivy, and new happenings only meant new creepers. People now said the single sure constant in her behavior was the fact that you could not predict anything about it from lunch to dinner.

And now she stopped going out; the tall black figure was hardly seen in the living room of her own house. The mailman's visits had ceased the day the two men came, so she was left quite alone except for them. She could not have been sick, because the men continued with their daily calls and stayed a while each time. And on the seventeenth day they stayed four hours; and when they left they went quicker than usual, not quite at a run—sour, angry in their faces. Loris Licia stood in her open doorway until they had disappeared down the next street. There was a line to the way she stood that looked fierce even for her. And Mrs. Charleston's maid, watching from the window across the Drive, said you could have felt those eyes three miles away.

The men did not go back to Loris Licia's house again. They did not leave town either. They lived on in their furnished apartment, and went out to make new friends.

Many might have thought they were tourists, or possibly businessmen. People might not have gone on thinking about them at all, if Mrs. Rhale hadn't remembered the name Bufardi. They were introducing themselves everywhere they went as the Bufardi brothers. Bufardi was not just the name Loris Licia had once used; it was also the maiden name of her mother, Edmund Choate's first wife.

Then gossip sank underground and liquefied, and spread like swampwater. It had become a certainty that the men were not in town on business, at least not proper business. They behaved as tourists should for a while longer. Then they never went any place during the day except to a restaurant for lunch or a coffee shop later: wherever they might be likely to meet Adrianne Legrange Choate. And, too, some nights they walked through the red-light district—always alone.

By the third week, people said they were enormously polite blackmailers working on behalf of Loris Licia Choate.

Lydell Wainscott's mother told Lydell Wainscott to invite Adrianne over for dinner. When he did, Adrianne said her father was not feeling well (he had taken the grippe) and had asked her not to go out alone for a few evenings.

After that, the tonal agreement—an unsounded note—was to help Edmund shield his real daughter from those two men. Doors and mouths shut silently. No one of any importance, man or woman, talked to the men at the Club. They were ignored; those who had been introduced to them snubbed them. The underground gossip choked and was left to stagnate: there were vermin in the deep water.

And the men stayed on. And Loris Licia still kept to the inside of her house.

And inside, things had not changed.

The seventh of December made a thick night, and a layer of cold heaviness that froze on glass. There was an animal east along the river, trapped or attacked, fallen—it was screeching in pain. The animal screeched every quarter-hour with an upturned, thrilling voice. Icy fog spread around the swamps, visible breath from the throat of the river; the barges and the boats called into it. They cut through to wail and whistle.

One small boat gave the sort of sound you always expect when you slice down a ripe winter melon.

Luthella crossed from the head of the stairs and threw open the bedroom door almost before she had knocked.

She waited then until Loris Licia looked. Then she told her, "You have got company."

". . . Frightened?"

"Little bit," Luthella said.

Loris Licia watched from the mirror. She held a comb three-quarters of the way down in her loose hair. She pulled it further down, and out, before she turned on one foot. "You are," she said. "You are frightened."

"I said I was. A little bit."

"Is it the house again?"

"Not unless something got to be over five feet tall and dressed in dark gray," Luthella said, "which it has not done so far."

"I mean to say it is the house that frightens you."

"Not likely," Luthella said, "any more. Not that old haunt."

"It is just the company."

"Correct," she said. "Shall I say what I did last time?"

Loris Licia let the comb drop behind her on the bed. "You are playing games. Is it they?"

"No I'm not, I thought you could figure. Not the Italians, no."

"I did not mean the Italians."

"Correct," Luthella said. "But just her. Without him. He wouldn't likely try to see you again; it's just her. Shall I go down and say like I did before? She's outside the front door, I didn't let her in. Hated to leave her out there, it's too cold."

Loris Licia jerked the sash of her robe tight, and retied it. She leaned her head back to shake the hair free.

"It's too cold out there for a person, and she's alone. You know?"

Loris Licia said, "Yes." The one word sounded a mile long.

Luthella said, "Shall I take your message down that you ain't at home? Not to keep her waiting. It's much too cold."

"I have no message," Loris Licia said.

"I know how you feel and all," Luthella said, "but you wouldn't feel the same about her if you'd ever met her. About him yes, and you got your reason. But not about her." Luthella moved a step to the side. "Let me go down and tell her right quick before she catches her death in that cold."

"Tell her what? Thank you, there is no message."

Luthella said, "No, ma'am. No," she said; "you would not want to let her stand out there waiting. You don't know her, or you wouldn't want to. She is not a thing like the father. Not her. Let me just tell her to go away quick, you wouldn't want her to catch a cold if you knew her."

Loris Licia passed, and put a hand up ahead to the master switch outside the bedroom. She let it rest there for a second, and then peeled it off downwards.

"Wait," Luthella said, "not you. Hey, most surely I do not think *you* should go. What are you doing without no light, why did you do that? I didn't intend for you to go, and you can't see without a light besides; wait now."

"Stay there," said Loris Licia.

"Not you, wait, watch you don't trip over that robe. Watch what you doing. What are you doing?"

But Luthella could hear her moving steadily down the staircase. "Wait now," she said.

Over her shoulder, Loris Licia said, "Stay there and be quiet. Where are Mady and Viola?"

"Went to bed."

"Good," she said, "stay there." Then she went on. The taffeta gathered loudly, electric around her legs in the darkness.

Luthella followed; she felt her way to the cool oak banister, and stopped at the top of the stairs. "I am quiet," she said.

"Stay quiet. And stay there."

"I ain't saying a word. I don't like it. He might come after her, think about that. She's a lovely person, but you never met her and suppose he comes after. It's him I'm worried about. These are not proper hours."

"Be quiet."

"I'm quiet," Luthella said.

Below, she thought she could begin to see shapes in the dark. Luthella was acquainted with every detail of the house so well it was possible to imagine it all in place. And she did not know if she was imagining. She opened her eyes wide as the skin allowed, and still she was not sure.

There was the staircase that wound down. There was a wide space of carpet on the first floor and an overcoat closet on the right. Ahead was the front door, with curtained thin long windows on either side, beginning to shine. To the left, the living room; over to the right was the rest of the house. A dark brown table set under the stairs and a mirror for seeing yourself as you went out or came in, for taking your hat off. A long white glazed china urn for umbrellas. There were three faint blue ladies painted and baked in the china, she knew.

Luthella said, "I am quiet. Now I am right here being quiet, but I don't like it and I can't see. And if you just use my name I'll hear it and I will be right down there. You just call me."

Loris Licia went without slowing to the front door. The turning of the handle made no noise. She pulled it back.

A misty white light swam softly inward; the night had a cover on it. You couldn't make out the farthest trees, nothing you could see in the sky. That swath of fog stretched over the dark earth, distant and deep, soundless. Like a blindfold on the city.

But the river was calling and screeching.

Light from the street lamp touched, lingered around the two women; not between them. It held them together in the night.

Luthella listened to the screams of the injured animal from the east.

And Loris Licia said, "Are you cold?"

"No," said Adrianne. "Not at all, thank you. Never."

"How do you do? Give me your hand, please," Loris Licia said.

Luthella saw the other woman stretch her arm out, and hold. Then Loris Licia stepped backwards.

Then she led her sister after her into the house.

When the front door was shut, from upstairs Luthella saw the shadows move past the patch of hazed light that came through the curtain on the south window. She heard the taffeta fading, and she heard another door close.

And then there was only the living-room clock, and those measured, raw cries in the night.

Luthella said, "That God damned river."

A boat was turning into the east bend. The wail was double, and the second half stayed for half a minute in your ears. When it ended, the sound went on floating like a dim murky tone in the memory.

Luthella took a firm grip on the banister, and spread her feet farther apart. Her pupils were getting accustomed, and now she could begin to make out the lay of the house downstairs. "Oh, Jesus. Damn that river," she said.

And close to an hour later, she said out loud, "Attend."

There were voices again moving in the hall.

Beyond, such cold wet noises as a boat can make were once more floating frozen through the fog. Like the slicking over of new ice, you could hear the thick winter breathings come wet down the air.

The sounds of winter, and the wind.

"No, by the front," said Adrianne. "Thank you."

Loris Licia said, "You remember this house well."

"I remember it."

"This way."

"Yes, I know."

Loris Licia called, "Luthella."

"I'm right here."

"You are still alone?"

"Yes, ma'am."

"She will not say anything."

"It wouldn't matter," said Adrianne.

"For my own reasons," Loris Licia said.

"I'll tell him if he asks, it couldn't possibly matter. He doesn't worry about me."

". . . Not since these men have come?"

"He has the grippe."

"Conveniently."

"No," said Adrianne, "he isn't like that. He really has the grippe. He doesn't worry, I go wherever I like."

". . . Not here."

"Anywhere. It wouldn't matter, you don't understand."

"No," Loris Licia said.

"He truly doesn't worry."

"He doesn't know you are here."

"It wouldn't matter; this is my mother's house."

"No," said Loris Licia. "This is my house."

Adrianne said, "I am sorry. Yes." Then as if she had turned, her voice came louder: "I'm glad to have seen you. I can't see you now."

"Me?" Luthella said. "You mean me?"

Adrianne said, "Yes."

And Loris Licia said, "Goodbye."

There was a silence like the darkness of the house.

Luthella gripped the railing, and leaned. Up from her feet she felt a tingle and a rush—a swarming sense of blocked blood.

Adrianne said, "And please don't worry. Please. I will tell him if he asks, it won't matter. There won't be any trouble."

"No," said Loris Licia.

"You won't? You won't worry."

"About that," said Loris Licia, "I imagine not."

". . . Thank you for letting me come in."

"Goodbye."

"I'm glad," Adrianne said, "I'm glad. I am so glad I know you now." Then with the door open—cut out against the frail white light from the street, she reminded Luthella of one of the pale figures on the umbrella stand. She said, "This house isn't hollow any more."

"The door is not locked," said Loris Licia."

"Isn't it?" said Adrianne. "They say it is."

"No, it is not. It is never locked. Don't bother to ring next time."

Luthella saw Adrianne lean quickly inside, and take her sister by the shoulders; she kissed her on the cheek. And she said, "I'll probably never come back. Thank you."

Then Adrianne was gone.

And Loris Licia watched at the door. She must have stood still and watched for three minutes.

Two thin feeler tips of fog waved up into the doorway, grayish green on the street lamps. Like the first tentacles: now the fog was like a great blind night-monster holding around the house.

"She . . . ?"

"Do not make noise," Loris Licia said.

The door snapped shut.

". . . Did you go outside?"

"No."

"You shouldn't of stood by the open air like that."

The light went on. Loris Licia was by the north wall, in the corner; she had both hands up to the switch.

Luthella squinted, and she shaded her eyes with her wrist. She said, "You were in there an hour."

Loris Licia pulled the edge of her robe off the floor, and started toward the stairway. She came to a standstill at the bottom step.

"You all right?" Luthella said.

"Yes," said Loris Licia.

She started up.

Luthella pressed a thumb in the small of her back; she had an ache there.

And Loris Licia said softly, "I do not believe."

". . . Don't believe what?"

"I do not. Not her, I cannot. I do not believe in her." Loris Licia said, loud: "I cannot."

"Who, Miss Adrianne?"

"I do not."

"A sincere person. About the only one you likely to find in this town, but she is. Sincere she is."

"I wish you would not employ vapid language," Loris Licia said. "You and everyone."

"But it's true. You can tell just from looking at her. She is sincere."

"Or be quiet," Loris Licia said, "or do not use that ridiculous word. Yes, she is sincere. Naturally. What do you think I was saying? Certainly she is sincere."

". . . Then what?"

"That is the most ridiculous word in the American idiom, and the one most used."

"No, it's not," Luthella said.

Loris Licia stopped again, on a step.

"It's not," Luthella said. "It means she means what she says. That's all. Might be a silly word in some other language."

"It is the same in any language," Loris Licia said. "Quite the same. It is an entirely useless word."

". . . She does mean what she says. Whatever she told you; she means it."

"But of course she means it. You are ridiculous. Certainly she means what she says. Yes, she is *sincere*, yes."

"Yes, ma'am," Luthella said.

Loris Licia went suddenly stiff. She turned full round to her right, and then went back down the stairs. When she got to the bottom she was running. The black sash of her robe flicked in the air behind her, and a few long surface hairs caught, lifting in the wind.

She moved swiftly through to the living room; and she entered from all sides, rushing from every mirror—converging on herself by the high windows that gave onto the street.

From upstairs, Luthella said, "Hey there."

Loris Licia pushed the heavy draperies back along the rod, bending low with the effort. They swung back wide, taking with them a vase from a round rosewood table; the vase sailed up and popped against the wall. It fell in three pieces.

Luthella had to reach for the banister to keep from dashing downstairs. "You prefer to be alone?" she said.

Then, into the silence, facing the choked night, Loris Licia said, "Yes." She strengthened her body and yelled: "I cannot believe in her."

"Goddam that damned river," Luthella said. The animal was screeching.

Yellow and the night met through the many-paned bare windows. They would not fuse. The near fog looked diseased, tinted the color of vomit from those raucous spangling bulbs.

Loris Licia let her arms go loose; and the furied stiffness left her as quickly as it had come. There was not much visible change in her stance. But you could see the difference.

She said, "I cannot believe, I must not try. I do not," she said, "I do not believe."

The end came seven months and five days after that.

At four thirty in the afternoon the living-room sofa was of a hue blacker than brown. It had been recently re-covered and dusted, and the light was bad. On the mantel facing this sofa were four brown wooden cocker spaniels in two poses, two on each side, and separated by a black calendar that was a marble back with a page for each day.

In seven months the weather had cracked and spread from inside. Heat smeared the feel of things with a sticky layer that did not evaporate. If you washed it off it was there again before you dried. It resided in the skin.

Late afternoon, and the living room lit by two wall lamps above the fireplace; the chandelier was not yet being used, and the windows were open.

In these seven months, and excepting the sofa, the room had not been altered by one article. The decoration was no different than Loris Licia made it the first week of her coming.

She was sitting now on the sofa, her legs together, right-angled at the knees, and her head was back. She was wearing a black

chiffon dress that came up to her neck and it had a full limp skirt.
It fell foolishly from her body, because again this queer tension had
hardened her; she looked rigid. She seemed not able to move.

Both hands were taut on her thighs, eyes toward the mantel.

Luthella sat next to her and watched her, and Miss Mady sat
on the other side. The three were alone in the room. Miss Mady's
arm was stretched out like a plume over Loris Licia's right shoulder.
She wanted to touch her, and might have rubbed the material. But
she couldn't complete the movement. The three were frozen in
the heat as ladies in a daguerreotype: they appeared to have been
slapped into silence.

It was as if the room were holding its breath—a kind of inflated
stillness.

Then:

"Let her alone," Luthella said, "don't touch her."

"I wasn't."

"Let her alone. Just let her be."

Miss Mady explained, "I was not touching her."

Luthella bent forward and pointed her lips for careful pronuncia-
tion. "Just let her be," she said.

Miss Mady lifted her eyebrows, with her eyes closed. She took
her hand back. Then she crossed her legs.

Miss Viola came in with a coffee tray, and laid it on the round
table by the windows.

"She don't want coffee," Luthella said.

Miss Viola lifted the pot and poured out a cupful of thick
liquid. The coffee was darker than the sofa. She cocked her head
out of the steam. "Do her good," she said, "good and hot. Mostly
chicory."

"Did you hear what I said?"

Miss Viola sifted two spoons of sugar in the cup, and stirred four
times around. She said, "It's here in case she wants it. I am having
some now anyway. I think it's all wrong," she said, "I think she
should go on out to the hospital and wait there."

"Nobody required you to think," Luthella said. "She should do
like she wants to. I phoned up the maid at the other house.

Nobody in town knows about it, they are not telling anybody now. She will phone me back right here if there is news."

"She at the hospital?"

"At the other house, I said."

"Then how will she know?"

"Don't preoccupy yourself," Luthella said. "She will know."

Miss Viola took up the cup. "Third hand ain't the same as being at the hospital. I don't care who says what. That's where her sister is, that's where she ought to be if she cares this much. To me it is funny she should care so much, she never met the man. She refused to meet him."

"I say the same. I will second that statement," Miss Mady said.

Luthella said, "Don't talk so much."

"I wasn't," Miss Mady said. "I am not. I hadn't opened my mouth."

". . . And don't," Luthella said.

"She doesn't hear us anyway. Not listening. Off some place else."

"Keep quiet."

Loris Licia pulled her head up. She got to her feet in a slow unsure way, like the unwinding of a mechanical toy. Then she walked to the mantelpiece and stood there with her back to the three women.

Luthella said, "See? All of us are making her more nervous than she already is."

"Not all of us," Miss Mady said, "I'm not."

Loris Licia reached up and tore one page from the calendar. She crinkled it into a hard ball, and gripped it in her fist. And she stood holding onto the mantelpiece.

"Right," said Miss Viola. "We clean forgot to do that today. Clean forgot what day it was." She frowned and nodded at Miss Mady to take up the new subject.

"I didn't," Miss Mady said.

"We clean forgot."

"I did not forget," Miss Mady said. "Today was my brother's birthday. Before he died. It happened to be. No reason for me to forget. I know what day it is. I have got no reason to forget; it was never my job to take care of that calendar. If it was my job I would have done it. But I didn't forget."

Loris Licia turned, and went to the sofa. She moved in the same manner, and sat down exactly as she had been before. Her low chignon was set tighter than usual that afternoon; it sank a little distance into the soft cushion when she put her head back. From behind her lashes she stared again at the calendar.

Luthella whispered, "*All three* of us are talking too much."

Then as though the black marble had changed its position, they all watched with Loris Licia. And they sat and watched in silence for some time.

After a minute both the big black numbers swam and wiggled if you kept your eyes on them. Especially the one on the right: like a water snake. This was the number two.

It was the twelfth of July.

PART THREE

The Only Danaïd

Late Afternoon

OVERHEAD WAS a four-leaf, wooden fan, long in each leaf. It moved so slowly, it was like the day.

And there was Adrianne Legrange Choate, called Adrianne, and she sat below the shadowy air just outside the farthest reach of the fan; her hair was not disturbed by it. She sat the way she was given to sitting: centered in the wicker seat, simply, straight—her own back straighter than any chair, but not stiff. Into the damp dark (it had rained the day before), some shadow wafted without a sigh through two open windows—fading, in the dark of the room.

Beyond the hospital, the hard sun pulled up wet that had settled; it baked at the ground. Heat, the bottomless orange light of late afternoon, wetted and filled the air in that time of day. And you had to suck in to breathe.

But a thick oak, decades thick, older than the building, grew now to keep the sun from the waiting-room windows.

Mrs. Rhale shifted her weight in the chair. Mrs. Rhale said, "I doubt to smell mildew in such a place as this."

"It's mildew," Aunt Clothilde said. "Oh, it is mildew."

"Dear," said Mrs. Rhale, "maybe if you didn't carry on exactly like that, it would be easier on everybody, and you could be doing a more constructive thing by not crying than by crying, while we are waiting here."

Aunt Clothilde's lower eyelids had sagged loose and doubled over, years before: two curved gashes, like the gills of a fish. They looked as if she were about to bleed from the eyes. She said, "My eyes always look to be crying."

"Yes, dear," Mrs. Rhale said, "that wasn't my point. You *are* crying now. You are sobbing now. Not your eyes, I wouldn't likely pass such a remark. And they could have operated on your eyes years back, when the doctor told you. Not your eyes. You are crying now."

Aunt Clothilde said, "Doctors. I wish I could help it. No, I don't," she said, "what's the use of wishing? A thing happens. You're crying too," she said.

Mrs. Rhale lifted off her rimless glasses and held them away from her face. She said, "With me it isn't hardly noticeable, dear."

The two old ladies sat to the right of Adrianne, and the three of them were corners of a small triangle. Two in high white and black; Adrianne dressed in pale solid green, paler and clearer than deep water. The Gulf water around something silver, and you might have thought of Adrianne sitting there. There was no one else in the room.

"Oh, Edmund," Aunt Clothilde said. "Edmund. What a way to die in your lifetime."

"No," said Mrs. Rhale. "No, now, no, I never would suggest for you to say such a thing. The doctor doesn't know yet. I tell you and I tell you they don't know yet. They just don't know yet."

Aunt Clothilde bent low over her wandering fingers, and then sat back slowly. "I do," she said.

Mrs. Rhale frowned till her forehead got under her glasses. She dropped her left hand to where Adrianne couldn't see, and fluttered it.

Aunt Clothilde looked at the hand. "No," she said, "how gross of you."

And Adrianne didn't move. She sat, ankles and wrists crossed, her palms lying up.

"Stupid," said Aunt Clothilde. She shrugged at Adrianne. "She knows it too," she said. "Don't be stupid. Of course she knows."

Mrs. Rhale's hand was a butterfly stuck.

Aunt Clothilde said, "How gross." She said it more like a wail.

Then through the stillness, without plucking her eyes from a private spot in the floor where they had taken root, Adrianne reached to the right and cupped and held her great-aunt's bloodless, leathery elbow.

"Of course," Aunt Clothilde said.

Adrianne drew her arm back and lay it as it had been before. She didn't move again for a long time.

When she came back at nineteen, Mr. Spewack the grocer claimed that Adrianne could cut through the center of a shooting battlefield, and nothing would happen: the bullets wouldn't hit her. He said not even a bullet would strike Adrianne, not if she walked, not when she looked with those soft eyes. And it was true that when the measles epidemic swarmed through town and down to Gerville on the river where the colored poor live, Adrianne went to get Dr. Shepard in a taxicab, and she bought three carton boxes of drugs from Reese's drugstore, and groceries, and then drove off with the doctor and stayed in Gerville for the whole day. No white doctor had ever been in Gerville, much less a white woman; no policeman ever dared to go down there. But as Dr. Shepard told it, Adrianne walked ahead of him, and wherever she went the doors opened of themselves. He would not have stayed there two minutes if it hadn't been for Adrianne Choate. Edmund grinned when he heard about it, before she came back; and afterwards he was proud. Everybody acquainted with her was proud, excepting Aunt Clothilde. Aunt Clothilde said if Adrianne wanted to be a nurse, she should have been a nurse.

And since her return the focal point of veneration around town was the young lady Adrianne. She was also called, more naturally, Princess. Edmund said she was born to the wrong century: an antique porcelain girl of a strange, unbreakable quality, born to an age of violence. What Edmund said was thereafter what everybody else said.

When Adrianne moved, there was a thin, crystalline breeze that moved with her all year. She was cool to the eye in August; and in January her breath came in a tiny cloud to touch you like the crisp puff of warm toast when you lift the glass bell. She carried her own air. She did not perspire much in the summer, but if this happened the drops held cool and clear on her white skin. And if the Princess trembled in the winter wind, her tremblings were heat waves from her heart.

From the talk around, you might think she would go out with any young man who asked her. It might be a fact that she would. But Adrianne Choate was not in danger, ever, anywhere in the city. She might go where she liked, alone, or with whom she liked. She could go out on the streets at four o'clock in the morning in the red-light district; she didn't, but she could. Adrianne was made like that.

And the sense you got, if you saw her often enough, was that she was waiting for something. Lydell Wainscott and two of the Thomas brothers, they all wanted to marry her, they said she was waiting to make a choice. But then Richard Baron came to town to set up a shipping office, and he fell in love with her; Adrianne went out with him sometimes. Which is when people took to saying that any proper young man could get her to go out, just so he met her father properly first. She never stayed out very late, and she was never seen to look very differently at one person or at one thing than she looked at everything else. She seemed to have enough love for everyone.

Aunt Clothilde said, "Let me not have this heat." She said, "I have a bearance for troubles, I had it all my life, and I wouldn't be feeling faint or sickly inside right now if the air wasn't gluing me in on myself. Just let me not have this heat."

"No, dear," said Mrs. Rhale, "hush up the edge to your tone of

voice. Watch your control and it will be all right. You are not going
to faint."

". . . I might."

"Did you ever do it before?"

"No. But I might now."

"No," said Mrs. Rhale.

Aunt Clothilde looked up at the fan. She stretched the trunk of
her body, and moaned with more breath than sound, and then
settled back down in her chair. "Why build a big fan," she said,
"if it isn't going to act like anything at all? I ask you. Why didn't
we? Why didn't we go to Biloxi?"

"Nothing to be ashamed about. Some of the best people stay
here in town all summer," Mrs. Rhale said, "the best. Nothing to
be ashamed of, I guarantee. Just because you-all are used to going
away. Biloxi never was so much if you want my personal opinion;
dirty filthy beach. Look at the people are still here this year and
it's already near halfway through July. Most of us are still here.
You think about it, you'll find the right people are still here. Except
for that Mrs. . . . ."

The dark air in the waiting room did not seem to be coming
from outside. Only the shadow of that oak tree and its moss broke
through the open, gaping hospital windows. Air in the building
was heavy, and it was wet and clinging and dead, and its sterile
death had taken place in stagnancy. There was a wispish tinge of
ether in the dead air. The stillness, hot and silent, was all around.

"If we hadn't stayed here," said Aunt Clothilde, "if we had gone,
it wouldn't have happened. Yes, it would," she said, "things
happen. Why should I want to pretend? It could have happened
any place. It just didn't, that's all. Till now." She lifted a lace
handkerchief that was wound around her knuckles, and pressed it
tight over her shining lips; they opened, and she pressed it in between the two rows of perfect false teeth.

On the floor by the window were four small splats of sunlight,
bright blisters in the linoleum, too bright for the eyes. If you
watched them and then looked away, you still saw the shapes—

first in orange, then purple, then deep violet. Filtered through the window screens, their exact edges were thick.

The fan's center was a light shaped like the wider end of any coconut on one of the trees along the lakeside drive. The light was not on. For six inches below it hung a beaded metal chain, copper-colored, and a small striped lily-bell at the end. The slow hum from the slowly turning fan was a part of the stillness, not a noise. The light, the eye of the fan, was dead; and the chain was still.

"Ah-hah," said Aunt Clothilde; "when the wheel hit him."

"Dear," Mrs. Rhale said, "hush up."

". . . Why?"

"Just hush," Mrs. Rhale said.

Aunt Clothilde licked her teeth. She said, "You are stupid, Gwendolyn Rhale. Oh, you are stupid. You think Adrianne could care what I say? You think we're not all wide awake dreaming about it? You think you know me, but you don't know Adrianne at all. Nobody does. Not even her old aunt, completely." She tilted to the left. "Do they?" she whispered. "We don't, do we?"

But the pale young lady, paler and drier than the air, was fixed as she was, unmoving. She might not have heard. She might have had no answer.

Someone once said Adrianne *was* dignity.

Loris Licia Choate nearly said the same thing. But she found other things to say in time.

They stopped on that only night and they stood together and did not speak for a full passing minute. Loris Licia's favorite, the gray room was small around them, and deepest dull, and smooth. There was one thickly curtained window, and a fireplace; a long table; and three straight chairs and two deep ones.

And not far apart, Edmund's two daughters watched each other, like small children through a fence, in opposite, private ways.

Then Loris Licia said, "You are extraordinary to look at. Your mother was less so."

"Yes; I know."

"So am I, but mine was. That is less merit to me."

". . . You did find her picture?"

"Your mother's? Yes, in the attic."

"They say you have it on the mantelpiece."

"They say a lot of things," said Loris Licia, "they like to live on half the truth, they are parasites by choice."

"May I sit down?"

Loris Licia walked away the length of the table, and turned back. "You need not ask. The chair behind you is nice; I like it. Sit there," she said.

Adrianne bent and sank, without looking. The chair fit around her; the walls and the chair soothed their color into the gray of her dress.

Loris Licia said, "Do you smoke? I like that dress. I wish you would take off your gloves."

"Why?" Adrianne worked the fingers free.

"Everything about you looks the same . . . you are not real. Only the face and neck. And even those. You are more like a spirit."

"It's my dress."

". . . Is it?"

Adrianne said, "Yes." She laid the gloves in her lap. Then she said, "You never go to the cemetery."

Loris Licia sat directly opposite her sister on the table edge, with the width of the fire place between them. "I do not care for cemeteries. You know this house well?"

". . . I left the city just after I was five."

"You also? Do you smoke?"

"No, thank you."

"Neither do I. Very good," she said.

Adrianne folded her hands on the gloves.

"You want to talk about the two men."

"Yes. That was the immediate reason."

"You would have come here anyway?"

"Yes," said Adrianne, "eventually I would have come anyway."

Loris Licia ran an arm over her hair. "I was wrong," she said. "I did not think you would."

Adrianne smiled. She waited; then she said, "I think I am right. I hope you won't be sorry."

"Yes," said Loris Licia. "I agree. I hope not."

And they waited again.

"It is difficult."

"Quite."

Adrianne said, "Sometimes I wonder why I'm not able to help. When I want to, I mean, when I really want to be of help. I can't. Otherwise it's easy, the . . . impossible things. Those are the things I can always do. But as soon as it matters, no. Then I am ineffectual. I can't help you."

Loris Licia slid off the table, and pulled the back of her robe down, and sat again. "I'm not sure I understand," she said.

"No, there probably isn't much reason. But there never was any time."

". . . You know something about me?"

"Do I? A little. Yes." Adrianne said: "Listen, can you hear that? We can hear that same animal from our house. That is a dreadful sound."

"Sounds don't bother me."

"They do me. I am a coward. I'm frightened by pain."

"That is not easy to believe."

"No," said Adrianne, "not my own. I have none. You understand, I have no pain."

Loris Licia fingered a crease in the taffeta. "Confessionals by nature I find disgusting," she said. "Still I don't mind the way you talk. Strange. Tell me," she said, "what you believe you know. Why you do not care to believe what they say."

"I'm not sure. I sometimes know what I see."

"Ah. And what have you seen?"

"Not very much," said Adrianne. "I am often . . . stupid. I don't see how they can make so many mistakes. People don't mean to be vicious, but they . . . make mistakes. They say you are promiscuous. They say you came here out of a need to do harm."

"Yes?"

"It's senseless," she said.

"What makes you think it is?"

"I can't tell. A child would know. Children don't have the words, and by the time they learn them they forget the meanings. But a child could see. You walk like a virgin. And you don't hate."

Loris Licia looked above her head. She opened her mouth to speak, and then she laughed. "Which times are you stupid?" she said.

". . . More often than before. I think."

"That also is not easy to believe."

Adrianne smiled. She said quietly, "I expect not."

"You say *think*."

"Yes."

"Strange," said Loris Licia, "many things are . . . odd. You make me uncomfortable."

"I'm sorry."

"You should be, you certainly should be."

Adrianne stretched her two gloves between her hands. She lay them down and pressed them. Then she watched them.

Loris Licia said, "Tell me. I am curious. Or he thinks as you do, or else he believes what people say. Which is it? Does he? Does he think like you?"

"No," said Adrianne. "He does believe you hate him. He thinks that's why you came back. He has to; he isn't able to forget."

". . . You mean he hates himself?"

"No," said Adrianne.

"He is confused."

"Yes, he is," she said.

Loris Licia stepped onto the floor; she stood with her legs wide apart, next to the table. "That is not right," she said, "not right at all. And what makes you know? Then tell me why I came here?"

". . . I'm not sure."

"I would suspect you are quite sure."

Adrianne leaned on her gloves. She said, "It's not my business. I can't help you."

"No one has asked you to help me. Or did he?"

"No."

Loris Licia said, "Good. About those men," she said. "They claim they are related to me."

"Is it true?"

"I suspect not. They would seem to be lying. As far as I know, I have no family. I had an alcoholic cousin in Paris, but he died. They made me many communications and they have some of the facts, these men. But it is easy for them to lie. I have no family."

"Thank you," said Adrianne. "There was no way of finding that out. I had to ask you. I think they will be after Father next, if it's money they want. And they'll try to reach him through me. They do want money?"

"Yes. But I do not have definite information about them one way or the other."

"I won't need it. I can find out the rest from them."

"Can you?"

". . . I'll find out for you."

"Ah, will you?" said Loris Licia. "For me, or for him?"

Adrianne looked at her hands. She said, "Yes."

"Anything you thought necessary you could do. Could you not? For him."

"Yes."

"He is slightly bigger than your own way of life."

Adrianne shook her head. "No," she said, "I am a part of his."

". . . I understand." Loris Licia reached to touch the wall. "Now tell me this," she said. "You instruct me that I don't hate. Now tell me do you think I don't forgive? Do you think that? Do you think I can forgive him?"

"Oh, no," said Adrianne, "no. But it's different. Not as he believes. It's the good you won't forgive him, isn't that it? Not the bad. You see I thought as he did, I thought so too, until I saw you that day on the street. I thought you must have come here for a false reason. But then I saw you. It isn't the bad, is it? Or am I wrong? You don't care about the bad. It's the money. You don't mind about anything but the money."

Loris Licia began to laugh, lower than before, and harsh; she laughed till she had no breath left. Then she leaned back and filled her lungs. She said, "It occurs to you I am molested by that. You think I am disturbed by a thing like that. My mother was a whore, and my grandmother; I will never be sure which irresponsible man made the error responsible for my being born. Your father adopts me, he throws me away before I can decently talk, and out of all that you think I am molested by having money. You think nothing else disturbs me but the money. You imagine I came to cross an ocean three thousand miles to live with the money he sent away with me. My own money. For it is my own money. It is not his, no, it is mine. You think I would come so far to a town with bad memories and worse people, and you can conceive that I do it because I am not able to live with this money. You. You can imagine. In a city of so many thousand inhabitants, in the entire world. Only you. You think I came here to this house for that, to live. To this one special place; to be here in this place."

Adrianne studied her lap as if the top glove were alive and clawing up at the air. She said gently, "It was the place for you to come."

On the west end of the table was an oblong brown enamel box, more shiny than the wood. There was a deep red in it, and it had been recently polished. Loris Licia walked around, and stood still. She pushed a thumb on the enamel, then took her hand away and looked close to see the print fade in the gray light.

"You are left-handed?" she said.

"Yes, I am," said Adrianne.

"I thought so. I don't smoke," she said. "I don't. But I keep cigarettes in most of the rooms. I keep several different kinds of cigarettes in the house."

A door opened and closed down a passage, and twice the double cluck of a woman's shoe sounded; echoed; repeated from the beginning; continued; got louder, on the black linoleum. Then the shoes stopped, and there were whispers, and another door closed.

Then they started again, the same shoes. Neither shoe hit the linoleum a healthy knock, but rather gripped and settled into it each time; and after each time the echo, as each shoe was lifted—and the unhealthy echo was the sickening suck of separation, like adhesive being unstuck.

The nurse came into the waiting room. She was all white, even her stockings, and she was all wilted from the wet heat.

Aunt Clothilde said, "You have nothing to say. Not you."

"That's right," said the nurse. "I'm maternity."

"You look to be," said Aunt Clothilde.

"I knew you were, dear," Mrs. Rhale said, "I was here last year when Mrs. Millicent Page got her pains premature and dilated, and then closed up again and left. You wouldn't remember me, but I remember you."

"Oh, yes."

"There's no reason you should," Mrs. Rhale said, "but I certainly remember you. I have such a memory."

Aunt Clothilde looked down at the nurse's thick, heavy, wide shoes. "Twinkletoes," she said. Then she whispered, "Oh, my God."

"Now, dear; now, just be normal."

The nurse said, "I met Nurse Baldwin in the hall, that's your nurse, she asked me to tell you they still have him in the operating room, they're doing everything possible they can, he isn't in any pain, he's full of locals and they're giving him a general too, that's anesthetics, he should be down from there in about a half-hour outside, maybe less."

"Thank you, dear," said Mrs. Rhale. "We understand."

"We?" Aunt Clothilde said. "We? Speak for yourself."

"There, now."

Aunt Clothilde said to the nurse, "She always tries to make like she's one of the family, I can't imagine why. I don't do that around her family, I don't act like that. We've only been living together since February; ever since we each of us figured the other one looked too lonesome. So we each got sorry for the other one, and she came to live with me for company. We have a whole upstairs wing of Edmund's house just to ourselves. And I tell myself I'm doing her a favor because she was so lonesome with nobody to look after, and if you ask her separate she will tell you she is doing the favor to me, because Edmund and Adrianne don't need me or anybody else but just themselves, and I was so lonely. But you have to ask her when I'm not around. So each of us thinks we are doing the favor, and we each get rid of our loneliness like that, and the ugliness of knowing we don't have any reason to pump air any more. So we pretend we're doing favors, and that lends us a reason, and it makes it easier till we die, you see. But that's fine. Only why should she make out she's one of the family? That's no sense. It's just the two of us, you see."

"Oh, yes," said the nurse.

"Dear," said Mrs. Rhale. "Aunt Clothilde."

"I'm not your aunt, don't call me that. Just don't call me that. Why should everybody call me that? The only persons I know don't call me aunt are Edmund and Adrianne, and they're the only nephew and niece of mine that I have. So it's a mystery to me why everybody should call me aunt."

"Oh," said the nurse.

"Did you ever see an accident?"

"A what?" said the nurse. "What kind?"

Aunt Clothilde said, "I wish you could have seen the wheel hit him."

"No," Mrs. Rhale said. "Be normal. Think what you're saying. No, dear. Think: the girl."

Aunt Clothilde said, "Adrianne's not a girl. Nurse, I wish you could have seen the wheel hit him."

"No," said the nurse, "well no. I'm as happy not to have seen, I'm sure."

"I wish you could. I just wish you could have seen him when the wheel hit him. And the two of us there behind. Not Gwendolyn, she wasn't there, she had to write post cards, she only got here an hour ago to the hospital. Only the three of us this noon out on that bridge. Did they tell you about it, the other nurses?"

"Well . . ."

"No, please," said Mrs. Rhale, "please . . ."

"The three of us out on the bridge. They probably told you about it in there down the hall. I heard you whispering down the hall. Why must nurses always whisper down the hall? You see, it was the three of us. Us three. And Adrianne was in the middle, she had one arm through Edmund's and the other arm through mine. But when we came to that bridge, the sidewalk is so narrow, Edmund stepped ahead. And he walked a ways ahead, so I was with Adrianne when the truck came. And I remember how quickly Edmund walked, I remember thinking he wants to cross in a hurry so he can be with Adrianne again. Those old clouds in the sky, used up from the rain yesterday. I saw a cloud shaped like me when I was young. I had a habit to stand on one foot, you see, with all my weight on this one foot, and so was the cloud. But it was wrinkled . . ."

"Dear. No, dear . . ."

"It was, it was wrinkled and gray, and it was all used up, like all the rest, just waiting for the wind to take and break it into nothing. The wind was doing that while I watched. Right while I watched the cloud broke apart and changed its shape, and it looked like something else that disgusted me; but I don't remember what. But that was when Adrianne said, 'The wheel.' And I said, 'What wheel, dear?' I couldn't see but the top of the truck coming, because I was walking on the inside next to the railing and Edmund was in the way. Then Adrianne said, 'The wheel is loose.' She said that louder, in her usual voice. And I said, 'What do you mean, dear?'; because I really couldn't see what she meant. And she said, quite loud, she said, 'The wheel will never hold.' Well, when she said that, I looked at her, and I wish I could tell you what I saw in her face right then made my fingers cold. I saw she hadn't been talking to me. Or talking to herself either. She was just talking. Just out loud to nobody, you see. And I had no more time to say, 'Adrianne,' when she stopped, sudden, there on the pavement. And she slipped her arm out of mine, and she stood there. She stood, and she said once more, exactly before it happened, she said, 'The wheel.' And when she said it that last time, her voice was louder than anything else afterwards. But she didn't shout it; you wouldn't want to say she shouted it. She said it, that's all. And I remembered then when she was little, and she used to go open the window and look outside whenever there was a storm beginning, and she would cry and cry when nobody could tell her why the white wind wailed so around the house. And in that second I thought, she won't ever cry again, now she knows. Because I've never, ever, heard anybody use their voice quite that way. She wasn't talking to me, you see; or to Edmund. Or to that truck. She was talking like the wind talks, to nobody."

Mrs. Rhale said, "Stop it. I order you to stop it. You must use your control. With her right sitting here with us, and Edmund up there on the operating table, how can you even think to let go?"

Aunt Clothilde said, "I am thinking. Oh, yes, I am thinking. And Adrianne isn't here. She looks to be here, but she's not. Adrianne is inside her own self, look at her, she doesn't even know I have my mouth open. And Edmund is inside himself, and he's dying up on that table, and she knows it and I know it. We saw it, we know. But nobody knows Adrianne. Edmund thinks he does, but Edmund can be very stupid. And the two of them don't need me, it doesn't matter what I say; now or any time, it didn't matter. Yes, I am thinking, yes. I am wondering how many times you are going to ask me to tell the story, Gwendolyn, after he's dead, you and everybody, tomorrow and the day after and the day after and the day after that. How do I get by those days? How many times will I have to tell it before I can die too? And think it. How often will I think it? Take your hand away from me, don't diddle at me. There's nothing wrong with me. Nothing; I saw too much, that's all that's wrong with me, and I knew too much before, years and years before. I always knew too much for a useless, stupid, damned old female cripple. And I'm frightened. Now I am afraid. That's what's wrong with me."

"He won't pass over," Mrs. Rhale said. "I'm just sure he won't. Don't you be afraid, dear. You be normal."

"Over? Pass over? You mean pass back. Over where? You don't mean over, you mean back. Back to where he was before he was born. Not over. Over where?"

"I mean he won't die," Mrs. Rhale said.

"Yes, he will probably die," said Aunt Clothilde. "And it's not his dying I'm afraid of."

The nurse cleared her throat, and put one foot behind her to the left. She stepped on the base of a long-stemmed, standing ash tray. The base had a rounded bottom, filled with lead, and the whole stand tipped forward and began to rock. The nurse stopped it against her hand.

No ashes were seen to spill, but for an instant the air smelled of burnt cigarettes. Then the smell went away.

Aunt Clothilde said, "I wish I could tell what I'm afraid of. But I'm not afraid in words. I wish I could say it now for you to hear. Oh, I wish you might have seen what the wheel did. And us standing there; and Adrianne didn't move. She never moved. I saw one edge of the wheel wobble with my eyes, I saw it loose and wobbly. But I didn't see it come off, that was too quick. And Edmund spun around three times on the railing, like a dancer, and he stopped, facing us, exact, he stopped and stood like a dancer. With that twisted, round metal thing from the wheel stuck part way out of his side. And his arm near torn off at the elbow, hanging there by the coat sleeve. He stood and watched Adrianne, and the red gush pumped out of his arm and splashed all over the sidewalk, and it went on pumping. But Adrianne never moved. The rasp, the scream the truck made when it went down on one fender there, and the sparks, and the screams, the truck screamed before it came to a stop. And the driver was swearing, he certainly was swearing. He swore and swore, I hope to tell you, such words he did use, I never heard him then, but I remember it now. And Edmund and Adrianne just standing facing each other on the sidewalk, staring at each other. And Adrianne didn't move; not even when Edmund leaned back against the railing and dropped in his own mess. Not when all those people came, and there was a crowd, and some woman held Edmund's arm this way to keep all his blood from spilling out. Not till the ambulance got there, Adrianne didn't move. All that time, from right before it happened, she just stood there. Till the doctor took her by the elbow and led her and me to the ambulance, and then she let him lead her. But if he hadn't wanted to, she'd still be there. Because she did not move. She did not. You didn't. You didn't, you didn't move."

"Hush," Mrs. Rhale said, "for God. Don't get her upset too. Hush, dear, talk to me. Talk to us. Don't talk like that to Adrianne, you'll get her upset too."

"Right," said the nurse.

"Upset?" Aunt Clothilde laughed a sob into her handkerchief. "Adrianne? Upset? Upset? *Upset?*"

Mrs. Rhale said fast to the nurse, "I think she likely might turn hysterical, dear."

"Not turn," Aunt Clothilde said. She giggled and said, "I already am. Not turn. I'm just as hysterical as I'm ever going to turn. Blind, are you? You blind?"

The nurse said, "A bit of smelling salts, I think."

"No. Her pills."

"Just stand where you are," Aunt Clothilde said. "Don't think. Just stay there. I don't need smelling salts. I can hush up when I want to. You watch."

A stillness groped back into the room, and started to spread through the high air.

Aunt Clothilde kept her handkerchief tight over her mouth. Her choked sobs made her look and sound as though she were retching.

"Good for you," Mrs. Rhale said. "Fine."

"Right," said the nurse.

The stillness.

The nurse wiped her hands for business. She stepped under the fan and put her right arm up to the beaded chin.

From the window, out of the heat, somebody could be heard humming below. It sounded like Sterling, who sometimes hummed without knowing.

. . . And Adrianne said, "No."

"What?"

"Please."

"What?"

"No."

". . . What, honey?"

Adrianne said, "No, please don't put the light on." Her voice caught soft in the air.

"Oh," said the nurse. "I beg your pardon."

"Thank you," said Adrianne. She uncrossed her ankles and rose, in one movement. Then, lowering her finger tips, she touched the top of Aunt Clothilde's head, and she leaned down and kissed her there.

"Oh, Princess," Mrs. Rhale said.

Adrianne straightened. She moved forward, under the fan.

The nurse said, "Miss, can I do something to help?"

"No, thank you," said Adrianne.

"Did you hear what I came to say before, about their bringing him down soon now?"

"No," said Adrianne. "Yes, no matter. Thank you very much," she said.

"It's such a sad human tragedy."

". . . Yes." Adrianne walked past the nurse to the middle of the room. Then she turned sharp to the left. She walked two steps more over the empty floor, and turned to the right, and went directly to the window seat. When she got there, she eased down and slid into it. With the point of one shoe tucked behind the other ankle, she sat and watched the close screen.

The nurse shook her head. She shook it again, and came up to Mrs. Rhale. "His daughter?" she said.

Mrs. Rhale nodded.

"Such . . . such . . ." The nurse said: "Such a lady."

Reflected sun from the ground beyond the oak tree caught; held in a circle around the brown gold of Adrianne's head. The light shone on her like a chaplet.

"So gentle," said the nurse. "Look at how she sits there. Such a lady. That happens to be the loveliest face I ever saw."

"It's the way she uses it," Mrs. Rhale said, wiping under her glasses.

"Why," said the nurse, "she isn't even crying. She was smiling. She even smiled at me."

Aunt Clothilde lifted her handkerchief away from her mouth with care. "Of course," she said. "Of course. Of course she was."

"Smiling," said the nurse. "I never saw such a lady."

Aunt Clothilde said, "Of course. How stupid. You damn fool. Now go back down the hall and whisper some more. Of course she was smiling. Pass over where? Of course she was."

Four weeks after the men known as the Bufardi brothers came to town, it was noticed that Edmund looked tired and considerably older. Yes, he did look older.

The fourth week was when those men confronted Adrianne for the first time in a public place.

She was dressed in clear, steel blue that afternoon—the shade of a fading winter sky; having coffee with Libbie Mills and her daughter in the coffee shop on Court Street. Adrianne had to be home early, and she excused herself and said goodbye at five thirty. The two men were sitting at a small table by the side wall, behind her chair, right where she had to pass. And when Adrianne came near they rose from their seats together; they got up in silence, turned slightly outward, for her to walk by. The whole coffee shop was silent then. Libbie Mills (who had known the men were there for most of an hour) teetered on the edge of a sneeze, looked now as if she'd just been stabbed in the back. Even the lady cashier was frightened, all the fingers of one dead hand pointed up at nothing. Of the people there present, only Adrianne did not hesitate. And as the lady cashier made a croaking sound, Adrianne bowed her head down and to the side toward those two men; gravely, in her porcelain walk, she passed them with her head bowed low. The two men sat again as she wound between the silent tables and turned onto the street, moving with the quiet inertia of her humility. Then afterwards, nobody could say for sure whether she had bowed to them for any reason—even queens are known to bow. Mrs. Mills still could not relax for the sneeze, but she blew her nose back into action. She blew it loud.

Talk was sharpest after that. Many said they hoped Aunt Clothilde would take Adrianne on a swift vacation to New York until something could be done.

Two days later, Edmund was in Pierre's Restaurant, waiting for Adrianne to come and join him for dinner. It was late, eight o'clock of the evening Edmund always went to Pierre's. The restaurant was full to the back room, and Edmund was at his usual table reading a newspaper. He had already said hello to the Wistons, and the Wainscotts, and the Crabbes, who owned Maison Rose, and the Le Veys. The right people (the Friday people) were mostly there. And the men were there too.

They were in the Picture Room, and had not been observed before they entered walking in a decisive line to Edmund's table; they stood on either side of him. Then they spoke low, to speak of what was not heard in full by anyone but Edmund. But Elizabeth Crabbe thought she caught something about their all meeting the next day—about Edmund's seeing them if they would go away immediately from the restaurant. Edmund would not look at the men; he kept his eyes pointed into the center of his own table while he talked. His back was hard, and his muscular fist white and bumpy around the bunched newspaper. Mr. Crabbe, Mr. Wainscott, Edmund's friends were all ready to come and stand by him. But Edmund would not look up.

And then Adrianne was in the doorway.

Mrs. Wainscott grinned like a mad woman and waved to divert her.

Adrianne watched over every head to her father. Crossing into the room she only said, "Good evening," with that gentle nod, and smiling as she passed each table. Her gray silk skirt swished crisp and clean. She nodded to everyone. And she didn't stop walking until she reached Edmund's side.

"Good evening," she said.

Edmund got to his feet.

The two men bent slightly from the waist. Then they started around the table, their backs to her, heading for the other door.

Adrianne said, "Please, Father." She said: "Please."

Edmund said loud, "Gentlemen."

The men stood still where they were. The older one turned.

"I am quite sure," said Edmund, "you did not mean rudeness to my daughter. This lady is my daughter. Not a waitress." His voice was wrenched out, separated from him.

The other man turned; they both bowed again.

Edmund said, "Mr. and Mr. Bufardi. My daughter, Adrianne Legrange Choate."

Adrianne went forward. She said, "I'm so glad." She gave her hand to the older of the men. He took it and bent over it. The other one took it from him.

The Wainscotts and George Crabbe were standing at their tables.

Adrianne smiled. She said, "*Buona sera, signori. Finalmente.* My father does not speak Italian any more, but I have studied it. Perhaps someday soon we will speak in Italian, if you can excuse me for speaking badly. I have not had much practice."

The beautiful man swallowed, and seemed to have done it the wrong way. He coughed.

Adrianne said, "Are you ill?"

The man shook his head.

"This is the dangerous weather," she said, "you must be careful here now. The heavy cold will come soon. I hope you are not angry with me, I didn't stop to speak with you the other afternoon because you had not yet met my father. Did you understand?"

"Yes," the older man said. A smile grew against his face.

Adrianne said, "Thank you. I'm happy you have met him now. I did want to talk. I wanted to ask if you had found your way in the cemetery."

Nobody spoke.

Then the older man said, "Please?"

"The cemetery. I know the grave is hard to find. The cemetery has grown so much since then. And they've changed it, the west gate used to be the main gate, now it's not and they've let it rust; it isn't used, it hasn't been used for years. The grave is difficult to find from the main entrance now unless you know where it is. But it is the only one with red roses there. Did you have trouble? Could you find somebody to help you? I'm told my sister doesn't go there at all; I know it must be painful for her. Did you find somebody else to help you?"

The older man said, ". . . No. No, miss."

"You did find it?"

"No."

"You didn't."

The man said, "We do not know."

Adrianne frowned, smiling. "Pardon me," she said. "Pardon, it's my fault I don't understand what you mean."

"We do not . . ." The man said: "We . . . do not go there. We do not know this cemetery."

Adrianne said, "Oh." Her eyes watered. She said quietly, "Oh." Then she said, "I am awkward. Forgive me, I am . . . how could you go, knowing . . . knowing . . . knowing no one here? Not even Father, how could you go? You're alone here. I'm sorry, I should have thought. I am awkward."

The older man looked at his feet, and then he looked at his friend. But the beautiful man was staring at Adrianne; he had his mouth open.

She said, "I said I was glad we have met. Now I'm doubly glad, now you can go with me. I go every Sunday morning, you can come with me. I take white roses to my mother, and I take red roses to the other grave. Will you come this Sunday?"

The older man said, "We . . . ah . . ."

The beautiful man said, "No."

". . . No?" said Adrianne.

"No, we are leaving . . . soon. Before then."

The older man snorted his breath in.

"Yes," said the beautiful man, "we are leaving sooner . . . before this day, Sunday. We are leaving. *Scusatemi, signorina.* We are leaving. *Ci scusiamo di tutto, signorina. Piacere, signorina.*"

Then Adrianne's hand was taken, and the men had bent over it once more; and sooner than anyone moved, they were gone.

The men were never seen again.

Adrianne gazed after them. She looked at the vacant doorway.

Back of her, Mrs. Wainscott said, "My dear, what a horrible experience. Really honestly. Such men."

Adrianne pivoted, her face pulled taut and sad. She sat in her place by her father.

Two dishes clinked, then some glasses. Mr. Wainscott took his hand off a big waiter he had stopped in the act of serving. Sounds rushed into a vacuum of no sound.

Mrs. Wainscott came to the table, with a long white napkin dangling in her hand. Edmund remained standing. Mrs. Wainscott said to Adrianne, "Don't get up. Dear, you mustn't be hurt. You really mustn't. Don't fret, don't. Those men were just pretending to be . . . who you think. You shouldn't have humiliated yourself in front of them that way, you really honestly mustn't fret."

"She didn't humiliate herself," said Mr. Wainscott, coming up.

"Well, but she shouldn't have spoken to them at all. They were not what they were pretending to be. You comprehend, dear?" Mrs. Wainscott was a thin, embarrassed woman. She stooped over and patted the air around Adrianne, and the napkin bounced.

"I do," said Adrianne. "Yes, thank you. I see."

"How about some wine, Edmund?" said Mr. Wainscott.

"No, thanks," said Edmund, "we don't drink much wine." Standing behind her chair, he pressed close against Adrianne's back. He placed one hand on each of her shoulders.

"Oh, you," said Mrs. Wainscott. "Come on. A half-bottle."

"Well," Edmund said, "a half-bottle, yes. We might. Today we might, a half. A half-bottle might be nice, we accept. We do drink, you know, in moderation. We accept. Don't we, Princess?"

"Thank you," said Adrianne.

"We believe nothing too much can happen to you if you stick to the middle of the road. Don't we? Princess? We try to prove it."

"Yes," said Adrianne.

Edmund said low, ". . . Something wrong?"

"Nothing," she said. But she did not smile. "He was so . . . shamed."

Mr. Wainscott burst out laughing.

Edmund chuckled with him.

"I think not," said Mrs. Wainscott, "I doubt it. I wouldn't say say shamed. More like scared. But shamed would have been the least of what he'd have been if I had told him what I had in my mind."

"Whatever did you have in your mind?" said Mr. Wainscott. "Fie on you," he said. He laughed.

Other voices took the laugh and used it for different things. There was a quick merriment in the room; held, passed around; blown with the smoke in dense clouds—small tufts of clouds that wafted into a flat blue layer under the ceiling. The layer was of laughter and smoke.

Adrianne whispered, "I did. I shamed him so."

Edmund's fingers tightened on her shoulders while Mr. Wainscott went on talking.

$\mathcal{E}arly$ $\mathcal{E}vening$

1

IT WAS NOT that it was easier for Adrianne to sit straight. She could not have sat any other way.

The delicate, sharp-honed humming cut through the heat around the hospital with one last note, and ended.

Adrianne focused her eyes on the screen; then on a fly that was squatting on the other side, cleaning its front legs. She focused through the screen out over the bright ground beyond the oak—past the gray strings of swirled moss hung sleeping like bats, in green shadow. The earth was hazed, the grass was burnt. Old rain steamed up from deep to the sun. But the top earth was already dusty. Blistering orange had spread over the ground.

Adrianne pulled back her point in vision to the screen. And it was lost there now. The fly was gone. The screen had no center and no end. The screen beat gently against her eyes, evenly; bigger, smaller; light and dark and lighter; it beat with her own pulse. The moan of the fan behind was set in the sundown day. And the screen beat between her and the sheets of orange earth that shone and burned like hell-shadows, from the dying sun in her eyes.

Christmas.

Edmund's wide hand came between her and the candle. He lifted the candle in its long, fluted-silver stick, and put it on the

bookcase over her head. "No," he said. "Don't touch fire. Fire
burns."

Fire burns.

Everybody told her she was tall for her age, but thin; but beautifully proportioned, they said: she will be a lovely young lady someday. She was five years old and nine weeks.

Edmund slipped a hand under each of her armpits, and raised
her off the floor. He bent her back and dangled her there, himself
laughing, her waves of hair shaking straight down behind. Then he
sat her in the big, upholstered armchair, red and firm and moun-
tainous.

Fire burns.

Edmund pushed up his coat sleeve. He unbuttoned the round
gold cuff link, and turned the cuff back, and back again. "Look,"
he said. He held his arm down for her to see.

On the inside of his arm, there was a place where the hair
couldn't grow. A splotchy place—shaped unshapen, like milk
spilled on the carpet. The skin there was too pink, and it shone
too slick for skin. It was like the wax drops as they fell from the
pink Christmas candle.

Fire burns.

Edmund said, "See that? There? See?" he said.

"Yes, Daddy."

" 'Daddy' is for babies. Not for friends."

". . . Yes, Father."

"That's better. See that?"

"Yes."

"Fire burns," he said. "That's where I got burned. See? See
what it did?"

"How?" said Adrianne.

"I'm telling you, I was burned. When I was a little boy. I spilled
hot grease on me. It burned me."

Adrianne said, "Not fire?"

"It's the same thing," said Edmund. "Heat and fire. Fire makes
heat, and heat makes fire. But it all burns. Don't ever touch fire.
You stay away from the fire. And from the hot heat."

"When is it hot?" said Adrianne.

". . . Well, when it's red. When a thing gets too hot, it turns red."

The chair was red.

Adrianne looked up at the thin candle, long and yellow, held in silver—and the pointed oval flame on top. The flame was orange.

She shook her head.

"Now, look," said Edmund. "You don't have to understand about it now. Just believe me."

"I want to feel it," she said.

"No."

"I once felt it. I once lit a match all by myself. And I once felt the stove in the kitchen, and it was nice."

"No," said Edmund.

"It was. It was nice."

"No," said Edmund; "nice to stay away from. Only nice if you don't get too near. If you get too near, you get burned. Fire burns." He reached to the side, and took the candlestick. Then he squatted in front of her. With the candlestick in one hand, he took her wrist in the other, and held her fingers up by the flame, away from it. "Here it feels nice," he said. "But no closer than here." He let go her wrist.

Adrianne looked at him.

"No closer," he said.

"I just want to feel the burn once."

"No," said Edmund. "You mayn't. Fire burns. Fire burned Father on his arm."

"Grease," said Adrianne.

Edmund said, "It's the same thing, I told you. You don't have to feel it. It hurts, it's not nice. You don't ever have to feel anything that hurts; Father felt those things already, so he knows. You don't ever have to get hurt. Father got hurt for you, he won't let you get hurt. You don't have to feel it; just believe me."

Adrianne looked back at the candle. She closed her fingers flat. Then she couldn't see the flame. But the light came right through between her fingers, and it made the skin there glow like the sun through a red lollipop. The warm was nice.

When she separated her fingers and saw the flame again, it was shivering: laughing at her.

Two flies, both on her left, faced in the same direction, one higher, both on the outside; with granulated eyes, two flies were on the screen. They had big, busy heads, twirling them. One was begging—the simple one.

It takes a certain kind of fly to beg; not the kind that knows.

Behind her, there was another nurse in the room now, undertalking to Mrs. Rhale. "Dignity . . . real . . . Everybody loves . . ." "Yes, oh yes." ". . . only know a person, really, by how they behave during these difficult moments in life." "Yes."

It takes a certain kind of fly to beg. Fire burns.

Nurses can get red if they get hot enough; but they don't burn. Nurses never burn.

"I'm not a nurse," said Miss Duff, "I'm a nanny. I'm a British nanny."

"Yes," said Adrianne.

"Call me Nanny."

"Yes," said Adrianne.

"Yes, what?"

"Yes, Nanny."

"Right you are," said Miss Duff. "Now let's get our boots on, there's the dear."

Adrianne said, "Nobody wears high boots but me. Girls don't wear high boots, not even Evelyn Wisterwood, and she's lame. I can't run in high boots."

"You don't have to run," said Miss Duff. "There is no saying you have to run. Our daddy simply wants us to go for a walk with him. Not run."

"Father. 'Daddy' is for babies."

"What, love?"

Adrianne said, "I call him Father."

"Did he tell you to?"

"Yes."

"*Right you are,*" *said Miss Duff.* "*Father.*"

The first boot was for the left foot. It was thick, lined with rabbit fur. It was hard to put on, and it came all the way up to her knee; then it zipped. Then it cut under her knee. It weighed a lot.

Adrianne said, "*I would like to run in the snow.*"

"*You might fall,*" *said Miss Duff, panting. She was working the other leg into the other boot.*

"*I would like to fall.*"

"*Why?*"

"*I would like to feel the snow.*"

"*Make a snowball,*" *said Miss Duff. She squatted down and sat on the carpet.* "*This here is a bit of a struggle. New boots are always a bit of a struggle until they get used to us. Remember that. I'm new to you too, but I'm not a boot. Ha ha.*"

"*I don't want to touch it,*" *said Adrianne;* "*I want to feel it.*"

"*What?*"

"*The snow.*"

"*Yes, love,*" *said Miss Duff.* "*Now simply hold it out stiff, and point the toes, but not too much. Simply hold it out stiff.*"

"*I am,*" *said Adrianne.*

"*Right you are,*" *said Miss Duff,* "*simply keep doing it. Oo-ooble. Did I hurt you?*"

"*No.*"

"*Right you are,*" *Miss Duff said.* "*Nanny wouldn't hurt us for the world. Zippy wippy. There, now. Well done us.*"

Adrianne let her heavy foot rest on the carpet. "*I would very much like to fall in the snow.*"

"*Why?*"

"*. . . Because.*"

"*Because why?*"

"*Just because.*"

"*That's no reason,*" *Miss Duff said.* "*It's a silly idea. Fall in the snow, indeed. If we fall down, we hurt ourselves. Even in the snow. And the snow is too cold. Then we catch cold.*"

"*Fire is too hot,*" *said Adrianne, softly.*

"*Right you are,*" *Miss Duff said.* "*Fire is too hot, and the snow is too cold.*"

"*Oh,*" *said Adrianne.*

"*Do you know what our daddy, I mean to say our father told Nanny, when Nanny came to work for him? Do you know what he told Nanny we always do? And why we always do it?*"

"*Yes.*"

Miss Duff wrinkled her face. "*What?*"

"*We always stick to the middle of the road. So nothing can hurt us.*"

The wrinkles all went upwards. "*Quite right,*" *said Miss Duff;* "*how did you know?*"

"*I know,*" *said Adrianne.*

"*How?*"

"*It was what my mother said.*"

"*Oh. Do we remember our mother?*"

"*No,*" *said Adrianne.*

"*Erm. Well. Never you mind. Now let's get Nanny up on her feet. Nanny must go on a diet. Oo-ooble. Nanny weighs . . . too much. The-ere we are; well done Nanny. Never mind, now. You have two mothers now. Aunt Clothilde and Nanny.*"

Adrianne said, "*No.*"

"*What?*"

"*I don't want a mother.*"

"*. . . I didn't hear you right, love.*"

"*My mother is dead. I don't want a new mother.*"

"*Well. Erm. Well. Well, Dad-uh-Father is waiting downstairs to take us out to the park to play with the other little girls. Then we come back and have fried chicking for lunch.*"

"*Chicken.*"

"*Chicking.*"

"*Chicken.*"

"*Chicking,*" *said Miss Duff,* "*pronounce each word to its fullest.*"

Adrianne said, "*I can't play with these boots on.*"

"*Yes, you can,*" *Miss Duff said.* "*Try. Everything is a matter of trying. If we try, we can do anything we want to in life. Did Dad-uh-*

Father explain to us how when he was young he went mountain
climbing in Italy, and he sat down too long and froze his uh, and
he sat down and froze himself?"

"Yes," said Adrianne. "He showed me."

"No, love, he couldn't have," said Miss Duff. "Not there. He
couldn't even show Nanny. It's in an unfortunate place," she said.

"I know. I saw it."

"How?"

"He showed me."

"How? Never mind, I don't want to know. Now off we go downstairs. Father is waiting."

Adrianne leaned with a hand on the back of the chair while she
stood up. Then, when she was sure of her balance, she clumped
across the high-tufted carpet to the door.

"Aren't we going to kiss our nanny goodbye?"

Adrianne clumped around in a wide half-circle, and came back.

"There now. Right you are. Now don't we want a new mother?"

"No," Adrianne said, heading for the door.

"Well. Poor, poor Aunt Clothilde."

"Aunt Clothilde is an aunt," said Adrianne. She opened the door.

"I'm not an aunt."

"No," said Adrianne. "You're not."

"Well? What am I?"

Adrianne said, "A nanny." She went out, and closed the door
after her.

She closed it with one arm.

Aunt Clothilde was sobbing again.

Mrs. Rhale was not.

One of the flies was gone. Not the begging one. Let a fly do your
begging; please God is for flies.

The screen was dirty on one lower corner. Through that corner,
holding her body to the left, Adrianne could see the front half of
the Cadillac parked on the shell driveway. Sterling was there. He
was resting on the dusty black fender, slumped, his hands on his
legs. His uniform was neater than usual, and he had a new cap
she hadn't noticed before. The cap was the same as the uniform,

not as dark as Sterling. And he didn't have the radio on. Sterling always played the radio when he had to wait and was tired of humming. Edmund didn't like for him to. It drained the battery, Edmund said; but Sterling played it anyhow, because he was old, and he knew Edmund wouldn't fire him, and because he really liked music. But not now.

"Who is the best?"

"Bach, Beethoven, Mozart, Brahms, you can pick any one," said Edmund; "they're all good."

Adrianne said, "Yes, I know. But which is the best?"

"That's a matter of taste."

"I know."

"I can have my taste," Edmund said, "and you can have a different taste."

". . . No," said Adrianne.

Edmund chuckled.

Aunt Clothilde said, "It's taking too long. Why can't they let him finish? My God, why can't they just let him die in peace?"

"Hush up, dear," said Mrs. Rhale. "You hush."

In peace.

A matter of taste. Unburned taste. Never too cold; never used.

Adrianne said, "But I did use myself once."

"What, dear?" said Mrs. Rhale. "Did you want something? Are you all right?"

"No," said Adrianne. "Yes, I am. Thank you."

Mrs. Rhale said, "Dear. Oh, Princess."

Oh, this, Oh that. Tum and a tiddy tum.

> Princess Pea, Princess Pea,
> What have you to say to me?
> Princess Stocking, Princess Glove,
> What have you to say of Love?

"Father made it up."

"No, he didn't," George said. "I heard it already some place."

"No, he made it up."

"Well, and if so, so what? I wouldn't admit to it, myself. Precious, precious, and for what?" George shut his eyes, and got sing-song nasal. "Princess Pea, Princess Pea, what have you to say to me? Prin . . . Princess . . ."

Adrianne said, "Stocking, Princess Glove, what have you to say of Love?"

"Lovely. Wherefore is the deep meaning?"

"No meaning. It's a nonsense poem."

"Hear hear," George said, aiming at a British accent, and quite missing. "There I can agree with you."

The Lexington Avenue drugstore counter was better than Schrafft's for after school. George couldn't really afford Schrafft's, and he wouldn't go Dutch, and it was too cold for a park bench. And they let you sit at the counter with just a Coca-Cola for as long as you wanted. Adrianne and whoever was with her could sit there even without a Coke: the soda jerks both had a crush on her. Everybody who met her had a crush on her—men, women, chil-dren. She was seventeen, and people said she could charm her way into the National City Bank vault. She could because she didn't use charm; she was Adrianne, and she was just as she was.

George said, "Well? . . . when?" George was a man of twenty. The height of a man; eye-colored eyes, and hair-colored hair, a balding spot in the back ("I could have been a priest at no cost.") Hard, round, slender in his many muscles; steel thighs, long and full; a deep skin; big of face, and the bones in his face like morning eggshells, tender. A mouth as warm and painful as his eyes; thick hair shaven from his jowls, smooth and not smooth, sometimes blue. All together.

"When what?" Adrianne said.

"You know what. The date of the evening. Beautiful soup."

". . . Come home and meet father."

"Seems as if I've been saying no to that since the day before I met you."

"And today . . . ?"

"No. I'll always say no." Lightly using two strong fingers, he twirled his glass in its sweat-ring on the brown plastic. A glass will sweat in winter.

Adrianne said, "Then please don't keep asking me for the evening. We have lots to talk about, and we don't have to talk. We can be happy and not talk. It's the wonderful thing."

"I will keep asking," George said. "I will ask you every afternoon. I want to eat with you, and I want to dance with you, and I want you to come up to my salacious apartment, which is one palatial room decorated and furnished distastefully in early lack-of-American funds, and I want to go to bed with you."

"Father . . ."

"I don't want your father," George said, "me, I am attuned to women. Accidentally. Basically."

"Father would . . ."

"No, he wouldn't," George said; "or if so do let's keep it hush-hush. Anyhow, I wouldn't. He's not my type. You are."

Adrianne rubbed over her cheek. Then she pointed a finger and made one small rectangle in the brown plastic with her fingernail. "It's only a question of meeting him."

"That's a big only question."

"It's not his permission. He hasn't given me orders since I was a child. I don't need his permission. You just meet him once, and from then on we go out."

George said, "My intentions are entirely dishonorable."

"He wouldn't ask you that."

"He wouldn't need to, he could smell it. I emanate lecherous animal instincts."

"He wouldn't . . . care."

"Then he's a bad father. There must be enough of the man left in him to care."

"Don't," said Adrianne. "Please don't."

"Hell," George said. He flexed the ends of his fingers, and the glass slid two inches away. "Every single goddam afternoon. You adrenalate my digestion," he said. "I don't like arguing, and I hate arguing with you. It destroys the rest of the evening. And then all I think about the next day is five o'clock and you and here. So I can have my next evening destroyed."

Adrianne said, "I said let's talk about something else. Or not talk." She said, quietly: "That's all I think about too. All day."

"If you only hadn't made it a condition the first time I met you, that would have been that. If you'd told me to pick you up at your apartment, and arranged your schedule accordingly, I would have met your father, and that would have been that. But you made it a social condition. And I won't be social. Sociable, yes; social, no. I outflushed Park Avenue from my blood when I left my own family and got a job. I won't go back into that pitter now. I can't. I would do anything for you, but I can't do that because it would ruin me and you. I can't play the monkey to your father's plush rules. He's no better than my own father, and I didn't do it for him."

Adrianne said, "But you're wrong."

"What?"

"No," she said. "It isn't his rule. I told you, he has no rules for me, not any more. He doesn't have to."

George was holding a cigarette an inch out of the pack. He let the pack fall on the counter. He said, "You can't mean what I think you mean." And he said: ". . . Whose . . . rule is it?"

Looking at him: "Mine," said Adrianne, "I thought you knew."

". . . I don't believe you."

"Oh."

"I . . . don't . . . You don't lie; do you? You never lie."

"I never had to," said Adrianne.

The cigarette was bent double in his hand. "Not even to be kind?"

She shook her head. "Is lying kind?"

George said, "I won't be here tomorrow."

"Oh."

He said, "Or the day after. I've had it."

"I see."

"Do you, I wonder?"

"Yes. Yes, I think so."

George swung away from her. He put out his right hand, flat, *and flatly slapped it on the counter. His head was down, and he studied the hand. Then he took that hand and put it on his hip, and set his head in his other palm.*

She wanted to hold him. And she had not ever wanted to hold anybody.

And he turned to her again.

"You are the most incredible, guileless bitch I ever met," he said. "How the hell I fell in love with you, I don't know. Or care. Yes, I care," he said. "I care to know how I could have managed to live so well and then fall in love with the likes of you. How, how can I love you?"

"You . . . what?"

Princess Pea, Princess Pea.

"Whisper louder," George said.

She did: "You what?"

What have you to say to me?

"Is that all you can say?"

"I . . ."

Princess Stocking, Princess Glove.

"Did you hear what I told you?" George said: "I told you I'm in . . ."

What have you to say of Love?

Adrianne said, "It's a quarter to seven."

". . . Yes." George didn't budge. "Yes, that is probably just exactly what it is."

She slid off the stool onto her feet. Her purse was standing upright on the shelf under the counter. She took it, and then plucked at the skirt of her dress; which was unessential.

George said, "That was unessential."

But she kept on doing it.

"You're neat enough. Too neat. Leave, don't make excuses to stand there. If what you want to do is leave, then leave."

". . . It's a quarter to seven."

"Keep quiet. Did you hear what I told you before?"

Whispering: "Yes."

"Before that, I mean. I said I wouldn't be here tomorrow."

"*I heard you.*"

"*Do you want it that way?*"

"*I . . .*"

"*Yes or no. Plain yes or plain no.*"

"*. . . No.*" *The strap of the bag came off her fingers.*

George stepped down. He stooped, picked up her bag, and dusted it off. He handed it to her.

"*Thank you,*" *she said.*

"Damn thank you. Damn your whole goddam social being. Bearing. Social bearing. Can't you breathe? You can't breathe," he said.

"I don't know what . . . you mean."

"Yes you do. That was a lie."

It was. She said, "Yes. That was a lie."

"I thought you never lied."

"I never did."

"How romantic," George said. "Her first lie." But his tone was gentle when he said it.

". . . I'm going now."

"With your rule? Taking your rule with you?"

"Yes."

"You know," George said, "you made one slip. You said it wasn't his rule. You said he didn't hold any rules for you any more. But you said, 'He doesn't have to.' I think I begin to make sense of that."

"I'm going now."

"Go," George said.

But as she passed him, he put a tight hand over one of hers. He said, "Five o'clock?"

And the words made two hot breaths on her forehead.

"Yes," said Aunt Clothilde. "Of course."

Mrs. Rhale was coughing, and getting the spittle up.

"Of course," said Aunt Clothilde. "Of course. He's already dead. They're just cutting around on his post-mortem."

Mrs. Rhale choked. "Oh, dear God," she said. "Dear. Aunt Clothilde, Clothilde, please. Clothilde, hush."

Aunt Clothilde said, "That's what they're doing. Those doctors."

"Hush, dear, hush."

"Those doctors," Aunt Clothilde said; "those doctors, those stupid doctors."

Edmund said, "And what's his name?"

"George Solomon."

". . . A Jew?"

"I don't know," said Adrianne.

"Sounds to be," said Aunt Clothilde. "Solomon."

"Well, none of my business," Edmund said. "You have your own life."

"My own?" said Adrianne.

"You have your own tastes, I mean. Your own set of values."

"No."

"You're seventeen. You can take care of yourself."

"Yes," said Adrianne. "That I can do. That is all I can do."

Aunt Clothilde's glasses dropped, hanging on one ear. She snapped her hand up to the gold stem, and set it right. Then she went on with her knitting.

Edmund chuckled, low. He said, "That's a lot. More than a lot. If I've taught you that, I can die happy. What more can a father teach? The rest comes with time."

Thin of voice, Adrianne said, "Does it?"

"Yes, naturally it does. Better to you than to anybody." Edmund sat in the big sofa, and stretched his legs out on the floor. "You never made a mistake, know that? True, Clothilde? Never once in her whole life. I was thinking the other day." Edmund's voice went deep. "It's true. You don't have anything to worry for, Princess. You won't make any mistakes. Nothing will ever happen to you. You don't even know how to make a mistake, you never made one in your life. You never lied, and you never got yourself hurt, and you never once made a mistake."

"No," said Adrianne. "I never had to. You did all that for me."

Aunt Clothilde lowered her knitting into her lap.

Edmund said, "What?" He said: "For a second . . ." And he

chuckled another time. He said: "Well, however you meant it, you're right. I did do all that when I was young. And I've told you I did. Before I married your mother. I'm not ashamed of it. Not now. I made enough mistakes for eight people, let alone two. Yes, I did all that for you."

Adrianne whispered, "I know."

"Don't stand up there like you were on jury trial," Edmund said. "Come sit here by me. Remember when you were little? Come stretch out and put your head in my lap. Like when you were little."

Adrianne picked her way over the patterned carpet.

It was eight precise steps to the sofa.

And the cushions were the same. The feel of Edmund's groin under the back of her neck was almost the same.

Edmund said, "Go on out with your new boy friend. Let the Jew boy take you out, Princess. Why do I have to meet him? Do I have to meet him?"

"Yes," said Adrianne.

"Nuts," said Edmund, "why? Why do you always insist I meet them? You've got lots of time. When you fall in love, that will be time enough, Princess Pea. When you're ready to get married, that will be time for me to meet the man."

"No," said Adrianne. "That will be too late."

Edmund lay the round part of his thumb on her throat, and moved it. He stroked her there. "Princess," he said, "let the Jew boy take you out. I don't want to meet him. I know you, that's enough for me. I don't have to tell you what Jews are. Besides, this boy might be different. None of my business. You'll find out for yourself; you never made a mistake in your whole life. I've made enough in mine for us both, and I've suffered enough to value people, Princess. And I couldn't trust anybody evermore as much as I trust you." His deep voice made his entire groin buzz; it stroked her, like his thumb.

Aunt Clothilde rose. She limped evenly out of the room.

". . . care, I want Sterling up here now."

"But, dear . . ."

Aunt Clothilde said, "Don't dear me. Just get him up here. I'll go down and get him up myself. He's worked for Edmund's family twelve years running, and when we came back down South he quit his job and came to work for Edmund again. And I want him up here."

"Dear," said Mrs. Rhale. "They absolutely aren't going to allow a colored visitor on this floor. They wouldn't allow one in this hospital."

"I couldn't care less what they allow," said Aunt Clothilde. "I want him up here for Edmund to die. I'll go down and get him myself. I . . . want . . . him . . . up . . . here."

"Shhhh. Shhh."

"Don't shush me; I'll do it myself."

"All right, dear. All . . . right. I'll go see what I can do."

"Don't see," Aunt Clothilde said. "Just get Sterling up here. If they won't take him in the elevator, walk him up the stairs. But get him up here."

"All right, dear."

Princess Stocking, Princess Glove.

The dark smell of cooked garlic. The hall was cold, drafty; dark.

Soiled walls. Dust on the unwaxed wood floor. Some light up the stairwell, the sliced shadows of the railings and banister.

"There's nothing up there," the woman's voice said. "Hall closet's been shut for four years, already. Bottom half's full of crates. Couldn't fit anything in there if I wanted to, except up in the top half, and the rats are particular. There's nothing up there. If it was a letter, they would have put it in your box, and if it was too big to put in your box or if it was a package, and if you wasn't at home, then they would have left it with me. Same as always. You got me out of my bath."

George's voice sounded ten years too young for George. It said, "I just thought there might be some place else."

"No place else," said the woman's voice, "because it don't exist, another place. And anyway I'm here all the time. I was sitting in my bath when you rang."

"Oh. Sorry."

"Uh-huh. Maybe they slipped it under your door. Did you look careful?"

"No. I'm sure not. She wouldn't have gone upstairs."

". . . What's she, crippled?"

"No," George said. "But she isn't the type of girl would go upstairs alone to a man's apartment."

"Uh-huh. Is she by any chance between one and three years old?"

"No," George said.

The woman said, "That's the type of girl won't go upstairs alone to a man's apartment. After that they can walk."

"This one wouldn't," George said.

"Uh-huh."

"She really wouldn't."

"Uh-huh."

"You don't have to believe me."

"Thanks," the woman said.

George said, "Well, thank you, anyway. If she comes, let me know right away, will you?"

"Sure. So what's she extract from, the foreign?"

"No. American."

"She can read English?"

"Oh, yes."

"Ever see a bell button, the lady?"

". . . Sure."

"Well," said the woman, "now after she reads the name on your box and pushes your bell under it, I will know somehow and I will get up out of my bath again, and I will rush out here dripping wet in the cold with a towel wrapped around me like I am now; and whistle."

"Thanks," George said. "Sorry for the trouble. I meant if she comes here to your apartment."

"She's likely to do that," the woman said, ". . . through two closed doors and a shower curtain, she will recognize in me a mother. And it's no trouble. By then I'll be able to whistle on three different notes all at the same time, with my mouth wide open. I'll have triple pneumonia."

"*Oh. Sorry.*"

"*I can't imagine what for,*" she said. "*I haven't enjoyed myself so much since my husband died. Unless it was that time I was seven months pregnant and sat down naked on one of Mr. Shönberg's live lobsters.*"

"*Oh. How did it get into your apartment?*"

"*Everything gets into my apartment,*" the woman said, "*you shouldn't think of yourself as a priority. That's what landladies are for. Silly questions; dead men; and live lobsters.*"

George said, "*She left a message in the drugstore for me to come straight back to my apartment building.*"

"*Uh-huh. Apartment building. So do tell me more.*"

"*That's all. But there must be a letter around here someplace.*"

"*I see what you mean. Would you like to come in and look under the bed?*"

"*No, I . . .*"

"*Why don't you do that, already? She might have walked in here and left it under the bed. I was in the bath so I wouldn't really know. And there's only a double Yale lock on this door and a chain bolt inside, so she probably walked right on in and left it under the bed, yet. Most likely place. I never keep a thing under there. Not since Mr. Wielmann left for Chicago.*"

George said, "*Just look down, will you Mrs. Stein? Maybe she pushed it under your door?*"

"*I did, already. She didn't. Now what makes you think she would do an ordinary thing like that?*"

"*I . . . well, she mightn't have wanted to disturb you in your bath.*"

"*No? I can't imagine why not,*" said the woman. "*Can you?*"

George said, "*Mrs. Stein, I'm in love.*"

"*Huh-uh, you're kidding me,*" she said. "*Making fun with an old lady, already.*"

"*No.*"

"*Really? The amazement is too much. It don't show at all, I would never have guessed.*"

"*. . . I am, though.*"

"Ever been that way before?"

"No."

"You'll get used to it," the woman said. "Like getting triple pneumonia. It's just the first time it bothers you."

"Oh. Well, I'd better let you get back to your bath."

"What bath?" the woman said. "Whatever for?"

"I'll see you later, Mrs. Stein."

"Yes, indeed. Come back in about five minutes. And bring a priest. I'll be dead, already."

A door closed. A lock. A bolt.

His footsteps.

He might leave.

His footsteps on the stairs. Creaking. He came up slowly, creaking. One flight up. Then he coughed. Then he started up again, faster, with his shadow on the wall.

Adrianne leaned back into the dark corner, and measured his footsteps with her heart.

Aunt Clothilde said, "Sterling, is that you running up those stairs?"

"Yes, ma'am." In the waiting room now.

"Why were you running? Where's Gwendolyn, where's Mrs. Rhale?"

"She's downstairs arguing, ma'am. They didn't want to let me come up. She done told me to run it, and she stayed downstairs to argue."

"Good for her, I didn't think she had that much guts. You run fast for an old man. Now sit down over there. Anywhere. Sit down in one of those chairs."

"Ma'am, right in here with you-all?"

"Just sit down over there like I'm telling you. Sit down."

"Yes, ma'am."

Aunt Clothilde said, "And wait."

Wait. With a begging fly.

Marry is an interjection from Shakespeare.

Princess Stocking, Princess Glove, Princess . . .

The flat rolling of his hips—the flat, tender rolling, tense;

shaped to the outline of an egg; joining them in its own live rhythm. A rhythm for a swing, if you could swing up over the bar, around, back again. Wherever she put her hands, every section of his mahogany body moved in time. His mouth was one integral part of that. When she opened her eyes and saw the walls around them, the room was doing it too.

He said one thing, just once. A nonsensical thing, voiceless, and incredibly anxious. He said, "Baby."

But she did not speak: had not spoken at all.

And before—he had only talked once.

Before. After he came up the stairs; after he halted on the fifth step from the top and saw her feet in a patch of light, and looked up and saw her. After he held still and stared at her for half an age. And then walked slowly up those five steps and across the hollow floor, never halting again, slowly walking until he had walked right into her.

The door open; open for them both. Herself ahead into the blackful room and the stale, urgent air. Then dark yellow light from two small lamps. Nothing overhead. No snap from behind her; the turning, slipping hit of a lock; and when she turned, she did it in his arms. His soft hair. The strength of him, and his soft hair. And the darkness of the dimming yellow light.

George stepped back four paces. He grew taller; he was electric in his eyes. He said, "Now I cannot tolerate buttons." And this was not the young voice she had heard downstairs.

Then Adrianne put her hands behind her, and watched him while she undid her dress.

Naked, waiting on the bed. The bathroom light out, and George coming from the darkness. The yellow lamps red on his body, shining there. Smooth red light; and the red cut in him. Smoothly glowing skin. Skin that was warm and was soft and deep and dull and textured to the eye, shining where it bulged over round muscles. The shadow of hair only on his forearms and on his legs, around his long thighs, sloping in all the way to the hip. The most perfectly fit legs. There was the man's property, swollen, standing out ahead to point the way. And a body down from shoulders. And all this made a fist-sized rock inside her ribs, and it was so fantastic, it was all his.

Swinging down over her.

Then, in the fury of the room, the peace, the rightness. Showing her to help him. Screaming dumb with joy, then the first was over and done, and they were together.

And that part of herself left alone to wait, dizzy in doubt—to undream dreams of wild sensation. Feeling; and no sensation. Nothing but the roaring of his groins. Together and alone for her. The quickening roll, still he was so gentle. He was so much too mild till he lost his breath at the end.

And then the peace of the room was the fury. And the fury was better fear.

And still he held over her, in her, holding her there.

So fearful it was in that pain born from a used violence of caring, she knew she had never known real tenderness before.

Finally—lying back from her: "God. Good God."

His God.

On his side, one arm around her belly. "Darling; I did . . . hurt you."

". . . I . . . think so," said Adrianne. "Oh, yes."

"Darling, darling. Forgive . . . me." He rested his lips on her shoulder.

"No. No; no, oh no," Adrianne said. "That is why I'm here. Yes," she said. "Yes, I think it's all right. I think you did."

". . . Darling."

"Yes," said Adrianne. "That was there. I think so. I'm almost sure."

George said, "God. I never let loose that way in my life. Except when I was fourteen, one night. In my pants. When a grown woman made me kiss her. It was different then." He said: "I guess I never loved before. I guess . . . I never did it with love."

Adrianne shivered.

"Hey." He took the bedcovers in his hand. "Lift up," he said. "Cover up, quick."

"I'm not cold."

"Not . . . not much heat in here. Only three hours in the morning, and three in the evening. Got to buy an electric heater. It's always too cold."

"I'm not too cold," said Adrianne.

"You must be."

"No."

"You must be," he said. "It's cold in here. Everybody . . . It's cold in here."

"No," she said, "I'm not too cold."

"Darling." George opened a drawer in the bedside table; he pulled out something white. He said, "Here. Take care." And when he'd handed it to her, he said, "I am your husband now. Now you do as I say. It would be perfectly ridiculous for us to do the social thing and get married. I am already your husband. Marry is an interjection from Shakespeare. Marriage would be an insult to both of us that would require the greatest love and the greatest understanding to overlook. So let's overlook it," he said, "let's get married."

Adrianne said, "Oh."

"That all you have to say?"

". . . Yes." It was.

"You're not seventeen a month yet."

"Not quite."

"Near a year to go. No. Can't wait. Have to meet your father, get his permission. Never thought I'd be going back social wanting to. Nicey nicey; I can do it, too. Know that? I can really do it when I want. When I really want. Watch me. You watch me meet your father."

Adrianne said, "No."

"Huh? What?"

"No," she said, "Not now."

"What? Before it was every day, and now it's not now?" George lumped his big shoulders. "Crazy. Darling, cover up, you are going to catch cold."

"I'm not too cold."

"Well, you'd better get things ready with your father, that's all I can say. You must know what you're doing. But don't let it take too long, that's all I can say."

"...No."

He said, "I'm your husband now."

"Oh," said Adrianne.

"Do that again."

"...Do what?"

George said, "Make your mouth like that again."

And Edmund said, "I don't know where the hell I got this cold, I haven't been out more than five nights in two weeks."

"No," said Adrianne. "You haven't."

"Can't figure where I could have got it. Not in all this heat. So much steam heat in this apartment you can't get the dry out of your nose. Nobody I know has a cold. I've been using the camel's-hair overcoat, with the collar turned up, and I haven't been out of doors more than five nights in two weeks."

"...No."

"Neither have you."

"I haven't, no."

"But you stay out every afternoon late enough."

"Yes, I do," said Adrianne.

"Two weeks now, you can't make it home for supper."

"Yes."

"You stay out. And I catch cold."

"Yes," said Adrianne. "I see."

"Who is it, the Jew boy? What's his name?"

"Solomon."

"Solomon what?"

"George Solomon."

"That the one been keeping you out in the afternoons?"

"Yes."

"You stay out; and I catch cold. Still doesn't care to come and meet me, no?"

"Yes," said Adrianne. "He wants to now."

266

"He does?"

"Yes."

"You want to bring him?"

"I'd rather not," said Adrianne.

"No?"

"No," she said. "Not unless you tell me to."

Edmund said, "That's funny." He said: "Been out with anybody else lately?"

"No."

"That's funny." Watching her: "Mrs. Nelson's boy wants to take you out. Edith Nelson. Boy's named John. Edith asked me to fix it up for him. Boy's shy, she said. Wants to take you out."

"Really?" said Adrianne.

"Yes. He does," Edmund said. "How about this Saturday night?"

"If you tell me to."

"I wouldn't tell you to."

". . . If you want me to."

"All right. I'll fix it up for you. Nice family, the Nelson's." Edmund sneezed again.

"Are they?"

He said, "I don't know where I could have got this damn cold."

And George said, "I don't care who or why. I said no."

"I'm sorry," said Adrianne.

"It isn't a thing you can be sorry about," George said. "It's no. You can't do it. You can't go out with him."

". . . I'm sorry," she said.

"Don't keep repeating that. Is that all you can say?"

". . . Yes."

"You are not going out with him. Whatever your father says."

"Yes," said Adrianne. "I am."

George got up out of his chair, and came for her. He said, "I'm your husband now."

"I know," she said.

"And you're going to do what I tell you."

"I'm sorry."

George said, "If you say that once more, I'll knock you across the room. Now don't get me angry." He said, "I'm coming to meet your father; I'm going to tell him. I'm going to tell him we'll be married."

"No," said Adrianne.

"Why not?"

"Not . . . now."

"When?"

"I don't know."

"Why not now?"

". . . He's got a cold," said Adrianne.

"That's a lie."

"He does have a cold," she said.

George opened his legs, standing in front of her. "You're not going out with this boy."

"Yes," said Adrianne. "I'm sorry."

He did it with the back of his hand. He hit her across the face, and across the mouth.

Her neck snapped to the right: a loud snap. It made her swirl on one heel—the right heel—and fall over a bare wooden chair onto the floor, taking the chair with her. She lay there till the fog eased out of her mind.

And George was down beside her, holding her. He was saying, ". . . me, darling. Darling. Darling, forgive me."

"Yes," she said.

"Darling . . . my darling."

". . . Yes."

"I . . . I did it again. I hurt you."

Adrianne said, "I think so."

"Oh, darling."

"Yes," she said. "Yes, I do think so."

"I couldn't help it," George said, "you make me . . . I don't know why. I can't help it with you. I can't help myself with you."

". . . I'm glad," said Adrianne.

"Darling, forgive me. I know you . . . it isn't right, isn't . . . easy

*for you at home. You two, I know, even if I can't . . . I can know.
I won't do anything more to make it worse, I promise. I would do
. . . I would . . . would kill myself for you. If you wanted that.
Take time if you want it. Take whatever you want."*

"Thank you," said Adrianne.

"Don't thank me. Oh, God, don't thank me." George said: "Put
your arms behind me."

There was dust on the floor; the pattern was worn off the thin rug
in places. Patches like brown dirty gauze showed through, and
the smell was of old dust. "Here?" said Adrianne.

George said, "I can't wait."

And Edmund said, "From a cold to a stiff neck, I swear I can't
understand it. I haven't been out of the house since the morning
I first got this damn cold, and now I have a stiff neck. And I
haven't been out of the house."

"No," said Adrianne.

Aunt Clothilde said, "If you would only just stop talking to
her long enough to tell me about the tree, I could give the orders."

"What do you want to know?" said Edmund. "Yes. Get the
tree. Same as every Christmas. The same-size tree as always.
What's there to know?"

"I believe to my knowledge," said Aunt Clothilde, "I have
said two times in the last half-hour, they don't have the same-size
tree. This makes three: they don't have the same-size tree. They
have a tree that's a little bit taller, and they have a tree that's a
little bit shorter. But they don't have the same-size tree."

"Get the bigger one," said Edmund.

"You want the bigger one? You sure, now?"

"That's what I said."

Aunt Clothilde stood up. "You want the bigger tree."

"No," Edmund said. "The bigger cloud." He smiled.

Adrianne smiled.

"All right," Aunt Clothilde said. "Without the sarcasm. I just
hope you don't change your mind." She went out to the phone.

Edmund turned his head to the right, and grunted; he set his face. "I swear, I do not understand it. Not a drafty window, and I get a stiff neck. Haven't bent the wrong way; haven't done a thing at all. And I get a stiff neck."

"I know," said Adrianne.

"Plop down here on the bed," Edmund said. "How was the date? Nelson boy nice?"

"Yes," said Adrianne. "He's nice." She sat by Edmund's left knee.

"Comes from a nice family. Just as dull as his father, I suppose."

"I suppose so," said Adrianne.

"Meet his father?"

"No," she said. "I didn't have to."

Edmund chuckled, long and low. "My Princess," he said. "Take a lot of man for my Princess, someday. Just between you and me, it's going to take a lot of the right kind of man to satisfy you."

". . . Yes," said Adrianne.

"By the way, seeing any more of the Jew boy? Uh, what's his . . ."

"Solomon," said Adrianne. "Yes."

"Seeing him again?"

"This afternoon."

"So soon?" Edmund said. "See a lot of him, don't you? Not that it's any of my concern."

"Yes."

"None of my business. You know what you're doing. Just live the way you always have, Princess, just keep to the middle of the road. Nothing will ever happen to you, you know what you're doing. You know how to live." Edmund pushed the second pillow against his back, and sat up further. "The boy is a Jew, isn't he?"

"I don't know," said Adrianne.

"You never asked him?"

"No."

"Well, you're probably right. Jews don't like to be asked. Don't like to have it proved on them straight out. Ever meet his family?"

"No."

"That's sensible. You always are sensible. No point in your going around to where he lives. No more point than his coming up here; that's why he didn't want to come up here and meet me, I imagine. Jews don't like to have it proved on them."

The wind was a whine; it was whining white on the window.

Edmund said, "Easy enough to find out, though. All you have to do is pass a little harmless remark. See it right away on their faces, they can't hide it; none of them. Not that I have anything against Jews," he said, "like some people. They're ordinary human beings, the same as anybody. I just never had much dealings with them. We all have our faults. And besides, this boy might be different. You're a much better judge of people than I am, you have a sense for it. I wouldn't care if you wanted to spend the rest of your life with a Chinese laundryman, just so you chose him with your eyes open. I wouldn't open my mouth. It's up to you. If you walked in one day and said to me this is the man I want to marry, I wouldn't open my mouth. That's it and that's that. You make your own rules; you're better equipped than I ever was. I had my family against me. You operate from freedom. All I mean is Jews are easy to spot."

Adrianne said, "They are?"

"Hell, yes, if he ever does come up here, I'll find out for you. If he comes here to my apartment, I'll find him out. Easy enough. You could do it yourself if you wanted to."

"No," said Adrianne.

Edmund looked to the side for a cigarette, and groaned.

"Damn," he said; "damn all stiff necks. Well, just as you like. None of my business." He lit a match. "But if Solomon ever comes up to my apartment, I'll do it for you then." He grinned, and said, "I'm king of my own house, you know, Princess."

And George said, "I'm coming to see him tomorrow afternoon. Christmas Day."

"No," said Adrianne.

"It's a good time. The best time. Christmas is a good time for everybody."

"It won't make any difference with him," said Adrianne.

George said, "I can't wait any more."

"You have to."

"I can't," he said. "What time shall I come?"

". . . Don't."

"I'm going to. Having lunch at home? What time will you both be there?"

The wind against George's window was gray. Gray sheets of snow. Adrianne went up to it, slowly, and put her fingers on the frozen pane. She said, "I'm never there."

"Huh?" Geroge rolled over on his stomach. "What do you mean, you're never there?"

"No," she said. "I'm . . . only here."

George sniffed. He said, "Don't get you."

"I know," she said. "I don't expect you to. I don't know myself. I only know I'm here."

"Explain it to me. Explain to me about it."

Adrianne said, "What . . . what can I explain? I don't know."

She said, "I come down the street, and the air is white. Hard, and white, and transparent, like new ice. The way it is when I'm with him. The way it always has been. I walk, I cut my way through the white air. It is . . . hard; it grips me as I walk. It's hollow and hard all around. Sometimes I dream I'm walking through the white air on white sand, and there aren't any clouds, because the sky is white too. And I am white; I am a real princess, walking in white. And I can't stop walking. And I'm afraid to look behind me, because I know if I do I will see nothing but white air, and whiteness, and there will be no footprints in the sand. So I just go on walking that way. Without . . . making a mark. Then there are noises under me, and the deep ground grumbles, and all around me great cracks, great long fissures open in the sand, all around. And a white fire roars in those fissures, roaring round in the air. But not where I walk. Where I walk is between them, wherever I walk. Exactly between them. Then I look down into one of the cracks, down deep inside; and down there, miles down in sand, I see the beginnings of redness and heat down there. And I want to burn in the red.

I want the burning, I can't live without that to burn me. Then way ahead I see another great crack opening right across my path, right where I must go. I run and I run, I run straight there, I run. But when I get there, it is double, there are two, one on each side of me, and I am in the center again on smooth white sand. They just go on like that. I can't burn. It doesn't matter where I go, or how fast, whatever direction. It's always the same. Always white sand where I go, and the fire all around under me, ahead of me; and I can't reach it, any of it. And I go on, knowing I can't reach it, knowing I can't even leave any footprints in the sand."

George came up behind her. He pressed tight against her body, and he wrapped both arms around her and held her back to him. "Stop shaking," he said.

Adrianne said, "That's when I dream. But when I walk, when I really walk, the air is the same. All hollow and hard; all white. Wherever I go. Except here."

"Here? What is here?"

Adrianne said, "When I turn the corner into this street to come here, that's when it changes. The only time it ever changes. And it goes gray and soft, full: the hollowness is full. The air flutters on my face, and I can feel it fluttering. And I can feel it soft, like pigeons' wings. Then I feel the heat inside me, deep inside, I feel the burning. And I know then that I am here; I know that I have never been before. I know that I am and I know why I am, because I know that I am here."

"Darling . . ."

Adrianne said, "But when I leave again, and cross the street, when I turn that corner, it's all the same again. The white air; the hollow, white, transparent, the hard, the white air. And I am white. And sometimes I want to forget. And I am what I'm not. Walking in between my life, walking. But I can't help myself. Because I'm not myself."

"Darling . . ." George said: "I wish . . . don't . . ."

"Yes."

"It . . . darling; it can't be so important for now."

"Yes," said Adrianne. "Oh, yes. It's important."

"Not for now," he said, "not now. There's time. Someday we will both know. Someday, when we know each other so well, we can remember where a thought used to be. Then we will understand. Darling, there's time."

Adrianne said, "There is no time. Only when I'm here."

"Why . . . ?"

He let her go, and stepped back. She had to grab the dirty lace curtains in both hands, to keep from falling.

"Why don't you want me to meet him?"

The gray swirling snow, and the gray sky. The gray.

"Maybe I'm not quite good enough after . . . afterwards. Is that it?"

"No," said Adrianne. "It's not."

"Then what is?"

Just the deep grayness. Soft and gray, deep into heaven. Deep with no end.

George said, "I'm coming to see you at your father's. Tomorrow. Tomorrow afternoon; Christmas. You'll be there."

"I'm never there," said Adrianne. She called, loud: "I'm never there, I'm never there, I'm never there."

". . . in just a few minutes."

Adrianne said, "I'm sorry?"

"I said," said the nurse, "I'll be calling for you in just a few minutes. Soon as he wakes up. You'd better be . . . I think you'd better be ready, Miss. Perhaps it would be the best thing if you were standing out in the passage. Just in case. Sometimes a person isn't sure."

"Do you . . . have him in his room now?"

"Yes, honey," said the nurse, "I told you that."

"Oh. I see."

". . . Maybe you should stand out in the passage."

"No," said Adrianne. "I'll hear you from here. Thank you."

"Would you like a little smelling salts to hold?"

"No, thank you."

"Maybe you should stand outside in the passage, with a little smelling salts to hold."

"I'm quite all right," said Adrianne, "thank you very much."

"You didn't seem to be hearing me when I was talking to you. Even though you answered me fine, only you didn't really seem to be hearing."

"Thank you," said Adrianne. "I'm so sorry. I will hear."

"Now don't apologize," the nurse said, "please don't apologize. I know what these things are like. You'd be surprised the cases you see in a hospital. If you knew how some of the others act; all the time, they're all alike. In one way or another. Not anywhere near like you."

". . . Thank you," said Adrianne.

"All right, honey," the nurse said. "And I'll be calling for you." She went away.

Way far off, Aunt Clothilde said, "Where shall I stand?"

"What, dear?" said the nurse.

"I want to know where you want me to stand."

"No, you just sit there," said the nurse. "Right where you are. I'll let you know. It's Miss Adrianne he's been asking for."

"Of course," said Aunt Clothilde.

Mrs. Rhale said, tremblingly, "It's all just so awful. I might need some smelling salts myself."

"Oh shut up, Gwendolyn," Aunt Clothilde said. "You don't need anything. It's not as if it was your family. Just shut up. In a hundred years what will you care?"

Christmas.

Edmund took the golden candle out of her hand, and put his foot on the first rung of the ladder.

Aunt Clothilde said, "I still say, the tree's too tall this year. You can't get up there on that ladder. You had a big dinner."

"Yes, I can," said Edmund. "I can get up there. I've put a gold candle on top of the tree every Christmas Day since she was born. I can get up there."

"The tree's never been so tall," Aunt Clothilde said. "Never."

"Doesn't matter. It's not that much taller."

"Enough," said Aunt Clothilde.

"Sit down, Clothilde," Edmund said. "Princess, you got a good hold there? Keep one hand on either side, and press down."

"I am," said Adrianne.

"O.K., then." He bent and kissed her on the nape of the neck. Adrianne threw her head back.

"Ha," said Edmund. "Ha ha." He said: "Remember when you were little?"

" . . . Yes."

"The two of us, the way we used to sit around the tree. You remember? And nobody ever to spoil it for us? And that time when Miss Duff wanted to come in and sing Christmas carols and you said, 'No.' You said, 'No, Nanny,' you said, 'Father doesn't like but just the two of us for Christmas. Father doesn't like anybody else to spoil it for us; you can sing carols tomorrow.' "

"I remember," said Adrianne.

"Ha, ha," said Edmund. " 'You can sing carrols tomorrow.' Telling her she could sing carols the day after Christmas. Ha."

Aunt Clothilde said, "If I'm spoiling it for you, I can leave. I can go to my room. I've got a room."

"Clothilde, Clothilde, sit down," Edmund said. "I didn't mean you. I meant outsiders. I mean we never had any outsiders to spoil it for us."

"I've got a room," said Aunt Clothilde. "I can go to my room."

"Not you," said Edmund. "For goodness' sake. You don't count."

Aunt Clothilde sat neatly in the big chair. "Yes," she said. "I am aware of that."

"All right," Edmund said, "here we go, Princess. Up we go. Hold tight."

"Yes," said Adrianne.

"Up, up, up, up, up, up. And up."

Aunt Clothilde said, "Be careful, Edmund."

"I'm being careful. Aren't I, Princess?"

"Yes," said Adrianne.

Edmund put one hand on the wall. He had bent, under the ceiling. With the other hand he opened the metal clip at the bottom of the golden candle. And he held the candle out over the top branch. "All right," he said. "Princess. One, two . . . three . . ."

Edmund and Adrianne recited:

> "Princess Pea, Princess Pea,
> What have you to say to me?
> Princess Stocking . . ."

The doorbell chimed.

"Damn it all," said Edmund. And he turned.

He fell straight into the tree.

"Aye," said Aunt Clothilde. "Aye, aye. My God, I knew it."

Adrianne held tight to the ladder; she was a part of the ladder.

"Ayeeee," said Aunt Clothilde.

Then bony William the butler was there, helping Edmund out from the colored litter of smashed baubles and electric wire and tinsel, and sifting, loose pine needles. Helping to free him; straightening the tree—helping.

While Adrianne held to the ladder.

And Edmund said, "O.K." He said: "O.K., Clothilde, O.K. I'm O.K. Shhh, Clothilde." He said to William: "It's my le . . . my leg. My leg. Watch my leg, now. My leg, it's my leg."

"I knew it," said Aunt Clothilde. "I was sure."

Edmund said, "Jesus."

And Adrianne held to the ladder.

He said, "Jesus. No."

"Wait, sir, it is that leg. You want me to pick you up, Mr. Edmund?"

"Jesus. Jesus. Je-sus."

"O.K., sir. Got you now. Won't take but a second."

"In here."

Edmund said, "Cheeese."

"In here," said Aunt Clothilde. "Carry him right in and put him on the bed, I'll call a doctor. Here."

Then Adrianne was alone with the ladder.

They were gone.

And she was alone with the ladder.

The maid ran through from the hall, through the living room, and into the bedroom.

The maid came back, and ran for the pantry. She slid; turned. She stopped, and said, "Miss Adrianne."

The ladder trembled.

She said, "Miss Adrianne. Oh, Miss."

"Yes," said Adrianne.

"There is a young gentleman in the hall, said he come to see you. Said his name is . . . I don't remember, Miss Adrianne. Too much excitement. He wants to see you."

"Yes," said Adrianne.

"He's waiting out in the hall."

"That's right," said Adrianne.

"You want me to give him a message?"

"No, I don't."

". . . Just let him wait?"

"That's right," said Adrianne.

"I could tell him there's been a mishap."

"No," said Adrianne. "Don't tell him anything."

"Yes, Miss. I'm going to get an ice pack for Mr. Edmund's leg."

Adrianne said, "That's right."

Alone again with the ladder. There was a silver bubble, burst, in the middle of the room.

Edmund said, "Adrianne." He said: "Adrianne."

She separated her locked fingers from the wood—held them back. She moved them in the white air.

"Adrianne."

She stood, and the ladder stood: two separate things.

"Yes," she said, "I'm coming." She turned and walked quite easily.

Edmund was lying down with a pillow under the leg. "Princess," he said. He tried to smile.

Adrianne said, "Yes."

"Princess. Sit . . . by me."

"Yes." In a chair by his head—not to disorder the leg.

He did smile. "Stupid me," he said. "Trying to act like . . . I *was seventeen. Broke the leg, I think. Old stupid me. You wouldn't do a stupid thing like . . . that; would you? You know how to live. Stupid me, stupid . . . me. Da . . . damn. Damn the doorbell. If the doorbell hadn't rung, I wouldn't have slipped."*

"Yes," she said. "I know."

"It was the damn doorbell."

"I know."

"Christmas . . . present. Probably."

"No," said Adrianne.

"No? Is Clothilde calling that doctor?"

"I think so."

"She'd better be."

"I think she is," said Adrianne.

"Wonder if he can set it . . . here. Have to cut my pants off . . . almost . . . certainly."

"Yes," said Adrianne. "Almost certainly."

"Damn. It hurts."

"Does it?"

"Sure does," he said. He said: "It does."

". . . How?" said Adrianne.

"It just . . . hurts . . . like hell. It hurts like hell."

"Oh," said Adrianne.

Edmund grunted. He said, "Then who was it?"

"Solomon," said Adrianne.

"Oh. Ah-hah. Have you seen him?"

"No."

". . . Still out there?"

"Yes."

"On Christmas Day? Who'd he come to see, you?"

"No," said Adrianne. "You."

". . . He wants me?"

"No," she said. "He wants me."

"Oh. Ha, ha . . . damn," Edmund said. He pushed up to get his weight off the left leg. "Da-amn. You'll have to get rid of him."

"I know," said Adrianne. "Now?"

"Certainly, now. I don't want him hanging around here while

I'm hurt. No sense in a Jew boy . . . hanging around here . . . at all. Or is there?"

"No," said Adrianne.

"Jew, isn't he?"

"I don't know."

"Well. Better find out. Anyway, get rid of him."

"Yes," said Adrianne.

"And then come back . . . here to me. It doesn't hurt so bad when you're here, Princess. Here with me."

"Yes."

"Come right back."

"I will," said Adrianne.

Up; across; through the door; past the Christmas tree, and the sofa, and the big chair. Through the whiteness into the hall.

Past Aunt Clothilde, just hanging up the phone and following with her eyes.

Around the bend. Past three chairs, and the mirrored table with the flat silver powder box on it. And George at the end of the hall.

He stood up for her.

Newly pressed, in navy blue. Combed hair and water on it. Dark tie, a lighter blue, with three thin white stripes. Shined black shoes, new. No overcoat, no hat; in the closet.

The closet. Adrianne went in and turned on the closet light. The same brown coat. She took it off the hanger, and folded it over her arm. Six of Edmund's hats were on the shelf. There were no other hats.

She stepped back, and carried it out. Then she walked up to him.

She said, "You never wear a hat."

". . . I never do. No."

"I would, in this weather. None of my business of course. It's cold outside."

George stared.

"You have your own taste," she said, "take your coat, please."

He reached out slowly, and took it from her. He had a tissue-covered box in his hand, forgotten. Then: "Merry Christmas," he said.

"Thank you. Same to you," said Adrianne.

". . . He can't see me?"

"No."

"Sure?"

"Quite sure," said Adrianne. "Without a doubt."

"Did he . . . say he couldn't?"

"He didn't have to," she said.

"What? Oh, you mean he isn't in."

Adrianne kept still.

"Bad luck," he said. But he looked relieved. "Bad luck. On Christmas Day. I was wondering what you were coming at me with my coat for."

"Were you?"

"I'll say I was. Bad luck. Well, you're right, I shouldn't come in without his being here. O.K., get yours."

". . . My what?"

"Coat."

"My coat?" said Adrianne. "Why?"

George grinned. He said, "It's cold outside."

"Is it?"

"We can take in a movie or something, till he gets home."

"We?" said Adrianne.

And George said, ". . . Don't look at me like that."

But the air was white around him.

He said, "Don't look at me that way." And he said, "What time will he be at home? When can I see him?"

"You can't," said Adrianne.

". . . Yes, I can."

"No," she said. "You can't."

George said quietly, "Darling, what is it?"

"What is what?"

"What's wrong, what is it? What are you scared for? What are you acting that way for, with me?"

"Scared?" said Adrianne. ". . . Acting?"

Edmund's voice was faint at first. It said, "Adrianne."

"Who was that?" said George.

"My father."

"Your . . ."

"That was my father," she said.

"You told me he wasn't in."

"No," she said. "I didn't tell you that."

George was tensing. He said, "You never tell a lie, do you?"

Edmund called, "Adrianne."

"You just are one."

"I have to go now."

"Which is the lie?" George said. "Which?"

But the redness was too distant, and too deep. There was no time.

"Goodbye," *she said. She used the handle, and pulled the door towards her. She didn't even need to lean on it.*

"Which is the lie?"

Edmund called, "Adrianne."

"No lie. Leave now," she said.

". . . All right," *George said. "All right; I will." He stepped out. Then he swung back to her. "Darling, I am trying to understand."*

"Understand what?"

"You," *he said. "I'm trying."*

"There's nothing to understand."

Louder: "Adrianne."

"What did he say about me?" *George said. "What did he tell you against me?"*

"Nothing."

"That's not true."

"Yes," *said Adrianne; "what could he say that would matter? It's true."*

". . . He said something . . . to make you hate me."

"Hate you? How could he? No."

And louder: "Adrianne."

"That's a lie."

"No," *said Adrianne. "I don't lie."*

"Then what did he say against me?" George put a hand on the door. "I'll go in there and ask him myself."

"Adrianne."

"Oh no," said Adrianne. She wedged her back with muscle. "No, don't bother, I'm not lying. He really didn't tell me anything against you," she said simply; "not a thing at all. He didn't have to. I know what Jews are."

And she did actually see the change in his face before she shut the door.

"Princess. Oh, Adrianne."

Hard, she said, "Yes. I'm coming."

The carpet of the passage was tinged with white ahead of her. And when she turned the corner—

Aunt Clothilde said, "Do you know what you just did?"

"Yes."

"That was the one," said Aunt Clothilde. "That was the one you're in love with."

"Love?" said Adrianne.

"That's what I said."

"Me?"

Aunt Clothilde said, "Yes, he is the one. You fool. Go, go after him. Run after him. You don't know what you just did."

"I know," said Adrianne. "Yes."

"You . . ."

"Get out of my way," she said.

She did know. She knew about all the afternoons, and the walk, the long walk; the air that wouldn't change. The air that would never change again. Then the card gone from his box; the vacant apartment; the landlady in a wrinkled green rayon robe, smoking, the landlady: "So, I'm telling you, he didn't leave a new address. I'd like to have it myself, already. I liked the young man. But if he didn't want to leave one, what was I supposed to do, smash him or something? It's a personal world. You sure you want the right Mr. Solomon?" The emptiness.

The beginning to forget.

Yes, she knew.

Aunt Clothilde said, "Stop smiling. What kind of a smile do you call that?"

Edmund said, "Oh, Princess, for heaven's sake. What about that doctor? Princess."

"I'm coming," she said.

"Don't," said Aunt Clothilde. "I've called the doctor. You just leave. Run after him, run."

"It's no use running," said Adrianne.

"Why not?"

Adrianne said, "It's always the same. It's no use running."

"What's always the same?"

"You don't understand," she said, "I'd never reach it. Nobody can understand."

". . . Don't I? Do you remember who I am?"

"You're in my way," she said.

She put one foot ahead of her on the white sand.

Aunt Clothilde backed to the wall. She said, "Just stop smiling. What in the world kind of a smile do you call that?"

And Edmund said, softer, "Adrianne."

"I'm coming," she said. "I'm coming, here I am, Father."

But he wouldn't have said Miss Adrianne. Not Miss. Not Edmund.

He would not have called her Miss.

"Yes," said Adrianne, "I'm coming."

The nurse said, "This way, Miss. Step right this way, honey."

Great squares; small squares. No focus. A great beast waving its long crooked legs. Clutches of leaves, mazing, tangling—and only in the eyes; still leaves around the moss, still, in the stagnant summer. A rise to the fire-filled light like the wailing of fearful color—like the wind, seen. And a windless, loveless lake of living. Death is a long-legged beast washing its hands. Love never was.

Focus.

"Yes."

"Honey," the nurse said, "come right along now. Come on."

"I'm coming."

Adrianne curved one finger, tensed it, and flicked the fly off the black screen. She flicked it into the end of the afternoon—into the wide orange sun that had started to swell in its own heat, worlds away.

She folded her used hand.

Then she got up, and turned.

Everybody was standing. Sterling on the left, his cap dangling. The nurse in the open passage ahead. Gwendolyn Rhale, biting the diamond on her wedding ring, sobbing now. Aunt Clothilde, quiet and stark.

The fan made a low halo over them all. It was a darkness above, the circle not of heaven.

Adrianne began to walk.

"Hurry, dear," said Mrs. Rhale; ". . . hurry."

Aunt Clothilde said, "No."

Mrs. Rhale slipped in front of Adrianne, and took her by the shoulders. She said, "Be . . . dear, you be very brave. Be like you are. Smile for him, dear heart; smile exactly like you're doing."

Aunt Clothilde giggled. "Yes," she said. "Smile for him just like that."

Mrs. Rhale edged back, sobbing, and Adrianne went on walking.

She followed the nurse. Through the doorway, left, and straight down the passage, she followed the nurse. And as she went, the white nurse moved always ahead of her.

On either side, behind closed doors, there were the grumblings, groanings, coughings; there was laughter; and there was the warm light under nearly every door.

And the white nurse moved always ahead of her.

2

The doctor said, "Miss Choate; we've done what we can do."

"Thank you," said Adrianne.

"He's full of dope, but he won't sleep. He asks for you. All during the operation, when he was completely out, he asked for you. And he kept saying, 'Princess.' That's you too, isn't it?"

"Yes."

"So," said the doctor. ". . . I can see why."

"Thank you," said Adrianne.

"All right, now. Go on in. See if you can get him to go to sleep. If he sleeps, he'll probably be O.K. It's up to you now."

The nurse said, "I'll be right down here, honey, three doors down, at the end of the hall. The buzzer's next to his bed; or you can call me."

"I'll be around too," said the doctor, "I won't be far off. But you can help more than any of us, now. If we can get him through the night peacefully he'll be O.K. Don't touch him, Miss Choate. He . . . we've uh . . . he has no . . . we've had to, we . . . had to amputate the arm."

"I see," said Adrianne. "Thank you. Thank you both so very much."

". . . You're very welcome, Miss Choate," said the doctor. "Princess."

Adrianne went after the nurse into the room.

The light was out. The nurse bent over the bed; she whispered, "There's someone come to visit us, Mr. Choate. Here's the person we've been asking for. Here's your princess."

Fast, rough breathing. Like a distant engine.

"Here is your princess," said the nurse. She made a demure movement with her shoulders. And she took her whiteness out of the room.

Adrianne stood by the closed door.

And it was gone: in the dim of the room, she could find no more pure white. Shadows lay over all the bedclothes, filming the wall—glooming. The sickly smell, sweet in the air, was the smell of dying shadow. Colors; few colors dimmed into the black floor. The colors hushed away.

Then she saw it over the bed. It was contained in an upside-down bottle with a tube on the end that dipped down to the vein of Edmund's right arm. The white, transparent-white liquid that was dripping into his blood.

A voice—something like his, but full of shadow—said: "Adrianne."

"Yes," she said.

"Where are you?"

"I'm here."

"I can't . . . see you."

"It's all right, Father. I'm here. I can see you," she said.

The breathing stopped. Then it started, slower than before; the breath rasped out of his throat.

Edmund said, "Adrianne."

"Yes."

"Adrianne, I think I am dying."

Gently, she said, "Yes, Father. I know you are."

"Where . . . are you?"

"Here by the door."

"Come where . . . please come . . . where I can see you."

"I'm right here," said Adrianne.

"I can't . . . come where I can see you."

The shadow was deep on her cheeks.

"Come."

The deep shadow around her fluttered, blue and gray and soft: like pigeons' wings.

"Come where I can see you. Come," he said.

And Adrianne said, "No."

And the soft, caressing shadows laughed.

"Come . . . come here to me."

"No," she said. "I won't."

"You . . ."

"No."

"Adrianne. It's not you, not . . . you."

"Oh, yes."

"Not really you."

"Isn't it?" she said. "I think it is."

"Adrianne . . ."

"Yes."

"Adrianne, Adrianne."

"Yes."

Edmund said, "I'm dying."

"That's right," she said. "You are."

Edmund said, "Dying." He said: "Jesus, the . . . Jesus. Now I'm burning up."

"You would appear to be," said Adrianne.

"I'm . . . it's . . . burning. Jesus, it does."

"Does it?"

"Jesus, it . . . the pain."

"Pain?" she said.

"I . . . it . . . is . . . better now. It's better . . . now."

"Good," said Adrianne. She said: "That must feel good."

The breathing slowed again.

Edmund made a jerky sigh.

From over the hospital, the sinking sun sent tinted rays through clouds in by the window. They lit on Edmund's face, and faded there.

Edmund said, "Adrianne."

"Yes."

"Are you really here? Really . . . here?"

"I think so," said Adrianne. "Yes," she said; "I think I really am."

"I can't stop dreaming. I want you here."

"You have me."

"I want you here beside me. Princess."

"Oh no," said Adrianne. "I misunderstood. Not her, no. Not now."

"Adrianne . . . I'm going to die."

"I know you are, Father."

"Princess; I am. I am dying."

And the princess said, "How dare you tell me that?"

"Princess . . ."

"How dare you," said the princess, "how dare you die?"

"Princess; I . . ."

"How could you leave me? How can you die? How dare you tell me that?"

". . . Adrianne."

"Yes?"

"Please . . . come here, don't tease me. No, I have such . . . you never felt, you . . . don't know such pain."

"I never had to," said Adrianne.

". . . Such . . . Don't, don't . . . tease me."

Adrianne said softly, "No, Father. I won't."

"Just . . ." Edmund said: "Just love me now."

"Me?" said Adrianne.

"Princess . . ."

"What?" said the princess.

"Just love me. Adrianne. Just love . . . me."

Adrianne opened her mouth, wet it, and shaped it. She pronounced, "Love."

And the princess said, "Who?" She said: "Her?"

"Oh . . . my dear, I love you . . . I've . . . I tried; I have tried . . . for you."

"Yes," said the princess, "yes, Father. Yes, I know you have."

"I've . . . Adrianne, I . . . I leave it to . . . everything, my life, everything was all for you."

"Me?" Adrianne said: "Oh, no, what a silly mistake. Not for me."

"Yes . . ."

Adrianne said, "No. You are still dreaming, Father. For her. Not for me."

"Jesus," Edmund said. "Jesus." He said: "Jesus, I can't . . . Jesus. Now I can't breathe. I can't . . . breathe . . . Jesus, I can't . . . Adrianne."

"Yes."

"I can't breathe. You better . . . cut them, I can't . . . They're too tight . . . Adrianne, cut . . . I can't breathe."

"With what?" said Adrianne. And she saw the open scissors lying on the table next to the bed.

"Adrianne."

Adrianne said, "No. I'd better get the nurse."

"The . . . pain . . ."

She said, "It really isn't any use, Father. The bandages have to be tight. But I'll get the nurse."

Edmund craned his head up in the darkening room. "Now. Light," he said. "You turn on the light."

"Why?" said Adrianne.

"I want . . . to see you. It is a dream. It isn't you." He said: "Turn on the light."

Adrianne felt upwards on the wall with the back of her hand. When she came to the switch, she held still. Then she pressed hard against it.

The white that came from nothing filled the room, splashing on the walls; killing the soft gray. The white burned everything —burned out the blue shadows: burned all but one.

Edmund's face stayed blue.

And he said, "Jesus."

He said, "Sweet Jesus Christ."

He said, "Don't you look at me like that."

And the shadows were gone from his voice.

He said, "Jesus. Don't you look at me like that. You never looked at me . . . like . . . that in . . . your life."

"No?"

Edmund said, "Am I dreaming? Princess."

But there was only the white silence of the room.

Then he said, "Adrianne."

"Yes?"

"Adrianne."

"What, Father?"

Edmund slumped back on the pillow. He shouted, "Adrianne, Adrianne."

"Yes, Father," she said. "I'm here."

". . . Where?"

"I just have to get the nurse."

"Adrianne, I am dying. Now I am. I . . ."

Above him and to the side, the bottle was almost empty.

"Yes," she said. "You are."

"Adrianne."

In the doorway, she stopped. "What?"

"Jesus. Are you leaving? Aren't you . . . staying here with me?"

"If you tell me to."

Edmund said, ". . . I wouldn't . . . tell you to."

"If you want me."

Edmund said, "Oh, Princess."

And Adrianne smiled.

Then she walked out of the room, down the passage.

He said, "Princess." He called: "Princess, Princess."

Past three doors—down the black passage.

Adrianne said, "Excuse me. I believe you're needed now."

"Oh," said the nurse; "yes. Doctor. Dr. Weston, please. Dr. Weston." She said: "Honey, you could have called."

"I never had to," said Adrianne.

"Dr. Weston," said the nurse, "number twelve."

"With you," said the doctor. "Right. Just hold on, Miss Choate. It may be nothing. Nurse."

"With you," said the nurse.

Edmund called, "Princess." But there was something in his mouth with the word.

Adrianne stood alone at one end of the passage. Off at the other end, she could see Aunt Clothilde and Mrs. Rhale and Sterling. They were all standing in the passage.

Aunt Clothilde said, loud, "Is it over?"

"Not quite," said Adrianne. She raised her arms and covered her face carefully with both palms.

"Princess."

Aunt Clothilde shouted, "Is he suffering much?"

"I wouldn't know," said Adrianne.

"Princess."

"Dear God," shouted Aunt Clothilde, "I can hear him."

"Can you?" said Adrianne. "So can I."

"Princess."

"He's . . . he's calling for you."

Mrs. Rhale hollered, "He's calling for you."

Edmund whispered, "Prin . . . Princess." His whisper echoed wet in the passage.

"He's calling. Adrianne, he's calling."

"Yes, he is," said Adrianne.

"Princess."

Aunt Clothilde yelled, "Go to him. He's calling for you."

"No," said Adrianne. "Oh, no. Not for me."

". . . Dear God," said Aunt Clothilde.

"Not for me," said Adrianne.

Then the air was white around her; and it turned blasting, blistering black; and it turned white again. And then, very slowly, it began to fade.

Adrianne said tenderly, "Princess Pea, Princess Pea, Princess Pea, Princess Pea."

And the air faded.

She said, "Princess Pea."

And the air went out.

"He's dead now," said Adrianne.

"Miss," said the doctor. "Adrianne." The doctor said: "Miss Choate."

"Yes." Adrianne stripped her wet palms from her face. Then she had to walk again.

When she got to the door, the doctor said, "Miss Choate. Quick."

"No," she said. "It's no use running."

"Get in here," said Dr. Weston, "quick."

Adrianne said, "But it's no use running. It's no use." She said: "He's dead."

"No. Not . . . Hurry, will you?"

"No," said Adrianne.

"But . . ."

"No."

"She's right, Doctor," said the nurse.

"But he . . ."

"Doctor," said the nurse, "she's right."

Dr. Weston looked down and did something. He did two things, and he looked again. Then he did something else. After that, he let his hands drop.

He came around the side, and stood between Adrianne and the bed.

He said, "I . . . isn't very much I can say."

"Thank you for wanting to," said Adrianne.

"He . . ." The doctor said: "He kept calling. Right up to now."

"I heard, yes."

"He . . ."

"I couldn't come," said Adrianne. "I could not come."

"Surely," said the doctor. "Our bodies won't always do what we want them to," he said. ". . . We can love too much."

Adrianne looked at the bed.

"If it's of any comfort to you . . . I'm sure he understood."

"I'm not," said Adrianne.

"Surely," said the doctor, "surely he did."

"Certainly. Certainly," said the nurse.

The doctor said, "Miss Choate. Adrianne, he knew. He did know and he understood, he loved you the more for it."

"Yes," said the nurse.

"Love is . . . love can understand," said the doctor.

"Can it?" said Adrianne.

"He knew," said the doctor. "He will be in heaven right now thanking God for his daughter."

"Really?" she said. "Thanking who?"

The doctor took her by each elbow, strongly. He said, "Your father has to thank God now. God should only give all men a daughter like you."

"Amen, honey," said the nurse. "Amen."

"Thank you," said Adrianne.

"If there were anything . . . I know there isn't, but . . . if there were a single thing I could . . ."

And she could still remember his long whisper. Like a slow, slushy rock on the sea—sick-making with the eyes open; worse with them shut.

"Please," Adrianne said, "I would like very much to be alone here now."

"Surely. I . . ."

The nurse said, "Honey, just give us a second first."

"No," said Adrianne. "That isn't necessary."

"He . . ."

The nurse said, "We want to fix him up a little, honey."

"It isn't necessary," said Adrianne. "Thank you."

"We just want to make him appropriate."

"You don't have to. You can't," said Adrianne. "He isn't here any more. He went up to thank God."

"Oh," said the nurse. "Oh. Honey. What a lovely thought."

The doctor pulled back; he took his hands away. "Come along, Baldwin," he said.

And when the nurse had put out the light and gone, he said, "God won't forget you. You are a real princess."

He touched her elbow again on the way out.

Adrianne leaned on her arms, against the thick white paint next to the door. She listened there to the brittle singing of some bird, furious and busy in the fading day. Singing of night dew—of water in the night, through the black screen.

It was all too dark. The soft haze from the window sighed off in red, taking with it the sickly smell of sweet, lost life. The red of the haze was real in the unearthly shadows.

From her shoulder, Adrianne pushed, and went on pushing till the switch pulled in.

And that brilliant white gasped in the room.

Hardness was everywhere, shining. The haze that had been real did not exist. Only the watery black of night beginning beyond the window, and high above it something left of red. And the harshness of truth in the room.

The bottle was one inch full of liquid, but its tiny tube lay loose and useless on the floor.

Edmund's head was thrown back; open-eyed—blunt, uncovered marbles, slick, his eyes were open. His mouth like his eyes. Slobber creeping on his chin. Teeth, stained brown at the ends from tobacco, pointed up in long uneven rows to bite the ceiling, to bite back a forgotten word.

Adrianne said, "Look at you."

And the proud bird sang.

She said, "I did it for you. And I'm not ashamed of it. Not now. Yes," she said. "I killed him; I did all that for you."

By the bed, by his head, the open scissors glinted silver to her across the white air.

The bird had things to sing about. A bird to end the day.

3

The fan overhead growled once, and then went back to moaning. The country hospital was quiet for night.

Aunt Clothilde said, "Turn off that fan."

"Yes, ma'am," said Sterling.

He got up and went to the wall.

"Never mind," said Aunt Clothilde. "Never mind. I don't care."

"Yes, ma'am," said Sterling.

Aunt Clothilde said, "Gwendolyn, shut up. Stop that sobbing. You shut up."

"I can't," said Mrs. Rhale.

"It's not your family. Just shut up."

Sterling sat down on a straight chair that was covered in green.

Aunt Clothilde said, "She's been a half-hour in there."

"Yes, ma'am."

"She's had plenty time to do it, if she's going to do it."

Mrs. Rhale said, "Oh, do what?"

"If she's ever going to, she'll have done it now."

"Dear, do what?" said Mrs. Rhale. "It's all over."

"I hope so," said Aunt Clothilde. "No, I don't," she said, "I don't know what to hope. But I don't think she's done it, because I'm still frightened, you see."

Somewhere in the swelling blackness outside, two cats started to whine aloud. Then there was a shuffling on the shell drive that led off to the asphalt highway.

The moon sat in waiting, nearly full, high over the last bright edge of the sun. It shone there to look flat and pale in the red and the thickening gold.

Dr. Weston stepped out from the passage. He was an old man.

Sterling got to his feet.

"She's been inside a half-hour," Aunt Clothilde said.

The doctor said to Mrs. Rhale, "Is there anything we can do for you ladies?"

"Not her. She's not family," Aunt Clothilde said. "Just me."

"Can we do anything while you're waiting?"

"Adrianne's been in there a half-hour."

"Yes," said the doctor.

Aunt Clothilde said, "It's time now."

"No need to worry. She'll be all right," the doctor said.

"I think she will too. I think I do. No, I don't. Depends on what you mean by all right."

"I saw her face," said the doctor; "she'll be all right. You know that girl from just seeing her face."

Aunt Clothilde told him, "She won't do it, if that's what you mean. I'm pretty sure she isn't going to do it, you see. Or I wouldn't still be frightened."

"You mustn't worry . . . Mrs. . . . ."

"Aunt Clothilde," said Aunt Clothilde.

"You must not worry. She wouldn't like for you to worry here."

"Don't be condescending," said Aunt Clothilde, "don't soft-talk, what do you know? All you condescending doctors. You have faces like zombies and fingers like zombies, you doctors. Unhealthy, take a look at yourself. With your cold fingers. Creepy and your feeling fingers; all over everybody's stomach. All the same, and dead in the face. Why don't you examine yourself? You look like you have a short circuit in your test tube."

"Hush, dear," said Mrs. Rhale.

The doctor set his mouth. "Easy does it."

"Bloodsucker," said Aunt Clothilde.

"Hush," Mrs. Rhale said, "you don't realize what you're saying. She doesn't realize what she's saying."

"You fade away," said Aunt Clothilde. "You shut up and go on crying. I so rarely enjoy myself. Now I am going to tell off this doctor."

"No."

"There, there."

"Right now."

"She's frightened, doctor, she said she was frightened."

"I understand."

"Always washing your hands. Why don't you examine yourself? Only the people with repulsive thoughts always wash their hands."

"No, dear."

"Sadist. Bloodsucker. Surgeon. You've got a gooey mind."

"Clothilde."

"Oh; I could go on for hours."

"Doctor, she doesn't realize."

"Now," said the doctor. "I understand. Easy, now. We must calm down. Look now; see? See how calm I am?"

". . . See how calm the doctor is?"

Aunt Clothilde said, "Zombie."

"Easy does it. Nothing more is going to happen. Why would you be frightened? Nothing can happen to that girl."

Aunt Clothilde leaned back slowly, and shut her eyes. "Maybe that's it," she said. "Yes. Yes, indeed. Maybe that is it."

Mrs. Rhale said, "Ah, the way she put her hands up to her face."

"Will you shut up, Gwendolyn? For God's sake, shut up. What do you know? Just stop crying."

"I can't," said Mrs. Rhale.

"Just shut up, Gwendolyn."

The cats had ceased to whine. They were doing something else. They were holding a conversation.

And the gold thickening light had begun to go dense and tentative.

The doctor said, "Here she is."

"What?" said Aunt Clothilde. "Where?"

"I think . . ." The doctor stuck his head out into the passage. "Yes," he said.

Sterling dropped his cap over the chair he had been sitting on. Then he picked it up again.

"Here she is," said the doctor. "Here we are, Miss Choate."

Aunt Clothilde said, "Where?"

They were still; they listened to the cats.

Adrianne came into the room, smiling faintly at each person as she passed. Her hair looked like it never needed combing, and her eyes shimmered clear. She stopped in the center of the room.

"Oh dear," said Mrs. Rhale. "Princess, dear."

"Don't smile at me," said Aunt Clothilde. "I never did a thing to you. How are you?"

"Are you feeling well?" said the doctor.

"Thank you," said Adrianne.

Aunt Clothilde said, "What do you want here with those scissors?"

"Scissors?" said the doctor.

Adrianne said to Dr. Weston, "I do hope you will allow me to keep them. I had to cut the bandages," she said.

"What? I don't . . ."

Adrianne said, "Father asked me to cut the bandages. He couldn't breathe."

". . . I see," said the doctor. "Surely. Poor child."

"Dear," said Mrs. Rhale. "Oh Princess, dear."

Aunt Clothilde said, "It's happening."

"Is there anything we can do?"

"For me?" said Adrianne. "Oh, no. Thank you. Thank you so much."

"We would do anything we could to ease the pain of your loss."

"Would you?"

Sterling bent down. "Miss Adrianne, ma'am, it's a downright shame."

"Hello, Sterling," said Adrianne.

"It's a shame."

Aunt Clothilde said, "It's happening, it's happening." She beat the table with her fist. "Are you all blind?"

"Hush, dear," said Mrs. Rhale. "Don't upset her, dear."

"Upset who?" said Aunt Clothilde.

"Would you like to remain and rest here a little while before you start back for your home?"

Adrianne smiled harder. "Rest?"

"Yes," said the doctor.

"Yes, dear," said Mrs. Rhale.

Aunt Clothilde ripped free of her chair, and stood up. "It doesn't matter what any of us say," she said. "Does it?"

". . . Sweet Clothilde," Adrianne said.

"Don't you dare sweet me. And don't smile at me. Answer what I said."

". . . Sweet . . ."

"Now, Aunt Clothilde," said the doctor.

Aunt Clothilde put her face in front of Adrianne. She said, "Why didn't you do it, then? Why didn't you?"

"Please, doctor," said Mrs. Rhale. "She is likely hysterical."

"Keep away from me," said Aunt Clothilde. She said: "Why not? Why didn't you? You could have done it, you had plenty time. You could have pushed them right into your heart. Why didn't you use those scissors in there and send yourself to hell and get it over with? Why didn't you send yourself away from here straight to hell once and for all?"

Adrianne's smile glowed. Then it dropped off. "Don't be stupid," she said. "There is no hell but here."

"You fool," said Aunt Clothilde.

"Madam," said the doctor. He took Aunt Clothilde by the wrist.

"You fool, fool." Aunt Clothilde said: "Let me go. Keep away from me."

And Adrianne said, "I killed him, you know. You heard me kill him."

"Of course," said Aunt Clothilde. "You fool," she said.

"No," said the doctor, "now Miss Choate. He would have died just the same no matter what any of us did. He got excited; he . . ."

Aunt Clothilde said, "Not him. Not him, for God's sake. She doesn't mean Edmund. Why don't you all disappear?"

"Yes. I did kill him."

"No, Miss Choate, you mustn't ever say that. You must not feel that way at all."

"Feel?" said Adrianne.

She walked to the window. "Feel?" she said.

The cats were talking back and forth—taking turns on different tones. Talking about the night.

Adrianne raised one bare arm high in the air. She separated the scissors with the other hand, and gripped her fingers around the sharp end. Then she placed that end in her arm, back of the wrist, and she drew a line down to the elbow.

The line turned red.

Mrs. Rhale jerked four times, and reached for the doctor.

"Feel?" said Adrianne. She studied her dripping arm with a certain care.

Then she began to scream.

Balancing the scissors in her elbow, screaming on full lungs, Adrianne ran exactly midway between Mrs. Rhale and the doctor. She ran out, and down the stairs.

"For Jesus," Sterling said. It was a type of gasp.

"Stop her," said Aunt Clothilde. "You let her go. Let her go."

"Wait," the doctor shouted. He started towards the stairs.

"Yes, yes," said Aunt Clothilde, "let her go."

Two large nurses came out of nowhere and collided with Dr. Weston in the passage. "Damn," he said.

"You'll never catch her," said Aunt Clothilde. "Let her go. You damn fool. You damned stupid old man."

Sterling said, "For Jesus, ma'am. Where she going?"

"To hell," said Aunt Clothilde.

Mrs. Rhale slid down onto the floor. She stayed there, on all fours.

"She is going straight to hell," said Aunt Clothilde.

"For Jesus, ma'am," Sterling said.

And Aunt Clothilde said, "Look."

The moon had caught behind the screen of the far window. Below the moon, away from the hospital building, Adrianne was running along the pale white clamshell drive. She ran the short distance to the highway; then she turned to her right, without stopping.

She turned on an angle, and followed the white line down the center of the highway.

Sterling said, "I'll get her in the car, ma'am."

"You'll be too late," said Aunt Clothilde. "You damned idiot. She'll be hit and killed by then."

"No, ma'am," said Sterling.

Aunt Clothilde said, "She'll be killed."

"No ma'am, not like that."

"She will. She'll be killed."

"No, ma'am," said Sterling, "you wrong. You just wait here, I'll bring her right back. Ain't nobody going to hit her the way she's running. Can't help but see her a mile off. Ain't nothing going to happen to her like that now, Miss Clothilde, she's just running straight down the middle of the road."

4

Only a thin orange fan of heat touched the sky above the trees. The visible highway led directly into it.

The scissors and both her shoes had fallen off in the driveway, and the asphalt was warm to her feet from the day's sun. The long white line of warmth led to the fire.

But as she was running, that orangeness shrank together like a folded fan, and pulled down in the fissure between earth and sky.

And the last orange was flecked with black, as she had seen it through the black screen of the hospital window. Black of water beyond the screen; spots of water in the sundown.

The fire water was passing through the screen. She saw she could never reach it. But she couldn't stop. She knew that the warm white line behind her was as smooth and bare of footprints as the one that stretched ahead to the end of the world.

And the moon knew it too. The moon was laughing.

Adrianne screamed: "Laugh."

She ran on, feeling the wind pass her; and she was the maker of the wind with the movement of her own body.

She ran on, torn from herself, in the airless evening.

Epilogue: The Sisters for Love

1

As there can exist no north nor south without an earth, no more can there be a future and a past without a man. Still it is believed there is an ever-final place for most things that have occurred in the sunlit world, regardless of when or how. And somewhere through infinite space—traveling at its rightful speed to bend again from each new surface in its proper way—is the light of every person's hour, and of each event.

Then it may also be said that a man's death is his absolute—that it brings him to fuse the destruction of his future with the living hope of his past. For on a man's last breath, the days in his life are freed, and they must run wholly together to be and to travel as one. And these days and these hours make a single constant that for him is neither ahead nor behind, but only an indivisible new present, immutable and newly born no matter where it shines.

There is an aimless immortality in light, as there is in truth; not many external occasions will ever truly be lost though they have had no witnesses on earth.

May such be the doom of the heart: and so men pray.

This is the hour of the sisters for love.

. . .

A day was still by some minutes the twelfth of July. Opal wore her good uniform, without the apron or cap. She carried a purple plastic handbag she had picked up at the last second for no reason. The handbag had nothing but a chipped rectangular mirror in it, and fifty-five cents.

Keeping her head motionless, she tinted the room with red eyes and let them rest finally on Loris Licia. She said, "Excuse me. I came for . . ."

Miss Viola said too loud, "Talk with sense."

"They phoned from the hospital. Excuse me," Opal said. Her lower lip hung suddenly, wet.

In the night, the yellow from the chandelier was sour and heavy to everybody. It spilled over walls and faces with a spoiling bright cumbersome glow.

In a precise manner, and quiet, Loris Licia told her, "He is dead. Isn't he?"

"Yes, ma'am," Opal said through phlegm, "he's dead."

Miss Mady sat down. She stood again immediately, and leaned towards Loris Licia; but her feet were thick on the carpet. "You going to faint?" she said.

Opal cleared her throat.

"You going to faint?" Miss Mady said to Luthella: "She going to faint?"

"No," said Luthella.

Loris Licia was standing in the center of the room. She had got up to receive the news. And she had tightened in even more.

The motions were now folding into one, and she shrank smaller. She squatted several inches. Her body contracted to one hard length of muscular purpose, fists turning and pushing against her breast; she looked at her fists. Then she let go and relaxed, like that, in a sort of fetal position.

"Catch her," Miss Mady said.

"She ain't going to fall."

". . . Catch her."

"No."

"She is."

"What you think she's been waiting for all this time? She ain't going to fall."

"She is. She's fainting."

"She is not," Luthella called. "No."

Loris Licia looked over at the mantelpiece. She turned her head and looked at Luthella's waist in desperation as though she expected to see something written there.

After that she looked straight up at the chandelier. She stayed that way for a breath.

And then she began to unfold.

"There," Luthella said.

Her face was sprinkled with sparkling light from the chandelier; Loris Licia grew up into the sharp-cut gleams—she pushed tall. And the false yellow light shone clean, breaking to a small multitude of rainbows on her skin. Her fists opened and slid down. In one movement she grew high enough to touch any section of the drooping, angled glass. When she had reached her full length, all the tension had left her. She stood quietly, examining the maze of prisms.

"There, there, there," Luthella said.

Miss Mady said, "There what?"

"You did it," Luthella said. "There."

". . . What did she do?"

Luthella said to Miss Mady, "And you thought she was going to faint."

"I wish to know what she did."

"None of your business," Luthella said. "You thought she was going to faint."

Opal made a sound, and swallowed. She felt around the purple plastic on her handbag.

And Loris Licia walked out of the room.

"Where you going?" Miss Mady said.

Luthella said, "Just let her be. Going up to sleep."

". . . Sleep?"

"You heard me."

"At a time like now?"

"The time is for her to sleep."

"She can't sleep now."

"Oh yes, she can. She can now."

Opal said, "Miss Choate, please. Miss Choate."

"You let her be," Luthella said.

"But . . . Miss Choate," Opal said. "Miss Choate."

"You . . ."

Loris Licia said, "Yes, what is it?" She had come back to the doorway.

"You let her go to sleep."

"Be quiet," Loris Licia said. "Yes?"

Opal coughed, "I thought she was here."

". . . You thought?"

"She is supposed to be here," Opal said. "I wouldn't of come unless I thought my lady was here. I came to take her home. They phoned from the hospital. Sterling. That's Mr. Edmund's . . . that's the chauffeur. He . . . She won't come any place but here."

"Who won't?" Miss Mady said.

Loris Licia said, "Be quiet." The words followed each other across the room like bullets.

Miss Mady sat back to stare. "Yes," she said.

"I should have remembered." Loris Licia frowned. And she said, "When is she to come?"

"Don't know." Opal was trying to twist her purse. ". . . Supposed to be here now."

"Why isn't she?"

"I don't know," Opal said. The catch unsnapped, and the purse swung open a space.

Loris Licia went to the windows overlooking the Drive.

Luthella muttered, "Won't even let her get a little sleep, now she can. Won't let her be." Then she said, "Now don't you do that here."

"I won't," Opal said. "Not in this house. I already did it. I cried before I came."

"Don't do it again."

"I won't," Opal said.

"She don't require your tears."

"I said I won't," Opal said.

"But . . ."

Loris Licia said, "Now. Is that a car?"

". . . I don't hear anything."

"Me neither."

"Yes."

"I do now, wait."

"It is."

"Is . . . ?"

"Yes."

"I can't see out," Luthella said. "Is that her?"

"She has arrived."

"How can you tell?"

Loris Licia said, "I know that she has arrived."

". . . Do?"

A car door slammed, and quick feet scraped like a single shower of hail, on the driveway. Then no noise. A second door, and a deep voice, and different feet.

Then nothing.

Loris Licia turned. "Now go upstairs," she said. "All of you go up."

"Not me," Opal said. "Please, I would rather not. I came to take her home."

Luthella said, "Me too? All of us?"

"All," said Loris Licia. "Yes. All go up."

Miss Mady and Miss Viola glanced at Loris Licia. They bumped together in the doorway. "You first," Miss Viola said. "She means serious."

Loris Licia said, "Go."

"I'm going."

"Now go."

"Not me, please," Opal said.

Loris Licia said to Luthella, "Take her up with you."

"Yes, ma'am. And come back down?"

"No. And stay up."

"Not me please," Opal said. "I came to take her home. I didn't come to go upstairs. I have got no interest to go upstairs in this house. The things people used to see here, I came to take her away from this house."

"You heard. She don't require your stories."

"Not me please," Opal said. "I want to go home to my husband. I have to take her to her home, and then I have to go home to mine. I didn't come to go upstairs. I'd rather not. The way they talked about one of those two ladies appearing up around. And he is dead now too. Doesn't interest me to go upstairs."

They were out in the hall, and Luthella was pushing her up the staircase. There was a man's voice calling outside.

Loris Licia waited beside the bottom stair. She said, "There is nothing to be afraid of."

"No. But I don't want to go upstairs," Opal said, being herded.

". . . What frightens you?"

"She's talking about that old ghost," Luthella said.

"I know that. Did you ever see it?"

Opal said, "No, ma'am. I don't believe in them. But my own mother likes to say she did. I just don't have an interest in going upstairs," she said.

"We already here. Come on; you heard her."

"He's dead, Miss Loris. That's Sterling out there. He's dead. I just came to take her home."

Loris Licia said to Luthella, "Let her leave when the hall is clear. I will shut the doors to the living room."

"Without her?" Opal said. "Sterling says she's not feeling well. He said for me to come and take her home."

"No. There is no need."

"But I did. I came to take her home."

"There was no need," Loris Licia called up; "thank you. No need." Then she said, "She has come home."

Sterling used the bell before the upstairs landing was entirely empty. Loris Licia waited, standing where she was.

Then she went forward and threw the door open wide.

. . .

Sterling had his head around and was looking first to the living room. His mouth shone some. He chewed at it; he was not crying by a few minutes.

He said, "She would not go any place else. I tried, we all tried, and she wouldn't. And she refused to stay in the hospital. She has been screaming and carrying on ma'am, you don't imagine how she was, she has been screaming and screaming, she wouldn't hush till the doctor promised to let me take her here. She would not even let him sew up her arm nor put no bandage on it till he promised. She would not let him give her the injection for the pain either, or anything. She is . . . not in her proper condition. She is very upset, Miss Choate, she is . . . something went wrong with her back at the hospital. She wouldn't let anybody come with us here. Then she wouldn't say a word. I took her in the car with me, and she sat up in front with me, and the way she was screaming before and then she would not say a word. She . . ."

Loris Licia said, "Where is she?"

"Around in back, she got away. She ran from me soon as I stopped the car here. I don't know whether to go after her, the way she looked at me. She might run off again and get hurt. She is out in back now, I saw her. And before, you know she made me stop at the other house? She made me stop there and we went inside and she wouldn't let go my hand. And you know what, she wanted to change her dress? That's all what she wanted, was just to change her costume. Then when I asked her why, she said she had to put on a dress to match the bandage, and she did it. She made me stand there right next to her while she changed her dress. She didn't want to come here in that dress. Then she took me back out and got in the car, and we had to go down to the river. We drove all the way down to the river, she said so, and she is not talking in her natural voice. She said she had to go to the river. Then when we got there she showed me where to stop and she quit talking. But she made me hold her hand to get out, and we got out, and then she wanted to look at a tree. We went the whole way down there to look at a tree, me holding her hand. She stood and looked at it. And she held onto my hand. Did you ever hear of a person say goodbye to a tree? Then we got back in the car and came here; and soon as we got here, she opened the door and ran off. I don't even know whether to go after her. I don't even know what to do. I wish I could tell what to do."

"No," said Loris Licia. And: "You may go home," she said.

"I can't go back, ma'am, with her out there like that. I've got my other ladies waiting for me at the hospital, but I can't just leave her here like that."

"Now you can, yes. You may go."

"No, ma'am. Is Opal here? That's . . ."

"You will find Opal at the other house. I am sending Opal back."

"But how about . . . ?"

"You may leave," said Loris Licia. "I thank you, you may go home."

". . . You don't understand, ma'am, you don't know her. She don't even look like herself. Something is awful wrong with her."

"No," said Loris Licia.

"Something is."

"No. Nothing is wrong."

"Yes it is, ma'am."

"No, it is not," said Loris Licia, "I have told you, no. Nothing is wrong. It was wrong before. I will take care of her, thank you and good night."

"Miss Choate . . ."

"Good night."

Loris Licia moved against the wood; the metal caught.

And she walked into the living room. She pulled the sliding doors to behind her.

She walked past the square black yawns of the open windows, feeling the skirt of her dress bounce against her legs.

Loris Licia crossed the room between those two mirrors. And she had no time now to stop and examine the two locked series of reflections. Yet she knew: she saw that they were not the same. She could see without having to look. They were not the same as they had always been. And she knew that she would not need to watch the mirrored child again, or study her, or seek to find what was not there—the need was ended; she had no longer the necessity. For the stunted infant, the dressed-up child was cut off and gone with all the life it had never known, and the breathless love of the dead. The night was now, and now was all. This was the woman.

She went quickly through, out onto the gallery.

And there too she could see; the black was clear. Three-fourths of the moon cleaned the sky. It shimmered in the dust on the leaves, and magnified the mood of things. The greenish moon opened the darkness.

The garden stretched, rectangular; expensive bare burned summer grass moved sparsely against itself, tipping-long and delicately dying. A platform of grass. Beyond that, lined on all three sides were the high bushes. Like a frame. And because this was summer they held white blooms, and they were clipped and gray in the green moonlight.

Then she saw it.

The chalk-faced figure stood beside a tall bush in the northwest corner of the garden. The vacant black eyes were watching the house.

Loris Licia placed a warm hand wide over the back of her neck. "Yes," she said. "Before, yes. It must have been frightening. Before."

She called, "I am here now. Why do you stand out there, why do you wear white? Come in."

But she did not expect an answer, though she was certain her sister had heard. She knew there could be no words for an answer. She stepped off the gallery sole-deep down into the singed grass; and under the moonshine began to walk through the lacing lawn, tearing a path with her feet.

Then she said, "I can feel it for her."

And walking she saw the bandage and she said, "I can hold that. I can hold it too. I will take your ache in my own arm, I can keep it for you. Would you like that?" she said. "I can live for you now if you like. I am enough for both."

She said to her sister, "I will not forgive him for thinking I could be angry with him. That is the one thing I can never forgive. He was cruel; but he was never incorrect with me before. But how did he presume to think such a thing? Did he imagine I came here to haunt in a haunted house? Why are people so thoughtless, it is far more than cruel to be thoughtless. It is insulting, the idea is vicious. How could I possibly feel anything for him? He had no right to my anger. He was the only man I have known who never wanted me."

She faced her sister, and said, "I have been outraged all my life, but I could not hate. He never wanted anyone but you. It was you who hated him," she said. "Or is that true?"

But Adrianne could not prepare for questions. She was still standing next to the highest, most white-laden bush in the garden; she stood without moving.

Adrianne's mouth was not now painted. And almost under breath, that quietly, she was singing.

2

Before the sisters left town was Edmund Choate's funeral. They went there together.

It was held at two o'clock of an afternoon, on a Thursday. The cemetery was full of people—so full that many had to crowd in among the graves for hundreds of square feet around. Everyone wore black, and nearly everyone whispered during the service.

But not many could say precisely how Edmund's daughters had come to be so close, that soon after his death. People were generally informed about some change in Adrianne since the loss of her father; a few claimed the grief had driven her temporarily out of her senses. But nothing really accounted for her sudden attachment to Loris Licia, and she was not seen in public until the funeral. Aunt Clothilde and old Mrs. Rhale only came out of the Choate house long enough for the service—they were not receiving or answering the phone. As before during his life, there was an unleavened atmosphere over Edmund's last appearance in the city, and there were whisperings.

There were two grand topics for discussion, apart from the obvious. Mr. Samuel Vine had made some disturbing announcements. One concerned the old Legrange house, refaced, with its new furnishings, all of which had been given free to the two white women who lived there. Mr. Vine went so far as to say a certain amount of money went included with the house. It was known that the sisters were leaving town, taking with them the maid Luthella and no one else, two days after the funeral. Before then Aunt Clothilde was to become owner of the Choate establishment and of the two hundred thousand dollars from Edmund's life insurance—by order of Adrianne Legrange Choate, expressed for her by Loris Licia Choate (who performed all functions for her sorrowing sister), and carried out by Mr. Samuel Vine. There was all that to whisper about, and not much time for tears.

Edmund's daughters stood tight together, touching; Loris Licia supported Adrianne's bandaged arm across one of hers. It had been announced by Gwendolyn Rhale that the truck which killed Edmund Choate very nearly sliced his true daughter's arm right through the bone. Both daughters had thick veils draped over their high-held heads—and each veil fell in folds over lucent skin as if it might have been cut from one of those white nights that are so clouded it is impossible to see the surface of the moon. You could sense their faces, but you couldn't study them.

Aunt Clothilde and Mrs. Rhale stood with Jergen Wilson, all three dry-eyed, on the other side of the grave next to the preacher; and behind were Edmund's servants. Mrs. Wilson was off in the crowd somewhere, waiting. Jergen had made a long speech at the church that alternately moved and bored everyone except Edmund's daughters, who were not there. They did not appear until the actual burial. This was not thought of as bad taste, but only natural. Adrianne's hold over her distress was known to be tenuous, and it was said that any mention of her father whatsoever, within hearing distance, brought about a violent and uncontrollable demonstration.

So perhaps the most surprising sequence of things to take place at the funeral started with the fact that Adrianne stood quietly by during the entire ceremony; she neither moved nor spoke, not even to demand a handkerchief. Then before the coffin was lowered, people had guessed she was not likely to make the expected show, and everyone's eyes were beginning to water and wander and relax. It was at this moment the sound of a raw spasm tore out from between the sisters, a cry that could not be withheld. One single sob so deep it made the minister glance up from his reading and pause. And while foreheads spread to see Adrianne more clearly—to witness her expressing the hollowness, the loss felt by a whole city at the death of Edmund Choate—another hand was raised, and pressed savagely over the lower half of a swaying veil. Adrianne stood like a cold metal statue with its arm fixed out to the left. Holding to that arm and trying without success to block a convulsion of grief which seemed to center in the stomach, like the last contraction of a mutilated animal, Loris Licia Choate sank, weeping, to her knees beside the open grave. She knelt and wept until the service was finished.

After the coffin had been lowered, the preacher hushed for some relative to lay in the first handful of earth. Again every person in the cemetery was contemplating Adrianne, or wanting to.

And again not Adrianne but Loris Licia reached out—still fiercely gripping her sister—and clawed at the dirt around their feet. She crumbled a dry clod, loose, in the flat of her fleshless palm, held between them over the grass-mounted grave; and the way she did it, you might have thought the hole was fifty feet deep. You might have thought so even more when the rain of a little dry dirt came up out of there like thunder—and soared off in flying, rolling noise past all ears across the cemetery, away off to wherever it is such noises go. Then Loris Licia straightened up with ease and blew once audibly to clean the dust from her big-knuckled, wide, bony left hand before dropping it to her side.

The funeral was over at ten minutes after four and the daughters turned around where they stood. Loris Licia raised her veil up over the top of her head, and pinned it there. And she led her sister out of the cemetery.

Then the whisperings choked; people did weep to see the two

walk together. The sisters went, they matched foot to foot, and they were black queens walking there. Adrianne's porcelain face remained hidden—although there was a bit of sad talk afterwards from some who said they glimpsed enough to know she was smiling. Loris Licia kept her eyebrows and her jaw pulled tight; her face shone out, discolored and lumpy from dry tears. And at a distance of six feet, Aunt Clothilde limped after them. The crowd separated in silence for the three ladies as they went. And these were the only three left of Edmund Choate's family. The sisters took the long way around—marching with no haste, moving slow as weary; they went by each grave of each of their two mothers never halting and left arm in arm. They did not look behind them. They left Aunt Clothilde standing alone on the verdant edge of the cemetery to watch as they walked down Melpomene Drive. They went away like that for the last time.

And they departed from the city two days later—dressed both in white. For of the three, only Aunt Clothilde refused to discard her clothes of mourning within twenty-four hours after the funeral. The sisters were never known to be seen after that wearing anything but pure white.

Around town no person can say for sure where the young ladies are now, or at any given moment. Though most do agree they went to live in Europe. But rumor has varied to mention such far apart places as Paris, Rome, the west coast of England; and even Egypt. Then someone went touring one summer and saw two persons believed to be the sisters in the full compartment of an Italian train, heading north for the mountains. It is understood that they don't seem to care much where they live, just so they can be together. Also that they do not stay in one place for very long. And people say if you travel far enough, in any direction, sooner or later you are bound to see them somewhere: the two white women, who sit together and watch—and the third, the Negro woman, like a dark-skinned sentinel replacement, mourning there with them wherever they may be.

But they are hardly talked about in the city these days. The subject is no longer one of real interest. Gossip had begun to ebb within four months after their departure, because no listener would be likely to believe that they are ever coming back.

And at the end, people said Adrianne accepted Loris Licia as she did out of kindness and from the forgiving dignity of her heart. Word even had it (this came, it was said, from Miss Viola herself) that all the previous comments about Loris Licia had been way off: she was not a whore at all. She was some new foreign kind of virgin.

3

It must here be mentioned that the man who has so recently bought the old Choate establishment and gardens paid a price of one hundred and eighty-three thousand dollars, furniture included. This man is Jergen Wilson.

Jergen Wilson has become one of the most prosperous businessmen in town, and is among the most respected citizens. His sudden success with business affairs and in society started soon after Edmund Choate's death; at that time he wrote a series of ten articles which appeared in the local morning newspaper and were thereafter reprinted by other journals throughout the South. These articles made up a kind of eulogy, a tribute to his deceased friend. They were well-phrased, beautifully conceived expressions in writing. And they embodied both a knowledge of literature and of certain modern scientific facts. A quote from one of them has been carved on Edmund Choate's headstone in the cemetery. The articles caused much comment for over a year, and will appear soon in book form, to be published by a Northern firm.

Such talent and quality of feeling had gone theretofore unsuspected in Jergen Wilson. Before the tenth and last of the articles had yet been seen, he was already looked on in social circles with different eyes. People used a new respect in approaching him. Those who had not thought of Jergen Wilson as anything more than a comic and unattractive shop owner were forced to re-evaluate themselves with their opinions. It became obvious that a thick layer of deceiving fat had hidden and perhaps protected the frail tendrils of a sensitive soul.

Less than a year after Edmund Choate's death, the two old persons occupying his house found reasons to go elsewhere. First, Gwendolyn Rhale was discovered naked in her bed one hot morning, having died in her sleep, peacefully, of a heart attack, at seventy-three years of age. Then the lady known only as Aunt Clothilde had herself committed to a private institution some miles up from the city equipped to deal with all varieties of mental disturbances. In both cases, Jergen Wilson was present when he was needed to take care of the unpleasant details. After that, the chauffeur, cook, and other help working at the Choate establishment (all of whom had received bequests in Edmund Choate's will; and except for Opal, the maid, who declined) were transferred to Jergen Wilson's home. He fired his own servants.

In the months following, unsatisfied by all that he had done, Jergen Wilson ordered a special bronze bust of Edmund Choate to be molded and cast by a most respected sculptor in Mississippi. The bust was to have been placed in the library of the Century Club downtown, of which Jergen Wilson became president soon after the project was announced. But the bust took so long in the making, now it is to be saved and put in the replanted, formal garden of Jergen Wilson's new home.

He has given up his yearly trips to Rome, and is no longer seen around his shop. The younger Wilson boy, Warburn, has replaced his father in these functions. Jergen Junior is now a practicing pediatrician and will have an office soon in the forty-story building under construction on Lapaulette Street. Both sons will reside with their father and mother in a wing of the new residence. The girl, Justine, fresh back from a finishing school, is engaged to be married; and she will be living in New York City.

The second Choate house on Melpomene Drive has been purchased by a group of leading citizens which was formed expressly for that purpose. The price demanded was half again more than it should have been, but the two women tenants hired a lawyer and were obdurate. Then they departed for the North in style.

The house was to have become a public library at purchase, and still may. At the moment, not enough money can be raised; the leading citizens concerned have paid too much already. It has again been allowed to fall into ruin.

Jergen Wilson's physical appearance has changed greatly with his success. He is considered a financial talent second only to a man like the late Edmund Choate. Although he is not much thinner than before, he dresses now in exquisite gloomy materials which are hardly definable by color. He has not dressed that other ostentatious way since he first went into mourning for his friend. And his subsequent taste in clothes might also be likened to that of Edmund Choate; yet here Jergen Wilson need not rank in second place. His sense for the rare and matching necktie, his collection of shoes and socks, these things are extraordinary. He never repeats an outfit, and it can be said that he gives more thought to the final degree of his appearance than has ever been noted in the city. There is a last, perfect touch to anything he wears.

Mrs. Wilson is now nearly always with her husband; the two are often seen in public. They are making plans for the reconditioning of the Choate place, and they carry out their social duties at the same time, in quite as exacting a manner. Jergen pays a monthly visit to the mental institution, where he sits and talks with Aunt Clothilde for an entire afternoon. This he has done from the day she signed herself in. It is said they have become very close in the last year; the old lady speaks of him as her proper nephew, and it was she who suggested that Jergen Wilson be the person to occupy Edmund Choate's empty house. She did attempt through a lawyer to sign it over as a gift, but the gift was refused. A cash transaction was made, the price having been set in estimate by a realty company downtown. However, it is expected that the money is eventually to be returned; Aunt Clothilde has made known her unwillingness to leave cash or property of any kind to either of Edmund Choate's daughters at her death, even if the daughters were traceable. She has no other living relatives.

And before going up to the institution she had just finished making her will.

The old lady is in good health for an advanced age; she spends all of her time knitting a scarf. This idea was conceived for her by a doctor as a kind of creative and therapeutic activity seven months ago. It is a cerise cashmere scarf. She knits for several hours every day, and any talk of finishing seems to cause an eruptive emotional disturbance. The doctor is at present far less pleased than he was in the beginning at the therapeutic aspect of her work. The scarf is measured on Monday of each week, and this is not a simple matter. It is now thirty-five feet long.

You will find that the asylum is half a day above the cemetery if you go by car from Melpomene Drive—and it takes much longer by boat; but the trip is more pleasant on water for those who have the time.

Then back down the river, the city is no more quiet than usual under the trickling gray ice of a fresh, new year.

$\mathcal{V}$OICES OF THE $\mathcal{S}$OUTH

Hamilton Basso
The View from Pompey's Head

Richard Bausch
Take Me Back

Doris Betts
The Astronomer and Other Stories
The Gentle Insurrection

Sheila Bosworth
Almost Innocent
Slow Poison

David Bottoms
Easter Weekend

Erskine Caldwell
Poor Fool

Fred Chappell
The Gaudy Place
The Inkling
It Is Time, Lord

Kelly Cherry
Augusta Played

Vicki Covington
Bird of Paradise

Ellen Douglas
A Family's Affairs
A Lifetime Burning
The Rock Cried Out

Percival Everett
Suder

Peter Feibleman
The Daughters of Necessity
A Place Without Twilight

George Garrett
Do, Lord, Remember Me
An Evening Performance

Marianne Gingher
Bobby Rex's Greatest Hit

Shirley Ann Grau
The House on Coliseum Street
The Keepers of the House

Barry Hannah
The Tennis Handsome

Donald Hays
The Dixie Association

William Humphrey
Home from the Hill
The Ordways

Mac Hyman
No Time For Sergeants

Madison Jones
A Cry of Absence

Nancy Lemann
Lives of the Saints

Willie Morris
The Last of the Southern Girls

Louis D. Rubin, Jr.
The Golden Weather

Evelyn Scott
The Wave

Lee Smith
The Last Day the Dogbushes Bloomed

Elizabeth Spencer
The Salt Line
The Voice at the Back Door

Max Steele
Debby

Allen Tate
The Fathers

Peter Taylor
The Widows of Thornton

Robert Penn Warren
Band of Angels
Brother to Dragons

Walter White
Flight

Joan Williams
The Morning and the Evening
The Wintering

Thomas Wolfe
The Web and the Rock